Author's preface

This novel is the second book in the Black Leopard series. The first book, Black Leopard I, relates, through the voice of the principal character, Chár, the destruction of his village and genocide of his people. He is rescued and taken to France, where he develops friendships, loves and finds lovers. With their help he begins to discover the values of this country, it's customs and to consider them from his Suri, semi-nomadic perspective.

Black Leopard II begins with the repetition of the final chapter of Black Leopard 1, so that the reader will be fully informed of Chár's current relations with Western Civilisation and its own attitude towards him. In terms of his history, this is the Event Horizon.

CW01498917

Black Leopard II

The Partisan

Chapter 1.

The Event Horizon. London, U.K.

"So, where's our Chár?"

"He's out. He likes to go to the lake first thing, have a swim. He'll be back soon." Nathalie was preparing coffee for breakfast.

"And probably with something for a barbecue this afternoon!" commented Charles.

"Which is very nice of him!" Nathalie reminded Charles.

"Of course it is! By the way, we have a freezer full of game to consume," Charles explained. "take whatever you want back to Germany with you, Dieter, we're already supplying the local butcher!"

"It's his nature!" said Nathalie. "So, how was your trip, Dieter? You decided to go back again."

"I – er – yeah. I felt I had to."

"You can show us your photos later."

"I didn't take any this time. I haven't taken any for a while. I met up with Joseph. I decided to contact him before going. He's in Arba Minch now, in a shack along the road to the university. He's become a complete alcoholic, drinking Tej and running a Tej house. At least, that's what he calls his shack."

"What's Tej?"

"Local alcohol brewed from honey." he explained. "He reckons he still works as a guide also, but I didn't believe him. He was either too drunk or raving. He never goes back to where we were, where the village used to be. He's frightened, kept jabbering on about ghosts. The Dizis won't go anywhere near it either, nor into the forest where they took them, for the same reason. At least I got a better idea of what had happened, although considering his alcohol consumption, that cannot be certain.

They were in the kitchen of Charles and Nathalie's house in the Sologne and Dieter, eager to see me again, had just arrived.

"I think the world needs to know about what happened to Beyahola. That's why I'm here. I've been in touch with Survival International. I wanted to talk about it with you. And, of course, Chár." Dieter suggested, knowing nothing of how I had avoided being murdered myself nor how I had arrived back at the river near the burned out village, covered in sheep's blood.

"He's coming, said Nathalie. "Look. You can see from the window. He's just coming up the yard."

Dieter got up from the table to watch as I walked across the lawn towards the back door of the house, in one hand my bhirɛ and the other the corpse of my kill, a sanglier[1] piglet. I was no longer naked, but wearing red shorts, white T-shirt and rubber flip-flops. It was a clear spring morning.

The kitchen door pushed open. Seeing Dieter, I dropped the sanglier, ran the few steps towards him and, wrapping my arms around him, kissed him on both cheeks. It was now two years since I had last seen him and I was bigger, stronger, but still with my youthful good looks (no beard!).

"Chár! How are you?"

"Well. Very well! It is so good to see you!"

I picked up the baby boar, and put it on the wooden work surface.

Dieter found his chair and sat down.

"Go and take a shower," said Nathalie, "change your clothes and make sure you are clean before you sit down for breakfast."

"I had a bath in the river. "

---

[1] wild boar

4

"Never mind. I prefer you to take a shower."

"See! My clothes are clean."

"Chár, please!"

Was I really that same difficult teenager as we all knew Claudine believed my Rémi to have become?

I left and returned in five minutes, fresh, with new T-shirt and shorts and pushed my way between Nathalie and Charles on the bench at the kitchen table, as was now my custom.

As the morning progressed Dieter was increasingly astonished at how I had grown into this "confident, young man, intelligent, speaking French fluently and English also", although he had had no opportunity to hear it yet.

"So, Chár, would you like to go to England with me, to London?"

Marie Jeanne had arrived and I was standing with her next to a work surface, sectioning the small piglet. Dieter watched on. I had become completely at ease and at home with Charles and Nathalie and clearly the house and countryside had become mine also. Dieter spent some time explaining about Survival International and Amnesty while I stood in silence working on the corpse of the piglet.

The outside world and its demands had crashed in on my tiny cosy little family where everything was perfect, safe and loving. Not that I felt that this outside foreign unknown was a threat, but certainly, Nathalie felt it. She had by chance found her son. Her, Charles and I had become complete together. Who knew what risks and dangers might await me were I to leave them, even though she absolutely trusted Dieter? She had willed time to be frozen in a perfect moment. For her, I had learned so much about France, I now spoke two aranjinye languages as well as my own, I had a best friend who loved me and a beautiful girlfriend, Juliette, who clearly thought I was wonderful and why disrupt all that?

Even Marie Jeanne, who had found it very difficult accepting me, this strange black and foreign teenager, not just foreign as in the sense of from another country but foreign as in utterly different and challenging to her well sorted out and rigid values, even Marie Jeanne had softened and warmed to me. She had felt somehow side-lined, the great passion her daughter and I felt for each other (she excluded from her mind what we might get up to privately), the obvious affection her husband, Louis Marie also felt towards me; since saving Pacquerette and the calf and then going hunting together, he treated me as a friend and equal; now, even Marie Jeanne was obliged to loosen her attitudes and allow herself to perceive me in a more generous light, especially since I had asked her to help me understand the village, its people, all about them and how best to flatter or manage them; she had become my confidante in that respect, my ears and eyes into the little world of the Sologne.

"Let things just stay as they are, mon chou. No need to look for complications."

"But they cannot, Nathalie," I finally insisted, "Things cannot stay the same. Rémi and Juliette are at university. I didn't want that! Why did Dieter go back to Beyahola? It is the past! The past is calling him to act. Maybe he doesn't even know clearly yet, what he must do."

"You are an innocent, Chár! You are already a young man, but money makes no sense to you!" insisted Charles. "You only feel contempt for work! So much of modern life, for you, is absurd. You will be lost out there!"

"But, Charles, he will be with me!" insisted Dieter.

"Chas[2], Natha, it is true. I will be with Dieter. He saved me; he is my brother. I will be fine; it is only a few days. And I must go! It is my Komoro who made him Suri and who calls him now, and all the young men who welcomed him at the time of the donga[3], they are calling him also."

"They even gave me a bhirɛ[4], which I have in my bedroom."

"And it speaks to you every night, eh?"

"Yeh. True." A short 'ha' accompanied his words, acknowledging my understanding of the strange and special powers drawing him into action. "That is true."

---

[2] Chas, pronounced Shaz
[3] Stick fight
[4] Fighting stick

6

"And all that past, with its ghosts," I continued explaining, turning to Charles and Nathalie, all the time acknowledging their scepticism, "has sent him here to find me."

"Okay, fine! Do what you must do," said Charles.

"I don't want this," said Nathalie regretfully, "but if you need, if you feel you should, then go."

"Before I decide, I want to talk about it with my Wóhólò Tagí."

"Claudine's son," explained Nathalie. "Rémi. His best friend. They have been an enormous influence on each other. No one knows Chár better than Rémi."

"I love him. I know everything about him, and he knows everything about me. We are the same. He is Suri now."

"Chár, I want to know what happened before I found you at the river."

"I will not speak about it. I have not told Nathalie and Charles, only Rémi and Juliette. Juliette only a little, mostly I have spoken about it with Rémi Wóhólò Tagí, and why? Because he loves me and saved me from myself, from those terrible memories. If you want to know, you can ask him. But don't be surprised if he tells you nothing."

"It is better we don't know," said Charles. "He is protecting us with his silence."

I put my arm around Charles' shoulders and kissed him on the cheek.

There was a long silence as Dieter tried to accommodate to my determined views.

"So, what's this, Chas and Natha?" wondered Dieter, with a smile.

"He's changed our names!" explained Nathalie. "He doesn't use them all the time; usually when he wants to persuade us of something. He's changed everyone's name! What is your name, Marie Jeanne?"

Marie Jeanne was standing next to me, assisting the cleaning of the piglet.

"I can't pronounce it, Madame. Too difficult for me."

"Nyábí, or plus intimement, Nyábí nanu[5]," I revealed.

"And what does it mean?"

"Ah, it's a secret!" I asserted, grinning at Marie Jeanne, who blushed.

"I surprise myself how much I am in awe of this Suri leopard," reflected Dieter silently, "who has grown into a confident young man, intelligent, fluent in three languages and clearly loved by all around him. His friend, Rémi, is arriving at the weekend. Who is this famous Rémi who knows more about Chár than anyone?"

*   *   *

Dieter and the Leopard, he enjoyed referring to me in that way, giving my name an English translation, we were attending the Survival International meeting, co-hosted by Amnesty International at their Human Rights Action Centre. Dieter had been invited to make a presentation about the massacre at Beyahola and the murder of its people in Dibdib. We had both spoken to Rémi Wóhólò Tagí. Between us, Wóhólò Tagí and I had decided not to tell Dieter about my actions and the details of what had happened to my people, but Tagí was happy for me to attend this meeting.

"It is better you are free, Chár, without any opinion or advice from Dieter. If he is right about anyone, a politician or government department, from anywhere, Ethiopia, England, France, the US, instigating this clearly organised massacre, giving guns and uniforms to the Dizi, they will show themselves when it is made public. You will not have to look for them; stupidly, they will find you, not knowing what they are doing. And I want you to say exactly what you think you must say. They are like Zhukov, whoever they might be. I was a coward and I feel shame over that. But you were not. And you are never a coward. Stand up to them. Show them your courage. Be yourself! You are leopard! You are Chár! You are Suri! Remember, I am always with you! Whenever you want, you must send for me. Send your leopards to call

---

[5] Ear, or more intimately My Ear.

me. Now is the time to act. Nothing can stay the same. I love you!"

Now, in Shoreditch, the centre of London, Ray Ferrier stood at the back of the hall with his erstwhile partner, Jack DeLange. He said that was his name, but who knew? Everyone in their covert world had a multitude of false names, identities and personalities. Everyone was pretending to be what they were not. Mind you, such occasions as these were fairly straightforward. They were here to watch what was going on, hear what was being said, make a note of those whose ideas seemed troublesome, look out for known activists, photograph everyone . . . That was the easy bit, constantly arsing around with his mobile, like everyone else in the hall. How more invisible could you get?

Jack DeLange sidled over from the entrance to the side wall where Ray was standing. Slowly, the hall was filling.

"What's going on tonight? What are we supposed to be doing?"

He was looking sallow and drawn, the skin of his prematurely aged faced seemed covered with a thin film of slimy sweat. His intestines were twisting in knots. He had tried to eat something to find the energy for the evening, but his belly, so used to being empty was finding it too difficult to handle solid food. He would have to find a toilet to regurgitate his futile attempt at nourishment.

"Didn't you get the directive?" and then looking at him with a frown, "Are you ok? You look really rough?" commented Ferrier.

"Coming to another of these do-gooder get-togethers – it pisses me off. What happened to good honest assassinations? Don't we do that anymore? You know, James Bond shit!" His mouth twisted with another stabbing pain in his abdomen.

Ray smiled to himself at the straightforward hatred for the tedium of these moments.

You're not wearing the right clothes! In fact, you look like a down and out!" said Ray. "Amnesty wants to implicate Overseas Development in the disappearance of a village in Ethiopia. There's more to this than just tea and biscuits."

"Oh, right! Great! So, what do we do? A bit of disruption? Shouting abuse, stuff like that?"

"Don't be fucking ridiculous. We're just hear to watch. I'll be taking advice, anyway."

"You're wired up, eh?"

"Look, they're about to start. Who the fuck's that at the front there? There's the German photographer making the presentation, but who's that with him, the black kid?"

"What did Overseas Development do?" Jack was shivering and breaking out into a cold sweat. Starvation was having its toll. Since his wife had left the country with the children for somewhere in Canada, he had slowly become anorexic if not bulimic, the modern disease of control. His family never contacted him.

"That's Dieter Schliemeyer, photographer, even published some collections, East German communist and of course eco-campaigner. Overseas development? What did they do? They funded the freeing up of land for international development. What do you think?" Ray laughed at treating Jack as an idiot.

"Fuck! Fuck you, you fucking smart-arse!"

"And? " demanded Ray.

"Got rid of the tribals."

"And in Africa?" Ferrier was being objectionably patronising.

"Just fucking murdered them, eh?"

"That's about right! But not in England. You can't just murder people here!"

"Ooh, I don't know!" Jack tried to laugh.

"So far, the ministry has been able to counter the rumours that International Development was involved with accusations of the usual bullshit in the Daily Mail - Communists, Marxists, etc." he started laughing cynically, "People believe that bollocks, let's face it! But if the black kid is a survivor, or even a witness, the Minister and Department are in deep shit."

"Right!" Jack's imagination started to fill with violence. "Take control before the shit hits the fan!"

For Jack, things had been spinning out of control for a long time now. Losing his wife and children, he couldn't remember whether he had been drinking too much before they left or whether their leaving had caused him to drink more. He'd tried health, as if it were a dress code for making himself feel at ease in other's company. But whenever he checked, looking in a mirror, he only ever saw a void of disconnected anxieties. Then, everything went, the mortgage, the house, family, credit cards. He continued drinking heavily, to bring the days to a conclusion, to blunt the sharp edge to every tedium. Not eating was both the remedy for his failure and his punishment for failing. He didn't, like some, moralise it into a series of prohibitions to save the planet, for example: not eating fish, because the oceans were being depleted, not eating red meat, or any meat for that matter, because cattle fart methane. In fact, he ate everything, hoping the planet would fucking die. Then, eventually, he would force himself to vomit as a punishment. His hatred now extended way beyond his own body. Even control over his own body had slipped out of control. Wet shit was seeping regularly from his anus. The soreness and frustrated anger it generated, further incited, not just a personal death wish, but one that had been globalised to encompass all of humanity, or any random victim he might wish to pick on. It would be the final, ultimate act of control, his own death; the closer you come to absolute control, the more out of control absolute control becomes. Ugly life, ugly fucking England.

This was not how I felt. In fact, I had quite liked what I had seen of London. Dieter and I had arrived a couple of days before the event to meet some of the organisers. Shoreditch, I had liked; all the slightly anarchic wall paintings, little shops and cafés. And I loved some of the English pubs and the choice of beers, with so many different people of all different colours, languages, features and smiles. It was an adventure speaking English with whoever we met. On both evenings I had got drunk with locals and sent photos to Rémi of all my new friends. One afternoon we had visited the New Tate and on another . . . . was it Tate Britain? Juliette would have loved it, I knew.

11

For Ray, the issue of Ethiopia could be dealt with through honest racism. He didn't give a shit about black Africa. These tribals, running around naked with spears! What the fuck? Over the entire history of humanity, they had failed to make any progress. As far as any civilisation was concerned, forget it! They hadn't invented anything; they had no written language. Honestly! The West had been trying to help them out for centuries with education, farming, simple industry. It was fucking hopeless! So, for him, black women were sex objects. Like most women, this was the first and immediate judgement he would pass on them. Black men were at most a sexual threat. It was easy for him to despise the young black guy with the German communist. As far as he was concerned, his racism was the norm. It was natural. Everyone generalised. Without generalising, no one would make any sense of the world at all. Everyone he knew thought like him. Look after your own. Ethnic nationalism, that was his logical perspective.

He looked around the room and laughed with a short contemptuous snort. Everyone with all their different skins, hair, dress, religions, beliefs, pretending they were all the same, all equal, all decent, intelligent, compassionate, kind, considerate, educated caring members of humanity. They were woke! And how wonderful it was to be their type of human! His contemptuous mockery reduced thinking to its most obvious.

If International Development had blundered into assisting a massacre with a nod and a wink . . . what the fuck! Who cares? Cabinet ministers, Secretaries of State who had been around long enough knew the agency would clear it up. They would take on the dirty stuff. And since operations had been partially privatised, which suited him and Jack just fine, there was a lot more money in it, him and his addled partner would benefit. Violence pays well when you're selling it. Besides, nothing happens out of national interest any longer. You can lie about it if you want, but not really. Doffing your cap to authority, loving the Queen and shedding a tear when singing the national anthem, forget that shit! It's all about cash in hand, now. No one respects or admires anyone else anymore. It was just a globalised white man's free for all out there, mate. These people in here were just the deluded herd and quite right they should remain so.

The meeting took the form of an interview. The interviewer was Peter Manson, well known to middle class intelligentsia, writer, left wing independent journalist, TV commentator and reporter. His intention was to film the meeting as part of a possible documentary project. The usual approach. Everything he did was going to be recorded, both by him and plenty of others, he was sure.

It started with Dieter Schliemeyer presenting what he was doing in the region of Beyahola that January. He mentioned with whom he had met and visited the region. And the unfolding of events as he experienced them, with his photographic presentation. Already the smoke of righteous indignation was rising amongst the chattering classes.

"So, Chár, tell us, what is it like for you living in France after this terrible incident?" asked Manson.

"I have been incredibly lucky, now I am a French citizen. Claudine's husband, Robert, s'est occupé de ça. Robert took care of that. I feel good. Nathalie decided to take care of me. She is like my mother and Charles also, a father."

"And what does that mean for you, being a French citizen?"

"I like it. I like the spirit of their Revolution very much, Liberté, Egalité, Fraternité; these are ideas my people, the Suri people of Beyahola, would have liked. In fact, these ideas are our instinct, so natural to us we don't even have to think about them. They are your instinct also, which is why you have to think about them all the time." I was doing the English thing.

A hushed attentiveness fell over the Hall.

"So, what do you do, in France?"

"I hunt . . . . and take care of the cows of Juliette's family. They are neighbours . . . . . and I study. I learn a lot from Nathalie and my tutor."

"You speak both English and French fluently . . . ."

"Yeh, quite good. With French it was very quick, because I needed to learn, and I was hearing it all the time. I also found, and my teacher told me, at some point learning a language, you must read books, all the time. I remember when I read the adventures of Tom Sawyer and Huck Finn, I noticed how at the time, I started to use the same words as them, even whole sentences. It was as if their spirit had entered into me. I

13

became Tom and Huck. Even at night, they would come to me in my sleep, talking to me. It was exciting!"

I paused to sense the response to my words. From what I could judge people were happy and amused by my reading experience.

"This was when I decided I had to read as much as possible. In that way, I can become . . . many. Maybe only names stay the same. First I am Suri, then I am French, hunting in the forests, now I am English. And each time, I am different, someone new. When I take the cows out for a walk in winter, I take a book. I build a fire to keep us all warm and we stay until the sun gets low, or the cows get restless. I have learned to read fast. I think you call it speed reading, lire à vitesse. My tutor in France helped me with this. I have too much reading to do. Especially for Rémi, he pushes me really hard."

I could see this man questioning me, Peter Manson, was struggling. My multiplicity confused him. I was unconditioned, untamed by this world of lazy thinking that wants to hammer everyone, especially the unknown, the unidentified into a single entity. That I should refuse it, stand up, tall, and say 'No!' to this reduction, upset a lazy habit he had never questioned. It was the same stupidity as saying foreigners have made the English poor! I felt some pity for him. The laziness was not his alone, but something all-pervading.

The pinks and blues and browns of the hall were closing in on everyone.

"So, you have been able to keep some of your customs as a Suri man, looking after cattle. Where are you living now?"

"La Sologne. It's like a jungle, a lot of it is like that, but not so hot . . ."

There were clearly a few radical strong-minded activists present who wanted to ally themselves to my people. According to one Amnesty activist who had listened to a voice inside and needed to speak out, money from the Department of International Development had funded the massacre, pressuring the Ethiopian government to free up land for international exploitation. Euphemistically, this was called 'development', in spite of all the bloodshed.

"The only thing that would be developing," the activist concluded loudly and angrily, "was not the land nor the people, but its financial exploitation!"

There was a murmuring, a rumble as of distant thunder which rippled through the room. I had already been made aware of this deeply political and contentious issue by Dieter, but at the time, it had hardly made any sense to me. Now with it being repeated and even affirmed by others in the room, I started to realise that the Dizi were just stupid, cheated out of their lives by something or someone unknown. Even their captain, was as bad as them, maybe worse; he had been arrogantly stupid. Maybe, even the government in Ethiopia were stupid also, acquiescing to some strange power which offered to empty the land for them; after all, they don't get development cash unless they clear the land and then who benefits from that? Did they even know about the spilling of blood until it was too late? I had started to notice, even see and smell this strange body which hovered over all white people, sucking their strength, organising them, telling them how to think. And I was beginning to realise what it was, this strange thing which made no sense to me.

"And what about friends in France? You have friends there?" Peter Manson wanted to cool things down by pretending the world could be simple and happy.

"Of course! Rémi. That is his French name. But I call him Wóhólò Tagí. This is his Suri name."

"And does it have a meaning?"

"We Suri give names to people by what we see at the time of first meeting, for example, when a new-born comes into the world. When I was born, a small child ran to tell my father who was caring for the cattle. The boy surprised a leopard sleeping nearby on the branch of a tree. The leopard fell, terrified, right in front of the small boy. My father had to defend the child and drove his Bhirɛ, which you might call a spear, through its heart. Out of respect, he gave me the name Chár, meaning leopard, and I grew up sleeping on the skin of that leopard who died as a consequence of my birth. Rémi's name is Wóhólò Tagì, Naked Moon. The first time we met and danced together in the night, we were naked. And there he was, his name was obvious to me, my naked moon, Wóhólò Tagí."

I couldn't help feeling secretly amused at how the crowd responded to this information.

"And then of course, I have my beautiful Juliette. I decided a long time ago just after I arrived in France, she would be my wife one day. What amazed me was Juliette, just like the custom of young Suri women, chose me! We will make a new Suri tribe together, a new people. This is what my mother asked me to do when she was dying."

"Do you want to tell us about that day? Dieter has already told us about the shooting at the stick fight. Perhaps you could tell us what happened after you had taken Dieter, Nathalie and Claudine to safety."

"I went to our village to find my mother, knowing something terrible was happening. The village was in flames and she was bleeding from her side, already dying. I had already seen the bodies of the Komoro and Chagdo."

"Who are these?"

"The Komoro is like a wise leader."

"You mean like a king."

"No! Not like your kings and queens! He was just a wise old man everyone respected, and turned to for advice."

My tone had seemed indignant, offended, and Peter Manson, found himself, to his astonishment, suddenly reddening with embarrassment and apologising.

"And the Chagdo can sometimes understand the future." I continued, "I stayed with my mother until she died. At that moment, I knew I was also dying, but still I needed to see what had happened to the rest of my people.

"When their captain threw the children into the Akobo river, hitting them over the head to make sure they were either dead or would drown, I decided to kill him. . ." I paused.

No one spoke. Who readily talks about murder?

"Do you feel ready to continue?" asked Manson, his eyes wide with the cold horror of incredulity.

There was a long silence, but a silence so deafening, it created its own subterranean shudder.

"A storm was approaching and the forest of Dibdib was becoming darker. The captain's driver was left behind in his truck while everyone rushed forward to watch the children being slaughtered, so he was the first whose neck I ripped, dragging him into the bush for hyenas to consume." I paused again.

I had decided before attending this meeting that I wanted to wear my favourite costume that Nathalie had first bought for me and which I had worn at the barbeque when Juliette had chosen me. I wanted to dress to kill, as the English say. I was wearing my white Egyptian cotton shirt, perfectly fitting dark blue jeans, my dark leather belt with brass buckle, my red boat shoes and Nathalie's white pearls, which I had practically claimed as my own. The striking contrast of my white shirt and white pearls against my black skin added to the tension between my admitting killing and my relaxed, guiltless, guileless manner. I became aware of a possible danger in the room, my leopards had felt it also, and wanted that threat and whomever it came from, to be aware of the danger attendant within me and my accompanying leopard spirits.

"Then I killed two of the Dizi murderers." I waited for the weight of my words to sink into the hearts of all present. "The captain? I blinded him, quickly jumping on his back to tear his eyes out. When you know how to hunt, it is not difficult to do these things unseen. He stumbled, bouncing from one tree to the next, futilely trying to escape the bleeding blindness of the two empty sockets in his face. Finally, he fell into an ant's nest. The ants slowly killed him with their vicious attack, and no doubt consumed him. The Dizi were too scared of the ants to rescue him, and very soon they scattered, leaderless and lost, many, most even, to never find their way out of that madness and home to their families. I stayed the night in Dibdib. In the morning, my leopards woke me and led me to the edge of the jungle."

I paused again. And then, with a grin:- "But since the Ethiopian government denies the massacre took place, I must be either a liar or a madman. You can choose."

Manson had difficulty responding to this cold, wry sense of humour over the Ethiopian government's denials: "It is true, the Ethiopian government is not pursuing charges against anyone and your status in Europe has been legitimised by the French authorities, but as a refugee . . . ."

"I am not that word, your English word. I am not refugee!" My voice was raised. "I am Chár. I am Leopard. My two leopards who take care of me since Dibdib, my brother, Wóhólò Tagí, they are with me now and all the dead people of Beyahola village, my village, are in me and they will be with me until they are finally appeased through what is to come. I am many! I am Chár!"

Again, a stunned silence. What did he mean, appeasement, everyone wondered. I, this young man from a prehistory, before recorded time, before so-called civilisation, with the startling madness of what I had expressed, I, Chár, had silenced their minds and focused everyone's attention. Perhaps I was mad, or driven mad by history. My intimacy with my people, my relationships in France, my current friend, my moral decisions entirely and assertively my own, which theirs never were, nor had ever been, humbled and highlighted their inadequacies in human endeavour. At the same time, my fearlessness was a challenge, a challenge to anyone who may have encouraged, or profited from the elimination of my people.

Dieter was white with fear and anguish at what I had said. As for Peter Manson, he knew that what he had just recorded was completely explosive. Was it naivety? A sort of ridiculous innocence? The values of primitive culture without any imposing laws? Was it guilt without any feeling of guilt?

"May I ask a question?" I asked.

"Of course."

"I have already asked my Rémi, but it was difficult for him to explain. What is civilisation? Am I civilised? Did white man's civilisation kill my people? Who in that civilisation is responsible?"

There was no answer.

"It seems to me in white man's civilisation everyone is good at talking but they have lost their freedom to act." It was just coming out! So much

18

of what Tagì and I had talked about. "Who did you give it to, your freedom? To your God? To Money? Your king? Maybe I am not like you! Maybe I am not civilised. Your civilisation want me to write myself into its own fate, to fix my story in ink for all the machinery of power to nail me to your cross of servility, to sign its forms, to speak its own truths and accepted lies. But I come from a world where words live only as long as breath. We don't write our stories—we sing them, dance them, cut them into the earth with our feet. Our language changes like the river, like the wind on cattle skin, like the red dust after the rain. It lives in the body. In the mouth. In the scars. In the silence between things. You say your writing is civilisation. But the first writing wasn't song—it was counting. Grain. Taxes. Debts. Guilt. Who owes what. Who belongs to whom. Manhours. Slave wages. Weakness and submission instead of strength and freedom. All carved in clay, chiselled in stone, so no one could forget—so no one could escape. Your language doesn't move. It locks. It binds. It freezes. It says: you are this. It says: you belong here. But my people don't belong. We move. We vanish. We return. We have no alphabet. But we have the wind. We have the stars. We have the songs of the elders and the names we give when we see something being born. They fear that, your high-priests of morality, because our language cannot be owned. They fear our ambiguity, our change, our wildness. But I do not fear it. I carry it in my blood."

I paused. There was a long silence at this indictment. I could smell carrion, the rotting flesh of corpses after a few days in the sun, the stench that hyenas carry around their grinning, gaping, gasping, black mouths and on their poisoned breath. My leopards could smell it also and were becoming angry.

"Who killed my people?" I raised my voice again. "Who wanted them dead? Before I left France, my Wóhólò Tagí said, I didn't need to search; my enemy, my people's murderer would find me. The hunter should be careful, before he becomes the prey!"

Ferrier was on his mobile talking to the client, Secretary of State for International Development, Sir James Mercantor.

"You can't help but admire him," Ferrier commented, "He's just admitted to killing several of your local private soldiers, if that's what you can call them, including their captain, leaving them in complete disarray. He's fearless! And, he's just made a direct challenge . . . to you!"

"What happened in that forest was nothing to do with me, and don't you dare repeat it! My role as Minister is to help that country into the modern world through international investment." Mercantor was almost shouting. "This black tribal, whoever he is, has admitted to the murder of Ethiopian state police. Regardless of any disruption, arrest him!"

There was a cynical look of resignation on Ferrier's face: absolute power at distance producing decisions of rationalised insanity.

From one side of the hall there was a strange hissing, whining sound near to a panting baby's cry, even a laugh. People looked around to see what it was, where it came from, some even stood up.

"Are you OK, Chár?" asked Dieter, approaching me to offer both of us some reassurance.

Manson repeated the same question, "Chár, are you OK?"

I was quickly glancing around the room, expectant, apprehensive, at the walls, the pink columns, the windows, the blues and browns. This sterile place was not the jungle, nowhere to hide, no trees to climb into.

The audience were becoming increasingly agitated, like the waves of a troubled sea. Suddenly, a loud voice was heard to cry out.

"This is ridiculous! Why are we listening to this nonsense? Can't you see? This is just political staging to blacken the name of legitimate governments." It was Ferrier. He had stood up and was walking down wide steps towards the stage, pushing through chairs and guests.

On the other side of the hall, Jack DeLange was also lunging towards the stage, his dirty brown coat, smudged with grime and covered in torn threads, hanging off the material like the balding fur of a mangy dog, billowed out behind him, leaving an invisible odour of his sweat-covered, sickly flesh.

"By his own admittance, this . . ." Ray was shouting, "this . . . illegal immigrant . . . is a murderer! And killing members of the Ethiopian police, who were legitimately clearing government land of illegal squatters, makes him a terrorist!"

By now other members of the audience were on their feet attempting to restrain these two aggressors, who seemed intent on disrupting proceedings.

"Get your hands off me!" Ray shouted at the jostling crowd around him. He removed a gun from inside his jacket and immediately the crowd fell back like skittles. "Stay calm everyone! We are from the Police Antiterrorism Unit," he lied, "and have been investigating for some time these individuals!" he was panting and rushing his words in desperation to get them out before the room descended into further chaos. "As it is, the French police are questioning the people who smuggled him into France. He's under arrest!" His voice had reached an almost high-pitched scream. "Don't move anyone. I'm talking to you, you idiot!" he shouted at an old man on the floor.

The same whining cry which had so disturbed everyone in the hall earlier could now be heard in several corners of the hall. There was suddenly a loud bang and all the lights went out. Ray's agitation had reached such a point, knowing he had nothing to do with anti-terrorism and was just a cheap secret service agent, freelancing, that his gun started firing spontaneously in his hand. The bluff might have worked, but not now in total darkness with shouts and screams and panicking bodies scrambling to escape.

Dieter, who was right next to Chár, took his arm and with voice raised against the hubbub told him to run.

"I am sorry! I am sorry!" he cried.

Ferrier found himself on hands and knees, sliding in the blood of the old man he had just shot, when he felt the weight of two feet or hands, he guessed, land on his back. In the general panic of the blackened sightless chaos, he felt a sharp pain as the feet seemed to tear into his flesh. At the same time, teeth sank into his neck as his face was pushed into the old man's blood. With a violent twist there was a nasty thudding crack at the base of his skull. His body fell apart.

As for DeLange someone stabbed him in the heart with an elbow. A sharp pain shot across his chest, down his right arm and out through the ends of his fingers. He didn't even have time to scream before he collapsed, and his poisoned heart surrendered to the dark.

I followed my leopards as they ran, glowing with the same flames as

Wóhólò Tagí. Outside, police cars were racing to crowd out the street with howling sirens and flashing red and blue lights. We ran up some stairs and from the roof, could see the brightly lit New Inn Yard. Still no trees, except a couple protruding from the barren pavement and both behind bars. It was easy to perceive a multitude of pathways through a jungle, some used by many different animals, some restricted to the few, but here there were none. I needed to escape to the dark. It seemed impossible to remain invisible were I to try to flee through that arid manufactured landscape. I could see a bridge at a short distance and the road underneath it was in shadow. Maybe the other side of that, along the embankment, I would find a hole to creep into, until everything calmed down and I could . . . what? There were people starting to flood out of the main entrance. Perhaps I should join them and use numbers to hide. No. I had already seen what had happened to my people when they were forced into a herd, surrounded. Kettling, the English call it. In any case, how could I get to that bridge through the mass of police, security services and ambulances?

I walked around the flat roof, checking each side to see if there was an easy escape. There were several strange metal boxes centred at different points on the roof, which were humming the cry of the unknown. Where the police cars had accumulated, there was a sheer drop to ground level before the cycle racks and the road, but on another side there were lower roofs above what I realised was the entrance, and from which, were I to climb down to them, reaching the street would not be so difficult. I lowered myself over the edge towards the higher of the two roofs, onto a narrow ledge, then peering over, saw a window ledge. I managed to just reach down to put my feet on it. From there I knew I would have to jump; the roof was not so far. The Amnesty building butted up against another much older building of dirtied yellow brick. In the corner between the two buildings, I found a black drainpipe I could climb down.

What would I do once at ground level? I knew I would have to steel myself against the cold night air. Moreover, I was in the territory of my enemy and his private security. My instinct told me to remain motionless and silent until the cacophony ended. Opposite, the other side of New Inn Street, was a tall building with a red door, which called itself, Seven New Inn. To the left of it were various graffiti. For a few minutes, my gaze was captured. There were several works, some overlapping each other. I was innocent of street art, having never seen it before London, but one figurative piece held my attention.

22

*　　*　　*

Many times I had sat on Juliette's bed, in her warm chambre intime[6], in the roof of the farm house, with its heavy beech beams, the walls and white plaster of the pitched interior ceiling, covered with prints of great paintings by the masters. I would spend time looking through books, either my own, whichever I was currently reading, or of works by painters of all time periods, while Juliette would sit opposite making sketches, paintings and studies. I had become her eternal model. Some were brief and quick, others taking much longer with considerable attention. I was mostly naked, which suited me, and which Juliette needed to develop her skills of life drawing and painting. She needed to learn how to represent bodies, she explained, and it was true the way she looked at me then was quite different, studious even, to how she looked at me when she wanted to seduce or be seduced.

One major intended work was to turn me into a black 'Cupid Victorious', 'Amor Vincit Omnia', love conquers all.[7] Of course, I loved that idea, love conquers all, and was charmed and delighted that I should be the manifestation of 'Love'. Looking at the Caravaggio painting, it was clear Cupid was only a boy; my genitals were of course bigger and I couldn't help grinning as Juliette posed me on the edge of her bed and splayed my legs wide open, as in the original painting. Love was definitely about sex, my naked sexuality. She smiled back at me, sharing my excited, amused pleasure at the overt, eroticism of both the original and her arranging of my seated position, legs wide open, head tilted provocatively.

"How do you want to arrange my búrrà and dormì[8]?" I asked, laughing.

Sometimes it wouldn't take long before she weakened, surrendered and pretending to adjust the position of my head, or turn my torso slightly, her fingertips would end up sliding down my chest, my belly, her face ever closer to mine until we could taste each other's breath. My dormì, slowly swelling, would lift and rest upon my thigh, while, naked, I would delicately unbutton her blouse, moving slowly closer until my hot breath

---

6　　intimate bedroom

[7] https://commons.wikimedia.org/w/index.php?sort=relevance&search=amor+vincit+omnia&title=S
　　pecial:Search&profile=advanced&fulltext=1&advancedSearch-
　　current=%7B%7D&ns0=1&ns6=1&ns12=1&ns14=1&ns100=1&ns106=1#/media/File:Amor_
　　Vincit_Omnia-Caravaggio_(c.1602).jpg

[8] Balls and penis

23

caressed her nipples, and I buried my face in her pretty breasts, both of us surrendering to our passion. Other times, it could be much longer and she was able to make considerable progress with her work and I would end up studying the pictures on the walls and then the books of prints she presented me with to distract me while she was working. Many times, also, I brought my own books, recommended by my teacher and sometimes those offered by Rémi. These were much more difficult, stuff that Rémi was reading even at university.

"Look! Stop moaning about how difficult they are and just get on with it! I do not accept that you should know less than me! Just force your brain to work and don't be lazy! You have to understand everything, eh?"

Even if I didn't understand, I just kept reading and then reading again, until familiarity presented me with new worlds, new thinking. Sometimes Rémi's impatience annoyed me and we would end up arguing, shouting at each other until Nathalie had to intervene, sending us in opposite directions to the ends of the garden, not that we were separated for long, but immediately sought each other out to laugh, play silly games and chase each other between the fruit bushes or end up wrestling on the lawn. Nathalie would just leave us to it. I hadn't lost the child in me and Tagí didn't want to either. He was definitely Suri, who were much more fun than these sensible aranjinya.

"Okay, you want me to keep up with you, read these books, learn this stuff, then I want you to learn Suri!"

"I can! I will!"

If anything such disputes brought us closer, such that sometimes, overhearing us chatter, Nathalie realised how much of a bond was growing between us when half of what we were saying was with smatterings of Suri, incomprehensible to her.

If the black wings of Eros/Cupid were able to emanate their own light, it was going to be possible for my black body to emanate light also. Juliette opted for the black background of the original to become shades of dark red, often a preferred colour of Caravaggio's for drapes and clothing in many of his paintings.

Initially, I wondered how it was possible to give detail to a figure, like my own, which was black. It seemed to me there was no shadow or variation in the black to show shape or form and this contributed to the quality I possessed of being able to become invisible, but when I looked at Juliette's paintings, I was amazed at the extent to which they were me, undoubtedly images of me. The number of different colours she had used was so surprising, different blues, reds, browns, yellows, whites. I looked at her with disbelief:-

"Are there so many colours on my skin?"

"Er, yes!"

"Here," I pointed at the picture, "my leg has some dark blue, but I don't see that on my real leg. Where is it?"

Juliette had understood that in order to paint chiaroscuro, it was necessary to focus on the dark shadows and lines of a figure, a white figure, hence, logically, with my black figure, she would have to concentrate on the light contours, lines and highlights.

"The colours move and change. Your skin doesn't have a colour, it reflects light, so the colour changes. At night everyone is black. Different skin reflects colour differently. White people think they are white, but no. They are pink, grey, yellow, green, blue, many different colours. People don't look. You have to look carefully. I am looking carefully at you! That you are hot, for example, your skin moist, sweating, I have to show that for you to become real in the painting."

At which point the memory faded and I found myself sitting on that roof edge once more, above Amnesty International, in Shoreditch, looking at the graffiti opposite, no longer in Great Britain, but nasty England. I felt a tightness in my throat, such that I couldn't breathe. My eyes were burning.

Looking again at the graffiti, the one image which caught my attention and had carried me back to Juliette, was of five abstract figures, all naked, and although they reminded me of paintings by Bacon and Auerbach, Bacon's tended to be about isolation and individual suffering and Auerbach's were simple portraits, often wise, beautiful, here, lit by a street lamp, were older men and women, misshapen by an unknown history, crowded together and supporting each other, one figure appearing to be slumped over, the blues and reds on their naked flesh like bruises or wounds. Were they being herded somewhere? Somewhere like Dibdib? Suddenly, it seemed right that this image was there opposite the Amnesty building commenting on the violence it opposes, violence which had been brought into my own home, my village. By whom? By what? And why? And there was someone, or something pursuing me, even now! What was it that was so bad about me, Chár? Why were they, whoever they were, angry with me? Were they angry? Were they going to kill me? The vicious spirit of Dibdib still seemed to be roaming the Earth in ravenous pursuit.

*   *   *

Addendum: The staging of art.

Many claims have been made recently about Caravaggio turning his studio, no less, into a gigantic camera obscura. Sunlight through a hole in one wall, possibly assisted by mirrors, focused onto his models and then that image of the illuminated subject projected through a lens onto the canvas. There have even been claims of traces of light sensitive chemicals found in the canvas primer on which a faint image could have been retained for several hours. Certainly, scratch marks have been found on canvasses delineating an outline to figures. Over the centuries, artists have used all sorts of techniques to produce realistic representations. Regardless of this primitive outlining of figures, the art is in the application of paint to produce the masterpiece. It, therefore, seemed perfectly reasonable to Juliette to use her camera and then project and delineate outlines for figures. Critically important now was the staging. If she wanted her art to contain the power of the Historia Sacre and mythological paintings, then it would have to illustrate a particular historical moment and tell the story of that moment, just as the Caravaggio paintings were used to illustrate religious history in contemporaneous terms. She discussed this with me and Rémi; we would be her models. But this painting would come from my history. Already in her mind was the religious symbolism of the slaughtered sheep, sacrificed by Abraham and Christ himself being perceived as the Lamb of God and then, my sacrificing of a sheep to bathe in its blood and wash away any remains of death that might be clinging to me. The coincidence was simply too great! And then Rémi, painted with the same black wings as Cupid, but as my Bodhisattva, surrounded by flames emanating from his skin, the fire of purification, anointing me with the blood of the sheep . . . . Positioning them for this tableau was now critical if she really wanted to create her modern painting of myth.

Chapter 2

The Three Sisters

"I have found him! I have found him!" cried Amani[9], her long black curls bouncing around her sculpted face, dutifully following, shadow-like, the rapid movements of her head and shoulders as she rushed to tell Lihua and Jolanta.

"Who have you found, Amani darling?" Lihua's high-pitched gentle enquiry momentarily halted Amani's frenetic, agitated race through the rooms of Place Pigalle[10], the highly reputed and exclusive venue, hidden in a small backstreet of Shoreditch, for the wealthy and powerful to relax and recuperate from the burdens of state and management of financial responsibilities, under the careful and experienced massaging hands of the three sisters.

"What's happening?" Jolanta stepped out of one of the massage suites.

By now Amani was holding her chest and panting heavily, her head nodding back and forth with each breath.

"It's your baby, isn't it?" said Jolanta, glancing at Lihua and rolling her eyes.

"No! No! Don't break my heart again!" she cried, her face grimacing as if she were about to burst into tears. "I know my baby must be dead, falling through the blue mirror and I . . . I didn't follow him!"

Lihua and Jolanta exchanged looks of despair.

"Have you taken your medicine?"

"No! Fucking cheap quack doctor peddling poison! No! And now I can see! He is here!"

"Who is here?"

---

[9] a Kiswahili word meaning "peace."
[10] Pigalle is a district of Paris renowned for prostitution. But in this context, the name of a massage parlour in central London

"The black one! The black one is coming!"

"The black one? What are you talking about?"

"I have to find him! He needs our help!" Amani's wild hysteria turned to a madness as both Jolanta and Lihua saw with astonishment how her eyes had become deep black pools.

"You said you had found him. Now what do you mean, you have to find him?"

"He is here, I know, and I have some picture of the place in my mind, but . . ."

Amani turned and ran towards the front doors of Place Pigalle, with Jolanta and Lihua in pursuit, persuaded Amani was having another crisis, if not a full-blown breakdown, hallucinating and talking gibberish.

In the empty night streets of Shoreditch, when even the latest of gay bars, massage parlours and strip clubs had closed, a vicious wind was blowing horizontal icy rain to sting and burn the faces of the three wild women flying through the yellow darkness of bending street lamps, making it practically impossible for Jolanta and Lihua to shut and lock the entrance doors of Place Pigalle before chasing after Amani.

"Amani! Stop! Wait for us!"

"No! You just want to drag me back! I have to help him! You stupid white people know nothing! He is near! Just help me, won't you?"

By now the three women had passed several streets to New Inn Yard, their flimsy clothes clinging to their bodies, their sodden hair wrapped around and clinging to their wet and scorched faces.

Amani had stopped running, seeming disoriented and, was making her own incantation of insanity: "Amanirenas, Nawidemak, and Malegereabar, Queen Mothers of Nubia, listen to me. Fly with me! Show me where our prince is sleeping!"

"Amani," shouted Jolanta, "your prince drowned when your boat sank! Your little boy is dead!"

"Shut up, you stupid Polish witch! This is not about my baby! Now just help me or leave me alone!"

She had clambered over a rotting fence and was clawing her way up an embankment.

"He is here somewhere, I know it!"

*   *   *

When I returned to the world, I felt myself floating through the dark towards pinpoints of light, not the stars this time, through the jungle of Dibdib, but towards little flickering flames, floating in warm sweet perfumes. As my eyes became accustomed to the light, I realised I was floating in a warm bath surrounded by candles. Around me, supporting me in the water were the three sisters of Pigalle.

"Look! He is waking!" said Lihua, her high-pitched lilting singsong voice charming every muscle in my body for it to swoon into the embrace of these strange women's arms.

"When I picked him up, his heart had stopped, you know," said Amani.

"Why was he covered in creepers?" wondered Lihua out loud. "So weird! Did he do that himself? Did they grow over him? Was he hiding, or what?"

"He has hyperthermia, no doubt. He feels cold. His pulse is weak."

"Amani, why do you go crazy like that? Why go running through the night to drag a down and out from the streets? The last time we all ended up attacked, who knows what might have happened if Lihua hadn't hit him over the head with the frying pan . . . ."

"He is not a down and out! Look at his hair, how it is cut and styled. Look at his teeth, they are perfect."

Jolanta held my head and opened my lips to examine my teeth. I opened my eyes and stared straight into hers. She stroked my face, let her fingers play with my hair and smiled back at me.

I felt myself drifting into a dream. I had died again and now I needed to sleep.

"He is making pee-pee! I feel it on my leg! Oh, poor darling! Poor baby!" said Lihua. The three witches were holding me floating in their gigantic bathtub. Naked in the warm water with me, they were carefully sponging my body, cleaning away the polluted filth of the railway embankment, the mud, slime and black oil stains of industrial dereliction.

"Tch tch tch! Look at these bruises and cuts! His ribs, legs, chest! What has happened to him?" wondered Jolanta.

In my half-dream, half-sleep, semi-conscious remembering, I heard myself answer that voice, from the cold hole in the ground, where they had found me, my muscles made rigid through my cramped damp hiding. In my dream, my remembering, I was being dragged, kicked, punched and although my will was to respond, fight back, my body would not respond, trapped as I was in that tight, dank pit of mud. My clothes were being ripped, my wallet, bank cards, and identity torn from me. The rest was dark night.

"What is he saying? What is he saying?"

"He's raving! It's just garbled nonsense."

"I know some of these words!" declared Amani. It is not my language, but I know it from the south . . . Sudan . . . Ethiopia."

"What is he saying?"

"Nonsense. It doesn't make sense! Something about the moon, his brother, leopards . . . I am leopard."

"He's speaking French!" declared Jolanta. "You are as crazy as he is!" she said, glaring at Amani.

"Hey! Don't insult me! I have found him! The dark night is mine!"

"What is he saying then," asked Lihua, "if he is speaking French?"

"Long lost . . . Shipwreck . . . lost . . . in your thighs." Jolanta looked puzzled.

"That's Dylan Thomas!" said Lihua.

"What!?"

"It's very sexy!" commented Lihua. "It's from Under Milk Wood, Captain Cat talking to his lost love, Rosie, in his dreams. 'I tell you no lies, The only sea I saw, Was the seesaw sea, With you riding on it, Lie down, lie easy, Let me shipwreck in your thighs.'"

There was a long, astonished silence.

"What?!" demanded Jolanta, her breath taken away.

"I read it at the American language school in Shanghai where my parents had sent me to learn English. I used to learn by heart these romantic lines from the books we read."

Silence again.

"Sometimes, I feel like Rosie," Lihua murmured wistfully. "the girlfriend of all the sailors of Llaregyb and Captain Cat's true love."

"Right! Good! Thank you for that!" declared Jolanta. "But more importantly, how does he know that?"

"And why shouldn't he?" demanded Amani, angrily. "Racist, Polish witch!"

"Oh, look! He heard my words! He has tears in his eyes!"

I could feel the warm, soapy skins of their bellies and breasts slipping and sliding against the life slowly returning to my limbs and naked flesh, confused with the memory of laying my head between Juliette's breasts.

"Oh, look, look, look! His pretty penis is starting to stand up!" exclaimed Lihua.

She reached her hand out through the warm water, gently lifted my couilles, the ends of her fingers playing with the thin loose skin of my scrotum, and my partly erect penis, which lifted up to follow her hand. Lihua was completely charmed. She had not seen, let alone been close to

31

a young body such as mine for a long time, perhaps since she left China.

"So pretty, eh? You can see the head just peeping out of the foreskin."

*   *   *

"This is the BBC News at 6 o'clock.

"Police are still searching for the young Ethiopian migrant who was a guest of Survival International at a meeting at Amnesty's conference centre in New Inn Yard, central London. The meeting, which had an audience of invited guests ended abruptly and violently. Two people died and one male attendee, who was said to have initiated the disturbance, was severely injured. He is now at an unnamed London Hospital in an induced coma.

"The missing guest, said to be a refugee from the Kibish a remote region between the Omo valley of Southern Ethiopia and South Sudan, ..." continued the report.

"You were right, Amani, about where he comes from," commented Jolanta, "if that is him. Do you think that is him?"

" . . . purportedly witnessed the massacre and killings of everyone in his village, children, women and men, by Ethiopian police. The Ethiopian government deny this, saying, tribal disputes between villages in remote jungle regions of the south, which occur regularly, had been noted and few deaths were recorded. Survival international is concerned because it is rumoured that land in the region is being sought by international companies for mineral and agricultural exploitation. Survival International believe the Department for International Development is implicated through its policy of wishing to determine how aid to Ethiopia should be invested. We invited the Department to respond to Survival International's concerns, but no one was available for comment.

"The police have released an image of the guest speaker, so far unnamed, who disappeared from the venue, and whom they wish to interview in connection with the incident. "

"Look! Look! It's definitely him!" Jolanta was lounging in a huge armchair of deep red velvet. One leg draped over an arm; she was wrapped in a heavy pale green linen dressing gown. She appeared

32

completely unperturbed by the fact that they were harbouring someone hunted by the police.

Already Manson's interview, Jolanta noted, had been published on YouTube with over eighty-nine thousand views. Videos and photos from private phones were also published on YouTube, Facebook, Instagram and other media outlets. No video was published of the actual disturbance since there had been a general failure of power to the building. Nevertheless, someone did publish recordings of the screams, shouts, gunshots and falling chairs as people fled the scene.

*   *   *

After the bath, the three women carried me to Queen Amani's private room, of course, I was unconscious, and placed me gently on her bed. Jolanta had switched on the TV and turned down the volume, but with sufficient to hear and then to see that this practically comatose, bruised and injured body was in fact that of the current hysteria-led, media-obsessed fixation.

Amani started quietly chanting to herself.

"What is that, Amani, darling? Lihua asked. "Do I know it? Have I heard it before?"

"Maybe you've heard me singing it." said Amanishakhete. "His skin is night, his features, the stars and all who see him will renounce the garish light of day, quit its clamorous certainties to take flight into the dark arms of his heart, his open heart!"

"Well, where does that come from?" demanded Jolanta of Amani.

"It's a prediction. It's from an ancient Nubian tale told by slaves. You should listen. It is for us who don't belong, the un-English, the foreign, the borderless. He is here for us!"

"Sometimes, you say such beautiful things, Amani, darling," smiled Lihua.

"Why don't you put him in one of the guest rooms?" Jolanta wondered. "There are security cameras in all of them. We could check on him on our phones while we are busy. He would be perfectly fine."

"No. I am going to sit beside him until he is well. I found him out of my madness, if you like. That is all I have!" It was as if she was almost pleading. "But I did find him, through a premonition, waiting through my people's histories, myths and beliefs; finally, he came, he came to me, Amani! Without those convictions, beliefs and histories, without him, I am just a prostitute and would die a prostitute!"

Jolanta and Lihua could see Amani was close to tears. These women only had each other and Jolanta was aware the other two were still much closer to their ancient cultural values than she had ever been. Whatever had been Polish culture had been destroyed by modern wars and twentieth century political ideologies imposed with such utter brutality that as a child she had had to search bins for her needs. All that was left was Catholicism and as a child she had determined she would never join the ranks of weeping old women in headscarves.

"Fine!" she declared, still hiding her compassion. "We will see what he has to offer, what he will bring to our lives. He has fallen into our laps from an ugly world that hates him as much as it despises us. We will see."

*　　　*　　　*

When I opened my eyes, I saw the most beautiful black face looking down at me; at the time, I was feverish, surrounded by my people, my leopards and I even saw Wóhólò Tágì, and Juliette.

"Shh!" said Amani. "Don't try to speak! You have been sick for two days. You were dying when we found you, from the cold and your body is bruised and cut."

"Amanishakhete, Queen of Queen Mothers![11] Now I have found you!," I managed to whisper, looking up at her face, her full cushioned lips, slightly puckered towards me as if to give me a kiss, her high majestic cheekbones, proud nose and fine black curls framing her face. I remembered this look of an ancient people not so far from home.

"One of the Candace, Queen of Mothers." Was I speaking in Suri now?

---

[11] The name of one of the Candaces, or Queen Mothers, of the Nubian kingdom of Kush (now northern Sudan). This name could be shortened to AMANI, itself as mentioned, Kiswahili for 'peace'.

And yet, she had understood me.

"Nubian people. Kushite Queen of Queen Mother's Amanishakhete! Near to Beyahola!" I was still feeling lost in a delirium of imaginings and memories, If it was true, as Queen Amanishakhete said, that my heart had stopped, this time, it was not leopards reviving me but my Queen Mother! "You found me after I'd died. I remember. My mother, Queen of Meroë, I have seen you before!" my voice, still a whisper of slow recovery.

"How does he know these things? And how do you know where he comes from? And why does he call you Queen of Queen Mothers?" asked Lihua, who was looking over Amani's shoulder.

"Be quiet, silly Chinese bar girl!" Amani reprimanded, herself feeling confused. "Amanishakhete was an ancient queen of Kush, much respected." She finally explained. "He wants me to be his mother? I was right, you see! He is a prince!"

"You are lucky, Amani! Fate has brought you a new son!" said Lihua. "Perhaps the same will happen for me, one day."

Amanishakhete looked at me with considerable surprise. How could I know where she was from and about her people's past?

"It's him!" cried Jolanta, her hair squirming with a sense of thrill. "I was not sure at first because of his bruises, but now . . . ! Are you not listening? It's him from the Amnesty . . . thing . . . incident, that terrorist attack!"

"Ha, ha, ha." laughed Amani quietly. "Those who want him dead should be careful! They don't know who they chase!" I could see from her face how her world now had sense. Before, she had been mad, but now . . .

I realised I was naked except for a fine silk cloth draped over my hips and legs. I was lying on a very large bed, which seemed to occupy most of the room, the walls of which were concealed by a multitude of similar silk drapes hanging from canes suspended to the ceiling. The three strange women who had somehow either rescued, captured or charmed me drifted in and out, appearing and disappearing through and behind

35

the silks, the colours of which seemed to have run dripping, tearfully, with fading strengths of pinks and turquoise and greens and blues. As the three sisters glided in and out, the silks seemed to want to grasp them, embrace them, follow them, trying to cling to their thighs, shoulders and breasts.

"Where are my clothes?"

"Your clothes are finished, darling!" said Lihua, soothingly. "ripped and torn by violence unknown."

"And my wallet and passport?!"

"Gone! You have nothing!"

"How long were you in that hole?" asked Amanishakhete.

"I don't know. Two nights, three nights. I am not sure."

"And these bruises?"

"I remember, one night, waking and people were kicking me. I couldn't do anything, stuck in that tiny hole in the ground. Then I passed out. The next day, I couldn't move. I was sure that night . . . already my body was so cold . . . "I could feel my eyes stinging and pain sticking in my throat. I was on the edge of tears.

"And we came to find you!" declared Lihua hearteningly.

"The idiots who attacked you must have stolen your things and left you bleeding." said my Amanishakhete.

Lihua felt she had to reach down and pick me up, pulling my head into her breasts. I was still naked and the comfort of her perfume and breasts aroused the passion waiting in my loins. Her hands drifted up and down my stomach muscles.

"Oh, my poor baby! Let me comfort you!"

Jolanta, seeing what Lihua was doing, pulled herself away from the news report, found a tube of lubricant, which she smeared liberally over her fore and middle fingers. Determined to bring Lihua's erotic intimacy

36

under her own control. Whatever happened, this young man was not going to be Lihua's pet, nor anyone's!

"He is not going to be your plaything, Lihua! If he stays, it is for the sake of Amani's dreams. And we will all help him to fulfil that, for her. We are sisters, we care for each other. He is important for Amani. And we are here to help her."

Manipulating men's bodies was the everyday for these three. As ordinary as washing the dishes. She opened my legs and pushed both fingers carefully through my ɗolé[12], along the internal shaft of my dormì[13] to find that special place that makes everything happen. My head lifted away from Lihua in a brief moment of shock.

"Shh! Shh!" said both Lihua and Amani, knowing what Jolanta was doing. "Relax! Everything is ok! you will soon feel better."

Within a few seconds, my dormì was making its milk. The first jumped across my chest to my right nipple. Jolanta's palm was cupping my ɓúrrà:[14] while her two fingers moved back and forth inside. She felt the first throb of my dormì and, with the other hand, held it near its base to pull the skin back tight so that the head was fully exposed and glistening. The next shot up into the air and hit Lihua's chest and neck, the third across my face. I let out a small moan. The fourth, fifth and sixth again across my chest and starting to run down my ribs to the bedsheets beneath.

"My God!"

"Bloody hell!"

Still more poured out, this time to my chin and lips, seventh, eighth, ninth, running down my penis to Jolanta's fingers at the base and down to her other hand cupping my balls. One more into my belly button, making a small overflowing puddle of white juice.

"He hasn't had sex for a few days," declared Amani.

---

[12] anus
[13] penis
[14] testes

"Nor masturbated," added Jolanta.

"For a couple of weeks, you mean!" said Lihua.

They started laughing.

"More like a couple of months!"

I looked up from the bed at these cackling witches, my dormì still occasionally throbbing as it lay against my belly. Where was I? Who were these mad women?

*   *   *

Jolanta was famous amongst the clientele of Place Pigalle for her two-finger prostate rubbing technique, although some, with the memory of ecstatic moments, referred to it as the exploding prostate technique. A few would turn up just for that, forgetting about a massage or other benefits, and would be so aroused in anticipation that stepping out of their taxis outside the entrance to Place Pigalle was an embarrassment as they desperately held on to their crotch in attempts to hide what was going on between their legs. They would only be in the Place for five minutes, dropping their trousers without even properly undressing, and then out again, the taxi waiting, and back to work, feeling as high as a kite. Her service was not cheap, but what did they care, these bankers, brokers, lawyers and occasional politicians?

"He can't stay here,"

Jolanta had marched into my Queen Amanishakhete's room. Her announcement was for the other two sisters. Urgency had driven her to make this demand and as she did so, she glanced at me with wide eyes, unapologetic, knowing this could offend me and at the same time hoping to convey that this was meant for the two women and not intended to deliberately hurt me.

"The police are searching for you, Chár. If they found you here, we would be arrested also, possibly imprisoned and certainly deported; we would lose everything." And then addressing Lihua and my Amani: "He has no passport and even if he did, it would be no good to him. They're about to declare that Amnesty disaster a terrorist incident with him as the main suspect. At the very least he's an illegal. And all this within, what? Only five days after the Amnesty riot!""'

"That makes him like you, then, doesn't it!" retorted Amanishakhete.

"Someone wants your blood, Chár," Jolanta declared, making clear the gravity of my predicament.

"We could help him get a new passport, everything, just like us! Besides, I love him! He is so cute!" said Lihua.

"Vous êtes des hors la loi?[15]" momentarily forgetting which language I was supposed to be speaking, and feebly lifting myself onto my elbows.

"Yes, my dear," replied Jolanta, "we are outside the law. We are outlaws!"

"We have no country."

"No family."

"Same me." said Chár. "If I am so bad, so dangerous for you, why did you help me? It's fine. Don't worry. I can go."

"Don't be ridiculous! You wouldn't get to the end of the street; you can still barely walk!" Jolanta paused, realising she was already presenting arguments against her own emphatic declaration that I couldn't stay. "Did you kill those people at the Amnesty meeting?" she demanded, knowing she was already weakening, losing the ground beneath her feet.

"Who are you to ask such questions,"Amanishakete interjected.

Jolanta left the room before I could answer, leaving me wondering about the secrets held between these three, their mysterious and cloaked history.

*   *   *

"I need blood, cow's blood!" I very soon knew what to do to heal myself. "Mother Amanishakhete, I need to drink cow's blood to regain my strength!"

---

[15] You are outlaws, (literally: outside the law)?

Amani just looked at me, but was hardly surprised: "I'll do what I can."

Then later with Lihua and Jolanta: "He says he needs fresh cow's blood. I know these people, they regularly drink cow's blood, which gives them great vitality and stamina. We'll ask Skinner's, the amount of money we spend there, they can do this for us."

Skinner's was a local butcher who slaughtered his own beasts; he wanted to know where it came from and his clientele, knowing the origin, paid a high price also for his beef. The Ladies had been customers for years and Skinner himself was always obliging. He had to send a runner with the fresh blood in a small flagon three times a week, shaking it so it didn't coagulate. The tale of fresh bull's blood further added to the reputation amongst the street kids that these women were a lot more than just prostitutes.

Lihua assumed the responsibility of taking care of my bruised and battered body. She gave me a massage every day, using her secret oils infused with various herbs. She also prepared me different teas and tisanes some of which alleviated my pains and discomforts, others making me sleep, others affecting my moods, making me laugh a lot, sometimes helping me reflect on my past life, drawing tears, understandings, mental strengths. It was during these kind and loving sessions, caring for me that she explained about Amani, losing her baby boy, who fell through the blue mirror. This sounded to me like my Chaga Boyé, the blue lake where I had died and been rescued by Wóhólò Tági, and we had picnicked with my Juliette and Angeline, and briefly, Rémi Tági had become a rabbit, although when he had rescued me he had become the Flaming Bodhisattva. Strange that these blue mirrors are places of transformation. Since losing her child, she had been looking for me, so Lihua reckoned. And Jolanta?

"Jolanta . . . she seems . . . angry? An angry person?" I commented, worried. "I think, maybe, she doesn't like me."

"Non, non, non, non, non!" replied Lihua. "Jolanta cares for everyone! That is why she sometimes seems angry. If you care for the world, that is a big job!"

"But when she looks at me, her look is so severe, as if she is going to beat me."

40

"I have told you, Jolanta doesn't like people to waste their time doing stupid things. She has said she will help you get a new passport and new ID, in return, she wants you to become smart."

"What do you mean?"

"Look. Number one: You have nowhere to go. You have no passport, no ID, no money, nothing. Number two: The police are hunting you; Immigration is hunting you. Number three: the public think you are a terrorist. You have no choice; you have to hide. We can help you. We are all illegals. But Jolanta wants you to understand what is happening to you, to know the history of things, to become yourself."

"What?"

"Yeh, she wants you to learn. She will help."

"Learn what?"

"Look, I will tell you a secret about Jolanta. Why are we three here? What binds us, I, from China, Jolanta from Poland, Amani, the Sudan? Women, such as us, usually have a man to protect them. Where are the men who brought us here? Where is the pimp who guards us? Think on it with care, Chár, and you will know."

I fainted back into a euphoric reverie induced by Lihua's perfumed oils and healing caresses.

*   *   *

Le temps était morne![16] How do you say that in English – morne? What a beautiful word and which seemed to sum up the very miserable nature of the weather - of the day. Too often it seemed that every day was like this in England. Maybe it was my mood. I was sitting in my little wooden window seat, painted ancient grey many years ago. This same grey as the sky, which, cracked by the jagged black lines of winter's trees, became the mirror of my misfortunes. I would curl up foetus-like with my arms wrapped around my knees staring out of the small rippled old glass pieces framed in panels, composing the attic window. One time, at night, unable to sleep, thinking of my French family, Juliette and Rémi, I saw a couple passing in the street below and starting suddenly, wondered if I

---

[16] The weather was bleak, dreary.

recognised them. They disappeared around a corner. But then I saw my two leopards. I hadn't seen them since I couldn't remember when – ah, the Amnesty evening. They looked up at me from the street below, then turned and walked away. Fuck! I had to do something! I had lost count now of the number of days I had been living with the sisters. It had taken a long time for me to recover from my injuries, days which passed in an eternity of recuperation. And now, better, Amanishakhete and Lihua had prepared me a room of my own in the roof of the house. I was now part of this little family. The only restriction imposed was that I could never go out for fear of bringing trouble not just upon myself but everyone.

*   *   *

Rémi was passing one of those nights when you imagine you have not been able to sleep at all. He couldn't make himself comfortable, turning from one side to the other, sometimes lying flat on his back, another on his stomach. It was a long time now that he had given up wearing pyjamas, since early adolescence, when he had become obsessed with his own body, checking it, wondering if his muscles were getting stronger, were his legs too thin, when would he grow more pubic hair, did others find him attractive. He was lying naked under his quilt. He spread his legs open wide and pulled his feet, frog-like, up until his heels almost touched his buttocks. His right hand went directly down to rub his couilles[17], pulling them and his penis upwards and then pushing his hand further down so that his middle finger could stroke his anus. Any sense of childish inhibition or disgust with parts of his body which in his culture, in fact many cultures were taboo, these ideas had been thrown out the window the summer he spent with me, as we both laughed, explored and experimented with our own and each other's bodies. It was a sort of desperation, hidden from himself even initially, a desperate passion to reveal all and discover all. I had made all that easy. Lying next to me, sharing my bed, because I was foreign, with unknown, alien, incomprehensible ideas and values, puisque j'étais noir, quoi, Suri noir,[18] Rémi, in my bed became a foreigner in a foreign land; we were both foreigners in foreign lands, and as such, he could be anyone, everyone, free from all constraints imposed by this world, by religion, parents, the culture in which he had grown up with all its prejudices and idiosyncracies! He was no longer the Rémi-self, but the universal nomad, Rémi Wóhólò Tagí!

---

[17]   balls
[18]   since he was black, Suri black

His restlessness continued. He hadn't seen me for several weeks now and I was increasingly on his mind. As he turned from side to side, trying to find that state of repose sufficient to sleep, he started drifting into thoughts and memories, which became illustrated, exaggerated and decorated as he slipped into an unpleasant dream, not terrifying but menacing. He was in Delhi – he had been there years ago with his parents; Claudine had been interested in Indian miniatures. He was not with his parents in the dream but was looking for me. Worryingly, I had absented myself from his company. Then in the middle of a busy street he came across an entrance to an underground shopping district, which as he entered slowly transformed into a narrow lane, lined with small Indian open restaurants serving chapatis, chai and snacks and decrepit broken down shops selling cheap trinkets. He recognised nothing; he was lost. Strangely this lane opened out to a beach with an unusual structure of rusty girders, which might have been a pier at some time, where he had sort of expected to meet me. Then everything suddenly changed. Had he momentarily been aware of dreaming? He was now back inside these underground tunnels standing on a wooden wharf, or jetty next to a canal built of stone with clear, fast running water, it was a fairground type ride, like the water chutes at an adventure park. Anyway, he was encouraged by a strange invisibility to board a small boat, which presented itself and which carried him for some time through various tunnels until he shot out finally into a lake, or was it the Ganges? He was now in what he recognised as an extremely poor and dangerous part of this city, which was crumbling before his eyes and its miserable citizens appeared dangerous and menacing, old temples and mosques disintegrating. He decided he was dreaming and should switch on his bedside lamp to end the uncomfortable insanity. He leaned across his bed in total darkness to feel the bedside table and let his fingers find their way to the light switch. Nothing happened! He turned it on but there was no light! He got up to look out the window to check if there was a general power cut. Down below he saw a street he didn't recognise and a strange, twisted figure scurrying along it, a hunched silhouette in rags scuttling through the slime, mud and excrement deposited by the houses, pubs, brothels, thieves and murderers of Victorian London. It was icy cold and wet. He felt it in his bones as he struggled with his sense of loss and being lost. In front of him, now down in the street, he saw two cats, big cats, one black, he could only see its outline and green eyes and the other yellow, like his own hair, with black spots. They started towards him, slowly, like any friendly pet and then running until they leapt at him, their heads hitting him violently in his naked chest and, with a thud, disappearing. He woke up.

"He's disappeared!" Claudine announced as she threw open the heavy damask silk, lined curtains. Every time she opened them, she reminded herself with a moment of pleasure that they had come from the Palais de Fontainebleau[19]; an aunt had lived and worked there as a guardian; occasionally the palace would decide to part with excess from its stores and the workers would get first pick. This particular morning there was no such pleasure as she feared Rémi's response.

Her feelings, sentiments and emotions towards her son had changed over the last couple of years. He was no longer her little boy who would turn to her for everything. Too often now he was critical, dismissive, while at the same time taking everything, the home, his parents and their wealth had to offer. Now that he was a man, and this development had happened in the last two years, especially it seemed, during that summer she had travelled to New York and he had stayed with Nathalie, Charles and me, now that he was a man, he seemed to value her love, her devotions, far less. For a start, he was more muscular. What had happened to cause that was obviously not playing games on his iPad. He had been hunting, he had said. And . . . he had had sex, often enough while she had been away to feel confident in that respect. This had been laid bare to her by the very nature in which he had invited Angeline to their apartment in Paris to stay overnight, in his bed and without even mentioning it to her, Claudine. The casual, dismissive way in which he had spoken about it, in response to her enquiries, was as if it meant little to him. Was Angeline his girlfriend? Oh, no! They only got together now and then for fucking, nothing like a serious relationship, for goodness sake! Just fun! Grow up, mother! And she, Claudine, was left behind feeling that pain of loss; his pubescent virginity had disappeared, suddenly, while she had been away and without her knowledge. And then she had realised he had been having sex with me, which Marie Jeanne's heavy innuendos had led her to understand.

He sat up in his bed. She knew he was naked. He rubbed his eyes and then raising his arms above his head, twisted his torso to rid himself of the torpor of sleep, such that his back was turned towards her.

"What? What did you say?"

She couldn't help admiring his muscular back and the fine blonde down

---

[19] Palace of Fontainebleau

running across it. It reminded her of Robert when they had first met. Now, of course, Rémi's youthful masculinity also implied her ageing.

"He's disappeared! Chár! He's disappeared!" She felt fearful of my response, which was why she announced it with such cold detachment.

"What do you mean, he has disappeared? He can't just disappear. Don't be ridiculous, Maman!"

"Me, ridiculous? You've told me many times he knew how to be invisible." Her face and voice expressed contempt for her son's prior idealising. "But now it has happened! I've just spoken to Nathalie, it's all over the news . . ."

Claudine believed, still, she was wiser than her son, understood relationships, their complexities, better than him, simply through age and experience. She believed, also, that it was her role as his mother to advise, persuade, even coerce so that his life might work out for the best, that he would successfully complete his studies at the Polytechnique de Paris and pursue a successful career. These were perfectly rational desires of any mother and any mother would do her best to guide her son in such a direction. Hence, Rémi's close friendship with me really needed to end. I was an impediment, actually, an uneducated, illiterate native of jungles, who would only ever be a burden to Nathalie and Charles and seemed to have an unhealthy influence over Rémi. She had tried pointing this out to him perhaps too many times and each time, less and less tactfully.

"Mother, he is not illiterate! He speaks three languages, French, English and his own, Suri. How many do you speak?"

"But he is not educated. What can he know about our world? How can he even hope to be part of it, let alone join in?"

"He reads all the time! Far more than you! He'll end up as educated as me; already I am making sure of that! He's my best friend, my brother! Besides, he's a human being!"

She knew she was right. How can someone who has no concept of civilisation, has never experienced it, suddenly become civilised? It takes legally eighteen years from birth to maturity for a child to become civilised and even then, it doesn't always work, which is why there are laws and prisons. The point is the control of desires and passions, being able to defer desire and mitigate or even, in some instances, suppress passion. As far as she could see, over that summer Rémi had discovered passions which were completely alien to him. The relationship between mother and son had now slipped into a nasty little merry-go-round of narrow sniping. They almost couldn't see each other without falling into that trap. She could see he was becoming angrier but couldn't stop herself.

"You were too intimate. Look, Natalie wanted you to help her educate him a little bit in the customs and ways of France. At first, he was even unable to sleep in his own bed. He'd go to Charles and Nathalie every night! I don't think their intention was for you to jump into bed with him. Rather than him becoming like us French, you have become like him, a savage who runs naked in the forests!"

"You should try, Mum. It's beautiful! Too intimate! Too intimate! What do you mean?" He could feel his frustrated anger seeping to the surface again. Was this some sort of euphemism whereby Claudine wanted to censure the sexual relations, the physical intimacy Rémi and I had created which as far as he was concerned was nothing to do with vulgar gratification.

"Thick as thieves! That's what you became! Comme larrons en foire![20]"

Rémi jumped out of his bed naked, deliberately, so as to embarrass his mother. Turning his back and sticking out his arse, he slapped his buttocks.

"Cul et chemise, tu veux dire!"[21]

Claudine left his bedroom.

According to the students of Lycée Janson de Sailly, since the battle of Friedland between Napoleon's armies and the armies of Tsar Alexander 1st of Russia, the most famous battle between the French and the Russians took place outside the gates of Lycée Janson de Sailly. Tsar Alexander had lost about forty per cent of his soldiers and the same percentage had happened at the Gates of Janson de Sailly, leading to complete surrender in both battles. While Napoleon and Tsar Alexander

---

[20]   As thick as thieves!
[21]   Connected at the hip, you mean! (Literally translated it is: 'arse and shirt', you mean!)

had signed a peace treaty on a raft in the middle of the river Neman, the peace treaty between the Russian and French families after the battle of Janson de Sailly, had been signed in the office of the Directeur de l'École[22]. When truths came to light about bullying, extortion, and persecution of Jacob, stealing his kippah, Monsieur Zhukov was so angry with his son that he smacked him across the back of his head and publicly chastised him there and then in the Director's office. All the boys were about to be suspended until Robert took Monsieur Zhukov to one side and they came up with a solution to build a new technology department for the school out of an act of good faith towards the school and in amicable cooperation with each other, promising the boys would cooperate and work hard for the benefit of all school enterprises. And everyone shook hands.

After the signing of the peace accord and the agreement with the Directeur, Robert spent the evening demanding Rémi recount in detail the battle for him and Claudine, who, by the way, found none of it amusing, unlike Robert, laughing and congratulating him on standing up for himself. From then on, Robert looked at his son differently. He was no longer the shy little boy with his computer games, he was becoming a man. And slowly as the boy slipped out of the fingers of his mother, he became closer to his father as equals, as good friends.

Now, arriving for breakfast, it was to his father Rémi intended to turn. Claudine was already in full flow lecturing Robert on her position.

". . . . the neuropsychologist we met at Frannie's in New York? He claimed that children have an abundance of grey matter in the brain, which controls body function, memory, emotions, language etc. During adolescence, parts of the grey matter which is not used is eliminated and a greater amount of white matter which makes up connections between parts of the brain increases, so patterns of behaviour, function, understanding, etc. become fixed. Remember all that?"

"Vaguely, yes." responded Robert, already tired by this tedium at breakfast. "Are you sure it's not the other way round, the grey/white stuff? Anyway, what has that got to do with anything?"

"Well, if you've spent your adolescence in the jungles in Africa, your brain structure and function is going to be very different to someone who has been brought up in Paris."

---

[22] The school's headmaster/director

"Oh, right! I see where you're going with this now! Be careful, you'll end up justifying ethnic cleansing. If you've been brought up in a desert in Afghanistan in a male dominated society and had your foreskin brutally chopped off at the age of thirteen, or whenever, you're not going to be able to fit into a liberal-minded, sexually liberated society because of the way your brain is structured physiologically. Is that what you're saying? Or if you are brought up in a strictly religious Jewish community? . . . Is that what you are saying? Are you fucking mad Claudine?"

"No! But his brain is structured for jungles, not for Paris or London."

"Have you finished, mother?" said Rémi, who had been standing at the door listening, unnoticed.

Claudine glanced at the floor in embarrassment and then turned away to busy herself in another corner of the kitchen.

"What happened, papa?"

*   *   *

"What the fuck happened, you idiot?" demanded Mercantor's jumped up intern of Ferrier. "Do the police know who you were working for? DeLange is dead. Oh, you didn't know? At least he's not going to be talking – to anyone. He was already turning into carrion anyway.

"So, you'll never walk again? Is that the prognosis? And, it seems, there is little chance of recovering use of your arms, also. You'll be quadriplegic. Ah well, the Government always looks after its own and currently loves especially to look after their disabled enforcers– such as yourself.

"The Minister will want to see you at some point. How's your back, by the way? Still sore? You probably can't feel it anyway. But the doctors reckon you have these deep . . . claw marks? Strange, eh? Into a bit of S&M were you, in one of the sex joints around Shoreditch before the event – the disaster – your disaster? Ah well, you won't be doing that again, will you? Having sex, I mean!

"So, we're after the nigger. As much as possible, attribute blame to him for the deaths and the general – how would you say? - disturbance? - Riot? - Terrorist incident? - should anyone ask. Terrorism, I think that's the best term. That's how the police and reliably prejudiced media are putting it about, so . . . Yeh . . . he's considered extremely dangerous. The public are advised not to approach him since he might be armed. The police have been instructed to shoot on sight. Here's your gun, by the way. We picked it up from the, er, hall floor. You might want to shoot yourself. After all, you don't have too much to live for now. Do you have family? No, I didn't think so. With any luck, you won't have to see me, and I won't have to see you, again . . . so, er, . . ."

Ferrier's hatred and contempt for this arrogant little Home Office servant, cheap errand boy, dragged out of his cupboard and fucked over a desk every now and then, only increased his sense of anger and impotence. He made as if to whisper something. The gofer leaned forward. Ferrier collected as much phlegm in his mouth as possible and spat it into the cunt's face.

*   *   *

"I want to dream."

Ray Ferrier hadn't always been a bad person, so he remembered. It was now, many days, perhaps a few weeks, he had been lying in this hospital bed. Every day nurses came to roll him over, massage his buttocks to prevent bed sores, his legs, feet, elbows and upper back. Mostly, he couldn't feel anything in his hands and arms. Were there occasional twitches? He had been completely catheterised, told he might get some function back in his arms, but not the lower part of his body. He would have to learn how to manage his bodily functions. If he could regain some use of his upper body, then moving around and exercising would help with bowel movements.

He just wanted to die. It was stupid. Anal plugs? Or would they decide to simply sew his A-hole shut? Emptying the urinary catheter bag, laxative suppositories, enemas? Unable to feel the need to shit or piss? The possibilities and their combinations were endless! His body was useless. There was no pleasure in it, only discomfort.

When he was young, he remembered, there were clear waters moving slowly through oak and beech bowers, sunlight darting through dark leaves piercing their surface illuminating gems on the soft silt of the silent riverbed, or reflecting ripples on the old, stained, yellow brickwork underbelly of a Victorian bridge – how clever the laying of bricks had been, beautifully curved and angled! Here lurked the dark backs of trout watching the shadows, allowing the cool summer waters to caress their pearly scales. Hours in the long sun fishing in happy boredom, or becoming pirates with friends, nailing together old pieces of wood to make a raft, which immediately sank. Arcadian paradises belong to children and should be their right.

In early childhood, life had been beautiful. When did it happen? When did he reach that bleak mental state of 'no hope, no fear'?

That fucking boys school! "Become a bully, a tyrant amongst peers!" Like that, he had understood that he would be respected by older students and feared by the younger ones, a culture he later discovered was not inevitable but belonged to the shithole he had been born into. Sulphurous lava crept through the veins of his ghost body ready to bleed through its skin and poison that world. He had even felt hatred, resentment born out of envy, towards those who had not been deprived of gentleness and simple kindness towards others. He had wanted to hurt them, make them as bitter as he felt himself.

He had settled for a cheap and somewhat vulgar relationship of convenience. There was no love, in fact he was such a cynic that he denied love existed even for those who claimed to know it. It was just a crude generalisation for a bunch of selfish needs, drives and instincts, which had no place in the world into whose employ he had fallen. When his wife had left him, bruised, battered and humiliated, taking his pathetic girly son with her, the last signs of tawdry meaning fled him. At that point, he thought he had understood 'no hope, no fear'. But now, confronted with the idea of spending the rest of his life prisoner of a completely useless body, he realised just how much he had loved those tedious trivialities of his existence.

One thing he noticed: when he dreamed, he could still walk, his body was fully functioning. His dream age was as he would imagine himself in an ageless eternity; he was neither old nor young but perfectly fit, able to use his body as he had always been used to, and even more so. At times he could even fly!

"I want to dream," he had said repeatedly to his assigned nurse, the first time, tearfully. "There must be something, some drug, anything, that can put me in a dream state. When I dream, when I am conscious of dreaming, I can still feel my body, I can still walk, run, do everything."

he pleaded.

"Of course, you can," said a tall black nurse with long curling hair, looking down at him somewhat condescendingly. "And there are drugs especially for that lucid dreaming. Ancient. From the daffodil bulb. It is said Odysseus was given it by Circe on his way home from Troy." she explained as she finished his bath and reassembled the bed.

How could this black woman know such stuff about Odysseus, he wondered, that he, Ferrier, hadn't.

Queen Amanishakhete looked at him with contempt: "You think a black woman doesn't know these things? I know far more about the ancient times than you!"

It hadn't been difficult finding this abject and confused petty criminal, the agent, the paid assassin, the whore to his . . . , nor inveigling herself onto the hospital staff and finally his ward; for a witch, such complications are meaningless; in any case, hospitals were constantly needing temporary nursing staff from the so-called gig economy, in which everyone worked for themselves and no one really knew where these temps came from let alone their abilities and qualifications. It was a simple way that these parasitic companies could bleed the NHS dry and eventually kill it off. The greatest gift Margaret Thatcher had offered the country was measuring, counting the cost and resentment,[23] this translated as efficiency, with the continued impoverishment of those already on the lowest of incomes, who work extremely hard for what? Merit? While billionaires clearly merit their billions, after all, without them sucking up all the wealth with their genius, the poor and their children would die! Let's face it, why should they pay taxes for the children of the herd, the masses, to go to school, or get free health care, or even somewhere to live?

What did Queen Amani, Nurse Manchester, want to do with Ferrier? She hadn't decided yet. She would tell Chár later when he was stronger. In the meantime, she would keep Ferrier in a confused state where reality and dream, memory and hallucination slip and slide like the snakes through the hair of the Medusa.

---

[23] When Nietzsche is surprised to discover that ressentiment actually possesses 'Spirit', what was that 'Spirit' he had discovered? It had to be the religion of money, with all of it's political and moral tentacles, surely! It's so obvious! When investors lose 'faith' in the markets, what happens? Money, like the god we no longer believe in, disappears.

She leaned forward to whisper in his ear through the drug induced tilting of reality and imaginings.

"Tell your master, the Black Dionysus is coming. He comes from deep in jungles along the Nile. - Did you know that? - You want to dream? I will ask him to come for you, the Black One. You want that? The Black One you didn't kill! Tell your master, 'They who wrote the law shall drink its ink. His leopards prowl for those who chose the dead; their dance begins.'"

He felt frightened, vulnerable. She had seen into him somehow. He tried to dismiss the idea, but . . . had she even said those things? What were imaginings, dreams, thoughts, fears, lies and what the truth? The next time he saw her, he had decided to ask her about Odysseus, Dionysus and daffodils. As he did so, he felt stupid, delusional. She looked at him puzzled and smiled: "You really need stronger dreams?" she smiled coldly.

The room seemed to fill up with grey smoke and the walls spontaneously sprouted the dense foliage of creepers.

*   *   *

My Queen of Queen Mothers had overheard me in a feverish dream, say: "Tu veux que je redevienne Dionysus, Juliette?[24] " I had been dreaming of Juliette and her portraits of me. Amani asked me about it the next day and I explained about my Juliette, her paintings and Caravaggio, and then asked my Kushite mother to find me a print of Sick Bacchus. For her this took on great significance, it was a further confirmation of her premonition of a 'special one' arriving. It was my Juliette who had first seen me as Dionysus and for Amani that naming had seduced her. For her to fold these imaginings into her encounters with Ferrier gave amused spice and enrichment to those meetings. It was as if she was cooking up outcomes of which she was yet unsure, stirring a broth of the birth of strange worlds and future events.

*   *   *

"Bacchus is the same as Dionysus," explained Jolanta. "Bacchus is Roman, Dionysus, Greek. He's the god of wine, partying, upsetting the

---

[24] You want me to become Dionysus again, Juliette?

52

order of things, just to have fun. Sex, drugs and rock 'n roll!" She looked at me and grinned, the first time I had seen her usually hard exterior crack a little.

I was staring at Caravaggio's Sick Bacchus. I remembered being sick myself, when Rémi had rescued me. Those eyes in the painting were my eyes, kind, loving, but vulnerable, I could remember feeling exactly that. As well as the eyes of Bacchus, of Dionysus, my eyes, they were also the eyes of Caravaggio, Michelangelo da Caravaggio, Michelange. I loved him. I loved Caravaggio. He was twenty when he painted this self-portrait, the same age as me, so Juliette had said.[25] Someone in that crazy, dangerous city, Rome, trying to survive, as best he could, just like me who now found myself in an equally dangerous mad city, lost, were it not for my three ladies of the night. This Bacchus, this Dionysus was obviously Suri; he decorated his head, his hair with leaves and in other paintings, flowers, just like all young Suri men. In fact, Jolanta had told me, Dionysus had come from that same part of Ethiopia which had been mine, my home. Maybe he was Suri, after all. I later bothered Juliette over exactly this. Where did he come from? Too many variations! There seems to be some Apollonian consensus on Thebes in Thrace. Certainly Herodotus reckoned from his travels along the Nile:

"Then after having passed through this country in the forty days which I have said, you will embark again in another vessel and sail for twelve days; and after this you will come to a great city called Meroe. This city is said to be the mother-city of all the other Ethiopians: and they who dwell in it hold reverence for the gods Zeus and Dionysus alone, and these they greatly honour."

Others say he comes from India, although again the consensus seems to be that he conquered India by introducing wine.

Maybe Jolanta was exaggerating her bit on Herodotus, or maybe she was casting a spell.

Maybe he was . .from . . . that past, which is so familiar it is invisible . . Maybe he just appeared as if ex nihilo, out of nothing! Intoxications, imaginings made flesh! And who is Michelange? Who am I?

I was staring at myself. For a long time. I was staring at myself both as an object and as a being. Being Dionysus and being Michelange, Michael

---

[25] For me, age was meaningless, as far as I was concerned, I had always been present, here and now.

the Angel, Michel Ange, Italian made, from four hundred years before, looking out from his being, his heart, to the mirror[26], reflected as Bacchus/Dionysus, half naked, with only a white cloth draped over his left shoulder, then looking to the canvas and back and finally out, directly into my eyes. His right shoulder and head turned, his lips slightly parted, his eyes looking out of the canvas, and into my very being.

Time had always been cyclical in Beyahola, the sun rising each morning and setting each evening, the seasons following each other and repeating, birth, death, watching life tear itself apart to reassemble itself again, occasional big gatherings for Thyrsus[27] Bhirɛ fights, meeting other villagers, eyeing up the pretty young girls. All of this interrupted by occasional minor events, chasing big cats away from the herd, the funny tourists, occasional sicknesses, evening parties. Then there was a different time, the time of France, Europe, white man's time, measured by watches and phones and every watch, every phone, every clock, every timetable demanded synchronicity. They all had to report the same time. Everyone starting work together, watching the same TV programmes at the same time, trains, buses, planes all running according to determined times. Nature had been taken out of it, disregarded, eliminated, as if it were somehow a nuisance.

But now, suddenly, that transcendental time of machines, of industry of production had itself been superseded by something human but eternal, no longer the time of nature, nor the time of machines, watches and mobiles.

I remembered myself, as a boy, spraying red ochre, red ochre mixed with a little water and then with it in my mouth, putting my hand onto the wall of a cave and spraying paint over it to leave a painted outline of my hand and then doing the same on Bongáy's body, spraying hand prints on each other's bodies, using leaves as stencils or making wooden printing blocks to make more ornate prints. In the same way, my father had passed the spirit of the leopard he had killed into me, its skin

---

[26] Caravaggio has a mirror in front of him, which he uses to paint his portrait. So although the image of Dionysus seems to be looking out from the canvas at the viewer, in actual fact Caravaggio is looking at his own reflection in the mirror. The observer immediately deludes himself into believing Dionysus is looking at him.

[27] The staff often wound by ivy and carried by the Thiasus, the closest band of devotees of Dionysus, otherwise known as the Maenads, "wild" or "raving" women, more likely, made up of widows, ex-slaves and any woman excluded from civil life, very much like the three Ladies of the Night!

marking my spirit-body. When Caravaggio became Dionysus, perhaps that blurring was also part of me sharing a common spirit with both Caravaggio and Dionysus. The stepping beyond, the handprint on eternity. I had seen it with Nathalie, on TV programmes about the earliest cave paintings in France, the human will to step into the Uberzeit[28].

*   *   *

It was due to language. By now, two, almost three years in Europe, I could speak French and English fluently. I still felt minor weaknesses, new words were still appearing, mostly from books now, but others always praised me, especially my accent. It would take some time for most to realise I was neither French nor English. Certainly, I thought of myself as being French. I had been taken in by French people and the government had given me documents which declared me French. In France, I felt as free as any French citizen. Now I thought in French, and English, and Suri also, especially when teaching Rémi. One thing which amused me was how I seemed to become a different person with each language I spoke. I was Chár! I was many! And now, being many in a strange place, I was beginning to notice, a sort of "outside of time".

*   *   *

The three ladies, the three witches, the three Goddesses, the three courtesans, all titles adding to the mystique of women, which men attribute and some women enjoy and exploit, that strange difference, both alluring and intimidating, were taking their late evening bath together in their biggest hot tub, the same in which they had bathed me on rescuing me from that railway embankment; it was an ideal place for them to discuss their day and share management of their affairs.

"Fucking trousers! I hate them!" I ripped them open, pushing them down and stamping on them as I pulled my feet out of the legs which were clinging around my ankles. I glanced across my room in the roof towards my leopards and the naked Bacchus standing between them, a smile of great joy spread across my face as I reached out towards those golden curls. As yet the sisters were unaware, but Wóhólò Tagí had arrived. I had kept all of the arrangements for contacting Rémi a secret from the three sisters, but now that he had arrived, I would have to explain. Jolanta would be angry, I was sure.

---

[28]   The beyond-time.

For the first few weeks I was there, being cared for in their apartment above Place Pigalle, I was too ill, but now I had recovered my strength and will, I found myself ripping off my shirt and pants, my brow furrowed with my usual anger; I was about to join the three sisters in their bathtub. The mix of Suri contempt and the spontaneity of English cursing, tripping from my lips made Rémi laugh. I, on the other hand had the serious task of announcing Rémi's arrival and explaining I had been breaking their rules!

I crept down the stairs towards the big bathroom. I didn't know why I was creeping. It was my instinct, the instinct of a leopard, to move silently at night, hunting. I opened the bathroom door and immediately felt the warmth and steamy humidity on my skin. This large room, much more than a simple bathroom, was designed to seduce, and relax their clients. There was a permanent smell of coconut, the regular oil for massage, but also sandalwood oil, rose oil, jasmine, mint, different teas and a host of perfumed roots and flowers. In one part was a double bed with a mattress of black leather. Nearby, was a large tallboy with bed sheets, pillows, dressing gowns and toys. In another corner was a massage table, then through an internal door, a toilet and shower. But the centre piece was a large oval sunken bath, surrounded by multi-coloured fine silk drapes, big enough for a dozen people to laze and splash around without feeling confined or crowded.

"I've been expecting you," said Amanishakhete. "I know you Suri people well."

"I've been waiting for you also," said Lihua, with a big smile, turning her eyes into those of a Modigliani portrait.

"Well, don't stand there, bollock-naked, showing off your penis!" declared Jolanta.

"I don't like this word, bollocks," I replied, with a grin, feeling I must stand up to her. "They are 'mes couilles'," I said, cupping my hand underneath them and lifting slightly as if weighing them, "my cojones! Búrrà ganyu!"

"Oh, you speak many languages!" declared Jolanta. "Very clever!"

"Yes." I was now playing with my foreskin, rubbing it gently between my thumb and forefinger.

"Get in the bath quickly," demanded Amanishakhete. "that is why you are here, no?"

I slipped into the warm soapy water, smiling at the three ladies of the night, my doe-eyes seducing all three, but only Lihua allowing herself to show it. For me, it was so wonderful that I could be naked with these women. They had found me, my old clothes in rags, had bathed me, cared for my body, nursed me, healed my cuts and bruises, and healed my mind also. They knew my body intimately, like mothers, and I could be free.

"No, I am not here for a bath only. I have important things to talk about."

"Okay. So, what are these important things?" demanded Jolanta, to assume charge.

"Recently, I fell from the sky."

"Ohh, here we go! More obscurantism!" she declared impatiently.

"You are too harsh!" Amanishakhete retorted, always ready to defend me. "He is a poet! You haven't understood that yet? Beyond your dry rationalism!"

Both responses, I had expected.

"I am Suri. My name is Leopard. I cannot be locked in my room, forbidden to leave this place. From the window in my room in the roof, if you look long enough, there are paths. Paths to many places, other windows, roofs, even to trees. For a long time now, I have been exploring these paths. And I discovered a band of night people." I had decided to give them a block of information to deal with rather than piecemeal apologetic snippets, each drawing looks and exclamations of horror! That way, they would have to pause and think before admonishing me.

"You've been going out?!"

"Over the rooftops?!"

"Yeh." I replied, as casually as possible.

"I don't believe you!"

"What do you mean, night people?" demanded Jolanta.

"That is their name, my night people. They like it, their new name. You still don't understand the power of names, eh, Jolanta?" I could see she was feeling annoyed.

"I watched them for a long time. Many times. And then one time, I decided to fall from the sky. I knew it would be fine, I could always jump back onto the roofs."

Why did these women want to keep me there, to hide me, protect me? I understood the danger I could be in, wandering the streets, attempting to cross borders to get back to France, if the police, Secret Service and Home Office really believed me to be a terrorist. The Sun and Daily Mail were now accusing me of being a member of Al Shabaab, they had even found a member of the Ethiopian parliament who claimed to have evidence of this, that I was not Suri at all, but was originally from Eritrea and was part of a group which had massacred a village in the south and killed over forty Ethiopian police, who were trying to defend the village. The TV news even showed film and photos from the area where the massacre had taken place.

"It is very bad what you do, if it is true." said Jolanta. "You know what the newspapers say about you and the TV. This is why you cannot leave just now, nor visit your night people."

"If it is true what I do?" I responded indignantly, offended by her suggestion I was lying. "I can show you. They have given me clothes, many, very expensive, beautiful. Every time I see them, they give me something new. Waiting here, doing nothing, I have become nothing! I need paints and flowers! Make myself Suri again!"

I had still not yet told them about the Golden One. In spite of these concerns, my excitement for the moment was irrepressible; I started dancing, bouncing up and down in the warm water.

"Good!" declared Amanishakete at my eagerness to get out into the world. " You want to go out? You will have your flowers and paints and I'll take you to meet the devil himself!" she said, thinking of Ferrier.

I disappeared beneath the surface and suddenly popped up in front of mother Amanishakhete's breasts.

"Queen Mother Amanishakhete, royal dear, you are as much a poet as I, but in truth this is no poetry. For them, I really did fall from the sky! Now tell me, who is this devil?"

"I am truly angry with you, Chár. You must promise not to go out again with your night people. Now, have you read those books I gave you?" demanded Jolanta, her sharp cold eyes attempting to pierce my easy cool.

"You haven't let me finish my story! But, yeh. I have read them."

"All three books?"

"Yeh. First, I read them before at home in my Sologne. Rémi, my Tagí, gave them to me. But of course, I read them again for you, Auntie Jolanta."

"I don't believe you! The Iliad, Odyssey, The Histories of Herodotus? Don't lie to me! And stop calling me Auntie!"

"I don't lie. In France, I taught myself to read fast, to speed-read you call it. When I read Herodotus, especially the Euterpe[29], when he visits near where Amani and I come from, travelling along the Nile, I forget myself in this . . . " I needed to search for a word. "this now, and when I remember myself along with all these stories these myths, these imaginings, there they are in little pieces and I can put them together as my own. They become me and I become them. Not only can I do this, but I want it to be like that." I paused. "Like jigsaws."

Was I explaining it correctly?

"Minos, son of Zeus, who built Knossos, so big, his slaves believed it to be a labyrinth from which they would never escape, like me here, in

---

[29] Euterpe is a Muse, her mother was Mnemosyne, the Titan goddess of memory and was fathered by Zeus. Euterpe means 'to please well'. Herodotus perceives her as his muse for the 2nd volume of his Histories.

Place Pigalle, eh?" he laughed at the uncertainty in their expressions. "I remember, with other Suri boys, teaching his young slaves from Athens and many other cities of Greece, how to dance with bulls. That old king boasted his father was a bull, the most beautiful bull, the biggest and strongest, of course. He was too old to show his bull-power to his people, he needed us Suri boys to dance with his bulls for him, to teach his slaves, and to excite his people so that they would worship him, believe him all powerful. All those young slaves knew, once entering the bull ring, there was no escape. Already his ships controlled the seas and all those peoples who depended on the sea to survive. He had to make his power beyond ordinary man, it had to be magical, from the Gods. You can see, on the walls of the palace, black Suri boys showing the young Greek boys and girls how to leap over the backs of his bulls. The king's mistake was that we became heroes for his subjects – and one of us young men, admired by his daughter. She helped us find a way out of his labyrinth of power, his gigantic palace of corridors and rooms. I remember, because foolishly, he abandoned Ariadne, of the golden thread, and she came to choose me, making me her lover instead."

"How lovely!" declared Lihua, enjoying the story and filling in the gaps, as the imagination is accustomed to do, seeing herself as the daughter, Ariadne.

"Wait, wait wait!" Jolanta cried out. "You want to rewrite these myths to make them about you . . . ?"

"I don't want to write. Your masters want me to write, To fix my story in ink, to sign their forms, to speak their truth. But I come from a world where words live only as long as breath. We don't write our stories, we sing them, dance them, cut them into the earth with our feet. Our language changes like the river, like the wind on cattle skin, like the red dust after the rain. It lives in my body. In my mouth. In the scars. In the silence between things. These myths, these histories, I take them into myself and give them breath. The very same will happen again!

"They say their writing is civilisation. But the first writing wasn't song, it was counting. Grain. Taxes. Debts. Who owes what. Who belongs to whom. Just as all rulers, those who hold power, (like Menelaos and Agamemnon who lied to their people that the war against Troy was about the Gods and Paris stealing the most beautiful woman in the world) . . . maybe the Trojans had raided those Greek states for women, maybe Priam had taxed trade through the Bosphorus, maybe drought had hit them all. For me, the Iliad is about friendship and honour, like for my Wóhólò Tagí and me. I want you to meet him. At some point they built walls to protect their wealth and power. But maybe the Trojan horse was already there, maybe the Trojan horse was its own subjugated and cheated citizens. Maybe it was about the control of food production and accumulation or it was about the transport of grain being taxed by Priam or about laws carved on clay so no one could forget, so no one could escape . . . . the LAW , because, after all, it came from their God, burned into stone by his lighting? Or chiselled by their prophets? In any case, it was WRITTEN! How does it begin, one of those stories about Jesus? 'In the beginning was the Word, And the Word was with God. And the Word was God!' And this Word is their LAW"

"This is true," commented Amanishakhete. "I remember about these records, accounts and control from those ancient times in Kush and Egypt."

"Myths are not written, they are lived. They are memories of moments lived. You show disrespect to those moments if you say they are only writing. The best use of writing is to push these memories into the present. You say they are not Suri in those paintings, the black dancers of Knossos? Why are they not Suri? Of course, they are Suri! They dance with bulls! The same with Caravaggio! His spirit is Suri. He is the same as my brother, the same as Wóhólò Tagí. The same as my mother, my father. The same as Juliette, who has held out her golden thread for me to take! She is the same as your English poet, John Keats, who declared that Truth is in Beauty. That is his Golden Thread, and the same thread, Juliette has offered to me!"

"Aranjinya civilisation's written fate will never capture me. I am not going to be their refugee, their terrorist, their illegal migrant. They are not cutting up my body, my passions to make me, gay, straight, bisexual, transvestite, transexual, This is exactly the naming that suffocates. I am all these and more! My naming does not oppress, it opens new worlds, new possibilities. I am Chár. I am many."

" 'An act and how we judge it', " I was remembering words from one of Jolanta's books, " 'varies at different points in space and time and from different vantage points in any society'. This idea is from one of your books, Auntie Jolanta, I found on your shelves – I read much more than you demand - and I knew it was talking to me. But, mostly, these evaluations, judgments, remain the same amongst most members of a

61

society or group; and finally the lie can be applied: they appear to be "given", by God, or described as natural when really being imposed by the power structure of the society or group. Is it possible to drop these and make all valuations of art, beauty, history, experience, acts, one's own evaluations, rejecting imposed histories and values by Church and State? Is it possible to possess all the valuations that have ever been made and experience them, re-evaluate them as one's own? Becoming Tom Sawyer, becoming Huck Finn, becoming the bull dancers of Knossos. And what about Time? The experience of Time, the understanding of Time? I have understood the significance of names, and by renaming Time can I, can we, take it back and claim it as our own, instead of being stuck with the slavish time of plodding synchronic machines, the time of work, money, measuring and counting the cost, the time of resentment.

"How many times have I died? How many times have I died as Leopard? How many times has Dionysus died? What remains the same? What do I mean when I talk about menenge, spirit? Is it that between of bodies, how they connect? Perhaps, it was necessary to separate the world of shape, space, and matter from change, to define it, name it, manipulate it, but the point at which they absolutely collide in the present, the Now, which, out of all this playing with ideas, is the only idea which implies The Eternal. The Now is eternally present, after all! And just as the Now is present, so am I. This moment, this now, is mine. It becomes my time. And all that is in it is mine also. Find me a wreath of flowers for my crown. Tonight I want to dance!"

"You will have your paints and flowers! Now go and find the wine and some glasses," said Amanishakhete, her brown breasts glistening in the soapy surface water. They watched as I put one foot on the side of the tub and with both hands lifted out my wet, shiny, black body, suds sliding slowly down my back and inside my thighs.

"He seems excited, eh? Something's going on." said Lihua, remembering those whispers she had heard earlier, passing his door.

"What's he talking about? Is he crazy or just full of bullshit?"

Amanishakhete was beginning to feel annoyed by Jolanta's dry rationalism.

"No, he's not a liar and he is not full of bullshit! You criticise him too much. You've read "Ways of Seeing" by John Berger. Isn't that what he was reading from your shelves? You told me about it, so . . . You, the clever one, you just forget! You don't understand how memory works. Personal memory and group memory can be the same thing. I have a Jewish client who knows the same experience with memory that my Prince was talking about remembering the Theseus myth. Although this client was never there, the experience of Auschwitz had become a real memory for him in astounding detail. Sometimes group memory can be so intense, it becomes a vivid personal experience. You cannot deny this Jewish man his experience, the experience of his memory! Didn't you see that Simon Shama thing on TV recently, about the Jews being kicked out of Southern Spain? He mentioned a similar experience, that history had been so intense it becomes personal. Visiting the first temple these Jews had built in Venice, fleeing persecution, it was as if he had been there with them. You want Chár to be indoctrinated? Or educated? How does he become what he is? What is the difference between memory and dream? Or history, myth and memory? History is the written memory of power, of civilisation. If he wants to become who he is, he has to reclaim and free those myths and histories, making them his own. Eh? Isn't that what he is doing?"

"Thank you so much, Mother Amani," I re-entered the perfumed bathroom, "for buying me 'Sick Bacchus'.[30]" I moved around the tub filling their wine glasses. "But I have my Bacchus here with me!"

"I'm sorry! I'm becoming lost, here! Are we in mythology, in reality, in the present? Where are we?" Jolanta demanded.

"I like it!" said Lihua." I love these stories!"

What have you got in your hair?" interrupted Jolanta, scowling with anger. "Is that my creeper, from my bedroom?"

I wiggled my hips from side to side as I danced around the sides of the bath.

"I heard it call me," I grinned, "as I passed your bedroom door. Don't worry! It promised me it would grow doubly strong."

---

[30] A print of the painting 'Sick Bacchus' by Caravaggio. Actually, a self-portrait when he arrived in Rome at the age of 20 years.

I sucked on the chilum[31] I was holding between my fingers until vast clouds of intoxication poured from my nostrils and mouth.

"Thank goodness my Bacchus arrived with this."

"What are you talking about? Bacchus!?" demanded Jolanta, exhausted by poetry. "Something crazy has invaded this place since you arrived. Are you taking over or what? Amanish has gone barmy since she found you, talking nonsense and believing everything you say and Lihua . . . well, Lihua just adores you. And me, I don't understand anything that's going on in your head!"

I continued twisting my hips dancing, which infuriated Jolanta even more, as I pulled down some of the silk drapes and wrapped them around my waist, giving myself pretty Indian pink and vivid green skirts.

"What are you smoking? Where did you get that?"

"It is for you, Jolanta." I passed the chilum to her. "Taste! Smoke! This is the best in the world, from the foothills of my Kailash[32]. You think I do nothing every day? While you sleep, what do I do? There are many out there who know me. . . . Ok, Jolanta, that's enough, pass it to Auntie Amani . . . I am famous!" I laughed, mocking her frustrations. "Many young people know me from TV and YouTube videos. They like me. They want to help me. I want to tell you about my night people. Many are black – not as black as me, maybe, but black - and some from India, China, Iraq, everywhere. One time, I felt I was going crazy, shut up in my room, I climbed out the window to run across the roofs and as I have said, I had been watching this little group many times and suddenly decided to jump into the middle of them!"

I was laughing and at the same time acting out the little drama of meeting my night people.

"Two of them just fell backwards onto their arses. Another couple started to put their fists up at me and another took out a knife. I made like my angry leopards, putting up my claws and hissing. Then one of them recognised me.

---

[31]   Indian, usually clay, slightly conic pipe for smoking marijuana and hashish.

[32]   Mount Kailash, sacred to Buddhists and Hindus alike, is where the Hindu God, Shiva sits and catches the heavenly river, the Ganges in his hair and allows it to drip from his Jettas (dreadlocks) into the world.

""It's him! It's him," he shouted, "from that Amnesty fight! Hey, wait! Don't run away!" And then to his younger friend, "Put that knife away you fucking idiot before he kills you!"

""Dude, you really cool!"

""No one believes that terrorist bullshit!"

""They want to set you up, man, to confuse the public and hide what the Prime Minister and his twats are up to."

"I bet they paid for them guns!""

"Everyone knows," Jolanta once again interrupted my story, "the government offers cash through International Development to control third world governments; bribes, coercion through inward investment to influence policy. That's nothing new." remarked Jolanta. "But what I know from my Deputy Commissioner – he was here only the other evening . . ."

"Funny how clients will tell you everything, even their biggest secrets," said Lihua, laughing.

"What is this deputy commissioner? Who is he?" I demanded. "Wait! Wait! Before you say more! I have seen my night people many times and they wanted to help. They wanted me to stay with them, but of course, I am happy here with you, my beautiful mother/sisters. One of them was going to visit his family in Paris last weekend, so I asked him to bring my Wóhólò Tágì here to London. He should hear the words of your Deputy Commissioner."

I ran out of the bathroom quickly, before they had properly absorbed what I was saying, the Indian pink and green silks swishing around my legs, leaving the chillum in their hands.

"What is he talking about? I don't understand half of what he says!" declared Jolanta, frustratedly. "This wine is really strong, isn't it?" She frowned.

"I think he was talking about the moon" said Amanishakhete. "Naked moon, I think that's what he said, if I remember what is left of my Suri."

65

"What on Earth?!" said Jolanta even more exasperated; her head beginning to spin from the effects of the best in the world. "Naked Moons?!"

"I think he has someone in his room," whispered Lihua. "I could hear voices whispering behind his door."

"Why are you whispering?" demanded Jolanta, whispering. The intoxication from the cannabis was starting to impose.

"I don't know!" whispered Lihua in reply.

"Vous êtes ridicule, enfin![33]" announced my Amanishakhete loudly, startling the other two. "It's not possible for anyone to get into this place without using the front entrance and being invited in!"

"Shh! Don't shout! You'll wake the . . ."

"Wake who?" Jolanta demanded, again frustrated by everyone's miscomprehension.

"What were we talking about?" Lihua wondered, still whispering.

"He's already told you how he got out."

"From his window five floors up? Do you believe him?"

"It's not five floors, it's four."

Amanishakete passed the chillum back to Jolanta who, having difficulties smoking the thing in the manner of any Indian Saddhu, decided to simply suck on the end. Huge clouds of smoke poured from her mouth. Her eyes widened so much, stifling a fit of coughing, her cheeks like huge balloons, that Lihua burst out laughing, Jolanta's habitual seriousness transformed to absurdity floating in the bubbles.

"This stuff never works for me," exclaimed Amanishakhete, wondering why her new name was so long. She took another hit. "My name is so long, isn't it? I tell you what, why don't you call me Amani, or Amanisha, or Nisha. Nisha is nice." she said, looking dreamily romantic.

---

[33] "You're both ridiculous!"

"That's what we call you already!" declared Jolanta. "Isn't Amani your real name, anyway?"

This tickled Lihua even further and both started laughing uncontrollably.

"No! Really?" said the new Amanishakhete, surprised. "Well, anyway it doesn't work?"

"What doesn't work?"

Amanishakhete, Amani, Nisha, Nasha, Mina, whatever she was called, spent a long time thinking about this through the clouds of steam bubbling up from the bath and condensing onto the mango patterns of the silk drapes, forming tiny droplets of yellow honey, dripping slowly, stickily into her attention.

"I . . . can't remember. What were we talking about?"

"Names?"

"Yes, that's it! So, which is it?" she asked, profoundly. "Bacchus or Dionysus? White Bacchus, Black Dionysus!" It was as if realising a truth, she had suddenly understood everything. She had reached the mountaintop and, 'Eureka!', had suddenly become the enlightened one! The three women had completely lost their footing in the everyday as they floated through clouds of euphoria and hilarity.

"Where is he?"

"Who?"

"Chár!"

I re-entered the room announcing: "I told you, I have the real Bacchus. Please explain to him, Jolanta, who this Deputy Commissioner is and what he said to you."

He pushed the door wide open.

"This is my Wóhólò Tagì!"

I had taken one of the drapes from around my waist and passed it to Rémi. Even so, Rémi hesitated in the doorway, the light from the corridor creating a framed silhouette.

"Something sexy this way comes!" murmured Lihua, floating between the other two, stunned by the youthful sihouette of my Wóhólò Tagí, sculpted by the light of the doorway.

Of the three ladies, only their heads were visible above the suds, their wet hair turning into snakes writhing in the water.

There was a long silence as the presence of the beautiful golden-haired Rémi, sank into their intoxicated conscious minds.

Queen Amani spoke first:

"Approche-toi et n'aie pas peur![34]"

"Speak English, Nisha!" Jolanta demanded, and then to Rémi, "you do speak English, don't you?" The snakes appeared to turn and look towards him.

I took Rémi's hand and putting my other arm around his shoulders, kissed him gently on the cheek and led him into the room.

"Plutôt que la peur, c'est la crainte," Rémi whispered to me.

"What did you say? Eh? Speak up!" Jolanta's usual stern manner, like the serpents floating around her, raised its defensive head.

I smiled to myself. I could see my three ladies were lost in the vapours of Rémi's cannabis.

"Je disais, plutôt que la peur, c'est la crainte, Madame."

"In English, please"

"Rather than fear, it is awe, Madame." Rémi was relying on his French good manners.

---

[34] Approach and don't be frightened.

"Good!" responded Jolanta. "Well, you haven't turned to stone, so that is a good thing. Chár, I am very angry with you. You know it is dangerous for you to communicate with any of your friends or family in France who the police might track. Not only you, but all of us would be in trouble. You are not allowed to use the internet or mobile phones. And how did your friend come here? You must have given him an address."

"Of course, I didn't give any address! I don't know any address! My leopards wanted to go to find him, ... "

"No, no! I am not having this nonsense! Spirit leopards going to Paris to find your friend? Please! Tell me something I can believe."

"I told you, I sent one of the night people with them."

Jolanta felt completely exasperated. These stories of animals and climbing roofs and spirits. I was even claiming Greek myths as my own past. Her expression of severity angered Amanishakhete and disappointed Lihua, for both of whom I could do no wrong, thank goodness. For my Amani, my arrival, my discovery held a powerful connection to her people's historical longing, a liberation into a new world. A retaliatory skirmish was already in train when she had whispered into that crippled assassin's longing for dreams. As for my innocent Lihua, she loved me like a devoted elder sister and sometimes gave me looks which were a bit more than just that!

Jolanta needed time alone with Rémi and me, and Amanishakhete realised it.

"Come, Lihua. Jolanta needs to talk to Chár and his friend. You can play with them later."

Silence fell as Amanishakhete and Lihua left. Lihua could be heard complaining she wanted to spend time with the golden one, it wasn't fair, as the door shut behind them.

"And who are you?" Jolanta demanded. I had looked forward to introducing my Rémi to these kind sisters who had saved him. But now it had turned to chastisement. A frown fell across my forehead. Wóhólò Tagí could feel my disappointment. He put his arm around my waist and pulled me closer.

69

"Madame."

"Please! My name is Jolanta."

"Miss Jolanta, I have many names."

"Do not start fooling with me as well! Already I can see you two are inseparable. So even your minds are the same, are they?""

"Perhaps you do not understand about the names between us," he indicated me. I was leaning my head on his shoulder. "Suri people name their children after the first thing they see at the child's birth, so Chár is 'leopard'. He even grew up sleeping on a leopard skin. The first night we met, we got drunk and smoked a lot of ganja and went outside into the garden to dance naked under the moon. You have to understand, this was the spirit that united us. So Chár named me Wóhólò Tagí, Naked Moon. My mother named me Rémi. Juliette, whom Chár has decided will be his wife, the mother of his children, decided Chár was Bacchus/Dionysus, naming him after the famous painting of Caravaggio, the self-portrait. It was the flowers he put in his hair, as you see him now with your vine leaves, just like the painting, the Caravaggio self-portrait,"

"Ok, fine, I agree!" said Jolanta, exasperated. "There are worlds and there are worlds. Some live side by side with each other, some live inside others."

"It's what Chár says about his spirit leopards you find difficult?"

Jolanta leaned back, with a sigh of acknowledged difficulty.

"Chár is my brother, more than a brother, we are so close, it is necessary I am here now. Of course, you can understand leopards in dreams. But what if I said that I had also seen them in a dream, not long ago in Paris? Would that make them more real? Shared dreams? He had also asked one of the street boys of Shoreditch, one who was French and returning to Paris briefly, to meet me and bring me back here. Don't worry, we have not used phones, nor the internet, I don't even know the address of this place. Chár met me in the street. We came here over the rooftops."

"Ah, you, the French! You are all philosophers, aren't you?" laughed Jolanta with resignation. "The world you have invented with spirit

70

leopards, beautiful names, flowers, Dionysus and Caravaggio is very beautiful, but . . ."

Jolanta hesitated. She had to stop rationalising, always trying to explain.

" . . . we are all stuck in the world of work, all us poor human slaves, including you, the world of counting the cost, measuring, mortgages, financial consultants, efficiency, brokers, etc. Poetry has no purpose, no place."

"I think you are a communist," suggested Rémi. "We, Chár and I, Wóhólò Tagí, have more in common with you than you think. And, Miss Jolanta, I don't want to offend. You have cared for my Chár when he most needed it. But, since he came to our countries, he has made great effort to learn our languages, our customs and about our culture. It seems to me that in any connection of strong foundation between peoples, simply living together, if he learns willingly about me, I should willingly and happily learn about him, his world, his customs, ways of seeing, thinking and doing. I expect him to see reason and I dismiss his poetry? Is that the foundation of good relations? To expect him to submit, accept my demands and to offer nothing is perhaps tyrannical, racist even, don't you think? I love my Chár. He has shown me so much. I want to learn about him, his language, his ideas. For me, this is what it means to be human. I am because of him. I am because he is."

I lifted My head to look into Jolanta's eyes.

"Wóhólò Tagí is Suri, now." I spoke quietly." He is in me and I am in him. Nothing can change that, nor take it away, not even the end of worlds."

Jolanta had suddenly recognised the comfortable, solid certainty of her confident rationality was capable of robbing anyone of their spirit, their drive for connecting with others, identifying with others, their compassionate humanity; it makes sense for the businessman, the banker to not be a good Samaritan. It can become the logic of the insane. At its extreme, it could build concentration camps. Before her were two boys, young men whose bond was profound.

"You are right, Rémi, Chár, you are right. Sometimes, events, especially big events can make one hard, brittle." She reflected on her own history. "I apologise for being so hard on you. Now, we can join together,

71

become one family, eh? In fact, we must. Out there are terrible dangers, which threaten us all. There are worlds which destroy other worlds as Chár knows very well," continued Jolanta; as far as she was concerned, they needed to know, understand as best as possible that venal ugly world of their enemy. "This is what the world of money has done to Beyahola. And to hide it's vicious cruelty it is still wanting to kill Chár. He is still being pursued. The broker, the politician who was instrumental in all of this, is still pursuing Chár. If you want to keep your Dionysian world of flowers, art, Caravaggio, dancing in the moonlight, leopards, protect the people you love and even each other, you will have to defend them, fight for them. My Deputy Commissioner has told me who it is, pursuing you. His name is James Mercantor. He comes from a family of wealthy nobility. From the beginning of the eighteenth century, his family's wealth and power has increased enormously, making their money, initially, out of slavery. He is the Secretary of State for International Development. He is the one responsible for the destruction of Beyahola and the one who wants you, like your village, disappeared. He is someone we three witches have had matters with before. Now is our chance to do something together. This is why Amani found you. This is why I keep you, my Chár! There! I have even told him I love him!" she said, looking at Rémi. "And you, Wóhólò Tagí, you have so charmed me with your French good manners, your intelligence and thinking, I must embrace you also. So . . . now is our chance, between us, to deal with this poison that pursues our Chár."

I drifted across the bath, and Rémi followed, to embrace Jolanta and recognise this new allegiance. From that grave in the icy mud of the railway embankment, a little band of satyrs and maenads was emerging to tell the tale of the future.

"Sister Amani has found the one who disrupted the Survival meeting. She thinks like you, Chár!"

So, that's what she meant when she said she would take me to meet the devil!"

"I think Dionysus has done his work, eh, this evening! We are all sky high!"

"Black hash from my Kailash!"[35]

---

[35] Actually, this was an exaggeration, the black hash was from Manali, one of the routes towards Kailash. Still the best in the world. Kailash itself is too high.

Rémi laughed, looking at Jolanta.

"From his mountain, Kailash! . . . . Miss Jolanta, let me speak," he said. "We must address our ideas to the problem we are now sharing, this Government Minister. When the Buddha wanted to introduce enlightenment to the people of India, he didn't deny Hinduism with all it's Gods, which had descended into meaningless ritual controlled by the Brahmin priests, he by-passed it. Instead of confrontation, he side-stepped it by claiming that "if you want to find enlightenment, you can do this," and he provided a technique of insight meditation, Vipassana. Let us think like this. Let us side-step the enemy's advances. We will choose the moment, the field of battle and how it should be conducted. Let us think like the Buddha."

Lihua had managed to sneak back into the bath.

"I want to take the golden one with me for a short while. I have something for him, for both of them," she announced, taking Rémi by the hand to lead him away.

"Lihua, do not preoccupy Rémi for too long," demanded Jolanta. "These boys need to be together and they don't need you to upset things! If you make problems, I will be angry! You are not seducing him now!"

"Maybe Amani is right," she reflected on the evening and their conversations, now alone in the vast bath, the sea. "Maybe he has arrived, the Black One! Kailash, his mountain! Well, if the entire world belongs to you, I guess you don't need private possessions. His friend, Rémi, wants us to think like the Buddha. Who are these people who have entered Place Pigalle?"

*　　　*　　　*

All this time that Jolanta was setting about her inquisition, interview and questioning of Wóhólò Rémi Tagí, Amani's intoxicated mind was in a state of deep reflection on leopards.

"Every name in history . . . " wondered Amani. "Which comes first, the leopards, Chár, or Dionysus?"

It was only very recently she had discovered that, along with certain plants, ivy, grapes, marijuana and of course wine and cannabis as intoxicants, all associated with or attributed to Dionysus, he was also described arriving in certain places riding a leopard! She had discovered this after she had heard me talking in my sleep, my dreams, about becoming Dionysus and found that spirit leopards were a part of my world and had been since I had been born. It was as if leopards confirmed her suspicion, her wish. Desire had somehow back-pedalled into the past, into a different continent, even, to create a willed present, as if the ideal had already been working in a mythological past to bring the present to fruition. The ideal, which had always been present, although invisible, had manifested itself. The will for the Black One had manifested the arrival of Dionysus! His leopards confirmed this!

Everything was now seen in a completely different light, even the drape, which Rémi Tagi had been wearing and which I had put around my own waist earlier, making myself look like a girl, even the way I had moved wearing it, had been exactly like the representations on Greek vases of the youthful and at times pretty girl-like Dionysus.

". . . . . make myself Dionysus again." had she heard him say this?

"Yes, yes, yes." Amani sounded almost impatient. "Disputes with the Egyptians as to who were the first humans! . . . Meroe, origin of Ethiop and all peoples of that country![36] We knew! We know even now!"

She was walking around Place Pigalle making sure everywhere was locked up when she suddenly noticed she was talking to herself.

"We three sisters, us witches, we are all as high as kites! We took him in, but he has cast the spell. 'Every name in history am I', isn't this what he had been saying? Maybe we are leading each other, but tonight was his!"

*   *   *

---

[36] See Herodotus travels in Egypt and who first discovered the Gods.

Chapter 3

Jolanta's brief history of the Mercantor family.

"My Deputy Commissioner of Police revealed to me that James Mercantor MP . . ." and thus began Jolanta's elucidation of my persecution and the history of my enemy.

"Sir James Mercantor is the sole remaining direct descendant of Maurice Louis Francis Mercantor, the first Viscount of Bone. He was until recently Secretary of State for International Development and at that time was seriously involved in freeing up land in Ethiopia for 'international development', in other words, acquisition and exploitation by global corporations and foreign countries. Sir James, or simply Jimmy as he is known to fellow old boys and graduates of St. Peter's Oxford, found this ancestor, the first Viscount of Bone, of particular interest, worthy of admiration, like all his early ancestors of the eighteenth century. The powers-that-be have a peculiar fascination with that period in history. Ask the right wing of the Tory party." explained Jolanta.

The Mercantors had owned the Isle of Bone ever since the defeat of the clans and the establishment of the Union. It was a large island populated by a few crofters and fishermen and, of far greater interest to him, Maurice, possessing a large herd of red deer. The castle, originally constructed by the MacLellan's whose clan, through internecine clan wars, had eventually disintegrated and dispersed, was falling into ruin until Maurice Louis Francis repaired it with tobacco wealth from the Americas. In fact, the family had at one time owned most of Massachusetts. Maurice had managed to sell his share to his younger brother who was then left with little capital to develop the territory and eventually drank and gambled it all away. There are still members of that side of the family living in the States and the last and most recent male descendent, leaving his family behind, fled the country, wanted by police for the production of synthetic drugs and currently teaches physics in a private Catholic school in Thailand, whilst developing his own brokerage for digital currencies. Sir James had never met this distant cousin and in fact knew nothing of him. Maurice Louis had had no intention of turning the castle into a permanent residence but to simply use it on occasions, as the royal family used their residences. For him, it became largely a hunting lodge, where he could entertain business associates, kill deer and over dinner make a killing financially with the latest cargo from East Africa. Imperatorial nature is not long to follow great wealth, especially if it is made at the expense of humanity, hence, it became important for Maurice Louis not only to make his mark in society, politically and economically, but to scar the very surface of the Earth itself, just as he did the skin of the slaves he traded in. The Palladian palace he decided to build just outside Bristol, with landscaped gardens, follies, false lakes, Greek temples hidden in bowers, the whole works, was not his only effort to brand the Earth, he also invested in sugar plantations in St Kitts and a neo-classical mansion in Belgravia.

Maurice Louis Francis Mercantor lived at a time when it was possible to make vast fortunes very quickly. The British East India company was established in 1600. In order to finance acquisition and transportation of goods often at great risk and over great distances, it being months before a return on necessary loans for shipping etc., the London stock Exchange was established in 1698. Political and religious turmoil persisted in Europe in spite of various treaties, famously the Westphalian Treaty which established the modern notion of national sovereignty. Disputes nevertheless persisted through French expansionism; the Duke of Burgundy taking part of the Low Countries, disputes over borders with the Hapsburgs, Louis XIV inciting Turkey to attack the Austro-Hungarian Empire in the east, Spain controlling parts of Italy as well as the Low Countries, etc. etc. The fact that all these rulers were related made no difference to their greed for absolute power.

The situation in England was just as complicated. Charles II died with no heir. The Duke of York was the presumptive heir and became James II of England and VII of Scotland. Not liked by the public in England because he converted to Catholicism, nor by Anne and Mary, his two daughters, who held to their protestant faith. Mary, the elder of the two daughters, who had been living in the Netherlands, married William of Orange and Anne through an arranged marriage, Prince George of Denmark. James was eventually deposed in the Glorious Revolution (no blood was spilled), led by William who was no doubt happy to escape the trials and tribulations of Spanish control over Les Pays Bas[37]. The shenanigans that went on in London when William landed on the south coast were quite laughable. Anne's closest friend, Sarah Churchill, wife of John Churchill, later duke of Marlborough, had been ordered to be arrested by James. Anne and Sarah fled from Whitehall by a back staircase, and with various assistance arrived in Nottingham on 1 December. Two weeks later, Anne arrived in Oxford where she met

---

[37]   The Low Countries (Netherlands)

Prince George (of Denmark) in triumph. Parliament declared James had abdicated by default when he fled the country. On 19 December, Anne returned to London, where she was at once visited by William.

William and Mary were declared joint monarchs in 1689. Almost immediately relations between Mary and Anne deteriorated. With the death of Mary and three years later, William, and no heir, Anne became Queen in 1702.

"Good Queen Anne" was born in 1665, married at the age of eighteen to George of Denmark, had seventeen or eighteen pregnancies, eight of which were miscarriages, five were still births, two daughters died, around the time of her husband, of smallpox, a further daughter died at the age of only 2 years and her son, William died at the age of 11 in 1700. Another son was born but only survived for two hours. After all these stillbirths, miscarriages and short-lived children, it was hardly surprising Anne was physically destroyed. She put on a lot of weight. She was never considered a beauty, and by many, of less than average intelligence. Overeating and over-drinking, possibly to compensate for her personal tragedies gave her chronic and severe gout, such that she had to be carried to her coronation in a sedan chair. Only four years later John Clerk described her as: "under a fit of the gout and in extreme pain and agony, and on this occasion everything about her was much in the same disorder as about the meanest of her subjects. Her face, which was red and spotted, was rendered something frightful by her negligent dress, and the foot affected was tied up with a poultice and some nasty bandages. I was much affected by this sight."

Her greed extended not simply to rich food and wine, but her personal wealth. Under the rule of William and Mary she had demanded and obtained, much to their annoyance, a personal allowance from Parliament. When Anne was crowned in 1702 the War of the Spanish Succession was already well into its first year. Marlborough was given charge of British forces whose involvement was mostly in northern Europe. Mercantor and Marlborough were friends and had been since attending Eton together. Both of them had come a lot closer to Anne during that period when she was falling out with William and Mary and playing at being a commoner, giving herself the name of Mrs Morley, while her best friend, Sarah Churchill, Marlborough's wife, became Mrs Freeman. There were regular parties, much disapproved of by William and Mary because of the raucous drinking and often licentious behaviour of some of the guests, to which Mercantor was always invited.

The war was triggered by the death of the childless Charles II of Spain in November 1700. His closest heirs were members of the Austrian Hapsburg and French Bourbon families. Whoever inherited would possess a vast empire which included Southern Italy, parts of the north around Milan, parts of Holland, and an expanding empire in South America and Mexico.

Charles left his throne to Louis XIV's grandson Philip who was proclaimed King of Spain on 16 November 1700. It was impossible for the Grand Alliance (Hapsburgs, England, and the German States) to contemplate an ever more powerful Bourbon family uniting France and Spain under one king, controlling the Low Countries and thus the Channel, access to the Mediterranean, international trade, especially shipping, sugar and slavery, most of Italy and thus the papacy.

*   *   *

Jolanta's dramatisation of Mercantor's meeting with Louis XIV at Versailles, assisted by the imaginations of Chár and Rémi Wóhólò Tagí.

End of the war over the Spanish succession and control of the slave trade passing to England.

By 1710, fighting was deadlocked; the Alliance's victories in Italy and the Low Countries had driven the French back to their borders but they could not achieve a decisive breakthrough. Marlborough managed to get Mercantor invited to Versailles to discuss ways of ending the war.

He was there for a month. It took time to go through advisers and officials before meeting Louis himself, by which time proposals were already forming and waiting agreement. Diplomatic relations have hardly changed since those times of European rivalries. European rivalries have hardly changed either.

He was astonished at the number of blackamoors at the palace. A nephew of Burgundy explained that most of the nobles of France were away at the borders defending France and had taken their servants, private armies and kinsmen with them, which was why the palace seemed so empty and why there were more blackamoors becoming footmen, houseboys and domestics.

"They make particularly good servants, actually. They work hard. They are extraordinarily strong and when you beat them, they feel no pain."

The palace was strange. There was no one there any longer. It was empty and even Louis, when Mercantor met him, now seventy-two years old, seemed exhausted and bored by the loneliness of his vast palace of mirrors and gold. Maybe he was waiting for death. He had spent a lifetime building this glorious monstrosity to his own vanity and state bankruptcy, and to richly keep his troublesome nobles close. Now, like his own life in old age, it seemed tarnished and pointless.

"Monsieur Mercantor, nous vous souhaitons la bienvenue chez notre modeste demeure. Est-ce que Mercantor est un nom français?"

"Merçi, Votre Majesté, vous avez un très beau palais, et, oui, je crois que mon nom est français[38]." Mercantor seized the opportunity, which the king had offered him, to win his favour. "An ancestor in the line of my father was in the service of Catherine de Valois who married Henri V of Angleterre." He lied. He had no idea of his lineage.

"Ah, I knew it!" responded Louis with pleasure. "I knew that you had French blood." He paused and reflected. "What a war that was!! And your Henri Cinq, he was exceptionally talented in warfare, eh? Not like the idiot French nobles and our ridiculous Dauphin who confronted him!" He seemed to drift off into his own bitterness. "The same problem today! The Dukes, the Viscounts are all capable of treason. Liars and good-for-nothings! This is why this war has lasted such a long time!"

"And if we could stop the war ..."

"But how?" The king demanded impatiently.

"A difficult issue, your Majesty! But, if England withdraws from the Alliance, pretending it no longer has funds for the cause, the allies will be too weak to continue."

"And will be obliged to make peace!" Louis completed the logic of the idea. "Marvellous! You are someone of great intelligence. Ah, I knew

---

[38]   "Mr Mercantor, we wish you welcome to our humble abode. Mercantor, is it a French name?"
     "Thank you, Your Majesty, you have a very beautiful palace, and, yes, I believe that my name is French.

you were French! So, your Queen wants to haggle, I suppose, as your name suggests."

"Precisely!" Mercantor smiled as seductively as possible at the old King. "For the Alliance, it would be impossible for France and Spain to be governed by one king."

"Hm. Charles of Spain had said the same in his will."

"So, if Philip keeps Spain and France goes to another of your descendants. . ."

"The Netherlands is already lost." Mercantor added this clear observation.

"I don't know why Burgundy wanted this misery." continued the king. "First there are only ponds, clay and mud. It rains all the time, and the people are always sick."

"England has great need of a maritime base near Africa, for commercial reasons only. I suggest Gibraltar and Menorca, perhaps?" Mercantor was praying the old king would ignore the strategic importance of both of these islands.

"Yes, no value! Only two barren rocks, in fact."

"Spain will keep all its territories except those it has already lost in Europe. And finally, we want to help Spain find stability and for the young Philip to assume the reins of power and centralise the administration of the state around himself . . . and the same for France and eventually your heir. These wars have been detrimental for all of us and we need to deal with our own internal priorities and allow trade worldwide to expand and benefit us all. This is why I believe Spain should cede control of the Asiento de Negros[39] to Queen Anne. This would alleviate Philip of those logistical complications. It could be a temporary contract. Marlborough and I would ensure that profits are shared by both Philip and Anne, the greater part going to Philip, obviously. We will take charge of this task and ship slaves to Spain's

---

[39] The asiento was the license issued by the Spanish crown, by which a set of merchants received the monopoly on a trade route or product. The Asiento de Negros was the licence to trade in black slaves between West Africa and the Spanish colonies of the Americas. Such licensing was taxable. This gave England the opportunity to become the biggest trader in slaves in human history.

colonies and yours, in the Americas, giving our three countries the opportunities presented by exploration, colonisation and exploitation in these great territories we have discovered. There is considerable wealth to be made."

The old king felt surpassed by an ever-looming future. It was no longer important nor relevant to the present day to be building palaces to one's own glory, commissioning portraits of oneself if no one saw them, squabbling with neighbours over where the garden fence should go, trying to steal his vegetable patch. Global trade was now about to replace these silly monarchies. All he could do was affirm as best as possible a role for himself, his grandson, Philip and his other descendants by making peace with Anne of England and forcing a treaty.

Philip was confirmed as King of Spain and renounced any future claim to the French throne; Spain retained the bulk of its pre-war territories outside of Europe and their European territories were divided between Austria, Britain and Savoy. Of special importance was the successful secret negotiation with France to obtain a 30-year monopoly on the Spanish slave trade, the Asiento de negros. Anne also allowed, nay, encouraged, her North American colonies to make laws that promoted black slavery. She boasted to Parliament of her success in taking the Asiento away from Spain. The Stock Exchange and its investors celebrated her economic coup. Most of the slave trade involved sales to Spanish colonies in the Caribbean, and to Mexico. By promoting sales to British colonies in the Caribbean and in North America, England more than doubled its income from this trade and in fact became the biggest slave trader in the world. The agreement Mercantor negotiated, allotted Queen Anne 22.5% and King Philip V, of Spain 28% of all profits from the Asiento de Negros. Anne's connection to slave trade revenue meant that she was no longer a neutral observer; she had a vested interest in what happened on slave ships, encouraging their arrival at whichever destination to retain more than just fifty percent of the original cargo. Important nevertheless, was the fact that slaves already in the Americas did not produce sufficient offspring to replace their loss through death, disease, exhaustion, starvation or simple murder by their owners. This reproduction never in fact happened, which meant that the highly lucrative trade in blackamoors, negros, niggers, whatever abusive generalisation you wanted to use to reduce these people to commodities, was able to expand and persist.

Thus, out of gratitude, Anne rewarded Maurice Louis Francis Mercantor with the state of Massachusetts, the Scottish Isle of Bone and the title Viscount of Bone.

As for Churchill, 1st Duke of Marlborough, Anne had wanted to reward him as her commander of the forces of the Alliance and for having pushed France back to its borders, with a palace suited to his victories, thus began the construction of Blenheim. Marlborough himself contributed £60,000 with Anne personally contributing, and there was an undefined sum supposedly coming from Parliament. Anne fell out with Sarah Churchill and the Marlboroughs went into exile until after Anne's death. Only then could they resume construction of their Blenheim Palace, the cost of which was unending. Ever since, the descendants struggled with debt, but pursued political careers to keep the power of the family dominant throughout the history of modern politics.

*   *   *

The second Viscount of Bone; ideas on employment.

Viscount Bone embraced the future of exploitative globalisation with great verve. Through the Game Laws, he eagerly prevented the peasants on his estate from idling away their time hunting, fishing and growing their own food on small plots of what used to be called 'commons'. All of this 'common' land was privatised, stolen by an elite who wanted to turn the British populace into wage slaves. Maurice Louis offered to his peasantry the possibility of becoming indentured servants on his estate in Massachusetts. This meant he would pay their passage; they could work off the debt over an agreed number of years and then earn a plot of land in the Americas. Either that or they could work in the cotton mills of Manchester or any of the other industries setting up in the North of England. He invested in his own ships for the round trip from Liverpool and Bristol to the west coast of Africa, exchanging with African kings, cloths and manufactured goods, for slaves, gold and ivory. The slaves were shipped to the Americas and sold to white landowners for the production of cotton, sugar, coffee and tobacco. The indentured servants travelled this journey working on the ships until they arrived in the Americas with their cargo of slaves. This meant that Maurice Louis in fact paid nothing whatsoever for the transport of the peasantry of his estates to the New World; the debt for their transport was completely fictitious. He sold off the fictitious debt to whoever needed white labour, usually employed to manage black slaves. The ships would then load with raw cotton, tobacco and sugar for the return journey to England. Those peasants not indentured who became the wage slaves of cotton mills produced the very goods bound for Africa to exchange for more slaves bound for the slave markets of the Americas. The principal "cogs" in these "machines" for producing capital were cotton and slaves: cotton cloth from factories in England, shipped to African kings for slaves, shipped to the Americas to produce raw cotton, shipped to the mills in England. The vicious circle is established. Efficiency then fulfils an important role in the operation of this machine in order to produce greater wealth: the more tightly packed the slaves on ships, the longer hours of production with starvation wages for labour in the mills of England, employing children of labourers families, on starvation wages, the greater the production of wealth, this being the sole aim of any of these machines of production. So successful was this vicious circle that it provided Mercantor and the wealthy elite of England with the means to build huge palaces to their own glory, with the same vanity as Louis XIV. These new 'kings' were no longer ordained by God but by the Market. The vanity of this pompous crowd was staggering. They even imagined themselves great thinkers and important leaders of this enlightened, rational and scientific, global exploitation in which the rest of humanity becomes a commodity.

"Where did the money come from," demanded Jolanta, looking at her two students, Rémi and I, "to build Buckingham Palace? Without the slave trade, global capitalism would never have developed. We are all indentured through mortgages and debt and like you, Chár, driven from our land, our 'commons', unable to be 'indolently self-sufficient.' If future governments do not repeal the Enclosure Act, we will act ourselves and take it back!"

"I think you are angry, eh, Auntie Jolanta?" I commented.

Rémi just laughed at my innocent comment.

"Stop calling me auntie, for goodness sake!"

*   *   *

The second Viscount Bone spent most of his time in London, taking on increasingly the status of an exclusive member of the capital's intellectual élite. At his house in Belgravia, he held 'soirées' attended regularly by not only nobles, members of parliament, investors, industrialists, but artists, writers and thinkers of the modern age.

"The possession of a cow or two, with a hog, and a few geese, naturally exalts the peasant. . . . In sauntering after his cattle, he acquires a habit of indolence. Quarter, half, and occasionally whole days are imperceptibly lost. Day labour becomes disgusting; the aversion increases by indulgence. And at length the sale of a half-fed calf, or hog, furnishes the means of adding intemperance to idleness."

Jolanta had to spend time explaining to both of us some of the vocabulary of these 'thinkers' of the Enlightenment. But quickly I realised that most of what was being said of the British peasantry's way of living was also a description of what my life had been like in Beyahola.

Jolanta noticed my eyes widening in horror at the insult. This cycle, this brutal circuitry of enslavement and outright robbery as a necessary part of the mechanism of production seemed to repeat itself, over and over, just as the horrific circle of cruelty swept around the Atlantic from continent to continent.

Sometimes in Jolanta's own apartment, sometimes in my room, sometimes during the collective evening bath, sometimes around a fire in our small courtyard, with office workers gazing down at the little ritual of binding, with spells, of storytelling, both Rémi and I illustrated, dramatised, imagined, with the various voices of all three of these night witches, an unfolding of the history of the Mercantors.

At a soirée of the second Mercantor, Arthur Young turned towards an immobile black boy standing at the side of a large round mahogany table adorned with fresh fruit, biscuits, dried figs and dates, candied mandarins, a large crystal whisky decanter and several crystal tumblers, most being in the hands of guests. The little black boy, no older than six years, was dressed in the livery of the house and the Viscount's servants, that is to say, powdered wig with tight sausage curls which sat on his ears, giving him sores from the rasping horse hair, on the crown, a spiked stubble and at the back a short pony tail with blue velvet ribbon, the woven underside scratching his scalp, blue velvet jacket with gold braid, brass buttons and folded tails, white breeches, and black patent shoes with brass buckles. The jacket could only be worn in front of the Viscount, his family and guests. His role was ornamental, more than anything. As soon as the boy was away from those people and simply amongst servants, he had to return the jacket into the safe keeping of the housekeeper. Any mark on it and he was severely beaten. Other clothing could be washed, but not the jacket. His duty was to stand immobile next to the table holding a silver platter with a variety of cigars, Spanish cigarillos, and curiosities, tobacco rolled in dried corn wraps, and the latest French cigarettes, wrapped in fine paper, all of which were bought from exclusive tobacconists, Friburg and Treyer, at The Snuff House, in the Haymarket, the likes of which the Viscount never visited. Arthur Young never smoked, sticking to perfumed snuff, the mace giving him mild hallucinations of enhanced colours and a sense of well-being, which was fortunate because as a being he was very, very ugly.

"I cannot conceive a greater curse upon a body of people, a primitive tribe of negros, for example, many of which are found throughout Africa, where this boy comes from, than to be thrown upon a spot of land, where the productions for subsistence and food are, in great measure, spontaneous, and the climate requires or admits little care for raiment or covering. Women bare-breasted, of all ages, children running around completely naked with not a care in the world, young men showing off their bodies, in the most vulgar manner, to bring attention to their genitalia. No morality, no decency, no shame and no interest in improving their lot through effort." Young's indignance echoed around the room and thanks to the dense fog of tobacco smoke, hung in the air like a curse, until these intellectuals had solved the problems of both known and unknown worlds.

"Leave it to the market," said the Viscount with conviction, "it brings its own morality and order."

Several other guests gathered around.

"Importantly, we have to ensure that survival depends on employment. Once we remove the means of peasant self-sufficiency, entire families will be happy to subject themselves to industrial production, demanding their children be employed also."

"Everyone but an idiot knows the lower classes must be kept poor, or they will never be industrious, which is why all foods should be taxed as heavily as possible."

"Do you remember Temple?" demanded Defoe, "Sir William Temple? Of course not, before your time. Temple advocated very forthrightly that children be brought into factories to work from the age of four. Thus, subsequent generations would be so habituated to constant employment and factory conditions that such a life would at length prove agreeable and entertaining to them."

"Locke[40] thought they should be working at the age of three."

"As far as I am concerned," continued Defoe, "it seems reasonable that children after four or five years of age should, every one of them, be earning their own bread, thus being no longer a burden on their parents and coming to understand their utility to society at large."

William was the name of the little black boy in the livery of the Viscount's household, holding the silver platter of tobaccos. He had been given this name since no one was willing or able to make the effort to either discover or pronounce his real name, which in any case was attributed to some insignificant primitive jungle language which hopefully would disappear as soon as possible in the interests of the betterment of mankind.

"Does he speak any English?" wondered Young.

Mercantor was slightly concerned Young should be showing any interest in the boy at all.

"No! He hasn't been in the country long. We've only just got the livery tailored for him. I found him at the market in Bristol. No one wanted him. And the ship's captain, who in any case commands one of my ships practically begged me to take him off his hands. I've never heard him utter a sound. Maybe he's dumb. It's quite common amongst blackamoor children. He'll eventually become a servant to mine."

"Very Christian of you, Viscount," said Young, his slippery fat face, turning towards Mercantor. The little boy watched a louse slowly crawl across a stain on Young's embroidered red silk

---

[40] English philosopher 1632-1704. established the notion of private property, hence shared 'commons' and land used for anyone to hunt or fish on, was removed with the promotion of the notion of a social contract where the people surrender certain freedoms for protection by the state. All lands were then subject to laws of the state and use of or ownership of had to come with documented proof.

waistcoat. The cuffs of his jacket were worn to a black shiny stickiness. Since losing on investments in the importation of firstly black pepper, and then Indian silks, both ships had sunk in storms, he had been unable to even afford to replace his overused dress. It was his writings and modern theories on morality and economics that kept his place amongst the wealthy and powerful, as well as a feeling of pity and compassion, from those who knew him well, for his great personal family tragedy. Moreover, he was still able to impress with his knowledge of and ability to quote the Classics in both Latin and Greek.

"They call them pickaninnies[41] in the colonies," added Chatham, "Peculiar name! Pickaninnies, possibly Portuguese derivation, apparently,"

Everyone produced a sycophantic laugh, aware of Chatham's political power.

"The landowners, cotton and tobacco producers all reckon to a man that you can beat them, and they feel nothing. No doubt the boy here has already proved their point. Does he ever smile, by the way?"

And everyone but the boy laughed again.

Mercantor put his arm around Chatham's shoulder to lead him away and share a confidence, whilst Defoe abandoned Young to serve himself another whisky and light a cigar he had taken from the silver platter the boy was still holding. The boy stood immobile, holding out the silver platter as if in offering to the room, he had become the piece of baroque decoration intended. Since being captured with his mother, from whom he had been separated almost immediately, he had quickly become accustomed to being treated by traders as just an object, a thing, a commodity. Hence he was quite used to hands examining his body, forcing open his mouth to check his teeth, his tongue, pushing open his buttocks and pulling back his foreskin to look for infections, checking his hands and feet, the muscles of his legs and arms. The importance was the utility of this creature, in the same sense that a

---

[41]   probably ultimately from Portuguese *pequenino*, diminutive of *pequeno* meaning small.

dog might be useful.

"You have heard, haven't you, Chatham," whispered Mercantor, "of Young's terrible loss?"

"Someone mentioned it to me a while ago," responded Chatham, always comfortable with Mercantor, knowing he was not about to be lobbied for political favour, "something to do with his son who died, or disappeared in unusual circumstances?"

"His only son disappeared on the way back from school a couple of years ago now."

"Ah, yes, I remember."

"Particularly difficult for both him and his wife. Never expecting a child, they were blessed late on in their lives when most would never believe it possible. They doted on the boy! Being a man of reasonable means, the child really was a blessing rather than a burden, as they too often are for the lower classes."

"Do they know what happened to him?"

"They have refused to believe he was murdered. Who would want to murder a small child? I see no benefit in that and neither does Young. His poor wife, distraught with anguish, ended up wandering the streets looking for him, abandoning all propriety, disappearing for days on end and finally returning muddied, unkempt and literally raving. On such occasions, doctors prescribed laudanum to calm her, but not even that seemed to help, and Young had to have her confined to Bedlam. A similar madness afflicts Young, constantly looking for the boy, no longer caring for himself, his health, his financial security, even his dress. That's why you see him staring at the black servant now."

"I don't see how I can be of assistance."

"Not only in the streets, but with every child he comes across - look at the way he seems to obsess over the black boy - it's as if he is trying to peer through the skin to see if his child is there, as if some wicked magic has been performed to bury him in different features hiding his nobility, even knowledge and understanding, under a spell of ignoble ignorance, like any slave who has lost all sense of identity, no longer even human."

"I'm not sure you can talk about negros having a sense of identity . . . but it is true, even white slaves, from the lower classes, very quickly, apart from their skin, become indistinguishable from the negro, behaving no better than animals. I say white slaves, I mean of course indentured servants. No sense of morality except induced by fear or greed. You're not starting to question slavery, are you, like some of the French thinkers?"

"No , no, no! of course not! Slavery has been an important part of civilisation since its very inception. It has been a large part of my business affairs and the family's, the country's economy depends on it, not least the Privy Purse. It's the issue of children being napped."

"Kidnapping." interrupted Defoe, more familiar with recent etymology.

"Sometimes the children of gentlefolk get taken; the brigands and privateers perform this act quite indiscriminately. And of course, the law in this respect hasn't changed for a long, long time."

"Well," interjected Defoe again, never one to miss the opportunity to trumpet his views, "the established church has always kidnapped children from the streets to make up their choirs. And of course, it's considered an honour and blessing for the child to be, as it were, chosen by God, to sing His praise. Many of the parents are informed afterwards and are very happy for their boy to serve in that way."

"Likewise," pursued Chatham, "landowners and farmers in the Americas are crying out for white servants, indentured if your like, although, there is little distinction often between black slaves and white servants, but they are valued simply because they can speak English and can often take on the role of managing the negroes. Now, if there is such a need in our economy for white slaves and if there are so many children who are just street urchins, already thieves, pickpockets and even murderers by the age of twelve, then there is a tacit acceptance in government to allow this trade to both clean our city streets and find a purpose for children who would otherwise remain a burden on society."

There was a sudden clatter of a metal plate on the stone floor. The room fell silent and every head turned in the direction of the intrusive disturbance.

Young was on the floor, on his knees, scrabbling around amongst the scattered London cigars, Spanish cigarillos and French cigarettes, while the little black boy stood silently by, wide-eyed, as if, by a premonition so terrible, turned to stone.

*   *   *

William

The small slab of grey limestone resurfaced precisely at the moment young Jimmy, at the less than innocent age of ten was being pursued by his cousin of fourteen years. She had already shown him her developing breasts and her little clitoris between the few hairs of her vulva and now she wanted to see what little boys were made of, in spite of his immaturity. As he ran, a tuft of long green grass reached up and caught a foot. Falling, a knee was suddenly confronted by the slab of limestone. His knee started bleeding profusely, his blood pouring over and staining the stone. he looked down at the conclusion of the event and saw on the rectangular stone, worn by age, the inscription WILL and then underneath, IAM.

A few days later he went back to the stone with a bandage around his knee and in spite of the rain and even with his determined effort of rubbing, the stain would not disappear.

He had already asked his cousin, Sophie, what this stone was and who was WILL IAM? She had asked Auntie Jane who had said it must be a gravestone for one of the servants. But who was WILL IAM?

"William . . . William . . . well, I wonder if it might be the little William in the Zoffany painting in the hall." guessed Auntie Jane.

Auntie Jane and Sophie had immediately got up from the breakfast table to go and look at the painting.

"He's the little black boy in blue, almost in the middle?"

"Yes, that's right. And you've got all of the family around him . . . with great great great something grandfather Mercantor in the foreground. Lovely painting, eh?"

"And er, who is the black lady next to him? Is she his mother?"

"Oh, no! She's a wet nurse. See, she's carrying the family baby."

"What's a wet nurse?"

"She breastfeeds the baby."

"Why?!"

Auntie Jane leaned towards Sophie and whispered: "They say great great great something Grandma Mercantor, the true mother of the child couldn't produce milk." And then with more certainty: "Besides, ladies were not expected to breastfeed. They were far too busy doing other things."

"Doing what?" demanded Jimmy when the bruise and limping permitted him to pay attention to the world instead of his own self-pity. Sophie repeated what Aunt Jane had told her.

"I don't know! Managing the household, meeting other ladies, organising parties." said Sophie, thinking of her own mother.

"So, this black woman breastfed the children of our great great great something grandfather!" he realised with astonishment and slight disgust. "What about her baby? Did it die?"

"I don't know!" Sophie replied, irritated. "Probably."

"What about WILL IAM? How did he die?"

*   *   *

91

Jimmy never did find out exactly what had happened to little William. One servant, a kitchen maid, told him stories of a little black boy's ghost being seen in the cellars and once in the kitchens. But these were just stories that all old houses have. Others from the village reckon the Viscount had beaten him to death over a misdemeanour, again others that he had died of a broken heart, missing his mother. Whatever it was, for a long time in his childhood, Jimmy had been unable to prevent himself from obsessing over that tiny black hole of the unknown in his family's otherwise important, influential and admired history. Something had passed into his soul from that stone, marking his subconscious, the day he had left his bloodstain upon it. Just as . . . .

"What was the name of that village," scattering papers on his desk in his office in Westminster, Sir James demanded of his secretary, "where that Amnesty boy came from?"

"Beyahola, sir." replied the secretary, aware of his boss's irritation.

"That bloody massacre was nothing to do with this office, the government, nor me, nor you, nor anyone here, understood? There are more discreet ways of getting rid of intransigent tribals than drawing the world's attention to it. It's entirely an Ethiopian cockup."

"Yes, sir."

"At least they could have done a decent job and got rid of all of them. Instead, I am being persecuted by that little black boy constantly on my mind."

James had spent a fitful previous night of anxious guilt and when he had been able to sleep had been stuck in a repetitive dream in which little William appeared and was following him around the gardens of the country estate, Utrecht House, near Bristol, where he had fallen over little William's gravestone.

"He's hardly a boy and certainly not little, sir."

"Never mind! Never mind! They all have the same blood though, don't they? Genetically, I mean."

The secretary looked astonished, having no idea what the Secretary of State for International Development, Sir James Mercantor was talking about.

"He was supposed to have been detained by immigration over passport issues, but MI6 farmed it out to two independent agents so that no links could be made to us. I thought you had spoken to one of them, sir."

"My actions don't concern you, Chivers! What about the boy?"

"He escaped. . . . . . in the confusion . . . . sir."

"These agents, are they mad? Trying to detain him at a public meeting."

"Apparently, it was a confusion of orders, sir."

"Orders, my arse!"

"The agent who died had a lot of drugs in his blood., both cocaine and heroin."

"Will no one rid me of this disease on the skin of civilisation, this ignorant wild boy from the jungles? You wonder how many more there are of him? He can't be that difficult to find. He's not invisible, is he?"

"So far, yes, sir," responded Chivers, enjoying his master's discomfort. "There have been no sightings at all since his disappearance."

"Fuck you, Chivers! I know nothing about either him or any massacre, remember? Get out! And find me that boy! . . . . before he finds me," he added, speaking more to himself than the departing Chivers.

*　　　*　　　*

Who is Chár? Who am I? What am I? I was standing in front of a full-length mirror. Swallowed by events, I was no longer that little boy running through long dry grasses, playing hide and seek between the legs of the cattle, naked and black except for my beads, sitting on my buttocks and hanging just above my small child's genitals, the only bright colours in all that blackness. No longer the teenager, swept off to France in the loving arms of Nathalie, unable to sleep alone at night, having to creep into their bed, so that my body might feel it was amongst my family once again. If anything, I was my body, even if my body had changed, grown.

The night of Rémi's arrival in Shoreditch, everything had been so rushed, we had hardly had time to greet each other. Rémi was led to the small side-alley not far from Vice, where I had met my local friends, friends who had dressed me, helped me find the three who had attacked me along the embankment, which three had now completely disappeared from the Shoreditch and Hackney streets. The same friends had met Rémi at St Pancras and led him to the rendez-vous. Our almost tearful reunion was tearing at our chests and the only way to appease it was to cling to each other. Some of the boys of this little gang were taken aback by our intimacy, this long embracing. It is impossible to tell you that joyful pain in both our hearts. I, of course, had tears and so did my Tagì, who was not naked this time, but clothed for winter, whereas, I was wearing almost nothing.

"Are they gay?" said one, looking shocked.

A taller black lad with shoulder length dreads and saggers revealing the D&G labelled band of his briefs, immediately slapped the younger one down.

"Hey, fuck you! Chár comes from the Rift, man, from the jungle. He's not gonna have your fucking neuroses, is he?" he retorted and clipped the youngster across the back of his head. "And Rémi . . . . is . . . well, he's French! Okay?"

"Right!"

"I've signed up to learn French," said the tall one, Jackson, as the little gang watched us disappear into the starry night.

"Learn French?!" queried another with astonishment.

"Yeh! I don't want to be thick, like you," retorted Jackson. You can't even speak English! If you speak English and French, you can go anywhere in Africa, man, anywhere."

The boys stayed with us through the streets until we needed to climb a fence, a drainpipe, to reach the rooftop and find our way to the attic window of my room at the home of the three sisters of Place Pigalle.

"Place Pigalle! Oh là là! Ta bien tombé, toi!" laughed Rémi. "Ces garçons sont très dévoué, eh?"

"J'ai du charme et charisme, Tagí, c'est pour ça. Et en plus, je suis beau."

"Ah, bon! Je n'avait jamais remarqué." laughed Rémi. [42]

We had just climbed through the window when Lihua knocked and called me for the bath.

"I saw your interview for Survival International, was it?" commented Rémi, "It's on YouTube. You were brilliant, Chár! Fantastic!"

"Wait here. You can make your political speeches later. I'll be back to fetch you soon. Once I've told my three 'aunties', you are here, you can come and take a bath with all of us!"

"Jésus Christ! Marie, mère de Dieu! Chár, t'es incroyable! Alors, ces femmes font quoi comme travail? Elle sont des putes, ou quoi?"[43]

---

[42]   "Place Pigalle! Oh là là! You've fallen on your feet there!" laughed Rémi. "These boys are very devoted, eh?"

"I have charm and charisma, Tagí, that's why. And besides, I'm beautiful."

"Ah, really? I hadn't noticed." laughed Rémi.

[43]   "Jesus Christ! Mary, Mother of God! You're unbelievable! So, what kind of work do these women do? Are they whores, or what?"

"Des femmes de la nuit!"[44]

"Ah, bon! Très bien!"

I threw off my few coverings and went straight downstairs leaving Rémi behind.

Now, after the bath, I was looking at myself in a full-length mirror alone, waiting for Rémi! Where was this Chár who had never even seen a mirror until after all his people, his family, his friends, his history had disappeared? In fact, that past, that history seemed feeble now, like shadows at twilight.

Sometimes I am a stranger inside my own skin. I watch myself move and speak, and the words that come are not always mine. They are older, deeper—voices that echo from a time before names, before recorded history.

This body, once only my own, is now a place where too many spirits clamour to speak. Their stories flowing through my flesh like rivers under stone. I am both the hunter tracking the truth and the prey caught in its snare. Am I the master of this fragment of time I call my life? The words I speak seem no longer mine. Are they cries from shadows, from ancestors, from futures not yet born.

If I lose myself to this becoming, this my history, this multiplicity of creatures, beings, souls, will I discover the true voice beneath the silence? Or will I vanish, swallowed by the dramas, tales and characters I adopt, encourage, allow to grow? Maybe that is my gift and curse of becoming: to lose my self and find something more, something untamed. If I surrender, maybe Tagí, Juliette, my sisters here, my wild leopards will guide me. I can never despair! That would be betrayal!

I fell on the bed, pulled the duvet over myself, hiding underneath and curling into a foetus. I heard the door open and close, but remained silent, immobile. I could hear Rémi moving around the room, then the light went out. I felt movement on the mattress and the sudden warmth of Rémi's body as he slid under the duvet. I knew I was turned towards him, I could feel his breath next to my face and floating down my chest. An arm reached out around

---

[44] Ladies of the night.

my shoulders and slid slowly down my back. I started to uncurl, pushing my knees and feet further down the bed, so that our bodies could come closer together. Our noses touched and our lips came together.

Maybe I was too desperate to embrace him, make him part of me again, discover a lost self in him, but . . .

"Slowly, slowly!" urged Rémi. "Are you okay?"

"I miss you too much! Excuse me." I said, suddenly feeling my loneliness, then, "Where have you been? Why so long with Lihua?"

Rémi laughed: "Aah, you feel a bit jealous?"

He threw back the duvet and stood up.

"Do you have some candles? I want to see."

"On the cupboard and window ledge."

I watched as the elegant naked Rémi moved around the room lighting candles and returning next to me.

"So, did you fuck her?"

Rémi laughed again: "You are jealous!"

"Maybe."

"She wants me to give her a baby." said Rémi with casual flippancy. "Ooh! What's this standing between us?"

"She wants a baby," I explained, "me, you, she doesn't care. The others won't let her. And what's that?" I replied, moving Rémi's dormì to gently stroke it against my dolé[45].

---

45   anus

"You want me to come inside you?"

"There's coconut oil on the table next to you."

"Slowly, slowly! There's no hurry!" said Rémi. "And no, I didn't fuck Lihua. I want to be with you, of course!"

"Same me, Wóhólò Tagí."

We spent the next few minutes letting our bodies discover each other again.

"I want to come inside," he said.

"Slowly!" I whispered. I took in a short breath with an expression of discomfort.

Rémi could feel himself slipping further, deeper inside. He was breathing deep sighs. I, likewise, was panting slightly, waiting for my muscles to relax.

"Wait! Wait! Don't move! I just want to feel you there inside."

Tagí, the naked moon, came down to lie beside me, my right leg underneath him, my knee bent up and almost under his armpit. I didn't move. He was still deep inside. I felt an almost tight discomfort in my lower belly, as if my longing had reached overload. I was breathing deeply in and out, my eyes slowly closing and opening as my body adjusted to taking his dòrmi inside me.

"Are you okay?"

There was a long silence.

"Fine! You're not okay. What's wrong?"

"Being here."

"Ah."

"I don't want to be involved in Dieter's politics."

"Well, you are now."

"I just want to be Chár, look after my cattle, be with you, be with Juliette, make babies."

There was a long silence.

"So, how is Dieter, anyway?" I asked.

"He's fine. He's back in Germany now. My father is in contact with him. I don't know what they are doing. But whatever it is my father is up to, it is for you! You can be sure. And these three women, Lihua, Amani, Jolanta, they care for you. You're safe here. And they are fun. Besides, with the police looking for you and that mad - what is his name? – Mercantor. You might as well be back in Dibdib! We have to fight back! Otherwise, they will kill you!"

His body was becoming more desperate. He pushed further.

"Yeh. But they're crazy, you know, these women! I have seen before in my country, some people, it doesn't matter, men, women, it is like they are mad, but not. They know things others do not, things that history, even, has forgotten. Amani – you have noticed, Tagì? - she can see the future, and what about Lihua? She knows things about medicines, plants, herbs, even insects and animals that others do not. Jolanta, she has special powers over men, especially men who have power. They've captured me, don't you think? And seduced you also. They have their own plans. I don't know what they are! Maybe we are part of that! We don't know."

"Ben, mon cher, tu délires pas mal, eh?[46] Are they more crazy than you? You read too much between lines which don't exist. You're not their prisoner, they want to help you. We don't know their history, but clearly, they are making plans, even if they don't know them yet, and they want both of us, to be part of that, especially for Amani, so Lihua says, who thinks you are connected

---

[46] Well, my dear, you're really tripping out, aren't you?"

to her past somehow. They've got you a new identity, a new passport . . . "

"A new passport? They've told you they've got a new passport for me? Well, why didn't they tell me?"

"Maybe they've only just got it. I don't know! You might have a new name in a passport, but you are still my Chár! How many times have you told me you've died and then found me, for the first time again? Well, this is just another of those times. Lihua told me how they had found you, that Amani was sure your heart had stopped. So, let us start our hearts . . . . together again."

There was a silence.

"You are right as always."

Rémi grabbed my shoulders to shake me.

"Remember, I am Wóhólò Tagí! You are the best that is in me! Now, you're my prisoner! And I want, I need . . . First time! . . First time again!" Rémi held his breath, with a slightly pained expression on his face.

"Wait! Wait!" I pulled him back on top of me, wrapping my legs around him and pressing my heels against his buttocks to pull him further inside. I lifted my head from the pillow for Rémi to lean forward and our mouths to meet. We could play, talk, laugh, whatever, later. Now he had to let our bodies take over. Already, juice was leaking from my dormi's swollen head and creating a small wet patch between our bellies.

After increasingly difficult attempts to hold back, "Ah! Ah! I'm going to flood you!" Remi announced through the mounting tension.

I felt him swelling inside me, more than was possible and then the first pulse from deep inside Rémi to deep inside me, a pulse which seemed to stretch without end.

"Flood you," he managed to utter as his mouth fell upon mine and further pulses of semen spurted out into the warm forever of my

100

body. My own swollen black dormì started throbbing, following the rhythm of the pulsing biroute that was filling me.

"You'll stay with me, eh? I don't want to be alone again."

"Hey! Of course, I'll stay with you! We have to fix this! You have many friends ready to help, the night people, these three crazy witches, my father, Juliette, your family in France. Everyone you have met, they love you! At least we know the name of the enemy, eh?

"Ne t'inquiète pas. Le crépuscule de son pouvoir arrive![47]"

*   *   *

The pink fingers of dawn slowly lifted the veil of night over the frosted roofs of Shoreditch. A thin beam of yellow light floated up above the horizon sparkling along the river estuary until it found the window to my room and wriggled its way through the narrow openings of the ancient leaded glass to lance itself across the room illuminating tiny specks of dust hovering in the silent air. Everything was still. The beam of light had found my eyes and gently encouraged them to open. It had also found the golden down of the dorsal curves of Rémi's back, illuminating a diagonal line down to the small of his back where the down was slightly thicker before it gave way to the smooth, white, twinned cupolas of his sugum[48]. His body was, after all, for me, a place of worship.

My spirit had been lifted by Rémi's arrival and our first night again. It was as if Rémi's devotion, strength and optimism had been poured into me. I felt full now of hope and excitement at what we would confront together. Dawn arrived. The moment of being stirred to consciousness by the naughty beam of light that crept across our bodies, revealed to me the possibility of the great beauty my life could offer me. Beauty beyond egotism, beyond utility, beyond any value, except in itself. Not something after you die, nor clouded by memory, nor imagined futures, but a beauty that is clear and distinct, to find here and now. That didn't mean I could not play with it. Of course I could. Just as my hero,

---

[47] Don't worry. The twilight of his power arrives.
[48] buttocks

Caravaggio, played with beauty, so could I. And maybe become part of it, enter into it, become beautiful, and thus make the world beautiful. That must surely be paradise even now.

I turned on my side and propped my head in my left hand. I wanted just to gaze at the sleeping body next to me. My Rémi. My Wóhólò Tagí.

As usual, Rémi had ended up occupying most of the bed, lying on his stomach, his legs splayed out, his arms folded under the pillow supporting his head and his now long yellow hair falling down over his shoulders. As usual, again, I was awake with the rising sun and Rémi still deeply asleep. I smiled at the memory of how this had annoyed me in the past, how out of frustration, I had gotten up to go hunting and Rémi had remained in dreams. Eventually, of course, I had dragged him out of bed to go with me. I reached out with my right hand to let my fingertips run down Rémi's back until they reached the top of his haunches, his sugum, ses fesses. Here they paused so that my whole hand could caress first the further cheek and then the nearer with my fingertips sliding along the cleft where the two cheeks met, at the bottom of which they separated slightly more, to a keyhole entrance of a warm, soft

interior, son cul, son fion, his ɗolé[49]. Des poils pubiens, short pubic hairs, chó:ré, decorated his pretty anus and more, aligned next to each other led further down to his loosely resting búrrà. I moved closer to gently rest my face on Rémi's buttocks, the white skin, ineffably smooth, soft to touch, the feeling so magical. Only humans are capable of such tender sensations between each other. I kissed the perfect surface, of yellow peach. I, Caravaggio, Dionysus, Rémi, all shared the same worship of naked flesh. Looking over the rise of his cheeks, my right hand slowly stroking the inside of Rémi's leg, until it reached delicate soft tan skin carrying his tender bùrra[50], and just peeping from underneath, I found the head of Rémi's dormì, the frilled foreskin puckered for a kiss.

But now, although I loved kissing Rémi's dormì and playing with his pretty foreskin, my intention was otherwise. I took hold of the opposite side of his hips to carefully turn his sugum towards me,

---

[49] anus
[50] Balls

without waking him from his deep sleep. He was now lying on his left side, the right leg had been left behind and through the movement was now bent at the knee and the thigh at right angles to his torso, which resulted in the cheeks of his buttocks being slightly parted. I applied coconut oil to my own rigid dormì and to Rémi's ɗolé. As I pressed the head against the anus it slipped inside with considerable ease. I had known this from our time in France, how, when sleeping, the muscles of Rémi's ɗolé, although closed, were relaxed. I pushed my penis as deeply inside as possible, until my bùrra were resting on the top inside of Rémi's thigh. I reached across his hips to find Rémi's genitals, his penis already rigid and his couilles hanging loosely to one side. Wrapping my hand around his hard biroute, I started to pull the foreskin slowly back. Rémi's body stirred from sleep and as soon as he realised I was already inside him, he pushed firmly his buttocks into my hips to ensure my dormi was as far inside as possible, then twisted his torso, so that he could look back at me with a big grin. I put my arm around his neck and pulled him into me for our mouths to meet. Then, with both arms crossed around him and my hands grasping Rémi's chest I thrust harder and deeper.

Rémi forced his way under me and pushed his backside higher, lifting it away from the bed. I had to follow and slipped out.

"Si tu veux me baiser, il faut me séduire,[51]" said Rémi, turning on his back.

"You're so sexy, Rémi," I replied, smiling.

"I know!" he said, his head falling back on the pillow.

"Does Wóhólò Tagí want to fuck like a Suri?"

"Non, Chár nanu, I want our choga.[52] Tagì and Chár's loving."
With tenderness in his eyes and a short streak of pain across his brow, taking onto his shoulders and in his heart his brother's hurt.

---

[51]   You want to fuck me, you have to seduce me!
[52]   Nanu, meaning 'my'. Choga meaning, having sex

"D'accord!⁵³" I whispered, almost tearful, and fell on Tagì's breast, while he gently clung to me, running a hand along my dorsal muscles.

Then, extremely quietly at first, I could hear a faint purring in his chest becoming stronger, and with a fierce expression of eyes and mouth and a short laugh and growl, Rémi reached up and grabbed my buttocks with both hands. I looked down at his expectant, defiant face, grinning up at me, and then fell upon the cupid's bow that made his lips, wrapping them in my own and grabbing the beautiful white cheeks of his sugum with that same claw-like ferocity.

*　　　*　　　*

Sometime later - who knows how long? Time seemed to slip and slide in Place Pigalle in ways that avoided the regimentation of machines, clocks and timetables. Unusually early for this Bohemian household, Amanishakhete, wanting to invite us to a house meeting, looked into our room. She saw Rémi and I, naked and asleep and at the foot of the bed, two young leopards, also sleeping with legs and paws around each other. The cats immediately looked up with Chinese eyes hardly open, and that gentle smile cats have when content and needing nothing. She quietly retreated, leaving these wild creatures to their repose.

Lihua wanted a baby, it was true. Mind you, she was not at all interested in conceiving through any one of the clients who visited Place Pigalle. It was my arrival and more recently Rémi's that had woken a passion and desire for sex, which she had not felt for many years. Her body alone, without the interference of thought, had identified DNA it wanted for making babies. As well, we were very handsome, our bodies were beautiful, which clearly helped and having seen our penises, she knew she wanted them inside her. But what to do? She didn't want to choose one of us over the other, having no distinct preference, and in fact preferring both. Nor did she want to make either one of us her lover. It would be a onetime event when she knew her body had reached maximum fertility in her cycle. What about Jolanta and Amanisha? What might they do when they found out? Jolanta was far too concerned about the business and militant politics to contemplate a little child running around the place and Amanish . . . it was always her

---

⁵³　Here 'd'accord' means 'okay', but can also mean, 'I agree' – to be in accord with.

obsession with magical manipulation that came first. Maybe their hearts would soften when the baby was born . . . or maybe not, in which case she would . . . run away to China! How would she persuade us boys and which one? Would we help her?

Later that same morning that Amanishakete, Queen of Mothers, had come looking for us, Lihua was running from room to room in the upper part of the house, panting with anxiety and distress her red dragon silk dressing gown, tied tightly around the waist, fluttering around her legs. We boys had had to strip our bed and put all the linen to wash in the utility room. We were taking a shower and admiring ourselves and each other in the large mirrors of this mostly black and white art deco bathroom, when Lihua burst through the door, clearly in a state of panic.

"Here you are!" she announced and almost immediately was losing her voice, choking on tearful emotion. "I've been looking for you everywhere."

"Lihua, what's wrong? Calm down! Tell us!"

Straight away, both of us approached and put our arms around her. Lihua pressed her face against my chest and started sobbing.

"I love you! I love you both! You know that!" she managed to utter between sobs. "Jolanta and Amani have been making plans! Haven't you noticed how they have been spending all their time whispering together recently? "

"What are you talking about?"

"I heard them talking about a crippled devil," she said, at last catching her breath and able to express her distress. " They don't always tell me everything. We all have secrets, don't we? But few secrets escape them. They are scheming a lot recently and you are part of all that. They want to meet your night people! Prepare them for something. I never know what they are plotting. They were asking me about special medicines."

She sat down on the massage bench with us either side of her. We spontaneously put our arms around her and rubbed hands along her back as all creatures, when offering compassion and comfort, do with bodies and gestures. Lihua could feel our hot, hard, muscular bodies surrounding her, the muscles of our chests and bellies, shoulders and arms as they enveloped her.

"This is the moment when everything changes," said Rémi. "Don't you see? Already Amani has found the assassin and now their plans are for you and your night people to . . . . "

"And me, what about me? All I want is to have a baby! But they are against that!"

"No, they are not! Believe me," I reassured her. "You say secrets don't escape them, well, nor do they escape me. Secretly they will be happy for you to have your baby."

"And you know what?" she said, with a little tearful laugh. "You, both of you, either of you, you are the only men I have wanted to make that baby for me."

There was something not quite right about Lihua's desperation.

I was never apologetic about my body. Shame, guilt, embarrassment, not at all! This was one of the reasons why Rémi felt such admiration. He had been made free of all that moral and cultural oppression. Defining things, attributing function is necessarily reductive. So, reducing everything to a base functionality, ears are for hearing, not licking, anuses are for shitting, not kissing, penises and vulvas are for pissing and fucking, not sucking and licking. We had entered a world without shame or guilt about bodies, but loving them, worshipping them, admiring, exploring, playing, not only with each other but with Juliette and Angelique. We had discovered how bodies and parts of bodies respond to feelings, even express emotion. Our compassion, our need to alleviate Lihua's distress was expressed by our muscularity, our strength enveloping her, protecting her. Even and especially, our penises were already standing, ready to help. The body's instincts are sometimes strange to us, even though they are our own.

"On va en faire ensemble, alors.[54]" said Rémi.

I was not so sure. Did I really want to be a father to Lihua's child? Her desperation indicated something far deeper than the instinct to have a child. What I am trying to say is Lihua's anxiety over this, the fact that

---

54 We'll do it together then.

the other two women seem to forbid her from having a child, there was a lot more to Lihua's distress than was immediately evident. And a lot more to whatever tied these three women together. Even after having sex, there seemed no relief for Lihua. She seemed now to worry obsessively about her fertility.

"Wait! Wait!" demanded Lihua. "Don't move! Lie me down first on the bench, so I can keep your seed as long as possible."

We carefully lowered her to the bench, lying next to her to remain inside. Later, as she left, she was still in tears.

"Something terrible has happened to our Lihua, something which eats at her heart. I am not sure trying to become a mother is the right path for her just now," I commented to Rémi later.

When I spoke to Queen Amanishakhete, my third mother, about Lihua's troubles, she said: 'Don't worry Chár, darling, neither of you are about to become parents," which puzzled me even more. Why do witches have to be so unfathomable?

*   *   *

"We have never said you cannot have a child, Lihua, darling. But you know you cannot."

"Soon you will have all the children you want!"

"Do not reveal this to the innocents! Their actions must be their own, untainted by obligation, favour or deception."

"I wish they could be mine," said Lihua. "They understand so much about bodies and feelings, how to be kind with their bodies, how to be human, instead of like our idiot clients."

"I am sure," said Jolanta compassionately, "I am sure you are right."

"The time of ice and mists has arrived!" Amanishakhete declared. "Wóhólò Tagí was born in dance under a full moon. I have met Chár's night people. They are ready, eager. They love him, his magical difference. They have waited an eternity for this future to unfold, to liberate their bodies and spirits. The dance of the Satyrs! They are strong, supple, ready to meet their ideal: that open, invisible event, that their strengths, their perfections are made for."

"What is the name, Lihua," Jolanta took her in her arms, " of your theatre friends? The Chronicles Troupe, is it?"

"They're not getting enough work. They're breaking up. Why?"

"We're going to start a new business. We need you to talk to the Chronicles. Maybe we can do a merger. They perform anywhere, don't they? This is perfect for our Chár, eh, Amani? You who want him to be Dionysus. Maybe your dream, your Nubian myth, will manifest itself. The Black One has arrived, followed, happily, willingly, by his night people." Even Jolanta, rational Jolanta, was starting to be seduced by Amani's mythic imaginings: the devotees of Dionysus at the time of myth were spinsters, widows, women without conventional family support, who became Maenads, and the Satyrs were largely composed of ex-slaves, runaways, outsiders for whatever reason. That same pattern was repeating itself. She couldn't resist cosying it all into place. There was no need to take a hammer for this, events, times and coincidences all seemed to marry so easily.

*   *   *

"The sisters hate Mercantor more than we do! When will we know why? His life must be ended quickly, or at the very least, as it parasitically subsists at the moment. A virtual death, perhaps, in which he loses everything, including himself. What do you think, Chár, goona nanu[55]?"

"Strange country, strange people who lift up and fix in stone a rotting wound that is him and his inherited power. They hate him also, the people around him, but a peculiar hatred. To hate through gross injustice is one thing, but to hate through envy, admiration almost, a wish to be like him and finally hate themselves. Like parasites, their existence feeds on suffering and deprivation in a silly game of stepping on others, each other even. An ugly competing and a hopeless wish to be glorified like him. . . . The poor are not like this. They seem to accept their slavish fate in this strange country, but are poorer for being lied to, deceived, even believing he, Mercantor and his like deserve to rule. My night people understand well and know him for what he is . . ."

---

[55] Chár, my brother.

" . . . . that pustule on the skin of the Earth."

*   *   *

Chapter 4

The Visions of Ray Ferrier

"Aah, Aaaahuhuh!"

Two nurses rushed into Ferrier's private ward. His wheelchair was pushed up against the window once again. One immediately silenced the warning bleep of his intravenous drip, which had been trolleyed over, and was standing next to his wheelchair.

"Aaah, ah! Uh!"

"What is it, Mr Ferrier? Bad dreams again?" The nurse looked down at Ferrier's contorted face, now quite gaunt. The furrows dividing the yellowing skin, becoming waves of crushing agony, pulled towards the gaping black hole of his mouth. A poisonous vapour seemed to emit from this pit as if it might be the final expiration of bloated carrion before the vultures, unable to fly thanks to their over-full bellies, stagger away, in greedy contempt of each other.

"We'll have to do something about your halitosis problem, Mr Ferrier, just brushing your teeth doesn't seem to work. I'll ask the doctor. Maybe an emetic might help, or laxative." said one.

"Or both," whispered the other.

"Uuh. You have to call the police!" he panted with fear, his voice high pitched, begging. "They're here again! I saw them!"

"How did you manage to get into your wheelchair and over here by the window? Everyone is sleeping, Mr Ferrier. It's two in the morning."

He could feel them climbing up his skin.

One of the few pleasures in his state of almost quadriplegic paralysis was to be wheeled to the window of his private ward to watch the comings and goings of the everyday and its people. He had managed to obtain binoculars expressly for this purpose. His chair, as well as providing mobility could also lift his back upright or recline when he felt tired. He had also managed to have his binoculars attached to a support so that he could at any time take advantage of them and, like a type of camera stand, the support could incline at angles and swivel from side to side to take in the entire panorama. His room was about three or four storeys up, so he estimated, hence he had a very good view of the pathway around the hospital, with a small grassed area either side, plus part of the hospital car park, the small enclosed public gardens beyond and then a distant road with terraced Victorian houses and small shop fronts. He was not above the hospital main entrance, nor Accident and Emergency, both of which were no doubt busy and would have been too distracting. As it was, he could peacefully watch the few who used the gardens and even get to follow lives, loves and amusements of these daily passers-by, those arriving by car and their frustrations, satisfactions and even occasional disputes over parking spaces.

On occasions, Ray could almost glimpse in himself a sense of contentment and even acceptance of the many attributes, characteristics, foibles and peculiarities of this tiny corner of humanity if not humanity at large - at large entailed something far too vague, beyond the needs or capabilities of his wounded body and soul.

The various medications his regular night nurse - Nurse Manchester, was it?- had been providing him had greatly relieved the psychological trauma of suddenly becoming almost totally disabled and the Odysseus daffodil drug had given him such vivid dreams in which peculiarly he seemed of a non-age. He perceived himself as perhaps he had been when life was good, in his late twenties, generally fit and able to do everything any normal person could. They, his dreams, even seemed on occasions to provide great insights and understandings about pasts and possible futures.

Then there was a period of heavy mists. It became difficult for him to see much at all and the times of day when the mists lifted slightly just didn't coincide with those times when the humanity that had so charmed him was around. Had they changed their habits because of the now dreary weather? He would still look out for them in hopes of cheering his falling spirits, there in his chair, his binoculars fixed before his eyes, at the lonely window of his sheer and polished tower. Then he realised the more intently he looked he could actually make out shapes, the bare branches of the trees of the enclosed gardens, the empty pathways beneath the bushes, all a silvery grey in the cold, damp vapours.

It was getting towards evening. The weak and shadowless light of day was fading to blue when he saw something dancing, moving, turning at happy speed amongst the undergrowth of this little park. And then another. And another. Three shapes dancing together. And then they disappeared in the darkness.

This happened on several late afternoons, the heavy mist hiding the bodies of these ballet dancers; clearly, this is what they were. He could see only silhouettes, bodies, without decoration or ornamentation, without covering, just the outline of bodies. Then one blue evening, they stopped and were looking towards the hospital, his window.

He started to feel . . . uncomfortable. Why weren't they moving? Why were they looking at him? Were they looking at him or just the building? He turned away, deciding to try to obliterate memory of that sinister moment through the therapy of junk TV. Nevertheless, his chair, his body, his mind, his eyes were drawn back, in spite of his best resistance, to the now terrible window. The rancorous mist, stubbornly clinging to and suffocating the naked trees of his pretty park had turned a foetid orange in the streetlamp lit light of night. As the darkness deepened, the mist slowly sank back into the ground from whence it had appeared revealing no longer three, or sometimes five, but many black figures and now he could see that, yes, they were black, with their carefully sculpted, chiselled hair, their bodies almost completely naked in the winter air, laughing at the icy cold. They were jumping and dancing, a pack of young wolves rousing each other with snaps and cries to the anticipation of blood. Suddenly, they turned together and started running towards the wall of his hospital.

He woke the next morning in his bed. As memories returned of what he had seen the night before, he started to wonder to what extent it had actually happened or whether it was in part anxiety, turned dream, turned nightmare. He decided to speak to the nurse about it before she went off duty.

He caught her attention, beckoning with his head and eyes.

"What is it Mr Ferrier?"

"The weather. It's been very foggy, eh?"

"Yes! And cold."

"Did you see the . . . fog last night?"

The nurse looked puzzled.

"Yes?"

"Did you notice anything in the park? Any people?"

"Ooh, it was too dark and too foggy!"

"I thought I saw a gang of black youths fooling around."

"You shouldn't be spending your time so late at the window, Mr Ferrier. When I came in to check on you, you were asleep in your chair, still there. Goodness knows how long you had been sitting there. And who put you there? Your visitor? We had to lift you back into bed ourselves, Nurse Benton and I, while you were sound asleep." She paused, then reflecting on what Mr Ferrier had said: "There are too many of these black gangs hanging around the streets at night, if you ask me. Why doesn't the government make a curfew, that's what I want to know."

"What visitor?"

"The tall lady, big black hair."

"The pharmatherapist?"

Again, the nurse seemed puzzled.

"Pharmacotherapist, you mean. Do you have one?"

Ferrier didn't reply. He felt as if he had therapists for everything.

The next night, after Nurse Manchester had left, he was sitting at the window again looking intently into the mists, when slowly he became aware of being laid out on an X-form cross. At either end of his ankles and wrists, he felt thick ropes pulling. Of course, any sensation in his limbs was only a ghost, but here he was being stretched out flat on a wooden rack. Previously, in the dreamworld, the daffodil-Odysseus medication had in fact been of great therapeutic value enabling him to be alive in a fully functioning dream-body and with the lucidity to manage the dream, but now in R.E.M. sleep his already useless body had somehow invaded the dream-body and he found himself frozen, unable to escape the medieval rack on which he was bound. He didn't even know he was dreaming; he was in hell. Slowly the ropes around his wrists and ankles were being pulled apart as the rack was raised for him to witness the creeping mists climb the walls to penetrate his window. Joints started to creak and pop, bones crack, arms and legs stretched to the limit of endurance as if being torn apart. He tried to scream but could not, only a silent groan struggled from his mouth.

Three faces, three women, appeared from the mist before him, in swirling grey and crumpled rags, hardly distinguishable from the swirling clouds, fading in and out of vision like the ghostly silhouettes of the dancers as their voices spoke, whispered, threatened.

"Where is he now, the one?" demanded the first with bitter slanting eyes and jagged red lips.

"The one you wished dead!" declared another, accusing Ferrier and pointing with crooked fingers.

"The one you intended to vanish, deprived of his life by your bloodstained greed."

"Where his leopards that cracked your neck?" asked another, tall and black with gigantic curling hair. "They are coming soon, for you!"

The voices raised, accusatory, each utterance on top of, overlapping the other, with the vile croaking of black vultures, leaving the sicken feeling in Ray's stomach that he was reviled, and were the world to hear and understand, hated by all.

"No! Not me! I wanted nothing! It was just a job!" screamed Ferrier, the small child, the weak, vulnerable, terrified victim of vicious sorcery, of the writhing distorted fear that only nightmares can bring.

"Mercantor! He's the one! He was going to send him back, back where he belongs, like all the other illegals."

Who were they, these witches? They might as well have given him acid, or a part of the red and white dome of a fly agaric. So powerful was the daffodil drug, he could not escape its visions, nor their terror.

As he spoke, screaming out his panic, his vision suddenly exterior to the building, he saw the same black insects that had been crawling over his skin, the ghosts of the enclosed public gardens, climbing the walls of the hospital and through his window until clearly six stood before him, at the foot of his bed, bloodied and bruised from the Akobo bridge and the cursed and anguish-ridden Dibdib.

"And where's the seventh?" he screamed out, terrified. He'd even researched the terrible outcomes of Dibdib, such was now his febrile obsessions with events he normally would have forgotten.

And then Ray's voice, austere and righteous dared to question what might happen returning to Dibdib, when the black ghosts of that place, falling, bleeding and dying in front of him, reached out to grasp his legs and drag him inexorably into the mire of fetid, parasitic vines and creepers of the jungle: "Why take me there again?"

Had he suffered a mad transfiguration, transubstantiation. Had he slipped into the ghost body of that Ethiopian captain the tortured forest had killed? His attempts to backtrack, his soundless pleading, his craven apologies, admittance of guilt, meant nothing to the bleeding and dying. More and more, ants started to consume his skin. He could hear himself howling.

And from out of this terrified bleeding multitude stepped the one connection, the heaviest of visitations, which would forever join his ugly life to the annihilation of Beyahola.

"Hello, Ray." His painted face and torso distinguishing him from the bloodied corpses at his feet.

"Keep them away, keep them away!" Ray's skin was wet with the cold sweat of panic.

"I am bringing you into my world now. You understand?" smiled the black spirit. "But first you have to die!"

As this black spectre of death reached out to stroke Ray's cheek, a gentle smile on his face, Ray's crippled vulnerability, overwhelming guilt, caused him to burst into wailing tears, a child about to be admonished for self-injury. Darkness impinged upon his peripheral vision until he was gradually swallowed into the void. He passed out. When he came back to consciousness, he was lying in his bed, no longer being stretched on the rack, no longer dragged into Dibdib, the pain he had felt throughout his ghost corpse had disappeared.

Ray felt his body relax. How could he have that sensation? He was surrendering. The ghost of Beyahola, the Black One with painted face, started vigorously massaging his legs.

"What is real often hides what is true. The black ants!" said one of the witches.

"Your masters wrote it down to make it true. But ink is not blood, and paper is not fate. We read the body - bruises, breaths, broken sleep. Their history is neat. Ours is hungry."

Ray found himself slowly slipping into the hypnotic rhythm of the wraith's strong black hands.

" The black ants are real enough for you, they will gnaw at you from the inside, but what is true often confuses what is real." said another. "The pen scratched lies in time. We licked the wounds they left behind. Now the script runs backwards, watch how its author weeps."

The vision stepped back away from Ray's bed.

"What is happening with your body?"

"Leave me! Leave me alone! I am just a poor idiot, a lackey!"

"This whining does nothing for you!!" said the painted ghost. "And your doctors, what have they told you!"

"Nothing. The doctors say nothing, but I know what they think."

He lifted the sheets covering Ray's feet and scraped a fingernail up the sole of his left foot. Ray felt a thin fine tingle run up his leg.

"Your body's changing and you don't even know! You lie to yourself about it and you think it is the truth!"

There was a long silence. Ray was looking into dark black eyes, trying to see what was real and what was true.

"All you have to do," the spectre insisted, "is tell the man who wanted

116

me dead exactly what you have seen tonight. Tell him he doesn't need to look for me, I will find him when I am ready."

"Of course! Of course!"

"You are one of us now, Ray!"

"One of us!" echoed the witches, cackling with laughter. "One of us!"

And slowly the mists and creatures of the night faded into blackness.

*   *   *

Ray and Mercantor

Since his encounter with the black ghosts, the witches and the black avatar, Ray found himself in a state of beatific reprieve.

He was listening to St. Matthew's Passion. Klemperer's ponderous and meticulous attention to the very human suffering, the passion of Bach's interpretation of what at the very least could be described as great tragedy, lifted him to a transcendent plateau of tearful bliss. He was both the individual characters represented, the Christ, Mary, mother of Jesus, the Evangelist and everyone in the collective of both choirs.

Nurse Manchester (that couldn't be her real name, could it?), who seemed to run a private nursing and therapeutic agency for people suffering long term disabilities and consequent psychological trauma, PTSD as they say, had brought in Nurse Joli who was particularly adept at therapeutic massage. It was she who had given him the CD copy of the Passion. As for the stereo player, that had been brought to his room and set up by two young black men:

"Don't worry where it comes from, mate," said one, whose jogging bottoms, black, with two white stripes down each leg, were sitting deliberately low, revealing the elastic band of his Dolce et Gabbana underwear, clinging to his athletic strong black buttocks, "stuff like this just falls off lorries all the time."

"How do you think eBay keeps operating, eh?" grinned the other, smaller, younger and clearly imitating his mate's bluff manner.

"Who's giving me this?"

"It's from the ladies, mate, the ladies, some police commissioner, or something. I don't know. Don't worry about it!"

"You're alright with them, in't yer Mister, eh, those ladies?" the younger one said, again with a grin.

Ray was being invaded. The world, its raving insanity, refused to leave him alone. Of course, he had reflected a lot on his night of hallucinations. Perhaps his own crucifixion, bound on that rack of burning pain, had been cathartic, absolving him of all sin.[56]

In his listening, he was getting close to movement 27 sections a&b. The Passion had reached the Christ's betrayal. Already he was anticipating the aria "So ist mein Jesus nun gefangen (So is my Jesus now captured!)", with the beautiful overlayering of wailing harmonies as the alto repeats the soprano line and the loud demands of the chorus "Laßt ihn, haltet, bindet nicht! (Let him go, stop, do not bind him!)"

As movement 27 reached "Mond und Licht (Moon and light) Ist vor Schmerzen untergangen, (have set in sorrow)", the door to his private ward was opened for Secretary of State, Sir James Mercantor, followed by his private secretary and the same intern who had visited Ray Ferrier shortly after the incident and his injury.

Mercantor spoke:

"So, erm, Ray . . . may I call you by your first name?"

"Weil mein Jesus ist gefangen." cried the soprano and alto.

"Laßt ihn, haltet, bindet nicht!" demanded the chorus.

Ray's eyes slowly closed with contempt at Mercantor's request, as he

---

56 The classic dream of being bound upon a rack is very common if the drug extracted from the daffodil bulb is swallowed and the subject passes into R.E.M sleep. This is why companies producing this drug recommend sleeping first, waking in the middle of the night, after R.E.M sleep, in order to then dream lucidly, which is what Ray had experienced until that night.

turned his head away. There was a look of vexed frustration on Mercantor's face.

"Can't we turn this music down?"

Immediately the intern turned towards Ray's stereo.

"No, you fucking can't!" shouted Ferrier, angrily. "And if that fucking idiot touches it, I'll call security and have him thrown out, and you!" he said, glaring at Mercantor and pausing the Passion with his remote.

"They told me you were quadriplegic, but you have some use in your right arm." observed Mercantor, attempting to show some concern.

"What do you want?!!"

Mercantor took off his leather gloves and walked over to the window of visions.

"The Deputy Commissioner passed on a message that you needed to see me urgently," said Mercantor, "although he couldn't say what it was about."

Ferrier started laughing loudly, almost hysterically.

"Deputy Commissioner! And you believed him?" he continued his high-pitched laughing, as if Mercantor were an idiot. "Let you out of the broom cupboard, has he?" he was addressing the intern. "To bend over his desk for him?"

"There's no point in this!" Mercantor looked down at the pathetic cripple. "If you just want to be offensive, I'm leaving!" He made towards the door.

"There were seven of them!" shouted Ferrier hurriedly.

Mercantor paused, waiting for more.

"There were seven. Seven who escaped from the Dibdib. Do you want to talk about this in front of your . . " Ferrier then turned to the assistants. "How do you feel about all the dodgy, dubious and ugly information you must overhear or discover about your boss? When does it become

119

collusion, I wonder," he said, looking at Mercantor's secretary and grinning wildly.

"Presumably you don't mind discussing Beyahola in front of the gimps?" he said, turning back to Mercantor.

Mercantor indicated to his secretary and intern to wait outside.

He was trapped. Mercantor wanted badly to leave that disaster of a body lying on the hospital bed. As far as responsibility was concerned, he had been trained to assume the distance of power and status and the corrupt rationalisation of greed. It was not important that the vagaries of money were not only ugly, even murderous, but what was important was what his venal world gained. He had to know about the seven.

"Tabula rasa is impossible. You can never wipe away every trace of any one thing, any act, any person or people. Only the very stupid think that. Pol Pot, Pinochet, Hitler and you, so it seems."

"Less of the lectures! What have you got to say?"

"There were at least seven who escaped your massacre in the Dibdib forest, I've done my research. Not just the one you wanted me to deal with, he wasn't the only one!"

"Dibdib! Honestly!" muttered Mercantor. "A measure of cultural wealth, no doubt, that monosyllabic repetition! So, where are they? Scratting around in the undergrowth of Dibdib forest?"

"Maybe they are here. Maybe I've seen them. Maybe they're scratting around in that park opposite." said Ferrier laughing madly again and looking to see how Mercantor might take the idea.

Mercantor had not sat down and inadvertently glanced again out of the window.

"Ah, you never know! Maybe they're looking back at you even now! The seven. Or is it only three?"

There was a heavy silence. Mercantor saw lovers on a park bench, sharing sandwiches, two mothers pushing pushchairs and three black teenagers in jeans and zipped puffer jackets against the frosty air, their

sculpted hair standing proud. One seemed to have . . . a feather? . . .
pushed into his tight curls? They were pulling each other around,
laughing and then they stopped and looked straight at the window.
Mercantor shrank back and almost stumbled on the corner of the bed.

Ray started cackling again: "You've seen them, haven't you?"

"What was his name, that little boy in the Zoffany painting?"
asked Ferrier his eyes slanting with contempt.

"What? What are you talking about?"

"The little black boy in the family portrait at your house near
Bristol. It's very famous, quite . . . haunting, really. I've seen the
picture on the internet. Are you the seventh generation? . . . .
Unto the seventh generation . . . You remember what the Bible
says?"

Mercantor had paled and his skin had become clammy, like wet
fish.

"I don't know what you're talking about. I never look at those
paintings, there are too many."

"When you think of the amount of blood spilled! How was it your
family made its fortune? It must be haunted, don't you think, that
house near Bristol, your family estate? What's it called? Utrecht
Hall? Inasmuch as ghosts are in your head, what about the little
boy, preserved forever in the family painting and what about those
boys in the park just now? You saw them, didn't you? Are they
ghosts? Just locals fooling around? Are they three of the seven?
And where are the others?"

"Fuck! Fuck! Fuck!" thought Mercantor. How did Ferrier know
there were three out there and not seven? . . . Seven? What was
his mind doing?

The private ward started to fill with clouds. Mercantor felt cold
and damp.

"I don't even know what he looks like," declared Mercantor,
angrily, and to himself. "I've looked at those YouTube videos a

hundred times, but I still wouldn't recognise him."

"They think they can be invisible, his people. Any hunter has to be. They use their paints and the plants of the forest as camouflage, as any professional soldier would."

There was a heavy silence as they stared at each other.

"In any case, he's wanted by the Metropolitan and Immigration, so, he's not going far - unseen," said Mercantor, with as much conviction as he could muster.

"Sind Blitze, sind Donner in Wolken verschwunden?
Sind Blitze, sind Donner in Wolken verschwunden?
Sind Blitze, sind Donner in Wolken verschwunden?
Sind Blitze, sind Donner in Wolken verschwunden?"

Ray had lifted his right arm, the only part of his body with partial mobility, and with the remote control, resumed the playing of movement 27 b. The powerful overlaying of different voices bringing progressively greater strength to the invocation: "Have lightnings, has thunder vanished in the clouds?" He could feel choirs, the crescendo of repetitions fill his limbs, his ghost limbs, with an inner sensitivity, more alive, present, than ordinary consciousness ever was.

He paused the music and turned to Mercantor again.

"Those young black guys you saw," said Ferrier, quietly, "You know why they are there?" He paused. "They are there for me. Protection. They're my guardians. Guardian angels! My black angels!" Ferrier was shaking with hysterical laughter again. "Look, I'm going to try to be completely honest with you. I have every reason to hate you for your part in where I find myself today. And I do. I wish the worst for you. Needless to say, I am taking all sorts of medication and some which play with the mind," he paused, "dream states."

"You're hallucinating."

"Mmm, maybe. The good thing is, in the dream state, my body appears to me fully functioning," he said with a smile, "which is beautiful. Recently, I had a very vivid dream, a nightmare. Although it was a dream, I am persuaded he was here, the Suri boy, with those nurses I see every evening. As I was slipping into that medicated sleep . . ." Ray related the story of how the mad black dancing figures had emerged from the mist, run over from the park to the hospital wall and had started to climb it, how he was on a rack, his joints and bones cracking as they were stretched, how the three witches (had they been nurses only minutes before?) had been accusing him, how in terror he had denounced Mercantor for the massacre, and how suddenly from behind the crowd of black naked ghost dancers, appeared the painted face of him!

"Maybe it was entirely hallucinated, entirely my imagination. Maybe there were only a few here. Was he here? I think so. Maybe the nightmare was a setup.

"He spoke, the black one with painted face, the one who died in Dibdib." Ferrier was still trying to work out what had happened. "He touched my foot. I felt him touch my foot." It was as if he was astonished. "It was so vivid, the sensation. I'm not supposed to feel anything at all in my lower body!"

"And what about now? Can you feel your foot now?"

"Maybe. Sometimes." he wondered. "When are those sensations just my ghost body, just an hallucination? When do I take them for the real world? Those nurses . . . " Ray stopped short. Such fragile intimacies he might have experienced were precious and not to be shared with all.

"Okay! Dream world or real, he asked me to tell you, you don't need to waste your time looking for him, he will find you . . . when he is ready." He started laughing again, laughing madly all through the chorus.

"Sind Blitze, sind Donner in Wolken verschwunden?
Eröffne den feurigen Abgrund, o Hölle,
Sind Blitze, sind Donner in Wolken verschwunden?
Eröffne den feurigen Abgrund, o Hölle,
Zertrümmre, verderbe, verschlinge, zerschelle
Mit plötzlicher Wut

123

Den falschen Verräter, das mördrische Blut!   "

Mercantor stared at Ferrier long and hard, knowing full well what the chorus was singing. As it called upon hell to open up its abyss, his hard stare turned to contemptuous hatred.

"Do you know what he said to me? He said: 'Ray, you are one of us, now!' Your deputy commissioner? No, he's not yours, he's one of us also. Like the three black boys outside, like the seven. We are many!"

The Bach chorus continued as Ray laughed at Mercantor's confusion of disbelief.

Outside the private ward, Mercantor rejoined his staff.

"He's hallucinating like mad! He's fucking crazy! Anyway, he has nurses who visit him in the evenings. I want to know who they are."

"Yes sir."

By the following afternoon, Mr Ferrier's private ward had been vacated.

*   *   *

Chapter 5

Closer

In Bristol, there was a thin, cold, grey rain. It was not a determined rain that wishes to affirm its existence with decent noticeable drops hitting puddles, or splashing flagstones with certainty, no, it couldn't even clean the grubby paving slabs at the exit of the shopping arcade where I was sitting, propped against the exterior wall of Sports Direct.

How long I had been there, sitting, of course I couldn't remember. The paradox of my quite deliberate position was that the best way to be invisible was to remain as open to public view as possible. All the other beggars I had joined, equally, were never seen. No one looked at me at all. Even along the river, which flowed through a deep gorge where the invisible people gathered often at night, sheltering in caves, lighting fires and entering into a shadowy state of being, even then their existence seemed to fade in and out of a presence.

With the sisters, we had all agreed , I needed to learn how to hunt through bricks, on concrete and roads, and amongst all the cracks and dirty corners of that country. I knew here in Bristol I was approaching everyone's intent. I knew also that the sisters would want to find me again. But this living here on the streets? Maybe they had wanted me to witness the catastrophe. The catastrophe of divided, deprived, and resentful England. We had persuaded Rémi to return to France with express orders to care for Juliette, Nathalie and Charles, whilst I, Chár, should seek out the devil's warren. He was only going to leave me knowing he would be back once I had penetrated Mercantor's territory.

What had Defoe, Young, Locke, Chatham, Mercantor and their inheritors done!? Jolanta had become my teacher, but had she understood me, Chár? This Mercantor, if he bears any responsibility for the death of my mother, father, Bongay and everyone I had grown up with, did I want to kill him? What sort of dimwitted revenge is that? If I am to take revenge, I need to see him, meet him face to face, perhaps then I will know what to do. Very quickly, just as before in Shoreditch, I had lost everything, money, (false) passport from the sisters, all identity. For a long time now I had been keeping my name to myself; no one knew I was leopard. From now on I was just . . . Black!

*   *   *

Ms Evelyn stepped down from the driver's seat of her new Lexus SUV and at exactly that moment the sun peeped out from behind clouds, in its shy English way, to bathe her with its glance. There was regality to her affirming and acknowledging the sun's admiration before it had to hide its face, out of deference and humility, once again.

She was meeting a pauper sent to be under her care by the local council, which had no doubt been bullied into making provision for him by local do-gooders who went to church and attended committee meetings. She had a fortunate relationship with the housing department of the council; she was one of the landladies who were used to accommodate the poorest in need of shelter, the so-called vulnerable. The rent was guaranteed. Believe me, as Ms Evelyn would say, these were truly the dregs: dirty, rotting, smelly, passed their use-by date.

Her daughter she instructed to remain seated in the Lexus. Ms. E. glanced back in triumphant admiration at the reward, one of many, for her compassionate generosity in taking care of the poor and verminous of her world.

There was a shadow in the doorway of 113. Black was crushed, hiding himself in the sheltered corner of the small porch of 113 in that angle with the least light where the door hinged against the wall. It had become his custom, now alone, to make himself the least noticeable possible. He had been perfecting it for some time.

"Yes? Can I help you?"

He noticed her dress which seemed more like vulgar evening wear than the everyday. At the back it reached down to her heels but then curved upward to above her knees at the front. It was some sort of black synthetic, the sweeping curve of the hem decorated with small bows. He glanced at her studiously tanned legs and then looked away.

"Mr. Black, is it?" She had made a mistake over his surname. "Christine from the Housing offices has sent you here, is that right? What is your Christian name, your first name?" she corrected, wondering if he understood what a Christian name might be.

"Black," he whispered.

126

She looked confused momentarily and smiled to herself.

"Fine. You can call me Miss Evelyn."

Black slipped to one side to avoid her as Miss Evelyn confidently stepped forward, reaching into her Louis Vuitton for her collection of keys.

She opened the front door and led Black into a claustrophobic entrance of cold maroon and black tiles and walls papered with beige chip leading to stairs further down the dim interior. She switched on a yellow light. Black felt her too close to him in the confines of the narrow hall.

"All right, Kevin?" she called out to a thin figure with bent shoulders in the twilight beyond the stairs. "Kevin, this is Black."

Neither Black nor Kevin said anything.

"He is moving into the room upstairs, at the back of the house. Zelusz's old room."

Once again silence.

"So, Kevin, have you been looking for work?"

Kevin seemed to squeak something and then turned to disappear through the door behind him.

"That's the kitchen," Miss Evelyn pointed out; just as the one toilet was shared between eight adults, which she didn't mention. "It's shared. For you as much as for all the other people in the house, so don't be shy to use it."

She smiled.

"Kevin seems to like it in there," she commented, with a wry smile. "He's always there with a tea towel in his hands." She looked at Black, expressing her bemused incomprehension. Black just hid his face.

Upstairs, she unlocked the door to the back room where Black would now be staying. Inside, there was a mattress leaning against a wall and a wooden bed frame. In a corner was a small sink and mirror and another corner, a brown wooden wardrobe. Next to the sink was a small

127

chipboard shelf, covered with grubby self-adhesive red and white flower-patterned plastic, and in the middle of which sat a pale blue plastic beaker. The cream, wood-chip papered walls, which were not hidden by the vertical mattress and brown wardrobe, had been spray-painted with meaningless graffiti, initially green and then superimposed with gold. Was there an expletive hidden there? It was as if some alien creature, trapped in the room, or made prisoner had ejaculated its howling anger there in a night of dark frustration.

"Speak to Kevin," said Miss Evelyn. " I'm sure there are some pots of paint somewhere. You'll be able to smarten it up in no time. The bed and wardrobe were left behind by the last tenant. If you don't want them, by all means just throw them out." She looked at him suspiciously. "But not in either the front or back gardens. Make sure they are taken away."

The door opened, interrupting the callous privacy of induction into the grim accommodation on offer. Ms Evelyn turned quickly with icy look and pinched lips to see her small daughter standing in the doorway, a twelve-year-old in dark blue uniform holding a large black rubbish bag.

"You forgot this, Mummy."

Issola appeared surrounded by a bubble of light, which protected her from the contamination of the room.

"Darling, I told you to stay in the car. I don't want you walking into these places."

"But you forgot these things."

Miss Evelyn took the black bin bag.

Issola looked at Black and said, "These are clothes and stuff from one of Mummy's friends." Her mobile phone called her attention; she took it out of her jacket pocket to look at it. "She works in a charity shop in town, Mummy's friend. What charity is it, Mummy?"

"Issola, go back to the car. It's called Shelter." Ms Evelyn turned to Black with the bin bag. "Here. Some clothes, towels, toothbrush, toiletries etc., to get you started."

128

The idea of giving old clothes to wear to someone who had a deep dislike of clothes, even though, as Black, I had become accustomed to my rags and had even taken care of them, made me, Black, almost laugh.

"The things you are wearing, I suggest you throw them away. They are finished. Take a shower. Get yourself clean. If you need me or have any questions, I will be downstairs for a short while with the other tenants. The bathroom is here, just next to your room. Keep it clean. Remember, it is shared." Ms Evelyn was quite used to organising her tenants, telling them what to do. They were so weak, completely lacking in any confidence to do anything, even opening a window, and certainly never picking up a screwdriver. She hated their clothes! Always those grey, faded colours, misshapen, grubby, if not downright filthy. She despaired! She had been puzzled by Black's private amusement at being offered this charity, but quickly attributed it to the madness induced by abject poverty. Without her and people like her this miserable lot would be completely lost. Their skin was always sickly yellowish and slimy. You couldn't come close to them because there was likely to be a smell of decomposition. But of course, Black had not yet been coloured yellow by deprivation. Would he ever be, she wondered idly.

Issola's mobile clicked, pretending to be a single lens reflex camera as it took a photo of Black in his rags in the middle of the traumatised room.

"Put your phone away and go back to the car straight away!"

Black suddenly found himself alone. The western sun was slowly changing from orange to red and flooding his room with warm light, eliminating the ugliness of the walls. There was a desolate moment when, no longer part of other people's world, no longer buffeted and dragged here and there by needs, fears or desires, I felt a sudden anger and started to rip off the stinking rags that hid me, disguised me as Black. An anger, a hatred for all things and all people was driving me to tear at everything which outwardly defined me, until I stood naked in the red light. I was no longer going to be Black. There were bits of newspaper still sticking to the skin of my legs, trying to become part of my living flesh. I quickly emptied the black plastic bag and pushed into it the detritus I had peeled from my body. I would never see nor touch it again. Squatting on my haunches, I quickly and carefully arranged the gifts of charity from Miss Evelyn's friend in ordered piles on the floor. The newspaper sticking to my skin, which I had used to keep warm, was falling like tiny confetti around my feet. I rubbed my shins vigorously, picked up towel, toothpaste, toothbrush, shampoo, and a bottle of oil from my own separate plastic bag. Standing up and looking out toward the setting sun, I let out a long solitary howl of isolation and pain.

Hearing the howl, Miss Evelyn and Kevin stood in silence, looking at each other.

"What was that?" asked Issola and walked out of the kitchen towards the bottom of the stairs.

"Remember, Kevin, you are in charge. Keep an eye on Mr. Black. Make sure he is okay. If there are any problems, call me. You've got credit on your phone?"

Kevin shuffled and looked guilty.

"Well, get some credit, then! And tell Brankovitch if he doesn't pay the rent he owes me, he'll have to move out. Let him become a nuisance for people he knows, his friends, and sleep on their sofas again. Honestly, what's wrong with him? Still doesn't have any work, does he?"

"I fink he does anyway."

"What? Have work?"

"Sleep on sofas. He's never 'ere. 'Ow can I tell him anyfink?"

Evelyn felt a shudder of disgust as she caught a glimpse of Kevin's teeth.

*   *   *

I was standing under a hot shower. At last my muscles were starting to relax. Too long, they had been tightened in a fixed position against cold and shame, so much so that my body was in pain whenever I moved. Now I could stretch and feel strength returning to my shoulders and back. When would I have the courage to call myself by my own name again? The remaining fragments of newspaper from my legs were washing away. I bent down to rub vigorously my calves and shins and between my toes. I remembered how I liked my feet, not thin and sinuous, but solid with stronger fuller heels and thicker skin of my soles and under my toes. I had to touch every part, to make sure it was still there, to rub it with shampoo, to rinse it and see the water make it shine.

I needed also to oil my skin, resurrect it Lazarus-like from the clinging decrepit rags which deliberately had been becoming my flesh and transforming it into carrion.

Issola and Evelyn were at the front door, about to leave when the warm moist air from the bathroom reached them. Evelyn looked up the stairs to see the outline of Black, with white towel around his waist, cross the landing to his room. She could smell coconut, mixed with　　　. . . what was it? . . . cut grass? . . . hay bales? . . . late summer fields? Something deeper than that. What perfume was that, she wondered.

*　　　*　　　*

On their way to the supermarket, before going home, there was silence in the Lexus SUV RX450h. Issola was looking at her phone, disappointed that she couldn't really see Black clearly in her iPhone photo. She guessed it was because the sunlight was behind him, making his image only a silhouette. Evelyn was feeling irritated. Her boyfriend was coming for dinner and staying the night. Fireman Sam! Well, no, not really. Fire chief Bryn. They had met over certification for fire safety for her several properties. The favours were mutual, they both understood. They sort of got on and even had fun, on occasions, but tonight she felt . . . bored. Was this really what she had to look forward to, X Factor, Chardonnay, and Bryn grunting in bed before eggs and bacon next morning? Perhaps if she bought him some of Black's perfume . . . How could a down-and-out afford perfume?

*　　　*　　　*

Kevin walked up the stairs with a cup of tea in his hands. It was now night. He tapped on the door of Black's room.

"I've brought you a cup of tea,"

"Thanks. Come in."

The room had no light.

"Oh, no! Have the lights gone again! I keep telling her about it. It happens all the time on this floor. Don't know why. Wait! There are

131

some candles in the kitchen. I'll go and get them."

I could hear him rushing around on my behalf. I smiled to myself. A strange humanity. What horrors had happened to this Kevin?

"You'll have to get yourself a side lamp you can plug into the socket. The main lights just keep fusing all the time. She sent her boyfriend, Bryn, to fix them, but he reckons there's nothing wrong with the wiring at all. She even wanted to charge us for calling him out. No one's paid her for that!" laughed Kevin, as if it was a sort of victory. "One time, we could all smell gas, everywhere in the house. Gave me headaches, it did. We phoned the gas people who said we had to get out of the house immediately. That was when Zelusz still lived here. He phoned her and you know what she said? She said Bryn would come and check it the next morning some time."

He lit a candle and fixed it to the middle of a saucer with drops of hot wax and then stood it between them in the middle of the floor. Their monstrous shadows terrified the graffiti of the mad scrawlings of previous tenants into a quiet passivity. I was squatting in my usual position, haunches on heels, elbows on knees, palms and hands turned towards eternity, as if the candle had become a camp-fire in the night. Kevin sat down and stretched his legs in front of him, his body now so fucked by drug abuse, he could no longer sit cross-legged.

"How's the tea?"

"Good, thanks."

"I guessed you'd like plenty of sugar."

Kevin saw Black's eyes look up at him from the candle flame. That was just about all he could see. He'd seen plenty of black people and never understood why people called them black when really, they were just different shades of brown. But Black was very black.

"So, where'd you get a name like that - Black? Just a nickname, is it?"

"Yeh, just a nickname." Black licked his lips revealing white teeth and pink tongue.

"Where you from, then?"

"From London."

"No, I mean, like, your family. No offence, but I've seen plenty of black people but . . ."

"From Africa, man! Where do you think? From the original primordial gene pool of humanity, from where all you English are descended before you bleached yourselves weak and coloured yourselves a dirty pinko-grey, calling it white." I laughed quietly, watching the confusion on Kevin's face.

Kevin remained silent.

"Tomorrow, you and me . . . you see all this dirty stuff?" I made a wide gesture encompassing the room. "We are going to burn it!"

"No, no, no! You can't do that! She'll be really pissed off!"

"So, throwing out that infected, infested rubbish called furniture and burning it, that makes me what? . . . Uncivilised, maybe, because I don't care about her private property?"

Kevin shifted uneasily in the doorway.

"Already the neighbours think we are a bunch of thieving, dirty, drug addicts, unable to work. They hate us. For them, we are vermin."

"Well, that's true isn't it?"

Kevin looked mildly frustrated being interrupted with this agreement to their public condemnation.

"Miss Evelyn doesn't want them complaining to the police and the council and phoning her to moan about us. She'll push us out of the house if there's trouble."

On my haunches, I shifted across a few floorboards and turned towards Kevin.

"Vermin!" I snorted a laugh of contempt. "Don't worry, I know I'm vermin. And you? Are you vermin too?"

I had changed my name . . . . rather, it was other people who had
changed my name . . . .Napoleon, the name, that old alcoholic, Joseph,
had decided on for my first passport. . . all the terms of affection Rémi
had used . . . the game of names with Juliette, the three wild sisters . . . .
My name had been changed so many times now that I wondered,
laughing, when I would completely forget who I was. Not so long ago, I
had even been forced to change it myself.

The bare room, wooden floor scrubbed (Kevin helped), walls painted
white, woodwork also repainted. I now sat cross-legged in one corner
facing the curtainless open window. I could feel my spirits returning.
What had become my secret name, remained my secret name and for
good reason. Once I had thrown out the old stained yellowish (or was it
beige?) wall to wall carpeting, (moquette as I had learned to call it, from
Nathalie,) once I had thrown out the urine-stained stinking mattress and
already broken wooden frame of the bed, once I had cleared the room of
every last bit of ugliness, I could feel all the names in history, in my story,
returning. I had been many throughout history and was already now
multiples of myself.

Kevin had panicked seeing me throw everything out of my (bed)room
window (my room was what these English called a bedsit, I guessed, or
was it rather, officially, multiple occupancy accommodation?).

"Don't worry," purred Black to Kevin. "Miss Evelyn will be happy. I
know." I was astounded that these English people could live in such
dirty, infested, infected hovels. Better to have nothing than share bad
smells with disease and fleas.

As I sat in the silence, I noticed through the smell of drying paint and
bleached floors a very faint perfume of dry grasses, long dry grasses,
chestnuts or acorns as Juliette had wondered, the drying bark of old trees
in the hot sun. I was happy. In fact, I had almost seen them, out of my
past, a disappearing glimpse out of the corner of my eye as they moved
back into the undergrowth of my mind. My leopards! I was becoming
myself again.

Evelyn had turned up the morning after I had thrown everything out.

"What's going on, Kevin?"

"It's him! Black! I told him not to do it!"

At that moment, a black shadow appeared in the doorway of the kitchen, which opened onto the neglected backyard. It was strange to them that they could see little in the shaded doorway but Black's red shorts, his burning eyes and occasional blue flashes of light on his smooth black skin.

"Mr. Black," Evelyn turned to address him. "What are you doing with these things?"

"I am going to burn them."

"What?!"

"They stink of piss, shit and vomit."

"So long as you replace them . . ."

"No."

Ms Evelyn hesitated, unaccustomed to being categorically challenged.

"Where will you sleep."

"On the floor. I have cleaned it. It's dry now, I can sleep there."

Evelyn was flummoxed. What was she to say? She was embarrassed Black had confronted her with the filth she put others in and just wanted to walk away.

"Here, Kevin. Go to B&Q, here's some money. Get white emulsion, rollers, brushes whatever is needed. It is about time the place was smartened up."

"My room is already painted," I said.

"Elsewhere then, the kitchen, the hall!" she insisted confronted by her own callous indifference.

"But what about the stuff here out back?" wondered Kevin.

She thought for a minute realising no one would want to touch it and since relations with her fireman boyfriend were wearing slightly thin, she didn't want to completely rip the veil of illusion between them by asking him to cart away a vomit stained carpet and the urine drenched, menstruation stained mattress.

"Burn it. Burn it tonight when everyone is asleep. Don't let it get out of control. If you get arrested, it is nothing to do with me." She was aware of surrendering an injection of power into the abused veins of these down and outs.

By the time the filthy clouds of poisonous smoke had rolled away towards the town centre and the spire of the least redundant of churches, Kevin had been filled with an ancient excitement and passion. Every man becomes a primitive pyro on such occasions. I, Black, I, Chár, looked at him. I had learned enough about Jesus to know he had made a career out of being weak and Kevin, who had been totally enfeebled by drug abuse and the violence of others, including the state, had occupied the only space left to him, minor acts of kindness and self-sacrifice. He had become Jesus. But now, watching Kevin swing around the midnight flames and acrid smoke of purification, I, Black Chár, saw something reignite inside this crumpled, enfeebled frame, a spark of joy, a tiny moment of love for being alive.

Evelyn had felt this condition of victimhood about Kevin, his weakness, his vulnerability. He even looked like Jesus, she thought, his ragged beard and long hair, blemished face, just taken down from the cross. She felt mildly sorry for him, although victims were often to blame for their own victimhood, so she thought. It meant she could use him and using him would be a kindness. By giving him little jobs to do, it would bring him into the world, almost turn him into a human being.

*   *   *

Back in town, at 113 Bishop's Gate, Ms Evelyn's property, home to Kevin, Black and other lost, economic nomads, Zelusz had turned up. When he had first arrived in the country, he had stayed at 113. Now that he had money, he had moved into a big Georgian apartment with his girlfriend. Zelusz was a businessman:

he didn't work, he just made money. On his arrival, the obvious way of making quick cash was to sell drugs to the wounded and traumatised, like Kevin. His girlfriend also was one of the walking wounded. Goodness knows what ugly childhood or adolescence she had suffered but a long time ago she had exchanged her body for the false comfort of regular drug abuse. Inevitably, their relationship was not based on anything resembling affection, but rather a resigned acceptance of Zelusz's psychological and physical abuse in exchange for chemical release. In fact, this was his preferred relationship with much of the world he encountered.

It was benefits payday. Kevin always hated it. Firstly, it was only about survival, and secondly, Zelusz would turn up to claim some spurious debt, leave behind more heroin, crack or amphetamines so that Kevin remained in debt, and ensure other parasitic addicts, supposed friends of Kevin, would turn up to scrounge, whine, steal or simply find somewhere to shoot up. Since their brains were destroyed by addled addictions and paranoid delusions, they all carried knives. Zelusz always accompanied his extortion with violence, humiliation, and threats. Demanding money was always accompanied by slaps around the back of the head, insults and pulling of ears. Kevin had to just take it.

The first time I encountered Zelusz was when I was with Kevin. Zelusz, having let himself in, still possessing keys, marched into the kitchen.

"Where's Majek?"

"Majek? I . . " spluttered Kevin.

"Brankovitch! Moved in upstairs!"

"Don't know. I haven't seen him."

"I've been trying to phone him. Is he in his room?

"I dunno."

"Well go and look then!"

Kevin left the kitchen to go upstairs and knock on Brankovitch's door. Zelusz stood in silence, staring at me, Black, with brutal menace. I made to leave, but Zelusz blocked the doorway. We stared at each other for a few seconds until I stepped back and Zelusz felt a rush of satisfied power with this childish bullying.

"Evelyn, the landlady, tells me there's a black cunt here who wants work. Are you the black cunt?"

There was a long pause while I decided how to respond.

"I want work, yeh. I am black, that's true. But I am no cunt."

The cold indifference to Zelusz's provocative insult forced him to explain and repeat.

"Anyone who lives in this shithole is a cunt and anyone who works for me is also a cunt."

"How much do I get?"

"No. I get the money and you get some. The money comes to me first. Understand?"

Zelusz could see me turn my head away with a grimace as if a poisonous stench had been emitted from his mouth.

"Six o'clock tomorrow morning at the corner of Wharfe Road, outside the Polish supermarket." He turned and shouted to Kevin up the stairs.

"He's not here," came the reply.

*　　*　　*

Secrets. Hiding. Having to hide had never been my condition until now, except when hunting. Now it had become a permanent state. But the hunt was on. I knew I was getting nearer.

One foot on the green sparkling, then the other. Gently crisp resistance to the pressure of my feet, my bare feet, on the wild blades of different grasses, the tiny crystals of early morning rime occasionally glinting but mostly providing the grasses a white dusting. The icy tickling to my feet offered a perceptive lucidity and eager attention to the present early spring morning. The darkness was over. I was cheerful and more than awake and others in the gang were amused at the way the frozen dew made my feet dance.

"I love my life, my day, my morning," I thought as I smiled back at the amusement of others.

It was one of those beautiful early English April mornings. The sun was only just above the horizon, so the early frost had not started to melt. There was a gang of around ten or twelve young people standing at the corner of the cabbage field. Most held their shoulders hunched and muscles tensed against the cold. The sky was crystal clear; it was possible even to see forever. And just like that forever, the field of regimented cabbages itself was so vast it seemed to disappear over the horizon, like the uniform parade of the armies of dictatorship.

The little band of nomads were all laughing and joking with each other in the cold morning air, all brothers and sisters, comrades in their position of the least valued and most exploited. None of them had mortgages, none of them had debts, none of them had bank accounts, none of them lived in a fixed abode, none of them rented. They were part of that mythological mass of illegals, foreigners, migrants, minorities of all hues and orientations, sexual, moral and indefinable that the illiterate and ignorant believed threatened not just the social order but they themselves. I wondered when they had lost their homes and families.

*   *   *

I quickly learned that half of the cabbage pickers did not travel in and out of town for their accommodation but were staying on the estate in an old barn that had been rudimentally converted into migrant living quarters. Occasionally, someone from the group would take a trip with the van returning the town workers in the evening to do some supermarket shopping and back to the estate by taxi. On a daily basis, the estate manager sold them fresh milk and eggs, both produce of the Utrecht estate farm. There was also a garden centre which sold fresh produce. I started to stay over. The open space, the fields, the green, mixed skies of blue, rain showers, rainbows - les giboulets de Mars, comme on disait en

France, içi c'était les giboulets d'Avril[57] - lifted my spirits. And there was something special about the camaraderie of this little community, a unity in an indubitable equality, a sort of fraternal and sisterly care for each other and a freedom to be oneself without fear of oppression or censure. There were a few children there also, who became everyone's responsibility. There was little that was private. I found a haystack and spread a bale on the floor of the barn for bedding. Someone from amongst the crew found me some spare blankets.

After a couple of days, I decided to return to town. I needed to collect money from Zelusz. Walking away from the town centre towards 113 Bishop's Gate, I noticed an ambulance parked outside. I quickened my step and as I arrived, Kevin was being stretchered out and into the back. I ran up to him and took his hand. Kevin turned to look at me through dazed eyes. He said nothing but managed a weak smile.

The hall stank of vomit. A stranger, a new tenant who had just moved in, greeted me. He had heard Kevin fall down the stairs and when he discovered him, he was lying face down in a pool of his own vomit, unconscious. Fortunately, the hall was not carpeted but simply covered with those cheap Victorian tiles of varying ugly shades of brown, beige and black. The new tenant, a teenager had just been kicked out of care and had been placed in 113 by the local council, desperate to accommodate the homeless. For Madam Evelyn this was a brilliant way to parasitically profit from the lack of council accommodation since privatisation; she could demand whatever sum she chose, such was the council's desperation, and randomly doubled the rent that she would normally charge private renters. I found buckets, mops and bleach to clean up the disaster. No one could trust anyone else in this household, anyone who was an addict was necessarily a thief. I glanced into Kevin's room, a mess of dirty carpet, an old and torn sleeping bag, a broken chair and scattered dirty clothes. I found the padlock, locked the room door, and went back down to the kitchen to find out more of what had happened. The teenager didn't know but didn't want to leave my side. His loneliness and desperate anxieties about the place he had been moved into, I had read across his face. He was only sixteen and the local authority, by passing him on to Evelyn was washing their hands of him.

---

57 the showers of March, here it was April showers

I remembered Charles and Nathalie taking me in when I was that age. The boy was already looking at me with the eyes of a dependent.

"It's ok. You can come with me away from this festering disaster. We'll go to the farm where I am working. Tomorrow. There are other good people there. Here is too dangerous for you."

Later that evening, Zelusz turned up. With him, he had a young girl, mid-teens, perhaps. She seemed scared and out of place, someone unaccustomed to either the place, the country, or the company of Zelusz. They sat around the small kitchen table. I had wanted to confront Zelusz about what had happened to Kevin. From the bottom of the stairs, I noticed the young girl was reaching across the table and taking Zelusz's hands in hers. I was not sure whether she was begging him or humbly thanking him.

"Don't worry, you are safe here now. I'll look after you. Just do as I tell you and everything will be fine. You have to stay here tonight and be nice to Mr Brankovitch."

Zelusz then turned to the young teenager, Marlon. Although the boy clearly didn't want to, Zelusz insisted he sit down on the chair right next to him. He put his hand on the back of his neck and squeezed slightly, while explaining how important he, Zelusz, was and could get anything for the boy as favours and how the boy could help him sometimes with odd jobs around town, helping each other out. If he was interested, he had a job for him tomorrow.

"Ah! The black bastard! What do you want?"

I walked into the kitchen.

"What are you doing here?" I demanded. I could feel the fine, imperceptible hair down my spine standing in anger.

"Be careful, shithead, how you talk to me. I'm visiting." Zelusz's voice was raised in the assumed authority of a bully.

"Oh, yeh? Visiting who?"

"My mate Kevin."

"Kevin's not here."

"When's he back, then? He owes me money."

"No one knows. He's in hospital."

"Overdose is it?" he laughed. "Happens all the time here. Always an ambulance or the police turning up. Can't believe it, can you? Respectable middle-class people like that, always in trouble."

"About money, I need what you owe me."

"Listen, fucking Coon! I don't owe you anything. I never owe anything to anyone. I'm going to give you some money, sure, but I haven't got it right now. Maybe tomorrow, or the day after. Besides, perhaps I should look after your money for you. I mean, you black cunts are too thick to manage your own affairs. You need someone like me to look after you."

I was ready to jump on Zelusz and crush the life out of him, but hesitated, concerned about the frightened young girl and the boy. Zelusz could see his suppressed anger and grinned noticing my glance towards his frail and frightened possession, the girl and his future victim, the boy.

"Pretty, isn't she?" Zelusz's lascivious menacing grin seemed to drool the words slipping from his lips. "She's come all the way from Kenya to study English and go to University. Haven't you, darling? And I'm going to help her. What do you think? You fancy her? Or maybe him? A bit of fucking, eh? I bet you don't get it often, a down-and-out, like you, living on the streets. Where've you been these last few nights? Not here, under a roof, like any civilised person would be. Back on the streets, were you? Infecting doorways with your overnight stench?"

I stood in silent anger, waiting for Zelusz's insults to be over. I needed the three sisters.

"Well anyway, Brankovitch is looking after her tonight, so hard luck. He does favours for me; I do favours for him. That's how it works, isn't it, between white men?"

Zelusz left the kitchen leading the girl by the arm upstairs to Brankovitch's door, insisting she just do as he, Zelusz, had told her and everything would be fine. All her problems would be over in just a few days' time. As she was led away, she managed to turn her head to catch the looks of both me and Marlon, with panic and despair written all over her face. We heard a slight whimper as Zelusz forced her along the hall to the stairs.

I was leaning against the sink and Marlon stood opposite, propped on the corner of the kitchen table. We could hear banging and shouts from upstairs as we stared silently at each other, Marlon's eyes wide with horror.

Zelusz left, the front door slamming behind him. Immediately I started searching under the kitchen sink.

"We have to help her!".

Amongst a cardboard box of old tools, screwdrivers, nails, there was a small hammer and a roll of duct tape. I ran upstairs with what I could find at hand and knowing Brankovitch's door would be locked, immediately started to kick at the lock. Marlon, unthinking, instinctively followed. With the third attempt the door gave way, breaking the frame. Brankovitch was already naked and standing in the middle of the room waiting to defend himself, waving nervously a big clip point bladed knife: the smashing down of the door had served to cause his erection to fail and his arms to shake with tension. Behind him stood the girl, clothes ripped, and her brown skin scratched and damaged. There was a bruise near her mouth where Brankovitch had had to punch her to get her to cooperate.

I stepped into the room, howling wildly, followed by Marlon. Incomprehensible gibberish and globules of saliva spat from Brankovitch's mouth. His ugly oily face, terrified. He lunged at me clumsily. I whipped the small hammer in the direction of the blade and cracked Brankovitch's forearm. There was a scream of agonising pain and shouts of abuse. The knife fell across the room towards young Marlon who bent down to retrieve it, by which time I had hit Brankovitch in the middle of his forehead with the small hammer which sent a burst of red light through his brain. Brankovitch fell backwards and I quickly wrapped duct tape around his mouth to stifle the stream of howling invective. There was an explosion of hot panted air, muffled whines, snot from his nostrils and burning tears from his eyes as I taped around his arms and torso, pinning him down to the legs of the bed.

"Marlon, look through the wardrobe and cupboards for something . . . " I insisted loudly, then turned to the young girl, "I'm sorry, I don't know your name."

"Lankenua," came the subdued and shaken reply.

"Look for something," I said turning back to Marlon, "for Lankenua to wear until . . ." I didn't want to give any indication of destination, so paused.

Looking through Brankovitch's ugly Victorian wardrobe, Marlon found a shirt, sweater, and jeans, all vastly oversized, but enough until they reached the farm, and gently passed them to the terrified Lankenua to put on.

"I know this language, not far from my homeland. Lankenua means Lucky, eh?"

Lankenua nodded.

"Well, finally, you are lucky. You are one of us now!"

Marlon was nodding his head in agreement and smiling reassuringly to the girl. I ripped through Brankovitch's jacket and trouser pockets to find cash for a taxi.

"Now listen!" I said to the quivering body before me. "Tell Zelusz when you see him, I'll be here tomorrow evening to collect the money for all the workers he is cheating. If he doesn't turn up, I will find him."

With that, I took Brankovitch's right hand, pressed it to the floor and hammered a roofing nail through the back of the hand and into the floorboards. Brankovitch's face turned purple as he

144

attempted to scream through the duct tape over his mouth, only snot and tears spurting down his red face with every attempted howl. I took the left hand, which Brankovitch tried to hold back, hit him across the side of his face and hammered the roofing nail through his second hand. When would Dibdib leave me, I wondered with a cry of anger. Brankovitch looked at my face and could see from the cold indifference to his suffering, the nails through his hands, my absolute determination and direction, and that his arrogant stupid friend, Zelusz, was in considerable danger. It was as if me, that black cunt, was at war, such was my anger, a war I was not going to lose.

The two children stood side by side, watching, with eyes and mouths wide open.

*   *   *

Jackson was pacing anxiously around the barn when a taxi drew up at the farmyard gate. A couple of children threw open the barn door to see who had arrived.

"Chár!"

"Jackson! Nyàbà Bulí nanu!" I said, throwing my arms around him..

"What? Bulì what?"

I smiled: " My blood warrior. Nyàbà Bulí nanu."

"Nyàbà Bulí? You give me this name?"

I was capturing Jackson's desire to be closer; I felt it in his body. The sisters already had plans of their own for him. Unfolding worlds, expanding universes! Suddenly everything changes, even though it stays the same.

"What are you doing here?"

"The sisters sent me to find you. You haven't called them for a long time. They have news. First, from France. You are going to be a father."

"Juliette!"

"Of course, Juliette. How many other lovers do you have?"

"Only Tagì."

"And he can't have babies, I guess!" Jackson grinned.

"When can I see her? And how can . . ." New needs, puzzles, labyrinths presented themselves.

"Calm! Calm! Soon. You will see her soon. Sooner than you think. This is what the sisters told me. Second news," continued Jackson, "Place Pigalle has burned down. The police think it was arson. The three sisters are fine. In fact, Jolanta has seen this as an opportunity to move up in the world. They have become event organisers. The deputy commissioner of police helped them find a new place to live and work from and they have too many clients from Place Pigalle who want to help them. So, guess what, the next 'Event' is here. The big house that owns all of this. Utrecht Hall. It's Mercantor's place."

"Fuck! How do they do that, get themselves invited into the house! It's like the Trojan horse! They have depths and powers that neither you nor I can understand!"

"I know! Some party that's gonna be! He wants to sell a painting, so there'll be interested guests. But he also wants to suck up to so-called friends for his leadership bid of the Tory party. He wants to be Prime Minister! Imagine how lucky the entire country would be then! Bloody Hell!"

I laughed almost madly. "Look. Can you contact them, the sisters? I've lost my phone. I need them to be here tomorrow evening. Did they know where I was? How did you know where I was?"

"Well, they knew you were looking for him, Utrecht Hall becomes obvious as a starting point and I worked it out from there. Not so difficult."

"Nyàbà Bulí nanu, you are a great hunter! One day we will go hunting together!"

"We are already, aren't we, hunting, I mean?" said Nyàbà Bulí, grinning. I grabbed his head in both hands and kissed him.

"I love you, Nyàbà Bulí nanu!" I laughed. "Clever and funny. When it happens in blood and flesh, I want you with me, by my side."

"When what happens?"

"The party! The Event!" I laughed again with excitement, all the time wrapping myself around Jackson Nyàbà Bulí.

"Believe me, Jolanta and Juliette have thought long and hard about this party. They know what they want to do!"

"Jolanta has been talking with Juliette?"

"Yeh, Juliette is in London now with Rémi." Jackson paused. " She has told me some of her plans. You are lucky Chár."

"What plans?"

"I cannot tell you. It's a secret. Juliette is an artist, you know. For Juliette, Amani, Jolanta, none of this is coincidence. Although the three sisters are very good at keeping their cool, I can tell they are increasingly excited. You'll be amazed at what they have been doing with the night people and Lihua's troupe of actors. Everyone is eager to see you again."

*　　　*　　　*

By the time Zelusz arrived at 113, it was mid-morning and Brankovitch was lying in a pool of his own piss and faeces.

"Where the fuck is she?" shouted Zelusz, stupidly, his head fuming with anger. He took out his knife to cut the duct tape around Brankovitch's mouth. The stench of piss, shit and the sweat of fear made Zelusz wretch. It was astonishing the extent to which a body can make itself so repugnantly putrid; a final line of defence against the threat of death.

"My hands! My hands!" whined Brankovitch, weeping.

It was only then, Zelusz noticed the full horror of what had happened. He immediately turned away and took out his phone.

"Who's taken my bitch?" he shouted.

"Black. It was Black."

"That fucking loser? There's only one place they'll be then."

On his phone, he quickly gave out instructions.

"For fuck's sake, help me, can't you?"

Zelusz, in a state of violent anger jumped down the stairs to find whatever tools might free Brankovitch's hands. He found a claw hammer and some pincers. It was impossible to get either the claw, or the teeth of the pincers under the head of the roofing nail without causing excruciating pain to Brankovitch's swollen and bloodied hand. Finally, Zelusz forced the pincer head around the head of the nail, ignoring Brankovitch's screams, then pulling with both hands and pushing up from a squat position, slipped on the pool of piss and fell backwards as the nail popped out of the floorboards. The howls of pain only seemed to infuriate even more the blackened, bruised, coagulated wound as the pierced hand began bleeding again.

"There's no point," Brankovitch panted, "No point going after him if you're thinking about the farm. You'll never find him, nor her. He said to tell you, he'll be here this evening."

"Look, you fucking loser, I don't need your advice. I'm sending the Romanians."

Brankovitch started moaning and crying as Zelusz tried to free the second hand.

"He wants all the money for all those workers. Fuck! My hands! Get me to a hospital, quick."

"The money in exchange for the bitch?"

Brankovitch laughed hysterically: "He's not giving her back, you fucking idiot!" he screamed as he got up and staggered to the bathroom to try to wash off the piss and excrement.

*   *   *

I knew that the ugly battle with Zelusz had only just begun. I explained to Jackson what had happened and knew that when Zelusz discovered Brankovitch, things would kick off fairly immediately. I expected also that Zelusz might use other thugs to try to retrieve his prize, Lankenua.

"Fucking hell! You nailed him to the floor?!"

"To send a message to Zelusz. Otherwise Brankovitch would have just run away. Let me use your phone. I want to speak to Jolanta."

I moved away from the others to speak privately. My new blood warrior, Nyaba Buli nanu, could see my frustrations and echoed my concerns about Zelusz. I knew I could deal with any thug who turned up at the farm looking for the girl. The next evening when I intended to confront him over pay to workers, especially if Zelusz had not regained his girl, would be more difficult.

"Marlon! What's Evelyn's phone number, the landlady. Have you got it? Jolanta wants it."

"I've got it on my phone. It's . . . here, look." "

When the two youngsters, Lankenua and Marlon had arrived with me at the barn, Jackson had immediately assumed responsibility for their care. First, he had carefully helped clean and disinfect the bruised abrasions to Lankenua's face, while Marlon talked at length about how I had rescued both of them and what had happened to Brankovitch. Horrified as he was, he couldn't help laughing, a slightly excitedly hysterical laugh, at Brankovitch's being nailed to the floor, after all, he had never witnessed anything so overwhelmingly terrible. Jackson stayed with both of them the whole time, sleeping next to her and Marlon at night. Her English was fairly limited, but they had managed to communicate, and

Jackson had been gentle and kind to this fifteen-year-old Kenyan girl who had barely escaped the worst of drug addicted slavery and prostitution.

All his life, Marlon had kept away from blacks, in fact anyone who was not white. He didn't really understand why, but it had just happened like that. Now, he loved black. In fact, he wanted to be black, wanted to be like both myself and . . .

"What's that name Chár gave you?" he asked Jackson.

"Nyàbà Bulí."

"What language is that? Does it mean anything?"

"Suri. It means Blood Warrior."

"Fucking hell!" said Marlon, who knew that now in his heart he was black. He had decided!

*   *   *

That evening, John, the gangmaster employed by the estate to manage and direct the bands of migrant workers, was out for his evening stroll with a visit to the barn where the migrants were staying. He was carrying a large bowl of coleslaw prepared by his wife, from the cabbages of the field and some skewered pieces of shoulder of lamb to barbecue; there had been a huge cast iron barbecue plate there for years for the migrants' use. He'd changed out of his blue overalls but was still wearing the same flat cap he always carried. It was not yet dark but getting there. A few stars were appearing and with the disappearance of the sun the air had become fresher.

I was at the door of the barn with Jackson watching the evening descend when John arrived.

"Alright boys, you're okay?"

"Fine! And you John?"

"What's your name now? Oh, it's Chár, isn't it?"

"That's right." I was no longer needing to hide as Black, being now surrounded by nomadic partisans, les vrais camarades[58].

"Chár Black. Black as charcoal, eh?" said John, with a smile.

"His name means Leopard." said Marlon, interrupting.

"And who are you?"

"I'm Marlon. I came here today with Chár and Lankenua. I think she's from Kenya. He saved us both from this really nasty guy and his mate. What was his name?" he said, looking at Chár. "Sounds like Jealous."

"You mean Zelusz." said John. "Yeh, I know him. He sends people here to work. Most of the people here are through him, aren't they, Chár?"

"That's right, John, including me. And all these people here still haven't been paid by him yet, you know."

John had known me for a few days now and had warmed to me. There was a sort of affinity between us. Although we knew little of each other, there existed a sense of something hundreds of years old that we shared. As far as I was concerned, John and his wife had grown out of the very land itself and were as ancient as many of the trees of the estate. He had the same wisdom and compassion as my Komoro of Beyahola, and I immediately felt part of him and that he was part of Beyahola and the Suri people. For John, I guess I was equally ancient, as at ease in my own body, with nature and the natural wilds that left to my own devices, here in the forests and fields, I would always survive. My nature was as ancient as humanity itself. At least, that was how John saw me. He could even smell it on me, the wild, he had called it.

"It's my leopards," I explained.

John just laughed.

"They say there are leopards around here, in the forests. Some

---

[58] True comrades

reckon they've seen them, but I haven't."

"If they are here, they'll find me." I said. "Anyway, John, are you eating with us?"

"No, no! I've already eaten, thanks. But I thought I'd better bring you something otherwise you'd be off hunting your own kill on the estate." said John, smiling. It had amused him how, watching me for the first-time barbeque raw meat, I had simply throwing it onto the hot coals. He promised to himself he would try it one time with his wife and family.

"Anyway, John, I need to warn you, there might be some trouble from Zelusz tomorrow."

"He's always up to no good, that one. Nasty piece of work. I don't know why the owner, you know, the lord, has anything to do with him."

"He was keeping this young girl, Lankenua. She's here with Marlon. It was pretty obvious what he was going to do with her."

"So, you brought her here."

"That's right John. I guess Zelusz might send some of his mates here looking for her, I don't suppose he'll come here himself. But don't worry, I'll deal with it."

"I'm sure you will, Chár." John laughed. "Do you want me to call the police?"

"No, no! The police will just arrest Lankanua and hand her over to Immigration. She'll be put in an immigration detention centre and who knows for how long."

"I'm sure that's true, Chár. We all agree with the law, don't we, all of us, until . . . we don't. Some know what to do and others just end up bitter."

*   *   *

The three Romanians had never before entered the carefully

tended mud of early English spring cabbage fields and had consequently arrived in standard dress, black zip-up jerkin, black creased trousers, white shirt, black tie, black glasses and black lace-up shoes.

They had initially visited an enclosed farmyard at the end of a rough track sparsely repaired with soft sandstone hardcore. The empty grey stone buildings, the yard with occasional unidentifiable pieces of rusting abandoned machinery, mostly overgrown with stinging nettles, a heap of rubble in one corner, an old and rotting straw stack elsewhere, moreover, the total silence of this uncared-for place amplified the notion, the anxiety, that they were being watched. Even the birds were hushed in trepidation. They backed away towards the tubular iron gate, half-worrying a couple of Dobermanns or Alsatians were about to leap from behind an outbuilding. The sinister nature of alien deserted sheds and the foreignness of unrecognised empty fields made them hasten to their black hatchback and drive out towards recognisable civilisation. They spent the next twenty or thirty minutes driving around narrow country roads with views blocked by tall hawthorn hedges, unable to even estimate where the fuck they were, sitting in repressed silence, moodily arousing their ugly brutality until the two passenger thugs started blaming the driver for the inanity of their lostness. After a short while of pointless frustration, the driver slammed on the brakes and stepped out of the car to make a stand against the abuse he had been receiving. The passenger from the back seat also stepped out. There was a moment of incomprehensible altercation and vulgar insults, whereupon the passenger jumped into the driver's seat and drove away leaving the other behind stranded in the middle of nowhere, waving his arms in ridiculous star-shaped frustration. Driving rain, a short spring shower, appeared from behind the sun and scudding spring clouds as the two remaining thugs laughed their way down a hill, over a small brick bridge and past a long abandoned railway platform that had stopped serving a purpose many decades ago.

Finally, at considerable distance, they noticed a field with workers in it, bent over whatever crop they were harvesting. With considerable difficulty, they eventually found their way to an entrance to the field. At first, they were confronted by two tractors, one with a water bowser, another with a trailer of trays. The cabbages were being hand-picked, carefully trimmed by the pickers, spray-washed and stacked in trays for immediate distribution to supermarkets. They had to look beautiful.

Everyone was waiting expectantly. Jackson Nyàbà Bulí was surprised to be handed a huge knife by the gangmaster John, which later he discovered was a 'short-handled' machete. Being handed the machete by a white man, he, still a teenager and black, he almost burst out laughing.

John noticed his surprise and said: "Things are different here in the countryside. Don't worry, we're still racists, though."

Jackson looked up from the huge blade to see the gangmaster grinning and laughed.

"Okay, so take off your shoes, the mud will cling to them," I explained to Nyaba Bulí, "but it won't stick to your bare feet. Take off your clothes also, you don't want to get shit all over them. Keep your boxers. After all, this is England, and the English are funny about naked bodies. The sun is shining! It's warm."

Nyaba Bulí laughed at my instructions.

"Are you any good at throwing?"

"Yeah, man! I'm in the basketball team at college."

"You go to college?"

"Yeh. I'm learning French."

"Ah, bon ?! Ils me cherchent, moi, il faut dire, un seul noir. Ce qu'on va faire complique les choses pour eux. Au lieu d'un seul noir ils vont être confrontés par deux noirs ! Ça suffirat pour confondre ces gros cons.[59]"

Jackson was flattered he should be spoken to in French and proud he could understand. Lankenua and Marlon watched in awe as the two young men undressed, the two who had saved, protected, and helped them.

---

59 They are looking for me, one black. What we are going to do complicate things for them. We're going to become two blacks. That'll be enough to completely confuse these idiots."

"Listen," I reassured Nyàbà Bulí, "we're just going to have fun. You don't need the knife. These two are idiots."

As the Romanians approached, John called out:

"Hello. Can we help? This is private property. You can't just come here without permission."

They stopped their approach, now standing between the cabbage pickers and the field. Jackson and I were hidden behind the group of workers. We quietly took a cabbage each from one of the trays.

"We're looking for a black girl and the black guy who took her yesterday."

"I think you'd better leave before I call the police."

"Look, old man. How long for the police to get here, do you think?" said one of the Romanians, laughing cynically at this faith in the order of things. "We just want the girl."

Suddenly the crowd parted, and two black figures raced towards the Romanians, howling and shouting some wild war-cry. The Romanians' mouths fell open and eyes almost jumped out of their skulls, so surprised were they, they almost fell over the cabbages at their feet as they stepped back. Nyàbà Bulí and I were running at speed, head and torso leaning forward as if we had started from racing blocks. Nearing our target, we straightened our backs to throw our one cabbage each at the two Romanians, one hit the side of the face and ear of the first and the second, managing to turn to protect himself was hit on the back of the head, the cabbage bouncing with a loud crunch into the blue sky. We raced straight past the infuriated Romanians who immediately gave chase across the field.

We ran in two large arcs in opposite directions with the over-weight thugs panting behind, until finally we returned to the group laughing at the humiliation. Leaning bent forward hands on their knees, panting to catch their breath, the two silly gangsters straightened up, took from their jacket pockets extendable batons, and started walking slowly towards the crowd. Immediately, every one of the cabbage pickers produced from behind their backs their machetes. The Romanians paused and a small girl of perhaps ten or twelve years of age ran at them screaming and threw another cabbage. More cabbages followed. It was like a stoning, but without anyone dying, a biblical miracle, not frogs, not locusts but cabbages, raining down upon the sinful, until the Romanians, battered, bruised, slipping in the mud, finally staggered to their car and drove away to the sound of cheering and laughter.

*   *   *

In the very simple way in which the farm labourers had been able to laugh and congratulate each other on their triumph over an ugly enemy and the return of peace, so Zelusz, as was his habit, always sought a more complex victory. A victory that was parasitic. It was never complete. It would feed off him, sinking its teeth into the open wound that was the heart of his being, the gaping black hole that sucked all joy, satisfaction, and health into itself. In feeding itself, it also fed off the worlds of others, turning them into misery and suffering that became his perverted pleasure, his victory. Very easily this parasitic pleasure turned itself into making money, which, as a businessman, as far as he was concerned, involved the exploitation of others, feeding off their need, their weaknesses, their fears, their stupidities.

This is why, returning to 113 Bishop's Gate in the evening, he was hungry for violence. The black girl from Kenya was still missing, the black cunt from 113 was still missing; the girl had been expensive. Just in Kenya, she had cost six hundred dollars and paying agents to get her here had cost just as much. Luckily, he knew the traders. After a visit to A&E, Brankovitch, had disappeared to find a serious dose of morphine and pass out on a supposed friend's floor. Zelusz had tried phoning the Romanians at least a dozen times, but the call went directly to an answer service. The first few times, he just hung up, but eventually ended up shouting abuse down his bejewelled mobile to an innocent recording of his vulgar invective. He took an old brass Yale key out of his wallet and inserted it in the lock. He tried turning it, but it wouldn't move. He was aware of this problem with the lock and tried jiggling the key and forcing it to turn. His rage was such that his violence was out of control. The key snapped leaving the stem inside the lock. The world of events was conspiring against him.

He looked up at the sky and screamed and then started banging on the door with his fists. Where the fuck was Kevin?

After a short while, the door opened, and he was confronted by a complete stranger. A beautiful woman with long curling red hair, wearing a fitted dress with a voluminous skirt and thin shoulder straps over her naked shoulders.

"Yes?" she said, with a slightly quizzical look.

Her elegance made him wonder for a split second whether he was at the wrong door.

"Erm, is the black guy here?"

"Who is that?" said Jolanta.

"Er, I think his name is Mr. Black."

Jolanta laughed.

"If you're looking for who I think you are, no, that's not his name. He is black, but he is not called Black. No, he's not here." Her look of condescending contempt withered him. He could feel his scrotum and penis shrink.

"Are you a friend of his?" Zelusz asked, slyly.

"That's none of your business."

"It's just that he has something of mine, and I have some money for him."

"Is he expecting you? Are you expecting him to meet you?"

"Er, yeh."

"Well, do you want to come in to wait? You can sit with us, myself and friends."

Zelusz hesitated, wondering who the 'friends' might be."

"Two ladies, such as myself." she had read his mind.

Zelusz followed the elegant lady into the recesses of 113, her long curling red hair, waving, squirming, menacingly, invitingly down her naked back as the zebra-like black and white stripes of her swirling skirts narrowed into convoluted zigzags at the waist and tightened around the bodice of the dress as if narrowing into the confused heart of a labyrinth.

He felt peculiarly shy, looking at her bare calves below the hem of her skirts, and averted his eyes as he followed her upstairs. Instead of going to Black's room, which he had half expected, the beautiful lady led him into Brankovitch's larger room.

"What's happened? Where's Majek?"

"Who?" asked the small Chinese lady, moving seductively towards him. "Come in."

"Brankovitch. This is his room."

The tall African woman took him by the arm to lead him to a large cushion on the floor.

"He ran away. I think he had a bad experience." she said.

"The owner of the property, a Ms, Tutt, Evelyn Tutt, was very upset about the room." said the woman with red hair.

"She was so relieved and pleased when we offered to help her," said the Chinese woman, sitting next to Zelusz.

"We'll manage the property for her over the next month, while we have business in the region, get it sorted out and in much better condition. You were managing it before, weren't you? And managing the tenants, so it seems." The lady in the zigzag dress looked at him with the contempt she would feel for a flea.

Ms Evelyn had hesitated at first, but when the three sisters offered to get her an invitation to the party at Utrecht Hall, she eagerly agreed. Besides, when she had met them outside the property, following their phone call the evening before, they had arrived in a

Bentley, which had made her red Lexus look embarrassingly cheap. Having agreed, Evelyn immediately warmed to the three mysterious women, feeling a sisterly camaraderie with them all.

The room had been completely transformed. Gone was all the ugly furniture, the bloodstained carpet, curtains, and ugly pictures of naked women on the walls. The walls had been repainted, new drapes in the windows, a new bed, and a large carpet, the slight odour of drying paint completely hidden by the perfume of musk, marijuana and sandalwood.

"It's from Morocco," said the tall black woman, noticing Zelusz staring at the carpet.

Next to the Chinese woman was a low, black lacquered table with stone inlay depicting a scene where small chubby Chinese figures, men, in ancient dress, were fighting over a woman. This was taking place on a wooden bridge over a blue stream. To protect the inlay a sheet of thick glass lay across the entire top of the table. The red-headed woman had taken out a packet from the folds of her dress and was dividing up lines of cocaine on the table's glass surface.

"It's amazing how quickly you can transform a room, " she said, "from a shithole to actually something quite pleasant . . . . if you have the right help."

"When is the black guy back?" Zelusz asked, wondering about the women's relationship with him. He knew he sounded like an uncouth peasant from an obscure, unknown Polish village.

"We don't really know. He was here earlier and then went out."

"How do you know him?"

"We don't." said the lady with red hair and jagged zebra-striped dress. "We've only just moved in. What is your name, by the way?"

"Zelusz."

"Ha, ha, ha, ha!" laughed the lady with red serpents in her hair.

"Your name means Jealous, doesn't it? Envy. I am Polish also, you see."

The Chinese lady leaned closer to him and bending over the table snorted a line of cocaine with a prettily decorated silver straw, which she then offered to him with her seductive Modigliani smile. He had watched the red-haired lady divide it up, so, following the Chinese woman, he knew it was perfectly fine to join in. Why be suspicious? In any case, he couldn't imagine these beautiful, sophisticated ladies having anything to do with a black down-and-out. They had said they didn't know him, and why should they? Besides, he was a businessman, he remembered.

"I can get more of this stuff for you if you want," he suggested taking a small packet from his jacket pocket and putting it on the table as the Chinese lady divided up more lines. "So, what are you ladies doing here in Bristol?"

"Organising a party," said the tall black lady. "Do you know the big house about ten miles out of town, Utrecht Hall? It's there."

"Oh, yeh. I know him, the owner. What's his name? Sir James, init? I've helped him out a few times. Not him directly, you understand, but someone from the estate, or the house. Workers on the land. I got some there now. He likes this stuff, as well," he added, indicating the coke. "That black bastard was supposed to be working for me too."

"Ah! So, he's on the estate already, is he?" said the tall black woman.

Zelusz looked puzzled. What did she mean, there already?

"You mean he's there now? I doubt it!" he declared, thinking of the Romanians he had sent. He frowned. He still hadn't heard from them. The coke had considerably boosted his ego. He no longer felt angry and was enjoying being expansive in front of these charming and beautiful women.

"So . . . what was this something that Mr Black, as you call him, took from you?" asked the lady with snakes in her hair.

"Well, to tell you the truth, it was not really, a something, it was a young girl, a refugee. I like to try to help people, you understand, people like me, who've lost home and country, even family, help them to get back on their feet, to find their place in the world."

"Oh yes, we understand."

"So, what were your intentions for her?" asked the tall black woman.

"Partying?" smiled the Chinese lady.

"Partying with your friend at the big house, Utrecht Hall?" the red-haired woman asked, her dazzling labyrinthine dress and writhing hair hypnotising him. "He likes young girls, doesn't he, without commitment, without obligation, just a big tip at the end of the night?"

"Here," said la Chinoise, "take the last line."

He took the silver pipe she was offering and snorted the last fat line.

"We had a friend exactly like you. We were refugees, also. He wanted to help us." she continued.

"He was Polish also," interrupted the red-haired lady. "So where are you from? Let me guess, a small town, grubby village even, where there's no future except hunting in endless dark forests with other directionless village men and at night around a camp fire in that wilderness singing sentimental old folk songs and weeping into your vodka until you pass out with a surfeit of endless stupidities. Is that right?"

He suddenly felt the rush of the drug through his body and brain. Although sitting on the cushions, it was as if he was floating. His heart had started pounding fast, too fast. He wondered if he was going to be able to handle such severe intoxication.

"But it turned out he just wanted to hire us out," said the tall black woman. "He was a pimp, you see." Her black mouth, her black lips looked bitter, cruel, callous.

"He thought he was clever. He had plans to make big money, unlike those village idiots with their vodka and folk songs he had despised and left behind."

Zelusz found himself trying to look concerned, as if he were upset for them, as if he would never do such a thing. His heart was slowing down now, even though his head wanted to explode. Slowly, the dark was creeping into his peripheral vision. He tried to blink it away.

"So . . .

"We . . .

"Killed him . . . Funny how history repeats itself, isn't it?"

"Are you feeling ok?"

"What was that last line?" he asked feebly. "I feel the . . dark is coming in." He made a strange gesture with his hands as if they were surrounding his head. "Too much darkness!"

"Some people call it a highball, some, a speedball . . . It's very dangerous, actually."

"It's getting darker," he whispered. A terrible panic had gripped him. He was too terrified to verbalise it and too fearful to flee.

"No one cared! Not his family! . . Did he have one? The pimp, you know. He had no friends, only people who hated him. The police cared even less! No one! No one! No one ever cared for him. There was nothing of any worth in him at all!"

"Which was quite lucky!" said the black one.

"Of course, a highball is a mix of alcohols, whereas a speedball is cocaine and heroin together. . . . Are you ok?" asked the woman with snakes in her hair.

"It's the dark! The dark!"

162

The three women leaned over him continuing to talk about recipes, he imagined, just jabbering on about nothing he could understand.

Slowly, slowly, the dark crept in, he was unable to control it now, until it completely enveloped his vision, every sound, every sensation, every understanding, and finally all consciousness. The moment of absolute forgetting had arrived.

*   *   *

When Kevin finally returned to 113, having spent a few days with his parents, on release from hospital, he was surprised to see the transformation in the house. Even his own room had been cleaned, repainted and old furniture replaced.

"What's going on?" he wondered.

"It's the three sisters," I explained. "They wanted to welcome you home."

"Three sisters?"

"They've moved in to Brankovitch's old room."

"Where's Brankovitch?"

"He's run away," said Lihua, standing at the door of Kevin's room, with a smile. "I'm Lihua and you are Kevin. We've heard so much about you."

She offered Kevin her hand.

"Has Zelusz been around?" Kevin looked worried. "I owe him some money."

"That's not his real name, didn't you know?" said the beautiful Jolanta with red waving hair, today in a startlingly red dress, again well fitted to her elegant figure. "His real name was Zeluszowski Jezkowiak."

"Was! What do you mean, was?"

163

"He's dead. Oh, you didn't know? Was he a friend of yours?"

"Not really. No, I know him though."

"And you haven't seen the local news? I suppose we're privy to more information than most, working at Utrecht Hall. They found his body on the estate."

"Quite horrible, really." said Lihua.

"Ghastly!" said Amanishakhete, joining the others.

"Something that will no doubt haunt the estate for a long time."

"From what we can gather, and some of it might be just scullery gossip, there was a lot of cocaine and heroin in his body, although the police pathologist seemed to think he had died where his body was found, there was a lot of blood in the soil around. How he got to where they found him, no one knows. Had he been to a party or something? The nearest property of course is Utrecht Hall itself. Otherwise, deep in that forest, he was miles from anywhere. Police speculate that perhaps he had got lost there, found a path, which happened to be a wild animal track and had passed out."

The ladies paused in their storytelling. I couldn't help smiling to myself at the manner in which the sisters were charming Kevin. I was rushing around, collecting a few things together.

"I have to go back to the farm, Kevin, to give my people their money, and to collect Nyaba Buli. The sisters will look after you, you'll be fine."

Kevin turned to look at the three sisters who all smiled back at him.

"Nyaba Buli?" queried Jolanta.

"Jackson." I clarified.

"Ah! You've named him, also, then!"

I looked back at Jolanta and smiled.

What had happened to the world, wondered Kevin. He watched as I embraced each of the three sisters on both cheeks before quickly leaving.

"Let me make you one of my teas," said Chinese Lihua. "It 'll help you feel welcome in your new home."

"Do you like your new TV, by the way," asked Amanishakhete. "It's one of those smart TVs. We installed it in your room, so that we could join you in the evenings and all watch TV together. Oh, and do you have a smart phone? No? So, we have one for you and have installed a modem also. It's good to be part of the modern world, Kevin."

"What about the landlady, Miss Evelyn?"

Ooh, she's very happy!!" said Amanishakhete. "She got her partner, Fireman Sam, - is that his name? - to come and take away the old stuff. I think she was a bit out of her depth, don't you, with Brankovitch and so-called Zelusz?"

"So, what happened to Z . . . zel . . ?"

"Terrible, really."

"Yes, awful!"

"Unimaginable!"

"Rumour has it, he was eaten alive!"

"What!?" shouted Kevin, horrified.

"Yah . . . . After passing out on that animal track, he was very quickly found, so they think, by a wild boar . . . actually, a mother sow and her piglets . . . and possibly other animals - fox, crows, magpies. In the bloodied mud around what was left of his body were wild boar hoof prints, large and small, the paw marks of fox and badger, even a large cat. Are there any lynx around here or big cats?"

"People say rich hippies released big cats in the forests in the 70s when it became illegal to own them. Plenty reckon they've seen them, but . ."

"Completely eviscerated."

"What? What's that?"

"He'd been opened up and all his intestines, heart, lungs, . . . " explained Amanishakhete. "Honestly, it's horrific! You don't need to know about that!"

"Ooh and the big favourite with pigs, of course, the liver!" interjected Lihua, who coming from China felt she knew a lot about pig's appetites.

"All eaten!" concluded Jolanta of the red hair and red dress. "Imagine, being eaten alive! Of course, he probably didn't feel anything, with all the drugs inside him."

"They still want to interview people. The local lord will be arriving in a couple of days, apparently. But so far, the police think it is probably death by . . "misadventure"."

"His eyes had been pecked out by crows, or magpies. His cheeks had been torn off. I feel sorry for the woman who found it, the remains, I mean." added Amanishakhete. "But wild animals are wild, savage, anywhere in the world. Some animal had shit and pissed on him to ward others away. It was her dogs, of course, which found him. She was so traumatised by what she saw, she's still sedated in hospital."

"Fuck!" was all Kevin could say.

"The police had DNA from when he had raped someone. The girl had dropped charges. It was lucky they had his DNA; fingerprints would have been useless, all his fingers had been chewed off."

Zelusz remembered the three women leaning over him talking about recipes, combinations of yeast and flour, the nobility of bread, sedatives and excitants, drug cocktails until slowly their

166

spidery hair transformed into the bare branches of trees, and a pig's snout pushed into his face to kiss him, to taste him. He heard himself scream as the troughing began.

*   *   *

Chapter 6

Birnam Wood to Dunsinane

Juliette had wanted to see for herself this man who, Dieter and others reckoned, had indirectly at least, incited, possibly financed even, the removal of my people from their homes and the destruction of our village. It just seemed so improbable to her that any current twentieth century first world politician would condone a massacre as part of a modernisation project. What would be the point?

"That is just fucking racist, Juliette!" said Rémi. "So, the third world massacres itself, but the first world has nothing to do with it, because, hey, we're civilised and they are not."

"Ce n'est pas gentil, ce que tu dis!" Nathalie réprimandait. "Excuses-toi! Tout de suite!"[60]

Rémi apologised. It was Easter break, so Juliette had come home from college and Rémi was visiting Nathalie and Charles. She came to see them almost every day and spent her time with Nathalie, in the garden, in the kitchen. Since she had become pregnant, they had become very close. Sometimes she went for walks with Rémi, but everywhere they went, through the forest, down to the lake, or the Beuvron, there was an emptiness. Often, they would return from their walks to find Nathalie sitting alone at the kitchen table performing minor kitchen tasks with tears in her eyes. Charles tended to hide in his bureau or sit on the divan in the salon listening to music, mostly the war symphonies of Shostakovitch. Occasionally, Nathalie would complain it was too loud, but in general everyone spent most of their time dispersed around the house, moving aimlessly almost, from room to room.

"It's like there is nothing here!" said Nathalie. "Nothing! The heart has gone from this place!"

"I know. said Charles, "I know."

---

60   It's not nice what you say! Apologise! Straight away!

Rémi had been told there was nothing for him to do but wait. But waiting was not enough. The others were getting on to him, Juliette, Charles, Nathalie and even Marie Jeanne and Louis Marie.

Marie Jeanne was still attending to her routines around the house, cleaning, tidying and occasionally preparing a soupe à l'onion for lunch. She missed the surprises and occasional shocks to the daily routines of the French countryside I had introduced. She had come to accommodate to the idea, and the fact that she was about to become a grandmother, and that the new baby would most probably be 'noirâtre', blackish. She had been admonished by Louis Marie to never express an opinion that could be construed as critical, ashamed, disappointed or in any way derogatory of either the forthcoming child, or Juliette herself, or me, repeating either her own or opinions expressed by the local priest and the silly reactionary and easily condemnatory churchgoing spinsters, housewives and bitter old ladies she met every Sunday. Besides, she persuaded herself, who could say that Jesus and Mary were not black? There were, after all, ancient icons and paintings representing them . . . as . . . black. The fact that Juliette was not at all interested in getting married in church in the eyes of God and that I found the notion of God incomprehensible were other obstacles in her relations with fellow born-in-sin gossip mongers, determined to go to heaven on the backs of their moral high horses. Losing those moments of shared and whispered secrets, was a hard brick to swallow. She had had to put on a happy smile and avoid all the wicked gossiping which had given her so much pleasure before.

In any case, she was in her heart so much looking forward to meeting this baby.

But, where was he? Where was the father of this soon to arrive child? He had disappeared somewhere in London. What was his involvement with politics? What did he know about any of that? Even the police had been looking for him. An illegal? Un hors-la-loi?[61] Wanted in his own country? A terrorist?

Rémi just avoided responding. In fact, he was increasingly annoyed and irritated by the constant questioning, inquisitions,

---

61   An outlaw

and remonstrations from everyone. He was very reluctant to talk about the three women caring for me at Place Pigalle, where, in any case, he had arrived uninvited and in secret. His secrecy about that visit made everyone else all the more frustrated with him. Then, within a few days:-

"Allô?" Nathalie was responding to a landline call. Everyone stopped to listen. "Oui. Oui. C'est de la part de qui?"[62]

She covered the mouthpiece and said:" C'est pour toi, Juliette."

"Who is it?" whispered Juliette.

"I don't know," Nathalie shrugged. "A woman with an extremely long name . . . Amanish . . something."

Juliette took the receiver.

"Bonjour." She listened for a long time, then, "Oui. Oui. Merçi. Tomorrow then. Au revoir."

Everyone was waiting in desperation to hear a full report.

"So, that was Amanish . . . "

". . . akete." completed Rémi. "Amanishakete."

"You know this woman?" demanded Nathalie, looking at Rémi.

"Of course!"

"The two of us, Rémi, are going tomorrow. Amanish has already sent the tickets to your email. The TGV leaves from the Gare du Nord around noon. She thinks we could organize our trip from here to Paris ourselves."

"Ah, no!" insisted Nathalie. "You can't take such a long trip in your condition."

"I agree with Madame Nathalie." interjected Marie Jeanne.

---

62   Hello. Yes, yes. Who is it from?

"Stop! I decide! She recognizes that I am pregnant, but I must not worry. It is very important that Chár starts to get to know his child. He needs my support and to see me right away. He misses me very much, that's what she said. He feels very lonely."

"Pauvre chou! Poor darling!" said Nathalie.

"I'll take them to Paris this afternoon," said Charles, "in the Mercedes."

"Who are these women who seem to be organising everyone? How did Amanish . . . this woman get our phone number? Did you give it to them, Rémi?" wondered Nathalie, slightly puzzled at how these three women had come to be controlling events, and what was their involvement in these affairs?

"No, I didn't give anyone your phone number. Maybe Chár. But they are amazing, these three sisters! They know many things! Many things that others can never know. Witches! Really! They've been so kind to Chár. What exactly their interest in him might be, we don't know. Maybe we'll never know. I know that for Amanishakhete it is something . . . . deep in history, in her beliefs. She's an ancient Queen, you know! Something to do with the Nile . . . I don't know. Something that connects her and her past to here and to Chár. But I trust them. I am sure they will come here one time to visit and meet you. Let me tell you, Aunt Nathalie, they have considerable respect and affection for you."

*   *   *

"Why didn't you tell me about the baby the last time I saw you?" My eyebrows were bent towards each other in annoyance, glaring at Tagì. I had spent a couple of days with my new people explaining we would be back with more family soon and then headed to London with Nyaba Buli.

"Because she said not to. She forbade me from speaking about it," explained Rémi. "She'll be here later. She's out with Jolanta. I don't know what they are organising, what they are up to! She wants to meet this Secretary of State."

"And your parents?"

171

"The sisters arranged an invitation. My mother is an art dealer, remember? And Mercantor is selling that family painting. They're flying of course. Uncle Charles is coming with them, I think. My father wouldn't miss this for the world! You're his favourite nephew! He loves you, Chár, as if you were his own!"

"And Nathalie?"

"No, she is not coming. It is too difficult for her, too painful, this political trickery, subterfuge. She is waiting in France. Charles and Robert have promised her they will bring you back with all of us."

*   *   *

Basically, Mercantor's grandfather had given up the title of Viscount of Bone in order to gain more power. It seemed to him the best way to influence the direction of the country, and his own personal wealth, was to get elected to the House of Commons and of course, eventually become Prime Minister. He did not succeed, neither did his son. So now it was up to Sir James Mercantor to fulfil that family generational wish. Of course, the family had always had considerable influence historically, since the brilliant political and economic success of the 1st Viscount of Bone. So far, James had managed various junior minister positions but as Secretary of State for International development, he had had considerable influence, with companies interested in investing globally, over where and how to place their investments. Moreover, that influence extended to governments in developing nations. You never get something for nothing in this world. More often than not, it was not the means of achieving an end that mattered, but that the end could be described as for the greater good of the nation or its people, even though that was a lie and not at all the real reason for exploitation. The only political system which guaranteed progress, lifting people out of poverty, so the lie went, was liberal capitalism. Inequality was actually good, since it encouraged hard work and achievement through the notion of merit and hence established a moral order: morality through inequality. Although the political establishment touted equality as a social ideal, especially the Labour party, even they, believing Thatcher and her spawn from hell, Tony Blair, accepted their lies that only equality of opportunity was a valid deception, achieving material equality would destroy the driving force behind capitalist

172

production, so the rationale went, and hence, it was to be avoided. Along with that inequality, greed was good, as Margaret Thatcher had said. As for the notion that billionaires were the wealth creators for the economy and hence for the general good, that lie was so obvious; they had only ever created wealth for themselves by extracting wealth from the majority, they were wealth extractors. Why else were they billionaires!? Any profit, surplus to basic need, being creamed off, meant that the majority were constantly striving to avoid starvation, or constantly paying off an infinite debt. There were surprising similarities between the Hindu caste system and the social and economic structures of liberal capitalism. Whilst liberal media wanted to claim the class system no longer existed, one only had to look at the way taxation and the benefits system were set up to see vivid distinctions between economic groups. But these distinctions were even more vivid during capitalism's birth and early development throughout the time of the Empire. Take Kenya and Uganda as examples, within the rigid colonial setup obviously the white English were the rulers, under them were Indian administrators, business people, merchants and so on, imported from the Indian subcontinent by the English to run things, with attitudes just as racist as their masters and then the lowest class were the indigenous tribes. Intermarriage between English and blacks, English and Indians, Indians and blacks was so looked down upon as to be the worst of possible sins. The Mercantors had always been particularly apt at manipulating and exploiting black Africa, that it was with a certain nostalgia that Sir James happily entered into the current rape of Southern Ethiopia.

Now that the scandals and outcries by do-gooder charities had drowned under the waves of prurient human-interest stories concerning royalty, pop stars and titillating TV game shows, interest in Ethiopia and its aggressive land reforms was fading into the past. The German photographer and his images of mass graves had been discredited. Local witnesses had disappeared having been branded as terrorists by the national press, which also invented tendentious links between the photographer and the remnants of the old East German Communist party and its Marxist/Stalinist politics. Now that the last of the agents sent to disrupt the Amnesty meeting had disappeared and the chaos had been put down to an electrical power failure, all of those worrying difficulties had faded to an insignificant corner of not only the nation's memory but Mercantor's memory also. The Prime Minister wanted the issue silenced and had made it known through leaks that the young Ethiopian at the Amnesty meeting was being pursued as a deluded illegal immigrant (and nothing more). Peace was restored and the hysteria of the Daily Mail, the Express, the Sun and the Telegraph returned to foreigners more generally flooding the country. The Ethiopian government was happy, Chinese investors were happy and Sir James' personal fortune had increased exponentially since the seizure of that land. All was for the greater good.

The Sisters would not have known about these changes had it not been for Jolanta's boyfriend, the Metropolitan Deputy Commissioner of Police. It was Lihua who had changed his status. Before, he had just been a client, gradually he had become a regular client, and then dependable client, and then 'with friendly intentions' and then finally, it was Lihua who declared it with great emotion and enthusiasm, that he was now Jolanta's boyfriend. For a while Jolanta had dismissed the idea with contempt, but Lihua was not giving up and finally, being caught several times looking at this handsome middle-aged man with starry eyes, she had to give in. It had already been a while since he had offered her first a beautiful diamond necklace and matching earrings and then a ring with a huge stone.

They were all happy about my change of status, which meant I could become even more invisible. But this would change neither my pursuit nor theirs of Mercantor.

*   *   *

Sir James' plans were to erase the old servant's graveyard at Utrecht Hall and to use some of his recent gains to build large stables and invest in some thoroughbred hunters. At the same time, he wanted to sell on the family portrait by Zoffany. The subconscious desire to eliminate the ghost of little William was rationalised in his conscious planning as simply adding improvements to the estate. Now that wild boar had been reintroduced and found propagating in the estate forests, he planned to re-establish an ancient tradition of boar hunting on horseback with boar spears. This was after all the sport of kings.

Of course, one doesn't exorcise ghosts by bulldozing a graveyard and selling a painting, but his ego was able to transform exorcism into the pursuit of his own greatness. For the sale, he would be inviting people of influence, especially in the party, as part of his campaign to bid for the leadership. He had many economic, political, and aristocratic allies who were already campaigning for him. After the PM's last debacle in Europe, Mercantor had stepped down from his cabinet position and could concentrate on his bid, as yet unannounced, for leadership. So, the occasion of the auction, when there would be collectors and dealers from different European countries as well as the US, there would also be the moment when he would make clear to senior disgruntled members of the party, his 'reluctant' willingness to rescue the party and the nation whilst swearing allegiance to the Prime Minister in the current extremely difficult relations with Europe. All of this would be in a quite informal manner, testing the waters, rallying around himself friends and allies whilst providing a lavish, exclusive, and flattering event for everyone to attend. He had already escalated his public appearances, TV, and media interviews. He was free to expound, elaborate and undermine, whilst the PM was a miserable victim of circumstance. Such were the thoughts of his scheming mind.

In spite of the best laid plans of mice and men, Sir James was worried. His estate manager had informed him of the corpse found in the forests. This was the last thing he needed, some random disaster, nothing to do with him, nor Utrecht Hall, nor anyone working there. Nevertheless, the police wanted to talk with him, informally of course, about the suggestion that he had met the victim on rare occasions because he, the now rotting corpse, had acted as agent for workers on his land. Shit! That was the last thing he needed! He also needed to speak with the event organisers about arrangements for the party. They had suggested a type of bal masqué in Georgian dress, which would suit very well the sale of the Zoffany, along with music and a series of tableaux to do with the Mercantor family history. He liked the idea. And as far as the corpse was concerned, the ladies had reassured him that they knew how to manage such public relations difficulties. He was fine in their hands.

Mercantor was on his way to Utrecht Hall to clear up any worries or problems the police had had with this corpse. He was waiting at

Paddington with Chivers when his estate manager called his mobile. Apparently, the workers in the cabbage fields had rallied together after the disappearance and death of their agent, Zelusz, and simply assumed responsibility for the harvest, in spite of the fact that Zelusz had not been paying them.

"Oh well, good. That's a good thing, isn't it? You can make sure they get paid."

But they had also successfully hunted boar themselves and most evenings seemed to be partying.

"Can't you stop them?"

"What? Partying?"

"Yes! Well, no. Killing boar. Whatever animal is on my land is mine since the time of the Game Laws."

"We can't find any more labour to finish the harvest any time soon, so I . ."

"You gave them permission?"

"Not exactly. Besides, they seem like decent people."

"Decent people?!" Mercantor practically screamed down the phone.

"The children and teenagers have taken over the job of looking after the cattle . . ."

"Have you got a band of gypsies there, or what?"

"I shouldn't have bothered you with all this. It's not that they are doing anything bad, it's just sometimes . . . a bit strange. You remember John, don't you? He's the worker who looks after the crops and the land-workers when they are here. He's very big-hearted and is generally a kind man. The youngsters really warm to him and follow him around the fields when he's looking after the horses and cattle. So, of course, he ends up giving them jobs, which they love."

"Well, it sounds like everything is fine, apart from them eating a wild pig one time." Mercantor was becoming impatient. He could see from the electronic departure board that time was approaching for boarding his train.

"Not only that," insisted the estate manager, "The older teenagers have started . . . well . . . dancing with bulls."

"What?"

"Dancing with bulls. The young bulls, actually. One time, so John told me, when the weather was threatening heavy rain, these kids herded all of them under a big oak tree; then they started this game of running across their backs, stepping from one bull to the next, as a sort of competition between them."

"And the bullocks let them do it?"

"Yeh, astonishingly. Then within a few days they started doing . . . acrobatics! Cartwheels and stuff like that."

" What!? I don't believe you! It's just that old farmhand making things up."

"No, I've seen them. It's like in ancient Greece. . . I saw it on TV."

"You mean Crete. Yes, yes, the paintings, Minoan wall paintings."

"Another time, one black kid, he's the tallest, when a cow was taking a leak, I saw him stick his head under her arse, so his hair got soaked in cow piss."

"Oh, for goodness' sake!" at this point Mercantor just burst out laughing.

"John reckoned it was a dare. They'd found out something about cow piss, you see . . . . . the next time I saw him, his mop of long black - dreads they call them, - his hair is matted together, like those pop stars – it had turned orange."

"Orange?!!"

"Ever since, the cows just love him. They follow him everywhere. It's weird! And he's really proud of his hair colour. Not only the cows, but all the girls follow him around as well. You just wonder what they're going to do next!"

"Are they circus people or what? Irish gypsies? So long as no one is coming to harm, leave them be. We don't want to fall out with them now, while the police are investigating the corpse problem. You know what they are like, these gypsies, land-workers! Their children never go to school. They steal and they're all liars . . . "

*   *   *

"We rented this apartment for you and Chár for the next few days, so that you might spend some time together." explained mother Amanishakhete.

The two apartments were in a small tower of perhaps fifteen or twenty floors right next to Tate Modern in central London and strangely looked as if they had been constructed from a Meccano set, with girders, beams and supports exterior to the building. Rémi guessed the architect had been influenced by Richard Rogers' Lloyds Exchange and the Pompidou Centre, where the body of the buildings, instead of being covered by a skin were transformed, inside-out, as if the intestines and skeleton were now exterior to the structure rather than hidden.

"Rémi will stay with us in the apartment below. We'll see you later, whenever you wish."

Juliette's hands moved slowly down my chest, each feeling a raised nipple as they slipped down to my waist. There was a mixture of anger, relief, and tears as she pulled me close, laying her head on my shoulder. It was my smooth skin and muscles underneath that reassured her, made her feel safe. Her hands moved back up, exploring, rediscovering the same moist armpit, the same dorsal muscles, and strong shoulders. She pushed me away to be able to look me in the eyes, slapped me across the cheek, and started to shake with the tears that come with the sudden release of months of distress and anxiety. I held her head in my hands and started to kiss her face, the pain in our hearts, our yearning for each other suddenly bursting out. All this time in England suddenly seemed stupid, irrelevant, a waste, compared to what was happening in my Juliette's body. I put my arms around her to pull her close, immediately finding things were different; I could no longer get so close, her huge belly was now in the way. Then I felt it myself, something kick me. A tiny foot, an elbow? I held her tighter to feel it again. And there it was! Something, someone making his, or her presence known again!

"You feel that? My back aches! And my legs!" Juliette moved carefully towards the bed and slowly sat down, manoeuvring her belly as she leaned back onto her elbows, unable any longer to sit with any comfort without first considering the size and weight of the gigantic pool of amniotic fluid and the child inside her.

"Let me help you. I'll run a warm bath." I knelt down in front of her and removed her shoes, helping her to lift her feet onto the bed. I hurried to the bathroom and started to run a bath.

"I can do that!" I started to help her undress. "I am so sorry! I thought you were at University. I didn't know you were carrying my baby. They tried to kill me, this lord, and his men. . . . . and yes, I felt . . ."

"You felt his kick?" she looked exhausted and then: "He can hear you., you know."

"What?"

"He can hear you!" Juliette repeated with more insistence. "The baby!"

"Hear me? No! I don't believe it!"

"He can hear your voice." She smiled. "He is listening."

"How do you know this?"

"I know these things! I am his mother. He knows who you are."

"He knows me?"

Juliette watched as she saw tears fill my eyes.

"All this time you have been here," Juliette continued, "I have had no one to talk to . . . about . . . you and me . . ." She hesitated.

" . . and my love for you?" I said quietly. I had failed. I had abandoned the one person I had wanted, that intensity of every moment with Juliette, of every touch, ever since we had met.

"Our love, Chár. Our love."

"So, you talked to him?"

"I told him about you, his father. About when we met, about the meeting at the lake, about the paintings, everything. I told him about your body, so that he would know you when first you hold him." She started to manoeuvre herself off the bed. "The bath, Chár. Don't forget the bath!"

I was openly weeping, overwhelmed. I helped her up and led her to the bathroom, again, assisting her to lower herself into the warm water.

"Your breasts!" I said, wide-eyed and with a big smile. "They are so big now!"

I quickly pulled off my clothes to join her in the warm water.

"He knows me?!!" I repeated, the sense of joy, affirmation and a feeling of victory, even, that life, our lives together had achieved its ultimate purpose to sustain itself beyond the limitations of change in an eternal present.

"I see your dormì still likes to stand up." she said with a smile.

"He is happy to see you! You think we can still make love? Your belly is so big now."

"Yeah! Of course! Like that he will get to know you better, your baby, your boy!" And then, more quietly, with a compassionate smile: "He will always admire you, you know that, eh? . . . and follow you everywhere."

180

The clatter of the high pitched cacophony of voices, tannoys, baggage wheels on stone, of loud announcements, shouts, sly whispers, moans, angers, frustrations, bounced around the great departure hall of Paddington station, alerting everyone to the urgency of the everyday, it's business, it's overriding importance. Personal identity was sucked away, everyone became a package on a conveyor belt, shifted, shunted, numbered, labelled and despatched. No matter how modernity tried to humanise this thing with slick fast food for the overwhelmingly busy, fancy coffees to reaffirm a lost choice for a lost identity, the callous indifference of its inhumanity shone through.

Regardless of its soundless nature, the order of departures clicked into place directing sudden commands to waves of people. Mercantor and Chivers followed instructions and hurried to their platform, finally able to leave behind the minor anxiety of securing their seats and resign themselves to a long period of self-reflection. The irritatingly self-important, or distracted, immediately occupying themselves with laptops and iPhones instead of drifting into the opportunity of dreamy, mildly cathartic self-examination.

On a Thursday afternoon, Mercantor had become accustomed to, and expected, especially first class, to be practically empty, which gave his often troubled thoughts - troubled by his schemes for party leadership, political alliances and foes, whether he was making the right investments in the current political turmoil, his guilt, his pride, his fears and anxieties - chance to expand into a gaseous void of soporific insignificance. Instead, all of that tangle of thorns had to remain locked inside; the carriage was full, every seat seemed to be taken. He always resented having to sit next to Chivers, rather than opposite and Chivers felt the same, but on this occasion, they had no choice.

"I think you've taken one of our seats," announced the young man with blonde hair. Mercantor looked at him, having initially sat opposite Chivers in a reserved seat, unashamedly showed his annoyance and moved next to Chivers.

The young men sat down around the table they shared with

Mercantor and Chivers and both stared directly at them. The handsome young blonde man smiled generously, especially at Chivers, who smiled back. His companion, a young black man, "Hm, unusually black," thought Chivers, seemed more reluctant to offer any social contact whatsoever, remaining sullen and silent.

Chivers was easily charmed by handsome young men and was pleased to have this distraction opposite him for the journey. He smiled.

Mercantor looked around. Sitting on the two single seats on the other side of the aisle were two young black people, a young woman and a very tall young man with exactly the same, or at least how he had imagined it, the same long orange hair the estate manager had described to him. He was puzzled. Were they real, or only imaginary these confusions, collisions of thoughts? He nudged Chivers, indicating the tall young man.

"Remember Geoffrey's story."

"Geoffrey? Oh, yes, yes. The manager. What do you mean?"

"The cow piss story."

"Yes, funny, yes, and?"

He indicated again the tall young man.

Chivers smiled.

"Coincidence, eh?"

As the train pulled out of the station, Mercantor took in the rest of the carriage, strangely full of mostly young blacks. Why were they in first class? Shouldn't they be in second class? Isn't that how you would expect young people to travel? He noticed himself thinking: "especially blacks." He felt reassured, looking up and down the carriage, there were also a few whites. The tall young black man with orange hair got up and went to the end of the carriage to the entrance where he appeared to be looking intently at the panelling next to the carriage door. He noticed Mercantor looking at him, grinned, winked and put up one thumb in greeting. Mercantor looked away immediately wondering if he thought he was gay.

"I guess we're all going to Bristol." declared the blonde young man. Then leaning forward towards Chivers and lowering his voice. "A big population of black people in Bristol, you know."

"Are you from Bristol?" Chivers asked.

"No, no. We're from France."

There was a long silence as all but Chivers sank into secret contempt, myself and Rémi for Mercantor and likewise him for us. Mercantor felt uncomfortable as I that young black man stared at him unceasingly with nothing but an expression of cold detachment, as if wondering what to do with the corpse of a dead fly.

"Déllé búgáʼ inye lé:thu. déllé kegeyndɔ múmɔ inye árrà, inye wolokoyndɔ." My voice purred like a wild cat.

"anye tággá." Rémi almost laughed at my words.

"Menenge chár nanu hídɔ kwáɔʼɔda noʼ" I exclaimed.

"Aggé cháchẚʼ gorí." said Rémi hoping to reassure me before my anger should boil over.

"Ingàrɛn. buhóginya woylenyɔ tággá tényéydá tiráyna."[63] I said, remembering what the three sisters had demanded.

"My friend was saying, he thinks he recognises you from TV in France."

---

63 déllé búgáʼ inye lé:thu. déllé kegeyndɔ múmɔ inye árrà, inye wolokoyndɔ. "I hate the stupid hyena. I see his stupid face, I am angry."
anye tággá "I know."
menenge chár nanu hídɔ kwáɔʼɔda noʼ "My leopard spirit wants to kill him."
Aggé cháchẚʼ gorí."We will truly take revenge."
ingàrɛn. buhóginya woylenyɔ tággá tényéydá tiráyna. "I'm not sure. I don't know. The witches know better when to make their play. (or: the witches are [better] able to know how to play [their hand].)"
Please note: for Suri people, witches are not necessarily considered evil, but certainly have special powers

said the blonde one. "He thinks you are a famous politician here in England."

"Yes, a member of Parliament."

"Mr Mercantor has been on political programmes quite often here in the UK," Chivers hurriedly added, wanting to join in and smiling at Rémi.

Mercantor looked annoyed.

"That's an unusual language you are speaking." he said inviting them to name it.

"Yes," responded Rémi, "Our secret language," he said, grinning at Mercantor. "Very few people can speak it nowadays. Of course, you, famously, speak Latin, I believe."

Mercantor recoiled, nodding, as if found out.

"So do we. I learned it at school in Paris and taught my friend at weekends. Not so secret as ours, eh?"

"It's part of Mr Mercantor's colourful public image," hastened Chivers with a big smile, as if his master's linguistic skills brought joy to his life, "much admired by many of the party faithful."

Mercantor wished Chivers would shut up. How he despised the ignorant public, Chivers and their pet dog admiration for his classics education. These two strangers were too strange, too foreign to have a right to any knowledge of him, whether it be his public image or anything else.

"Personally, I have always found it shocking to the level of idiocy, the admiration that still persists for Rome's first dictator, Julius Caesar, who was nothing but a lying over-ambitious, venal, greedy cunt. His Histories of the Gallic campaign, which was nothing but genocide, the seizure of wealth, and enslavement – I mean, his political movement was called Vox Populi - and greedy populism is exactly what it was, enriching his foot soldiers so that that would provide sufficient threat to the Senate that it would capitulate to his dictatorship as his armies returned to Rome, those Histories were nothing more than propaganda worthy of Goebbels."

Mercantor offered only a sickly smile, "I see you know your Roman history and its politics."

The handsome blonde young man had removed his jacket and was now sitting in a thin white cotton T-shirt. He lifted his arms and rested both hands with fingers interlinked on his head. His black friend bent his head and leaned towards him, putting his mouth and nose into the moist armpit.

"kálugey nunu a chàlli!"[64]

"anye tággá!"[65] replied the blonde, with a big smile, all the while staring at Mercantor.

Mercantor was horrified by this blatant intimacy, overtly sexual, overtly homosexual, overtly worshipful, completely discarding the sterility of convention. These were like . . . vulgar animals, dogs, sniffing around each other, between each other's legs. Chivers simply wished he could put his face in the other armpit.

While the two middle aged men were recovering from this moral trauma, I reached down between my legs to open my backpack and retrieve a large wooden canister, a simple water carrier, made of a section of giant bamboo, already fairly battered and polished by use. A crude leather strap was looped over the top of it, by which it could be carried. Pushed into the top was a large piece of cork. I flipped the cork and retrieved from my bag, a long thin stick and two wooden bowls. I inserted the stick into the canister and stirred. Mercantor and Chivers watched.

"Nyàbà ʷolé[66]" I said with a deep growl, as I retrieved the stick now covered with a thick red liquid. and grinned, lifting the stick and sliding it across my lips, my tongue curling around it to capture all of the liquid. I took hold of the back of Rémi's head, twisting it towards me and kissed him firmly on the lips. We both looked up at the two men opposite, our mouths now covered in red blood.

---

64   "Your armpit is beautiful!"
65   "I know!"
66   Bull's blood.

I turned to pouring the dark red liquid into the two bowls. Mercantor and Chivers watched in horror as I passed a bowl of blood to Rémi and we both drank, leaving our mouths stained red.

"Bull's blood." explained the blonde. " It is his custom."[67] He wiped the blood from around his mouth with a corner of his T-shirt, looked up at Chivers and laughed: "My mother would be horrified!"

The two English gentlemen had become strangers in their own land; their narrow-minded culture feeling under threat.

"Very spicy! Usually, we drink it as soon as we take it from the young bull, but for travelling you have to make sure it doesn't coagulate, otherwise you just end up with a jug full of red jelly!"

The blonde one's teeth were stained red and a thin strand of coagulate stretching across one of his two front teeth. He was sucking his breath in and out through tightly puckered lips, as would anyone eating very spicy, chilli food. Both Mercantor and Chivers felt their stomachs turning.

"We are lucky," he continued. "We have a good friend, Chinese. She knows everything about herbs, spices, traditional medicines, and more, a lot more! There are natural anti-coagulants, turmeric, chilli, cinnamon. She knows exactly how to prepare a mixture to keep the blood thin." he paused and burped. "I don't know. It is her secret. I think she is a bit of a witch, with her spells and potions." He looked at the two opposite and laughed, as if encouraging them to laugh at his funny story, his maw now dripping blood down his chin.

"Good thing it's not the blood of children!" he said, looking straight at Mercantor. "I'd hate to have that on my head!"

---

67 It is a custom amongst Suri people to drink the blood of cattle on special occasions, for example before entering in a stick fighting competition with another village. It is highly valued and considered to give great strength. It is obtained by shooting a small arrow into the prominent vein/artery of the bull or cow's neck. The arrow only makes a small opening. As the blood spurts out it is collected. When the men have sufficient, the bleeding can be stopped by simply rubbing the tiny wound.. Very quickly the blood coagulates and the tiny wound is healed. The cow feels almost nothing, certainly no pain.

At that point, the very tall young man with long orange dreadlocks approached and whispered something in the ear of the blonde, who stood up, lifted his T-shirt to wipe his mouth and left. Immediately, a small young woman, heavily pregnant, with long brown hair came to take his seat. Her big belly made it difficult for her to squeeze into the seat, the edge of the table distancing her from the two upright English gentlemen. The young black man, already seated opposite Mercantor, turned, and kissed her on the cheek.

"Chár, ça va si tu veux boire du sang, mais s'il te plaît ne m'embrasse pas avec tes lèvres ensanglantées !" said Juliette, with a frown and a smile. "J'en ai sur la joue maintenant!"[68]

"Bonjour," she said, addressing Chivers and Mercantor, with a warm smile.

Once again it was Chivers who was well-mannered and polite enough to respond.

"Bonjour!" he said.

Laughing gently at being told off, I pulled Juliette close, and placing my mouth on her cheek, put out my tongue to lick it clean.

"Arrêtes![69]" she laughed quietly, pushing me away and then addressing Chivers: "Il est méchant.[70]" She shrugged and smiled and then found a tissue to wipe her cheek dry.

Chivers and Juliette smiled at each other.

Mercantor slipped into brooding and staring blankly at the countryside zipping past. His entire life, he had been trained to enjoy privilege, the birth right of superiority. Freedom came with wealth and power, so he was free, whereas all others were not. Chivers at his side, for example, was he free? Certainly not. The idea of equality was absurd. Look at the two unfortunates opposite. She was clearly ready to drop his spaff accident any day,

---

68 "Chár, it's okay if you want to drink blood, but please don't kiss me with your bloodied lips!" said Juliette, with a frown and a smile. " I have some on my cheek now!"
69 Stop!
70 He's naughty.

and as for him . . . the claim by the vulgar blonde that he could speak Latin was clearly a lie! No! This couple of fools of stunted outlook and possibilities, about to give birth to their crossbreed, mixed-race mishap, even the idea that they should be his equals was for the dogs.

Inasmuch as his entire family history had been caught up in the exploitation of black Africa, he wondered why in his own mind he had not found the means to come to terms with their existence, their being human. How many times had he visited so many parts of that continent and found himself unable to perceive any of those dictators, politicians, priests, officials and peasants as any more than peculiarly alien, in spite of the fact that many were highly educated, yet seemed remarkably stupid, often moronic? They were nothing more than the black masses, cartoons of themselves, their children, picaninnies with watermelon smiles. He smiled to himself at successfully using recently, in his regular news column, these terms related to slavery. In any case, the Queen visiting her Commonwealth, how much more of a reference to slavery, exploitation and their inferiority to Her Majesty and the British State than that! He had either despised them or feared them. There was always something dangerously unpredictable about how they conducted themselves, how they related to each other. Here in this carriage, he felt ill at ease. He was nevertheless conscious, of the demands of his education to always succeed in making the other, whoever, white, black, brown, educated, stupid, rich, or poor, feel inferior . . . which of course, they were. Better they know their place. It was a matter of fortitude.

When he finally came out of his Churchillian brooding - who would have ever known what Churchill's 'black dog' mind state was offering him, apart from the deepest regret over the crumbling Empire? - Chivers was expanding on the experience of birth. He had been chatting away with the young French student about her pregnancy, when the baby was due, did she know its sex, what she was studying and so on.

I watched as the conversation developed. This person seemed genuinely interested and amicable, a warm heart. My hardened expression and forced distance, my willed silence, began to soften. I even glanced at Chivers with kindly eyes.

"Alors, vous êtes une étudiante des beaux-arts!" said Chivers. "C'est merveilleux!"[71]

I sensed a baleful, menacing arousal taking place within the fat somnolent body of Mercantor opposite and immediately felt the tiny pellicular muscles of my own skin tightening.

"The young lady is a student of the fine arts," said Chivers, turning to Mercantor, who had managed to sit himself upright in sour acceptance of his reanimation.

"And what particular field of art or period interests you?" asked Mercantor. "I'm sorry, I didn't catch your name."

"Juliette. And you are a well-known member of Parliament, I believe."

"Mr Mercantor was a member of the Cabinet as Secretary of State for International Development," interjected Chivers, as if that were something to be proud of.

"Looking after countries that don't know how to look after themselves, basically." added Mercantor with a contemptuous smile.

"Ha, ha, ha!" Chivers tried to laugh off the ugliness of what his boss had said. "Really it is to do with inward investment to help with modernisation and economic development."

"And where do you come from in France?" asked Chivers, trying to deflect Mercantor's offence.

"La campagne. Pas loins de Blois, en fait. Mon père est fermier."[72]

"So, he owns a lot of land?" wondered Mercantor.

"No, not at all! Enough for a herd of cattle and a small milk and cheese production."

"Un paysan! A peasant farmer, then," commented Mercantor.

---

71   "So you're a student of the fine arts. That's marvellous!"
72   "The countryside. Not far from Blois, in fact. My father is a farmer."

"That they still exist in France is quite amazing, nowadays."

"And your art, my dear young lady," said Chivers, trying to change the subject, "you were going to tell us your interest."

I opened the jug of blood again, offering some to the NyabaBuli with orange hair seated the other side of the aisle, then filling my own bowl.

"Let me guess," interrupted Mercantor. "You like Impressionism and especially Van Gogh," Like every culturally half-baked teenager, he thought.

"Of course! But especially, I love Caravaggio."

"Ah, really?" responded Mercantor. "Personally, I find him rather vulgar. Too much flesh, especially young men, and basically, he was doing portraits of prostitutes, their pimps, down-and-outs and all the vagrants and criminal elements of Rome and then calling them saints."

I could feel Juliette struggling under the barrage of offence. I felt my stomach tightening with anger, but knew I should wait.

Juliette was astonished at the extent to which the sisters, as Rémi and I referred to them, were able to organise events. Hardly surprising, they had become professional event organisers. Here she sat on this train to Bristol next to me and facing the man who had destroyed my village and attempted to destroy me. Clearly, Mercantor didn't realise who he was sitting opposite. Did he have any suspicion? Moreover, the carriage was full of my more recent friends. Was she going to let him know who he was sitting opposite, who surrounded him? It was as if they, the three sisters and I, were amassing all the lost tribes of the disaffected and despised. How did we know about the train journey? Which carriage Mercantor was in? Maybe we knew someone who could hack into ... ticketing ... Great Western reservations?

"So what type of paintings or artwork do you produce yourself?" enquired Mercantor.

I knew he was fishing to insult once more.

"Figurative. With chiaroscuro, like Caravaggio. The series of drawings and paintings of mon mari[73]," she said, gesturing towards me, "won me my place at the art school of Bordeaux University. My black Dionysus with flowers in his hair."

Mercantor almost laughed: "Chiaroscuro with a subject who is so . . . excuse me . . . so black?"

"Your eyes, Mr Mercantor," responded Juliette. She could no longer hold back from confronting this nasty man with some truths about himself, "you are that member of Parliament who used to be International Trade Secretary until that scandal over the village in Ethiopia, aren't you? . . . . "

Mercantor realised this girl, about to give birth, intended political warfare. Her partner, mon mari, as she referred to him, who still hadn't spoken, seemed as thick as the colour of his skin.

"Your eyes and understanding have been trained to dismiss distinctions. How else can you make decisions disregarding . . . "

"Disregarding what?"

"Detail. The lives of others. Individual differences. People call you white, but you are far from that."

Mercantor dismissed the criticism from this silly little girl, who had got herself fucked by someone from the jungle.

"So, your model became your husband? The father of your child?"

"We are not married, but, yes, Chár will soon be a father," Juliette responded with a smile.

"I've noticed" commented Mercantor, with a sour smile. "In my family, well, it must be almost two hundred and fifty years ago now, the sister of my great great great great, - however many greats, - grandfather, a great aunt, was seduced by a servant, in fact a slave, working on the estate."

---

73   my husband

Telling stories in such hostile situations can easily lead to insult; this much I know about civilised white people. I took another mouthful of spicy blood.

"Inevitably she fell pregnant. In spite of considerable upset to the rest of the family, she insisted she loved him, etc., and was sent away to give birth. . . "

"And the servant?"

"Oh! I have no idea! Sold, probably. Sent off to the colonies. Who knows?"

"And the baby?"

"No one knows. Disposed of! . . . No doubt with expediency and discretion. Of course, at the time, it was considered utterly shameful to give birth to a . . . ." he paused. He wanted to give as much weight as possible to the abuse intended.

Chivers was rigid and white with fear, awaiting his boss's explosive insult. Juliette could feel the adrenalin of her anger sitting in her stomach, her heart racing.

"Give birth to . . . ?"

A faint smirk crossed Mercantor's face.

"Give birth to a mulato![74]"

At which point, Chivers lifted his hands to his face to hide his eyes, Juliette leaned back in her seat, stunned by what she had heard, and I spat my anger, a mouthful of blood into Mercantor's face. There was a minor nuclear explosion around the table. The blood splattered onto his nose and cheeks, spraying into his eyes, and sticking into his fragile thinning khaki hair, spilling down his chin and neck to stain his white shirt.

---

74 The origin of mulato, mulatto, or mulatta (fem.) is uncertain, but certainly very insulting. A term adopted during the slave trade to refer to someone of mixed race, neither black, nor white, but a separate species, as in the equine species, horse, donkey and mule, being a separate species neither horse nor donkey - in Spanish and Portuguese, mulo and mula.

Both Mercantor and I immediately jumped to our feet, Mercantor screaming angry abuse and racist insults. Nyàbà Bulí, sitting on the other side of the aisle, also jumped to his feet, and reaching above the seated Chivers, took hold of Mercantor's shoulders. Wóhólò Tagí quickly arrived as well, blood stains down the front of his T-shirt, and moved Juliette away.

"You fucking black cunt!" screamed Mercantor. "I'll fucking murder you and the mule inside that frog you fucked!"

Mercantor's fists started flailing through the air. Infuriated by this idiot's persistent racist insults, I punched him on the nose to shut him up. Tears, snot and drool mixed with his own and the ox blood, spilled down the chin and shirt front of this jumped up little trou du cul![75].

"My eyes! My eyes are burning!" It was the chilli in the oxblood. He started desperately rubbing them, which only made the burning sensation even worse.

"Fucking do something, Chivers, you prick!"

"Move, sir!" insisted Nyàbà Bulí to Chivers, who squeezed out of the way from under Jackson's arms. And Jackson Nyàbà Bulí himself took his place to better restrain Mercantor.

"Let me out! Let me out! I need to get to wash this shit out of my eyes!"

Mercantor suddenly became the staggering, blinded Mihret, blood streaming from his ripped eyes, bouncing off tree trunks and falling into thickets and undergrowth until he collapsed on the ant's nest. This time, the arrogant narcissistic psychopath was reduced to a snivelling pathetic idiot, only temporarily blinded.

"You can't use the toilet! The toilet door isn't working." Nyàbà Bulí shouted at Mercantor who was crying as he struggled stubbornly, stupidly to free himself from Nyàbà Bulí's hands. "None of the electrics in this carriage are working."

---

75 literally, arsehole!

Rémi pulled off his bloodied T-shirt and threw it at Mercantor.

"Here, use this to clean yourself!"

Mercantor wiped his face.

"I still can't see! I need water!"

Rémi Wóhólò Tagí offered a bottle of water to Nyàbà Bulí who grabbed Mercantor by his hair and tipped his head back, pouring water over his face until his shirt had turned pink with the diluted blood and his jacket equally stained. Mercantor coughed and spluttered at this waterboarding.

"Chivers, for fuck's sake, phone the police!"

"My phone's not working. There's no Wi-Fi."

"I told you, white boy," laughed Nyàbà Bulí, "the electrics in this carriage are fucked up."

"Let me out! Let me out!" Mercantor's was the same childish scream that he, ugly James, had heard so many times when he had bullied and tortured the first-year fags as part of his training to become a leader of nations.

Jackson stood up and still holding Mercantor's arms, led him into the aisle, Mercantor staggered to one end of the carriage, guiding himself by the backs of the seats until he reached a door separating the carriage exit doors and the toilet cubicle from the rest of the carriage. It wouldn't open.

"Sit here," someone said. Mercantor still couldn't see. "No one will bother you."

Very soon, he realised he was sitting alone.

When Chivers quit his seat, shaken, he found his way down the carriage to where Juliette was sitting and was offered a seat with her.

*　　　*　　　*

"No, no! He deserved it. He was very rude." insisted Chivers. And then: "What did you say your partner's name was?"

Chivers was now sitting with Juliette, Remi and me, although I was standing taking off my T-shirt, which was also stained with blood.

"Chár."

"Ah. Unusual name."

"Chár, mon chou, n'oublie pas de te trouver une chemise, et pour Rémi, aussi."[76]

So, this was him, thought Chivers, remembering the name. All that time Mercantor, his boss, had spent trying to find the refugee from Ethiopia, to silence him, even to have him killed, so Chivers suspected; all that time of failure, blundering stupidities with the two stupid private agents at the Amnesty meeting, one dying at the event and the other ending up as a paraplegic in hospital, who had then strangely disappeared; all that time of lying propaganda in the Mail and the Telegraph, which Chivers had been dragged into; all that time from Paddington Station to very shortly, Bristol, the boy from, - where was it? - Beyahola, had found his enemy, Chár had found his enemy! He probably could have found him any time he wanted, imagined Chivers.

He had a feeling of awe and in that state, he started looking around the carriage.

"And all these people here, they are your friends?"

"Yes. Well, Chár's friends. And necessarily mine also." said Juliette.

"Fuck!" Chivers whispered under his breath. "Fuck!"

He looked up at us two young men cleaning each other of the blood on our faces. I was licking Rémi's face, whose eyes were

---

76 "Chár, my dear, (perhaps the reader has already appreciated this French term of affection) don't forget to find yourself a shirt, and for Rémi also."

closed with pleasure, and then rubbing with my hand and Rémi likewise for me.

"They're like a couple of kittens," Juliette commented to Chivers, "cleaning each other."

"Exactly."

Chivers felt lonely and his eyes were stinging. He had never known that intimacy, nor would he ever; his mind wandered in a mix of current and personal time-shot despair.

"You are a good man, I can see," I said sitting next to Juliette and reaching across the table to take Chivers' hands in mine. Rémi sat next to Chivers and pressed up against him such that Chivers, for the first time in what seemed forever, felt warm legs and a body next to his. He was lost at sea and the only harbour was here next to him.

"Unfortunately, you've been working pour un con," I said, "un vrai trou du cul.[77] Soon the train will stop at a station in the middle of nowhere, the doors will open and he will get off. It's up to you. You can get off with him or stay here with us."

Chivers was silent. What should he do? Abandon Mercantor? He'd only ever been treated like a piece of shit. Or should he worry about his future, his career as a civil servant? Servant! That just about summed it up!

"What happened to Ray?" asked Rémi. "You know, the paraplegic, injured at the Amnesty meeting?"

"What didn't these people know?" wondered Chivers to himself.

"Do you know?" continued Remi, "But we know this. The sisters who saved him, the nurses, remember? What happened to them? Their business was burned down!"

"He'd asked me to find them," remembered Chivers, shaking with memory of his own complicity. "I just found a private detective to search them out."

---

77   . . .for a cunt," said Chár, "a real arsehole."

The train was slowing down. The lights on the door leading to the carriage exit doors suddenly lit up.

Jackson put his mobile in his pocket and walked to the end of the carriage where Mercantor was sitting alone.

You're getting off here," said Jackson, addressing Mercantor.

Chivers had noticed the one with orange hair, using his mobile, and wondered why he could do that while no one else seemed to have any reception.

"He's a magician!" laughed Rémi, noticing Chivers watch Nyaba Buli. "He set up the train journey." He laughed again. "Amazing, eh? Hacking. Manipulating programs. You wouldn't know that, of course. He should be arrested, don't you think? None of this happens by accident, you know. He booked the carriage for us all, including you!" He said, looking at Chivers.

Mercantor pressed the illuminated button which released the door and it slowly slid open.

"Chivers!" shouted Mercantor, looking along the carriage "Get my bag! we're getting out here before they kill us!".

He sounded like a frightened child.

"Are you going?" Rémi asked. "It's not finished with him, you know. We'll catch up with him later. This was just a forewarning of what is to come!"

Chivers looked up at the smiling Rémi and smiled back, astounded at what he was hearing.

"Stay with us! We're not going to hurt him, just destroy him. We are Burnham Wood coming to Dunsinane!"

And that was it! Suddenly free! After years of tolerated abuse, the world had gone crazy! Chivers watched his nasty boss glance back at him from the platform as the train pulled out of the station.

The little band of bulinya[78] cheered and waved as they left their
bloodied baragaráy[79] in humiliation on a platform to nowhere.

.

> You may write me down in history
> With your bitter, twisted lies,
> You may tread me in the very dirt
> But still, like dust, I'll rise.[80]

"That was fun, wasn't it?" commented Rémi to Chivers with a big
grin. "Your boss wanted to tread us, our people, into the dirt, but
we will never surrender. Our spirit is too great for his petty envies
and greed! We will always rise again! You are one of us now!"

"Did you see Chár's interview at the Amnesty meeting? He said it
then, ""I am not that word, your English word. I am not refugee! I
am Chár. I am leopard. My two leopards who take care of me
since Dibdib, my brother, Wóhólò Tagí, they are with me now
and all the dead people of Beyahola village, my village, are in me.
I am many! I am Chár!"

Chivers knew not where he was going nor what he was doing, but
he had the most wonderful sense of elation, sitting surrounded by
these kindly, warm, intelligent people, who had happily
encouraged him to lose his job through the most stunningly
awesome of events! This lightness of being, this joy was untainted
by daily compromises, deceits, obligations, debts, and moral
compromises. He had suddenly stepped through a mirror.

*   *   *

Sir James Mercantor looked around. He might as well have been
dumped in a desert. His bag, laptop and letters, documents, and
programmes for his bid for the leadership disappearing into the
distance.

"Fuck!"

A stark Spring sun shone down on the emptiness of the single

---

78   warriors
79   enemy
80   First verse of 'Still I Rise' by Maya Angelou. The complete poem easily found on many sites of
     the internet.

platform. Mercantor felt his pockets for his wallet.

"Fuck!"

He felt again through every single possible pocket for both his wallet and his mobile.

"Fuck!" he shouted and this time he lifted his twisted bloodied face to the sky and screamed.

The solitary platform attendant, cum ticket-collector, cum station-master, cum cleaner of toilets took one look at the madman, locked himself in his ticket booth and called the police.

No matter how much he screamed at the police that he was Sir James Mercantor, Member of Parliament and how he would stuff their balls up their arses, the police seemed indifferent to reason:

"Yes, sir," said the older policeman, "And I'm the man in the moon. Been in the wars, have you, sir? Taking on the world and its auntie all at the same time, have you? I think we'll sort this out at the station . . . and not Waterloo. Haven't murdered anyone recently, have you, sir? There's been a very suspicious death, mutilated dead body on the estate of the big house not far from here. Nothing to do with you is it, sir?"

"No! Yes. No! That's where I live, you fuckwit! That's why I'm here! To see what's going on!"

"Returning to the site of the crime, are we sir?"

"Yes! No! Oh, fuck!"

The two policemen handcuffed him, bundled him in the back of their car and drove away. The platform attendant-cum-all-things-to-all-men had been discreetly filming this little scene and set about uploading it to his Facebook site, with the comment, "Murder suspect arrested covered in blood!" Within minutes someone had put it on YouTube and quickly it spread like an infectious disease to every social media site the frenzied public could dream of at the click of a button.

Mercantor spent several hours in a police cell, before he could phone the house for someone to identify him for whom he claimed to be, a local lord, member of the Mercantor family, Member of Parliament, ex-government minister, etc., etc. He had been so enraged at being arrested in the first place, so humiliated by his desecrated appearance, the stench of deteriorating, coagulating, warm, sticky blood, soaking through his clothes and clinging to his skin, the blackened blood in his hair and the reddish stains down his neck and covering his hands, that he had descended into a tantrum of childish rage and the only thing the police could do was lock him in a cell until he calmed down.

After an hour of screaming ranting and indignant lunacy, Mercantor finally quietened down, largely because no one was paying any attention. Two police officers entered his cell.

"Sir, we need you to remove all your clothes which have to be examined."

"Fuck! Haven't you idiots done enough? I'll have you fucking castrated when I next see your chief constable."

"Ok, sir, you are still not cooperating, so we will have to strip you ourselves."

After much wrestling, Mercantor was cuffed again and the bloodied clothes cut off him. Finally, he was left naked, still cuffed, lying on the floor. Thirty minutes later the two officers re-entered his cell.

"Are you going to be calm now, sir, in which case we'll remove the handcuffs and give you some clothes to put on."

"Thank you. Can I take a shower?"

"You can wash yourself at the sink above the toilet."

"What's this? These fucking cell clothes are made of paper!"

"We consider you are a risk to yourself and others. Providing you with conventional clothes, you might use them to try to take your own life, which would be a disappointment for all of us."

When, finally, Mercantor was able to persuade the police to find the telephone number for Solicitors Trelawney, Brunt and Meyer and to tell them that Herbert Brunt should attend the police station to advise and represent Sir James Mercantor, their office was already closed. The police had told him they already intended to charge him with assaulting a police officer, affray, resisting arrest and travelling by rail without a ticket. His ravings about 'black cunts' and 'that arse-licking camp queer of a secretary' who had betrayed him and robbed him of his wallet, bank cards, mobile phone and identity 'and the fucking train ticket!' hardly impressed either the station sergeant, or the arresting officers, those who had stripped him and all the others who had had to put up with his shouts, pompous indignations and abuse.

The following morning, late:

"My Christ, James, you stink of shit and carrion!"

Herbert Brunt, solicitor, had entered Mercantor's cell.

"What the fuck are you wearing?"

"A stupid paper suit they gave me after they cut off my clothes."

"What happened to the legs?"

"There's no fucking toilet paper in here. I had to rip off the legs to wipe my arse, if you must know, and now the toilet is blocked!"

Brunt started giggling.

"You're in an ever-deepening shithole, Jimmy, recently. What with that cadaver found on the estate, with whom apparently you had dubious business relations, the YouTube video of your arrest and now this! Witnesses state you were covered in blood and raving when the police were called out to deal with, dare I say, a dangerous madman at Hookwich station."

"It's on the internet? Fuck!"

Mercantor just sighed deeply. Herbert and James had known each other since attending Eton College together. They had formed a deep alliance as first years when bullied into becoming fags for a couple of fat (and ugly!) older boys.

"Anyway," Brunt resumed, "I've been up to the house, your place that is, and collected some clothes."

"Thank you!" said Mercantor with a bitter, twisted expression of sarcasm.

They told me your secretary - what's his name? - Chivers, had been to the house yesterday evening accompanied by a young woman who was pregnant. Is that his girlfriend?"

"He's a fucking queer, you idiot! Of course not!"

"Bizarrely, they arrived in a chauffeur driven Bentley!" said Brunt with an expression of curious astonishment. "They delivered your bag, phone, wallet, coat, etc., and left. Oh, Chivers has resigned, by the way."

Brunt couldn't help grinning at the state of his old school friend.

"About the charges," added Brunt, "we should be able to get them dropped. I offered a decent sum for a police charity for officers suffering PTSD. Apparently, the officers who arrested you are already completely traumatised and suffering symptoms." He laughed.

Back at Utrecht Hall, he knew the best way to reassert his authority was to be as objectionable as possible, criticise everything any servant did, insult them and refuse all conversations. For the next few days, whenever he appeared around the house, which was not often, it was with a scowl on his face. In fact, no one was allowed to talk at all. If he discovered any member of staff in conversation with another, they were threatened and abused.

He kicked the dogs. Then, on the third day, as if risen from the dead, collectively, the dogs bared their teeth, snarling with anger.

Was it a premonition? Even the walls, the curtains, the threadbare furniture from the nineteenth century, all seemed to oppress upon him, resent his presence, something which was new and surprising to him, since his family, his antecedents were responsible for their very existence. His response was to find ugliness in every wall, every brick. Why should it creepily want to take on an independence of its own? He was losing control of an environment which was absolutely his to control. Even his body was in revolt. Ever since that train journey, both in the police cell and now at home - was it home anymore? - he'd had the shits. He blamed the blood that had been spat at him, some even entering his mouth, slipping between his lips. It had seemed like abuse. On one occasion, loosening his trousers in desperation before arriving at the toilet, he had uncontrollably shat up the wall going up the stairs. Rather than clean up the disaster himself, he had blamed the dogs and left the staff to it, smirking psychotically to himself.

*   *   *

It was him! He was persuaded. It was him on the train, the one at Amnesty International. It must have been him! Of course, he couldn't talk about it with anyone for fear of being implicated in the Amnesty débâcle. Was he just being paranoid? After all, they all look the same to him those fucking black bastards. He tried to find YouTube videos of the event, photographs, but he couldn't find any, they all seemed to have disappeared, if they'd ever existed. In any case, what harm could some primitive nigger tribal bring to him, Lord Mercantor, Earl of Bone. The audacity of sitting opposite him on the train, the atrocious insult of spitting blood in his face, and who was that dangerous rabble he had had with him? It was impossible to imagine that some illiterate tribal would be capable of such organisation. Better forget that Amnesty issue and not allow absurd paranoia to infect his usual mental acumen.

*   *   *

Chapter 7

The Party

"Le secret des grandes fortunes sans cause apparente est un crime oublié, parce qu'il a été proprement fait."[81]

I was standing outside the front entrance to Utrecht Hall with Jolanta. Either side were curved stone stairs leading to a large balustraded balcony, which served as the stylobate for six, hexastyle, fluted columns, the capitals of which were in the sculpted leaved Corinthian style. Each was standing on its own plinth. Above the columns and resting upon them was a large pediment which held its own frieze of neo-classical Romanesque Gods.

"Difficult to work out exactly what Balzac was saying," said Jolanta. " The great crime against humanity, which was slavery, was capitalised upon to the greatest possible extent by the nobles and entrepreneurs amongst the English with their slave drivers using the most appalling cruelty, but yet this, built entirely on the back of that misery can stand, be admired and counted as one of the great monuments of British culture. It is that transformation which causes the crime to be forgotten. The notion of 'proprement fait', cleanly done, what does that mean? Did the fact that civilisations had made it law and practised it for millennia make it acceptable? In a way, one exploitation legitimised the next. The enslavement of the English peasants, pushing them off their land to live in degradation and misery as wage slaves, all of that was 'legal', made 'legal' by an avaricious establishment which wielded power. Each crime legitimising the next, culminating in the worship and admiration of this tower of cruelty. Oh, the wonderful architects! Oh, the wonderful landscape artists, the interior designers, the furniture makers!"

"Tonight, the walls will bleed," I responded with a grin, putting my arm around Jolanta's shoulders. The Cotswold limestone glowed a warm honey yellow in the morning sun, innocent of its participation.

---

81   Balzac, from Le Père Goriot: "The secret of great fortunes without apparent cause is a forgotten crime, because it was properly done."

"How far we have come since I walked along the banks of the Kibish, and in ancient memory, before all recorded time, the Nile itself, Jolanta!" I exhaled. "One thing I have learned, Jolanta, with words, with languages, my Suri, my French, my English, I name something, and it becomes itself. I name Wóhólò Tagí and he becomes Wóhólò Tagí, I name him Suri and he becomes Suri. Here now, when I look at my world, I designate things as they are and as they become, named in every possible way, painted into my vision. All the names in all of time, through the history of all things, all are in me in a present I cannot begin to describe.

"The word is 'ineffable', the history of all things, in an ineffable present."

"Ineffable. The history of all things, in an ineffable present." I repeated quietly, contemplatively. "I feel them in me, those ghosts and gods . . . and in you and the sisters, and in my Wóhólò Tagí and . . ."

"I know! I know! It is your big heart, my Prince." said Jolanta, openly showing her affection. "I was hard on you when we first found you and your journey has been long, but . . ."

"It's the vastness, the sum of every event, the vastness of things! We can only play our part, I guess, act out our portion of fate, our foolishnesses, loves and pointless self-justifications. Tonight, will be the return of all things, Beyahola, Akobo, Dibdib, Knossos, the drama, the play of all of history, alive again."

"Fear him not, for Mercantor, there is only venality, avarice, megalomania - his own obsessive madnesses. You and he are not the same. His moment in time will never come."

Jolanta looked deep and hard into my eyes and in her inner silence was naming me, Maha Atma, Great Soul. In her eyes, I could see reflected the same flames around me that I had seen surrounding Wóhólò Tagí, all the ghosts of the past and all the willing spirits of the children here with us now.

Jolanta had been explaining her contempt for Mercantor's fortune, when Jackson arrived in shorts and T-shirt, clear lines of sweat running through the dust in the furrows of his forehead, leaving distinct black lines against the fine, yellow powder.

"Nyàbà Bulí, what have you been doing?"

"The children want to perform this evening along with everyone else," he said.

"Yes, they should. It's their party also."

"So, they have been practising."

"And you have been taking care of them." I smiled at his predicament.

"Yeh. And they all want challanya beads to each make a derre[82] belt." he looked up to catch my eyes.

I lifted my hand to his forehead to almost absent-mindedly finger the dust that had coagulated at his hairline. He smiled at my distraction.

"I need a bath and to get changed for this evening." he said.

"Don't worry, we can take a bath together at the river later. I'll come with you, Nyàbà Bulí. I want to paint them myself, the little ones." I turned to Jolanta. "Jolanta, where can we find beads?"

"Ask Amanisha. No, wait." She took out her mobile to call Amanishakhete.

Although she was in fact the event organiser, she'd already surrendered any sense of directing the succession of tableaux planned. They had become self-organising in the hearts of all, including and especially now, the little ones.

" Amani has costumes for them," said Jolanta, "simple wrap-around skirts for both boys and girls, and cloth bands for the girls around their breasts."

"A lot of them want to dance naked," said Nyàbà Bulí, "which is what they have been used to anyway."

Jolanta rolled her eyes as if giving up.

"I'll talk to them, Jolanta," I insisted, "Don't worry."

---

[82] beads

"Amani will meet you at the field," she added. "She wants to help paint them and with the challanya and derre beads she intends to conjure up powers through little rituals and charms to give them confidence and strength. You know what she is like."

"I know! She saved me, remember? And you also, Jolanta. And I really don't know how. If she wants to do this? . . . good! Both the challanya and the paint will give the children those special powers she is seeking."

"Sometimes, Chár, I just don't understand her at all." said Jolanta.

"But I do," Nyaba Buli found himself saying, "and I think the children do, Jolanta. They can sense the Queen of Queen Mothers' powers, "she was right when she went looking for, Chár, the Black One, as she calls him, remembering him from her past!"

*　　　*　　　*

Jolanta, Nyaba Buli and I walked through the large double doors into the Great Hall, already set with large tables, joined in a U shape, and decorated with candelabra and flowers. At one end of the Hall was a grandiose double spiralled white marble staircase, precisely a copy of the Staircase designed by . . . .

"Da Vinci in the Château de Chambord, built by François Premier as a hunting lodge," I explained, knowledgeably. "I visited it with Nathalie. Then, on the roof, he had built small sidewalks, small paths, window to window, balcony to balcony, so that all the nobility, with the king, could visit their secret lovers, boyfriends and girlfriends during the night." He laughed. "How many of these nobles, billionaires, and kiss-arses will be chasing each other from bedroom to bedroom tonight?"

On the other three walls were small plinths with the busts of different heads of the family made to look like imperial Roman Emperors with laurel crowns and bare necks of toga-ed nobility. Above was a gallery, which the Da Vinci staircase joined, supported by scrolled, black marble corbels. Around the gallery were perhaps a dozen doors each framed by Doric columns supporting a heavy pediment. The doors themselves of dark red mahogany with brass door handles and hinges. All this glory had to be regularly polished by hand by labour of insignificant, unnoticeable, and contemptible existence. The tedium of the white marble floor was broken by the insertion of smaller black tiles providing decorative relief. From the gallery level were more stairs going to a second floor of similar design with gallery and doors on all walls. Above that again, by smaller stairs, was access to a glass pyramid to allow in light to the Great Hall, and for guests to be able to look out over the entire vast estate, with its avenues of limes and oaks. Nearer to the house in laid out lawns and gardens were several ancient cedars of Lebanon, spreading out their huge branches like gigantic green hands, providing beautiful shade for the ladies and children of the house as they wiled away summer afternoons gossiping and attempting to distract the children. Between these cedars and the river, what sins, deviances and secret rendez-vous had occurred to preoccupy the unemployed bodies, minds and passions of the delicate Mercantor progeny, wives, daughters and their wicked sons when they were not away being beaten, abused and masturbating in the dorms of Eton College?

Through further double doors, opposite to where they had entered was another large room, the parlour, entirely furnished and decorated by Thomas Kemp, the original Georgian interior decorator, replete with sofas, tables and upright armchairs with arms and legs curved and sculpted in the wood of "des arbres fruitiers"[83], rosewood, cherry, pear, walnut, to imitate the scrolls of Roman architecture, with the clawed feet of exotic cats of the expanding empire. Above the room was a huge dome, designed and decorated, again by Thomas Kemp. The scene within the dome, painted in the typically garish colours that Kemp preferred to use in all his interiors, was of a blue sky background with cotton wool clouds, as if he had never looked at clouds himself. At the centre, was the first Earl of Bone, dressed as Jupiter, enthroned, holding his thunderbolt in one hand, a royal orb in the other, usurping the position of the new unloved Hanoverian kings, and flanked by an eagle and a lion. Beneath his feet, ranked in descending status, were, wives, and children. It was a gross representation of generational tyrannical power, privilege, and over-arching egotistical self-flattery.

"We'll paint over it," said Jolanta, noticing Jackson's horror as he looked up.

"Can you do that?" he asked knowing this ugly ceiling was no doubt considered a national treasure.

"When the house is ours, we will. And you will help," Jolanta laughed.

---

[83] Fruit trees

"They have plans, the sisters. Don't worry!" I whispered with a smile, putting an arm around Nyaba Buli's shoulders.

The other side of the Parlour were glass-panelled doors opening out onto a terrace with steps leading down to the lawns. Nyaba Buli and I crossed the lawns and the field of cattle and wandered down to the river where the children were waiting.

He was quiet, pensive. We walked in silence through the strong green spring grass, speckled and decorated with meadow flowers, the blue forget-me-nots reaching up to kiss the sky. we were both barefoot. I reached out to hold his hand.

After a short while walking together, he asked:-

"So, er, after tonight, what happens?"

"What do you mean?"

"Well, you are going back to France, aren't you?"

"Yes."

"And er, me? I go back to being Jackson, eh?"

"No-oh! Never!" I said with a frown. "Why do you say that?"

"Because . . . I won't see you." It was very difficult for him to express such feelings, I could see. He was nearly choking on his words. "You are like a brother for me. I am happy now . . . before . . . "

" Hey! Hey! Hey! You will never leave me! I will always be with you! My Suri people have never left me. My leopards have never left me! You will come to France sometimes. I will come to England. The sisters have plans for you, I have said. They are not going to let you go. Besides, you have work with them now. They need your help with their business. They are going to send you to university. They have a place for you already, this Autumn."

"I can't do that! I have no money! It's too expensive! My mother wanted that before she died, but . . . . ."

"Look, Nyàbà Bulí nanu, we are not the same as those poor English slaves and their masters. We do not measure, count the cost. We do not think about debt and blame. Our spirit is generous. Since you are with the sisters, have you ever thought about money?"

"No."

"Don't worry. They have everything arranged."

The flowers of the meadow parted. We continued towards the river, making out Amanishakhete, Lihua and the family of children looking towards us, waiting. Nyaba Buli turned his face towards me to look at and take in the profile of his friend as if printing it to his memory. I turned towards him smiling.

"Are you ready for the dance?" I asked.

He just smiled and leaned his head on my shoulder.

*　　　*　　　*

"There's a lot of them now, aren't there, the children?" Nyaba Buli commented, puzzled. "where do they come from? When I first arrived at the cabbage harvest there were only about six or eight, But now there's almost thirty!"

"It's Amanishakhete, Queen of Mothers, and Lihua, who just loves every child she meets. They've been collecting them."

"What do you mean, collecting them?" he exclaimed, astonished.

"I don't know! You'll have to ask them! It's their latest project."

All the little ones quickly lined up in two queues, pressing their little bodies up against each other.

Some wanted to join in and help paint each other, especially the older ones, but the little ones wanted either Nyaba Buli or I to paint their bodies for them, standing silent and patient as prints from leaves, stencils, different grasses or just fingers were used to apply mostly yellow or white, sometimes ochre paste from stones and soils along the river bed. A little four-year-old watched Nyaba Buli's face and eyes as he carefully painted swirls and curls and tiny birds on his chest and belly, finishing with a quick brush of white down his little penis. Jackson looked up and grinned, while the little boy smiled back with his pretty doe eyes and skipped away to compare with others their painted nakedness, now made invisible in the long grasses.

"Does he speak?" he wondered. "I was asking his name, but he said nothing."

"No, he hasn't spoken yet. Auntie Amanish says he can understand some Arabic. But I don't know."

"So, no one knows anything about him?" said Nyàbà Bulí.

"No. No one knows."

"Poor little one!"

"He came with Oncle Robert, Wóhólò Tagì's father."

"They are here?"

"Yeh, they flew from Paris to an airfield near here yesterday evening."

*   *   *

I explained to Jackson Nyaba Buli I had wanted Rémi to take Juliette back home to Nathalie. This several days before the evening of the party. Robert also needed Rémi's help in navigating his plane to the small airfield Rémi had found for him near Utrecht House.

"If you try to send me back to France, now that we have found you . . ." initially Juliette had been very angry. We were all congregated at 113 Bishop's Gate.

"This is not the place for you, Juliette. You have seen Mercantor, how dangerous he is." Chár hesitated and then wondered, "We?"

"You talk as if he doesn't exist!" she scalded, pointing to her belly. "You think he wants to leave now that he has found you, and that for the first time?"

I sat down, knocked over by Juliette's anger. An anger I had never seen before. I was silent.

"You think he doesn't know what is happening now? You think he doesn't have feelings, wants?" Juliette paused. "Do you remember the day he was conceived?"

There was a long silence. Of course, I couldn't. I was now sitting with head in hands.

"Ever since then, he has not known you."

I got up, distraught, and went to the bathroom to wash the pain from my face. I was silent as I left and the little group of Lihua, Amani, Rémi and Juliette stood in silence also.

Kevin was amazed at how the house had suddenly been invaded by these exotic people talking about a baby not yet born listening to conversations, people flying back and forth to Paris. They'd even got him a costume for this party they were organising; he was going to be a pirate, and afterwards, they were going to get his teeth fixed, so they said.

"What have you done to him?" said Rémi, finally. "Already he has the world on his shoulders! It's easy to think he is so strong, his hunting, protecting others . . . he is my brother, more than . . . I hate to see his pain . . . maybe you don't know it, but my Chár, his heart is far more sensitive than anyone else I know. You have wounded him, Juliette!"

"I am NOT going back to France!"

"He just wanted to protect you and the baby."

"Stop, Rémi!" Lihua reprimanded.

With a look of fierce determination on her face, Juliette opened the bathroom door, entered, and closed it behind her.

Followed by Juliette, Chár finally emerged; it was Lihua who spoke: "We have decided, Chár, darling . . ."

Wóhólò Tagí immediately stepped forward and put his arms around me, his beautiful brother, kissing my wet eyes.

"We three," continued Lihua, "Rémi, Amani, and I will go to Paris. I want Rémi to show me how beautiful it is, take me to all the best places. They say, in Springtime . . ."

"We have business in Calais," said Auntie Amani. "I have spoken with Robert, your father, Remi. You both are going to help us."

"And Jolanta wants me here," said Juliette.

"So, that is decided," insisted Lihua. "Not you, this time, but we three, my darling. We are big people also! Juliette and the little one, waiting to join the world, they will take care of you!"

I breathed out a deep sigh as the self-imposed burden of caring for everyone was reversed and I could briefly sink into the loving arms of Juliette and all my friends.

*   *   *

"They have friends," I continued explaining to Nyaba Buli, "especially Auntie Amani, in the Red Cross in Calais and Dunkerque. They met up with Wóhólò Tagí's father who brought quite a few here himself from the camps, children that is."

Jackson was puzzled.

"But twenty or thirty small children is too many, isn't it? I mean, you can't really hide that many small children. The chatter for a start . . "

"Lihua reckons the rest they dressed them all in school uniforms, got on the TGV to St Pancras and just walked through immigration."

"What!?" Jackson Nyaba burst out laughing.

"Lihua is good at telling stories, anyway. But there is one thing you must remember, Lihua would do anything to have children of her own, as many as possible. Ask her and Auntie Amanisha yourself! Look, different people do different things. These children, I didn't bring them here; not everything happens because of me. And they are witches, after all!" I laughed.

"You don't believe that, do you?"

I couldn't help laughing, this time at Nyaba's consternation.

"Yeh, why not? There is no doubt, they have special powers. They just do. Most women do. After all, they are the origin of the world. Ask the little children about them being witches; they all know. Besides, I think Jolanta's Deputy Commissioner went with them in case there was a problem with border control. He knows officers there." I tried to explain as I greeted the next little child with a smile and started to put leaf prints on her belly, asking another child to fetch flowers for her hair.

"I met him, remember? When we were playing games with that ex-secret-service agent. Nice guy for a copper. I liked him. Liked joking and fooling around. He really loves Jolanta. Couldn't stop talking about her."

"They just love taking care of children! Anyway, you're going to be looking after them all soon , so . . er . . . "

Seeing the flowers decorating one little head then all the children were clamouring for flowers in their hair.

"Are you ready? This evening, it's up to you. The cattle love you, the children love you and Lihua has some medicine for you, to help you fly."

Jackson looked at me.

"Here. Lie down next to me. I want to show you something."

We both lay down in the long grasses. Some of the smaller children joined us.

"Look. See. Towards where the sun is starting to touch the trees. You can see? In the light? Tiny white, very, very small, little flies, hovering in the light. You see?"

"Yeh. I can see."

The children were looking also. Ah, yes! They also could see.

"They are . . .," Chár hesitated momentarily with his explanation, "they are angels! We don't know how long they live. Maybe one day. Maybe a few days. Their lives are fleeting. Nature's angels!"

Nyaba Buli wondered if he was catching up with events or being carried along. Things didn't make sense anymore. The world had changed. The way things had become, it was like a super-sense, a beyond sense. Would he really fly tonight, like nature's angels?

*   *   *

"Every night and every morn, some to misery are born. Every morn and every night, some are born to sweet delight. Some are born to sweet delight."[84]

The first time Chár read Auguries of Innocence to him, Nyàbà Bulí was unaware of Blake's spiritual and political opposition to the outrageous, gaudy avarice of the pompous, over-privileged presumptives of power; land-grabbing, financial greed and self-righteous exploitation of all peoples and properties of the world - like the Mercantors, their utter arrogance, lavishly extolled by Zoffany in that awful family portrait.

Becoming William Blake! The more Nyàbà Bulí read, the more he felt the spirit of William Blake seep into the cells of his body, his will, his passion. Maybe not himself becoming a poet, but perhaps this evening he could dance his own poetry. All these becomings! He had spoken to Wóhólò Tagí about the difficulty of Blake's mythology.

"Just take what you can," Rémi had said, "the rest will slowly follow as you read again and more. What you choose as important or beautiful will stay with you."

"Bull dancer becomings!" he recounted to himself. "Becoming Pan! Chár becoming Dionysus! The becomings of leopards. Chár must have been right: you have to reclaim history, make it your own, reclaim mythologies, live them, become them. Becoming Nyàbà Bulí, becoming Pan, becoming Suri!" He realised he was slipping into a special madness and laughed almost tearfully to himself.

He watched and as the painted children began to move the cattle across the field towards the house, themselves still hidden by the long grasses, so

---

84   William Blake, Auguries of Innocence.

the elite guests, billionaires, politicians, art critics and collectors, appeared descending the balcony of the parlour of Utrecht House to cross the lawns and enjoy the spectacle, dressed as invited, nay instructed by the event organisers, Jolanta, Amanishakhete and Lihua, according to the period of the first Earl of Bone. A type of Bal Masqué in which putting on the costumes of the first Mercantors, the Youngs, the Defoes, the Chathams, bowing, curtseying, fluttering their handkerchiefs and fans and adopting the pretentious poses of classical sculptures, they actually discovered their own true nature, becoming their entitled selves. It was time for Jackson Nyaba Buli to put on his costume.

As the delight and excitement abated at encountering acquaintances, monetary allies and exclusive groups of old associates, all dressed and decorated as if part of a theatre troupe or a circus of the lascivious absurd, the anticipatory breathing and eager sparkling eyes turned towards the field where a number of cattle had been herded together.

"Are there people on the backs of those cows?"

"What are they doing?"

"Are they children?"

"They're skipping across them! Oh, look a cartwheel!"

"They're dancing on them! Doing acrobatics on their backs!"

"Come on! Let's go closer!"

"Isn't it dangerous?"

"Oh, stop being silly!"

A group of eight or ten women, encouraged by their own and each other's bravado, marched forward, picking up their petticoats from under the full length flowing silk mantuas hanging from their shoulders, laced at the waist, billowing out behind them and delicately decorated with floral embroidery, birds, elephants the intricate famous mango pattern, original designs from Kanchipuram, and woven with the gold thread of empires.

"Jennifer, I forbid you! Come back!"

But by now, Jennifer and most of the invited were on their way across the lawns, even the reluctant, cautious husbands, like the latter-day Stuarts and early Georgians, swept up by the enticing winds of the exotic extra-indigene[85].

As they entered the first field of uncut meadow, small painted children began to appear from the ground around them to take hold of their skirts, coattails, or fingers to encourage and lead them further forward. Confused and charmed, the guests could not make out whether these children were partially clothed in skimpy underwear, or their little bodies simply disguised, appearing and disappearing amongst a confusion of long grasses and yellow, white and green paints, the faeric innocents leading the gaudy, momentarily guileless corrupt.

The small painted children, unnoticeably, had quietly disappeared into the grasses from whence they had arisen. There was a moment of uncertainty, hesitation. The acrobats and older cattle dancers froze staring back at the crowd of onlookers when suddenly from behind the herd of painted cattle, a clash of cymbals and trumpets announced a dislocation of mood and two satyrs leapt out between earth and sky, masked with wild eyes of desire and a grimace of erotic madness. Naked cream torsos and shaggy silvery white goat's wool leggings barely hiding genitalia, their howling cries of lustful passion, gesturing sexual innuendo and insult brought the mesmerised guests to a shrieking halt.

The satyrs turned their backs, bent forward, sticking their backsides out towards the onlookers and quickly pulled down their leggings to reveal their naked arses. Jennifer, who was the furthest forward of the crowd of guests, had indelibly and vividly printed in her memory, which, for years to come, she would often turn to quite deliberately to savour and make her heart skip, a pair of black muscular buttocks, which parted sufficiently for her to clearly see the slightly open short dark cleft of a black anus surrounded by a slight halo of tight black pubic curls.

She had never seen an anus before. She had never seen Richard's, her husband's. She would never be able to invite him to show her, either. Besides, would it be as beautiful as what she had just seen, except white, or would it be the brownish colour of nipples and scrotums? Then she

---

85   Extra-indigene. Using the French indigene meaning native or indigenous, with the suffix extra, i.e. exogenous.

worried about the buttocks. Were they white, pink, spotty, hairy or what, compared to the smooth black cheeks she had just seen? All of these thoughts had flooded through her brain cells within seconds of the event, and as if a sudden inundation had drowned out all sanity, she fell backwards into an ecstatic swoon.

At that same time, by snorting a fat line and expelling a short laugh at the absurd circus at the end of the lawns, James Mercantor attempted to obliterate from his thoughts the anxiety that his nemesis, the black avenging angel, the Suri devil, was invisibly present, disguised, hiding amongst the staff, the entertainment and guests.

Again, at that same moment, Nyaba Buli, ran up a ramp and leapt into the air above the herd of cattle. In his various transitions, his becomings, he had reached the perfect All, Παν[86], Pan, whose multiples flew into the air and hovered miraculously as Nijinsky's faun[87]; in white and black piebald ballet tights, dipping down at the waist to sit tightly on his suprapubic bone, under the distinctly sculpted abdominal muscles of his naked torso, now paler than his bleached jettas[88], painted with a yellow ochre paste, which, drying, cracked like the scorched bed of a dead lake and revealed the incalculable depth of his blackness, Pan Nyàbà Bulí. Behind him other fauns shot into the air, their shaggy goat's wool leggings twisting in the breeze, torsos painted variously, red, white, blue and green, bright fireworks exploding into the sky.

"As I reached my zenith, left leg bent at the knee, and foot against the inside right thigh, my hands reached across my chest to tear away the ochre paste, revealing my black, true nature. A gasp of astonishment went up from the transfixed crowd, as if I might be flaying myself. I hovered above the cattle and the crowd and watched as, from out of the undergrowth, reappeared the smaller children, this time armed each with a Suri ber[89] and, threateningly, brandishing them and shouting, started to herd the awestruck guests back towards the house, dazed by what they had seen!"

---

86 Παν translated means 'All'. It is also the name of the Greek demi-god. Pan is the god of the wild, shepherds and flocks, nature of mountain wilds, rustic music and impromptus, and companion of the nymphs. He has the hindquarters, legs, and horns of a goat, in the same manner as a faun or satyr. With his homeland in rustic Arcadia, he is also recognized as the god of fields, groves, wooded glens and often affiliated with sex; because of this, Pan is connected to fertility and the season of spring. The word panic ultimately derives from the god's name. (Wikipedia)
87 in L'Après-Midi d'un Faune by Debussy, costume designed by Bakst
88 matted dreadlocks, jettas being the Hindu term
89 spear

Nyàbà Bulí landed gracefully with the other satyrs, and ran at the spellbound, mesmerized crowd, herding or ushering them towards the terrace.

As they entered the Parlour through the terrace doors, they were met by Jolanta and Amanishakhete's elegantly trained household staff. For the usual function of Utrecht House, there was a limited number of resident staff and in any case, the management from Red Windmill Events had insisted they be given several days off and sent to the south coast to St Ives for a weekend of pleasure therapy, enjoying foods, entertainment and fresh sea air, which they would never consider pursuing on statutory leave. It was over a line of coke and reassurance that Jolanta had persuaded Sir James of his ownership of this original and personal notion of compassion and generosity towards his servants. He felt good, he felt . . . kind!

Each footman, formally waiting for the guests, was accompanied by a small houseboy, all dressed in identical livery of blue topcoat, carefully folded back to reveal white lining, the folds held in place by gold braid and brass buttons. Underneath this, they wore a long white waistcoat, white shirt with frilled cuffs and high collar, bound by a white bowed cravat. Beneath the waistcoat were white breeches, buckled just below the knee, white stockings and black patent, brass buckled shoes with a fashionable square heel of about 3 centimetres although at the time of the first Earl of Bone, one inch heels, and, of course, powdered short wig with short tail at the back tied with a ribbon of black velvet. The traditional livery since the title Lord Mercantor, Earl of Bone, Marquess of Bart was conferred on the first Lord by Queen Anne. From amongst the servants, since the beginning of the time of nobility, only the groom was expected to have a full historical understanding of these titles. As far as the temporary footmen and houseboys were concerned all these weird titles were meaningless. For Mercantor himself, from when he was of the age of the houseboys, they had always meant entitlement.

The footmen and houseboys lined up either side of the terrace doors with Mercantor comfortable enough to formally welcome his guests. Most had been arriving at different times, shown to their rooms, if they were staying overnight, to change into their late Stuart, early Georgian costumes, everyone becoming dramatis personae within their own drama. Others were being accommodated locally and, when prepared, all were encouraged to enjoy the grounds and gardens and encounter the other guests until the formal event began.

The tedium of formality was completely erased by the general excitement of the guests. Mercantor, who was as high as a kite, felt increasingly flattered as guest after guest praised him for the entertainment in the fields.

"Great acrobatics! And so young!"

"Where did you find these circus people?"

"Loved the spectacular presentation of Greek myth, James! Minos, the Palace at Knossos, those wall paintings! Theseus and all that! Wonderful aesthetics!" said the curator of the National.

James just smiled to himself and turned to nod in acknowledgement to Jolanta, who was at his side. He was feeling euphoric, blessed, beatific even.

"Let me introduce you to Jolanta, who organised all of this, should I?"

And Jolanta took the elderly gentleman by the arm and led him in amongst the other guests to enjoy caviar and champagne.

"I'm not so keen on blinis, are you?" said the curator.

"I know what you mean, a snotty version of American pancakes." Jolanta smiled.

"Yah, I prefer simple crispy tostes[90] rather than that flaccid limp thing. The caviar is outstanding, though, isn't it? I am guessing it's Persian."

"I'm sure you are right, sir."

The footmen led guests and partners to groups of neo-classical armchairs, uprights and low tables where large crystal bowls of caviar and porcelain plates, small bowls of sour cream awaited as the houseboys assisted everyone with service and the footmen poured champagne. The general hubbub of near hysteria became more subdued, giving way to the laughter of the second glass of Champagne. Some started to move to the furthest end of the parlour where the Zoffany family portrait was

---

90   French for crisp toasted thin squares of bread.

stood for contemplation.

"That's quite deliberate, isn't it?"

"What . . . what do you mean?"

"The image of little William."

"Who's little William?"

"The black houseboy at the centre of the painting."

"Same livery as all the other servants. Why deliberate?"

"Zoffany has managed to paint the houseboy to look like any or every houseboy, tamed, civilised, almost not black. Either that or Mercantor has arranged for every houseboy to look like William, tamed, civilised, knowing their place."

The companion of the self-appointed critic, to resolve his sense of confusion, found himself looking furtively around the room at all the houseboys present.

"Really?" he finally questioned. "What am I supposed to believe?"

The critic looked down condescendingly at his companion, with a sardonic raised eyebrow and wobble of his head.

"Why are they all black?" wondered the companion.

"Who?"

"The houseboys! Surely, they weren't all black at the time of the first lord, were they?"

"How do you think Mercantor made his fortune?"

"Black houseboys?"

James Mercantor approached. The critic and his friend immediately changed the subject to inquire about family members portrayed in the gigantic masterpiece. Size matters when you wish to include the entire

221

subordinate household and a vista of the vast estate. Mercantor was aware of the change of subject noticing fleetingly their slightly awkward self-conscious questions.

The critic, someone unknown to Mercantor, pointedly looked at little William and then towards the houseboys busy in the room.

"A lot of blecks, James, a lot of blecks!"

"Yah!" retorted Mercantor. "Once we've sold the painting, we'll be auctioning them off also." The others held his serious gaze, shocked into an uncomfortable uncertainty of incredulity. A few tense seconds passed before he burst into loud guffaws of laughter. "So make your choices now! You are staying the night, aren't you?"

*   *   *

As guests were ushered into the Great Hall, evening arrived, light began to fade, and more young servants arrived with candelabra for each table. The directors of Red Windmill Events had been quite insistent about creating an authentic experience of a Georgian party. Electricity supply was cut, mobile phones collected from the guests as they arrived; this was frustrating for some, but another source of excitation, trepidation and expectation for the majority. Amanishakhete and Jolanta had even discovered, with the help of household servants, four original gigantic crystal Chandeliers which had hung from the ceiling of the Great Hall but had been packed away years ago. These were carefully reassembled and hoisted, hanging from the original heavy hooks set in the sculpted ceiling. Further standing chandeliers were distributed here and there.

I was sitting in the shadows, head in hands, behind the balustrade, as if hiding, time slipping backwards, my anger, my hatred for Mercantor, which I felt under the surface of my skin, a cold and sinister curdling of thought, it was as if I no longer knew myself. This was not the me, Chár, I knew and loved. I struggled to see the point to this bitterness. For the sisters, would it be sufficient to expose him? Would it be sufficient enough for me, Chár, to expose him? I knew enough about this world to also know I couldn't kill him, or would I, even though it might, that brief ecstatic moment of vengeful justice, give me some satisfaction? I could easily have killed him on that train journey for his casual belief in his right to abuse, insult, demean my Juliette and unborn child. Too often I could hear the voices of the living dead, the cries of babies, the screams . . .

"The play's the thing!" declared the three sisters, appearing from between the dark shadows of a disappearing twilight and the gloom of his thoughts. "Already James Mercantor, cursed be that name, is persecuted, pursued through the darkest hours of the night by his Furies[91], golden, red and yellow, tearing through the blackness of despair to rip and consume what was never any true equanimity of the soul. His fate will be in his own hands. With the Scottish lord we only ever told him the truth, his own greed, his lust, was his downfall. He who wants to stand above the choeur, the chorus, the song of humanity, curses himself, signs his own death warrant, his own condemnation. Look at Caesar, Napoleon, think of Jesus. Tragedy is the nature of their fate. But we are not that. We are beyond that stasis, that dried and cracked clay, we are of the air, at the heart of humanity. Why do we choose you, Chár? You are both the first and the last, for Juliette too, our little God, our Bacchus/Dionysus. Wóhólò Tagí loves you. For Nyàbà Bulí, you are his hero. The children, our children, all follow you, they all listen to you. You have taken history, stolen from us poor mortals by great powers and co-opted into their service, you have taken it back to make it your own. Your nobility is immanent to your presence, while Mercantor's slavishness seeps from his skin; the immediate stench of generations of avarice and cruelty miraculously painted onto the Zoffany canvas! But we will make greater art, great intoxications, greater creations together tonight, dislocating the order of events, with our bodies and our actions. And all that has been taken away will be returned."

"Before you take the stage, to make the scene complete. . . . . "

"Here, take this yellow silk skirt, embroidered with Ariadne's golden thread[92]. Become the Avatar we all love."

The trees fell silent, the grasses hushed. No one spoke but Lihua who demanded I play a final game. Blindfolding me, they spun me three times.

---

[91] The Furies were female chthonic deities of vengeance in ancient Greek religion and mythology. A formulaic oath in the Iliad invokes them as "the Erinyes, that under earth take vengeance on men, whosoever hath sworn a false oath". The Erinyes task is to hear complaints brought by mortals against the insolence of the young to the aged, of children to parents, of hosts to guests, and of householders or city councils to suppliants—and to punish such crimes by hounding culprits relentlessly. Their victims die in torment.

[92] In the myth of Theseus and the minotaur, Ariadne, in love with Theseus, gives him a ball of golden thread which he uses to trace his way out of the labyrinth having killed the minotaur.

"We have a surprise for you, Chár! A special present! This is for that occasion when all things begin again!"

Lihua removed the blindfold and the three retreated as I slowly opened the barn door before me.

Leopards! When I first saw them and they looked back at me with their fearless eyes, that pure curiosity, free of any ugly sentiment, feelings of anger, violence, threat, I felt an overwhelming sense of having become myself. It was as if Dibdib had found me again and the whole history of what it was to become myself had brought me back to that moment in the jungle. All this time I had carried the spirit of my leopards with me. They had watched over me, guarded me, given me strength and assurance, and now here they were, no longer only part of my heart, my spirit, no longer spirit leopards but absolutely clear and distinct, here and now, present. It was as if they, too, immediately recognised me from their inalienable past, my leopard spirit, a shared common instinct of the innocent and perfect, invisible hunter.

They were lying in a nest of straw which they had discovered near some bales and clearly rearranged as they saw fit. As I opened the door, they lifted their heads to see who had arrived. I entered, closing the barn door behind me, and straight away they stood up and sauntered slowly towards me. I spontaneously pulled off my summer shorts and T-shirt, the will, the instinct to become animal, become jungle creature, be the Suri Chár I had been when the catastrophe had happened. The yellow one paused to smell my cast-off T-shirt, then looked back up at me. The other, the black, came straight over to me and started sniffing my legs, eventually lifting his head to sniff my genitals. I squatted down to sit on the barn floor; the two young leopards moved forward to embrace me, as I bent forward to whisper in their ears.

I slowly leaned back to stretch out on the straw next to them. Gradually they started to examine me, rubbing me with scent from their cheeks and eventually climbing on my chest with their front paws, to look down at me with an expression on their faces of laughter. I started quietly to laugh, in anticipation, with them.

*   *   *

Rémi, Charles, Claudine and Robert-Louis were dressed as all others, in

224

the attire of the early Georgians. Of the one hundred and eighty rooms in Utrecht House, approximately one hundred and twenty were devoted to accommodation, some as fairly extensive apartments with sitting room, often more than one bedroom, bathroom and facilities to accommodate through the centuries the often large extended family with brothers, sisters, cousins, aunts, uncles, and so on and so forth ad infinitum. There were always occasions when anyone of such enormous import would have visitors, colleagues, associates seeking advice, support, political or economic backing. This venal and ugly favouring was part of the self-flattering duty of the Lord.

Rémi skipped with delighted pleasure from the bedroom of his apartment within Utrecht House to the sitting room. He loved the huge, long wig of light brown and pale grey rolled horsehair curls he was trying on for the first time. The long silk waistcoat, intricately decorated with embroidered, small birds, elephants and peacocks, and the light green topcoat were equally beautiful and he enjoyed the white stockings, brass buckled shoes, and knee-length breeches, but it was the wig, framing his handsome face, that he appreciated the most, constantly stroking the lengthy pendulous front curls hanging over his shoulders.

"Where is he?" he asked with a frown.

The sisters faded back into the shadows from whence they had appeared and Rémi Wóhólò Tagí pressed against the barn door, arriving to help with body paint.

"Wow!" he whispered. "Where did you find your friends!"

"I don't know how it happened. Maybe the sisters found them in the forest! Who knows! Maybe the leopards just turned up, looking for me, following my scent!"

"What? Really?" Rémi laughed at both the idea of the audacious outrage of the sisters finding leopards and the alternative madness of leopards just turning up looking for me.

He knelt down next to me and the two youngsters.

"Don't worry. They have marked me already. I am one of them. They're still quite young, like teenagers really, full of fun. They'll not want to hurt you, nor anyone, so long as they feel no fear nor anger." I was smiling with contentment, feeling at last united with my magnificent and fearless namesakes. "They'll probably want to rub against you as well. Amani has left the paints we used for the children. I want you to paint leopards' paws on my chest and belly. I remember for the stick fight before my people were killed, I had wanted to paint myself into my name. Well, we can do that again now."

The young cats seemed fascinated by Rémi and what he was doing. One wanted to chew his wig and the other to steal his paintbrush.

"I think they like you. They must already know humans, don't you think?" I wondered.

"I think they already know you from Dibdib!"

The yellow one rolled on her back, inviting Rémi to stroke her belly.

"She wants to seduce you."

He ran his hand gently up her belly to her thorax. Straight away she used her paws, front and rear to grab his arm and lift it to her jaw.

"Don't pull away!"

"Non, non! Don't worry. I've been used to sleeping with a leopard for how long now? Two years? Three years? When have I ever pulled away?" He looked up at me and laughed. "Don't worry, my beautiful one! This evening, the best of future possible worlds is with us!"

Rémi could feel her teeth press into his arm, then suddenly she pushed it away, stood to her feet and rubbed her jaw around his face.

Ochre imprints of the four toes and pad of a big cat's paws with tiny lines left by the claws now decorated my belly and ribs.

I stood up, the cats on either side; Rémi leaned forward and wrapped the silk cloth around my waist.

"Who'll take care of these two after that entrance scene?" wondered Rémi.

"Nyàbà Bulí will be waiting."

"And now, look! It's time! Finally, the crowning moment!" announced Wóhólò Tagí, as he too faded into the shadows and the darkening seemed to fill with the green leaves of creepers and vines.

"My Chár! My baby! My lover!"

It was the voice of Juliette from behind me, her lips next to my ear, whispering, her hands and fingers sliding over my ribs and slowly down my abdomen, under the belt of the silk wrap to run her fingers through my pubic hair, her large pregnant belly pressing into the small of my back. My head rolled back onto her shoulder, my cheek next to hers and eyes closing.

"Juliette, what are you doing here? I thought you were helping Lihua with the little ones."

There was a kick from inside her womb into my lower dorsal muscles just above my buttocks.

"He wanted to be here," said Juliette, as the baby stretched and moved for space between us. "I see your leopards are happy to be next to you. The children told me all about them; you can't keep secrets from them for long. Some say the sisters got them from a zoo, others that they flew to Africa to find them, and the little ones claim they flew on broomsticks. Others say they just appeared from the forest, looking for you." She smiled. "Who is to deny them their worlds!?

"Now is the moment, as we create new worlds, we find our way to the heart of the monster and out of his labyrinth of cruelty. Are you ready my darling Chár, my leopard, my Dionysus. Your brow is furrowed!"

I breathed a heavy sigh: "Sometimes I feel like a stranger inside my own skin, as if the leopard that once died beneath my father's hand to become my cloak, adorning my shoulders, under my naked body as I slept, now prowls within me—not always tame, not always known. I watch myself move and speak, and the words that come are not always mine. The story shifts and folds beneath my flesh like rivers under stone. I am both the hunter tracking the truth and the prey caught in its snare. Am I the master of this tale we unfold? The lines I speak are no longer lines I compose. They are calls from shadows, from ancestors, from futures not yet born. If I lose myself to this becoming, will I discover the true voice beneath the silence? Or will I vanish, swallowed by the myth I helped create?"

"Maybe that is not the curse, but the gift," Juliette spoke, "to lose the self and find something more—something wild and eternal, beyond masters and slaves, limitless and free! Shake off that furrowed brow. I have painted you, Wóhólò Tagì made you, the children dreamt you, your leopards and ancient spirits will guide you. You are complete, embracing all!"

"You are right, Juliette! You and Rémi have always guided me so well! I am Chár! I am Leopard! Leopards have arrived to accompany me tonight. Every courtroom, with their lords and robes and wigs is nothing but fantastical theatre to sustain civilisation's vicious injustices. Our theatre is greater, the revelation of the historical cruelty of power and its collapse!"

She paused as she started to secure a crown of ivy on my head, inserting between the stems and leaves, bluebells, and anemones, white, blue and red.

"This drama we create of fantastical myth, history and revelation of Mercantor's venal cruelty, trust this theatre of justice to weave its own futures."

"We are all willing that outcome, however that flux within the spheres of multiplicity occur."

"You look beautiful, my darling." she said, "Time to go. Nyaba Bulí is waiting for your entrance."

*　　*　　*

"Of course, it's not worth a great deal," said the curator of the National Portrait Gallery to the other guests at the same table, "perhaps fifty thousand. With the board, this was the figure we decided would be the maximum I would bid."

"I quite agree," said the houseboy who was discreetly moving around the table filling everyone's glass with champagne, his youthful black face contrasting with the white horse-hair wig and white neckerchief around the high collar of his shirt. He was formally dressed in the livery of the

228

household, denoting his status as a servant. As the entire table understood, the most important quality of any servant was to remain invisible and not intrude in conversations. All were stunned into a frozen silence.

"The only painting of Zoffany's of any worth is the portrait of George III, which is in the royal collection." continued the houseboy, blithely ignoring the obvious offence that the curator and the rest of the guests at the table clearly felt.

"It's the informality of posture and its imitation of the posture of the politician, John Wilkes, in the Hogarth print that gives the Zoffany's George III its originality and value. The king becoming patriot, man of the people. Although it's hardly original if it's copying Hogarth, anyway."

The curator and a couple of his associates stood up and walked away, this being the only way they could avoid the clear lack of deference this black teenage servant was showing them.

Disguised as circus ringmaster, master of ceremonies, chief auctioneer, stroking the curls of his wig as they extended down over his shoulders (there was something wonderfully sensual about these pendulous curls, which made touching irresistible), Rémi Wóholò Tagì stood forward and cried out:-

"My Lord, James Mercantor, Earl of Bone, Marquess of Bart, Lords, Ladies, gentlemen, friends and guests, welcome to the House of Utrecht. We hope you have enjoyed your arrival and the introduction of the origins of drama from the chorus of nature and that you continue to enjoy our presentation of a history of the great house of Mercantor in the form of a series of tableaux. All are enjoined to participate. Assume the guise of characters and personages in this significant history. As our great poet and playwright insisted, we are all players, actors, strutting and fretting our hour upon the stage, our world, playing our part in the ever-unfolding drama of our lives. As you have seen, tonight we take you back to the classical origins of theatre and humanity's drama itself.

"Before the great God of imagination, dreams and intoxications opens the pursuit of our histories, we come to the auction of the Zoffany masterpiece and an announcement on behalf of our host, the establishment of his own charity for children, parentless, lost, without home or country, innocent victims of man's inhumanity to man. It has been determined by his lordship that desperate and lost children at our borders should suffer no longer! The final bid paid for the Zoffany portrait of the Mercantor family will be used to initiate his charity."

There was loud applause from the crowd of guests, such that James Mercantor was obliged to stand, acknowledge their praise with smiles and several short bows in all directions of the Great Hall.

"What's he talking about?" said Mercantor, looking puzzled and turning to Jolanta as he resumed his seat.

"The money from the sale of the painting would go to the charity you are intending to set up." replied Jolanta. "We spoke about it last night with Deputy Commissioner Henshaw and your solicitor, Herbert, Herbert Brunt. In fact, he had all the contracts drawn up for you to sign." Jolanta's expression of confusion and surprise that Mercantor had forgotten about this was enough to persuade him of its truth.

"Oh, yes, of course! Of course!" said Mercantor, with still no idea what Jolanta was talking about. All he remembered of last night was being excessively drunk and smoking a couple of lines of morphine.

"We all decided it would make a good impression in your bid for leadership of the party when the current PM resigns, if he ever manages to get his face out of his plate." She indicated with a nod in the direction of the PM who was slopping back mouthfuls of raw oysters. Mercantor turned, saw the PM, then turned back to Jolanta and snorted a short laugh of shared contempt. He had complete confidence in these three event organisers. His idea of a children's charity, if it had been his idea, he was persuaded it must have been, would hugely impress his support.

"Don't worry, James. We're looking after you now."

Typically, the bidding was slow to start. In spite of hoping to initiate bidding at thirty five thousand, our dear auctioneer had had to bring it down to twenty thousand. An agent from the Metropolitan started the bidding, followed by the curator of the National Portrait at twenty-five thousand. Mercantor felt slightly embarrassed, something from his family history being so cheapened. At the same time, he wondered if he knew the auctioneer from somewhere. Frustratingly, context can cheat and confuse memory far too easily, as he remembered had happened to that thug Ferrier, and where had he disappeared to?

The only person who had anything from the modern world was the auctioneer, since to maximise the sale, the auction was also happening via the internet. There was one bid from Ruanda for thirty thousand, another came from Nigeria and yet another from Sierra Leone.

"Ex-colonies and their leaders are just as interested in these paintings of slavery and black servitude as the colonisers, so it seems." remarked several of the guests to their company at table.

"So, who is in the painting?"

"The second Marquess or the third. Who the Mercantors were before being given titles and estates, no one knows. It's rumoured they came to England with the returning army of Henry VI."

"In the painting right centre is Mercantor, to his left his two elder sons, and at his feet two of his younger boys. On the other side, his wife, next to the wet nurse with the recently born and in front of the wife, two teenage daughters. Behind the family group are other cousins, aunts and uncles."

"And the little boy next to the wet nurse?"

"You mean the black boy in livery? I don't know. A servant."

At which point, the curator and his companion who had exhausted their knowledge of the painting noticed the knowledgeable houseboy who had spoken to them earlier.

"Let's see just how much he does know," said the curator, who had already abandoned bidding to anonymous parties on the internet and was expecting to embarrass the boy by revealing his ignorance.

"It is the second Marquess, sir, already in his late forties. And you were right about all his children."

The curator wondered if he was being patronised.

"The little black boy at the centre? A houseboy such as myself. William was his name. The name the family had given him. He was mute. Never spoke. Probably through trauma. Died in unfortunate circumstances shortly after the painting was completed. The story goes he was beaten by the head butler for an accident at a reception. The wounds became infected and he died of a fever seven days later. There was a headstone on his grave until recently when the Master had the servants' graveyard cleared."

"Good Lord! How do you know all this?"

"Well, I've always been interested in history, sir, especially represented in art, or literature. It gives me insight into different worlds."

The curator and his companion stood dumbfounded.

"Let me make you both a champagne cocktail. I'm particularly good at it, so people say."

As the young houseboy left the two critics with their champagne cocktails, unusually, in very wide Martini glasses, the curator turned to his friend and said:- "Do you believe him?"

"What do you mean?"

"Perhaps he's just inventing it. Maybe it's just . . . " he shrugged, "lies! Why should a black teenage servant know better about the history of a painting than the top art historian in the country?"

"Or be better able to lie about it?" added the companion, sardonically.

"Quite!" insisted the Curator with haughty indignation, not realising soon enough his companion's mockery. The champagne cocktail was making his facial muscles and fingers tingle.

The bidding was reaching its conclusion. Charles, who had been so angry that his son had found himself once again victim of the machinations of this atrocious English Lord, had insisted that he and Robert should attend this event to . . . he knew not what . . tuer le gros con (kill the fat cunt)! These two friends, with Claudine, were sharing a table with Amanishakhete and Lihua.

"I feel proud to be his parent!" he explained to the two women. "He has really become blood of my blood, flesh of my flesh. He has made me his father, Nathalie his mother. His manner with others is generous and kind. Anyone who wants to hurt him, we will destroy them, Robert and I." he added with a grin.

"Don't worry, Monsieur Charles, we have plans for this Mercantor," said Amanishakhete.

"I think his innocence and need, his dependence persuaded us to love him. In France, no doubt, he felt lost. In many ways, he was like a baby; he couldn't speak, he couldn't sleep alone at night. By the time he had crept into our bed between us in the middle of the night, it only took a couple of occasions, that was it! He would always be ours, our baby, our Chár. Of course, I am proud of him, proud to be his guardian, his parent, his father."

"Your love is profound, Monsieur Charles!" commented Amanishakhete.

"And me also, I am so happy he has become the best friend of my son, Rémi, who is no longer fearful and shy, but joyful." added Robert. "See, he is there at the front of this hall, conducting this auction, disguised in outrageous, Baroque fashion, stroking the curls of his wig! What are they up to, these two boys, this evening?!"

"The spell is cast!" said Amanishakete, with a laugh and a wicked smile that hid a secret.

""Yes!" rejoined Robert with his own gentle provocative observation. "Rémi mentioned with his enthusiasm and admiration of youth that you were . . . how should I say? . . . had magical powers."

"Robert, please!" Claudine reprimanded.

Lihua moved closer to Claudine and stroked her shoulder: "It is fine, Claudine. We love Rémi. And Robert is right. We women have special skills secret to us that silly men with their claim to reason, resent. You also, Claudine, I can see, have special magical skills. How else could you have produced such a beautiful son?"

"So, please tell us, Madame Amanishakhete, how did you come to find Chár and rescue him?" asked Charles.

"I am from Africa, Monsieur Charles, my country near to Chár's. I know some of his language, how he thinks." Amanishakhete paused wondering how much she could say to these people before they should think her mad. "Call it intuition if you wish, we found him in a hole, in the freezing rain, beaten by the storm. He had died. His heart had stopped. Jolanta refuses to believe me. But I know. He is a gift. A gift you share with us, Monsieur Charles." she smiled at Charles. Then her expression suddenly changed. "Mercantor will not stop. We have a special hatred of him, Jolanta, Lihua and I. Chár is a gift to us to end our anger, possessing every attribute, every quality to bring about the downfall of this ignoble lord. These are secrets I share with you!"

It was Claudine who first became aware that so many of the children helping out around the hall were staring at this little group of French visitors. She pointed it out to Robert and Charles. Finally, three of the very youngest just came to stand before them, staring.

"Why are the looking at us like that?"

I watched at a distance, concealed by an arras[93], which also hid the double helix stairs, our curtained backstage, as one of the older boys serving wine, hearing Claudine's concern, explained:

"You are the French people who rescued Chár. For all of us, you are very special, very important. Word has quickly got around, to everyone, who you are; secrets are impossible here. You are the real guests of the evening. You can see the little ones are in awe of you and what you did. All of us, we would do anything for you."

"Well, that has put me in my place," whispered Claudine, who had always expressed her resentment towards me and my friendship with Rémi Tagì. She glanced guiltily towards both Charles and Robert.

The bidding had reached forty-five thousand. The massed crowd of guests were losing interest. The politician from Ruanda had dropped out, and the land agent from Sierra Leone. The only bidding now was between an oil executive from Nigeria via the internet and the curator of the Stadel Museum and Gallery of Frankfurt, in fact, Zoffany's birthplace. Both bidders seemed reluctant to raise the bid by more than a thousand pounds at a time, but neither seemed ready to surrender. Servants were rushing around with plates of hors-d'oeuvres, caviar, more

[93] The term Shakespeare uses to refer to the convenient drapes, often tapestries, of the castle of Elsinore, behind which Polonius could conceal hmslef while spying on Hamlet.

champagne and some old bottles of Muscadet with more oysters for the Prime Minister.

"Fifty-five thousand!" Robert jumped to his feet.

The round face with thick glasses of the Stadel Museum's curator looked impatient, annoyed by this intrusion, and raised it to fifty-six. The Nigerian oil executive followed suit worried this newcomer was spoiling their game.

"Sixty thousand!"

"Stop it, Robert!" insisted Claudine. "I'll never be able to sell it on! And I certainly don't want it in Paris."

The Nigerian dropped out and the internet died. The Stadel's curator was now red in the face and sweating.

The Auctioneer was parading back and forth, waving and pointing with his Shillelagh[94]: "Am I offered sixty one? Sixty one, anyone? Sale at sixty, then. Sale at sixty!" The gavel hit the block to conclude the sale. "Come forward, sir, to collect your painting! And please introduce yourself."

The massed Georgian guests applauded.

"I am Robert-Louis Fontenay. Happily, I take possession of this painting, celebrating the power and wealth of the Mercantor family at its zenith. and wish to liberate our current Lord from its curse. I pay in cash!"

He waved a wad of notes, which he handed to the auctioneer. Producing a large pair of scissors from inside his topcoat, he paraded back and forth, with the scissors held high making sure everyone amongst the guests was watching and then stabbed the canvas to one side of the wet nurse and proceeded to cut out a central section of the painting which contained alone the wet nurse and the small houseboy, William.

Immediate screams ascended from the crowd of guests as the pointed blade of the scissors pierced the canvas. Gasps of shock went up at the desecration of this art object, the culturally sacred, illustrative of a historical moment of Britain, and British nobility as masters of wealth,

---

94 nobbled walking stick with a clubbed end.

power, empire, and peoples of the world. Even without its historical significance, in itself, as art for its own sake, it was the tearing of the temple curtain, the smashing of the altar, the rape of value in itself. The cursed veil of Mercantor's past and present history, everything that had made him what he was, was ripped apart.

"What are you doing?" screamed the curator from the Stadel. "Are you mad? If you didn't want the painting . . . "

He ran forward and tried to wrestle the scissors from Robert's hands. The crowd looked on with horror and excitement as the large blades waved and glinted in the light of the several hundred candles, the air stiffening with fine clouds of black candle soot.

Mercantor, who had just returned from sharing a couple of lines with the PM in one of the bathrooms and whose brain was sufficiently addled that all conventions of civilised conduct could be put to one side, was warmly reminded of the drunken brawls of his student days at Oxford and laughed to himself at these middle-aged men rolling and sliding around on the marble floor while the auctioneer ran around in circles hysterically flapping his arms up and down like a panicking chicken.

Eventually, four guests held them apart.

"You can have it!" shouted Robert. "I give it to you, the rest of the canvas. The only part I keep is with the black servants. In fact, I'll have an internal frame put around the hole. Let less than nothing, a pure negative, a pure absence, become art itself!"

All fell silent, while, what seemed like several minutes, but was only several seconds, they contemplated that idea. Could a frame around a hole be art? Could nothing, a big fat zero, be beautiful? Would a sheer absence, a negative quantity have value, as art? Would it have monetary value? Would it be possible to sell a framed nothing at a great price? Maybe it would be price-less? Such was their inebriated thinking of value as only money!

The auctioneer, no longer flapping hysterically was striding around the hall looking intently, demandingly, at the audience, crowd, guests, call that herd what you will since all meanings were starting to slip and slide drunkenly. As he paced around, he started to clap slowly at first. Some footmen and houseboys joined in. At the back of the hall, three men in outrageous wigs of dirty yellow, very pale pink, and a rich blue, stood up and joined in the applause. Slowly, slowly, more and more guests, stood up to applaud also. Taken aback, the Stadel curator turned to see the entire audience looking at him, awaiting his response. Hesitantly, he turned back towards the Frenchman and offered his hand. Robert stepped forward and held out a hand to the curator in a gesture of futile armistice. The masses all cheered!

Suddenly, loud trumpets cried out filling the golden air with their clear bright voices heralding the arrival of a great king, a god, a hero. Between crisp, distinct and certain phrases an awestruck silence now reigned, until the next loud blast imparting that realisation to the masses that it was they, who must wait. Satyrs burst through the balcony doors, running, and leaping around the room carrying large jugs of wine, which they used to fill everyone's glass at the same time carelessly spilling and slopping it over tables, chairs and floor. Two satyrs spread another large tapestry in the centre of the floor beneath the principal chandelier and between the two arms of the U-shaped arrangement of tables, indicating a change of scene.

"A small green bird who had flown in from Nepal," her voice announced. In brightly contrasting patterns of red, black, green, yellow and orange, her dress swarmed around her as Queen Amanishakhete stood up and approached the stage where earlier the Zoffany had been sold. She was shouting, almost screaming, above the dying trumpets and general hubbub of the hall. Five satyrs immediately surrounded her with flaming ancient torches, kneeling before her such that she was brightly lit from beneath her waist, appearing to float on the flames, her face contorted by long shadows seemed to twist and grimace as she spoke, her voice booming and echoing around the hall:

"A small green bird who had flown in from Nepal, along a cavernous gorge, twice the depth of the Grand Canyon, bringing news from the cries of the wind that the great Dreamer, through his intoxications of perfumes, leaves, flowers and roots, wanted once more to bring to the world for the delight of all great spirits, great souls, his will, made manifest in the bodies of children, great dramas of history. We three, the Sisters, the Witches," and immediately Lihua and Jolanta were lifted into the air by satyrs either side of them, hoisting them above their heads, this, accompanied by a long deep trumpeting of gigantic Tibetan horns, their deep green skirts billowing out behind them, giving the impression they were flying. Lowered next to Amanishakhete in the circle of torches, they spoke each, one after the other, while Maenads and Satyrs emptied the hall of standing candelabra and those on tables to focus attention and light on the three sisters.

"We come from many foreign lands, Queens of Orient, Africa and Asia. Such is our reputation amongst the many we meet."

"All the Maenads and Satyrs, the poor and dispossessed children of lost tribes, the children here tonight, confer on us great powers."

"Some say we can fly, others that we see the future and can change the past, others again that through our potions and secret brews we can offer dreams, hallucinations, revelations!"

"Barely realising, they are painting their world when they paint us thus."

"And through the power of their willing, their art, they offer you this mighty night's truths!"

More trumpeting as the satyrs disappeared and through the balcony doors appeared, bathed in the rich hues of light from a thousand candles, the god-prince of ancient myth, flanked on either side by two leopards, one black and one yellow with her leopard spots. A shout goes up from the darkness:- "Mahadeva Lingaraja Chár Dionysus Shivaji![95]". The witches returned to their seats. The crowd fell into the sort of silence invoked by fear, knowing these leopards could tear open any throat, but yet already seduced by the colour, exotic charms, and dramatic presentations of this fantastical Georgian evening. As yet, they were not willing, nor ready to turn over tables and run. Decorated, as I had left Juliette, with my crown of ivy, woven into my hair, between the stems and leaves, bluebells, and anemones, white, blue and red, around my waist the yellow silk wrap, woven with gold thread, my naked torso, with the prints of leopard paws, now lightly dusted with gold! The immutable calm displayed by the three of us, I, the painted Chár/Dionysus and the two leopards which sat either side of me, reassured the awestruck multitude as I turned to address them:

---

95   Great God, Lingam (phallus) King, Chár Dionysus, Lord Shiva. Like Dionysus, Shiva is
the Hindu god of intoxication who dreams the world into existence, as do we all. And if
by dint of compassionate effort, you have come to know this, to feel it, then you are free.
The riches of the world, that quiet sense of joy permeating your body, that surrenders you
to smiles and laughter will illuminate your presence, knowing: "I am because of you; I
am because you are.

"Behold! Here in these fields of the House of Utrecht, I arrive, I, Chár, born by leopards from blood-soaked forests, carried by leopards, as is Lord Dionysus, born of leopard spirit, those great nomadic cats who, like my people and I, left the birthplace of humanity to travel the world. Here I stand at the doorstep of the origin of fires and murder that took my mother, the rubble of her house still smouldering in undying outrage, the anger for revenge.[96] I, yes, I myself, covered with leaves and flowers from our trampled garden, the blood-stained bodies of our Komoro, our Chagdo, the head of our council, our soothsayer, and my mother, who together have sent me here. I, the black Dionysus, sought by Herodotus along the banks of the Nile, bring together through our spirit of celebration and play, the disaffected, deprived, and downtrodden. We are every colour, every sex, every sexuality, we are parentless children, we are the starving, the homeless, we have no land, no country, we are the Maenads and Satyrs of Dionysus, travelling from town to town, farm to farm, job to job, sleeping where fate puts us. This is my tribe, the new tribe my mother foresaw, I, Chár Dionysus, have willed it thus. My children wait at the gates of Calais. More truth in art, in poetry, in theatre, will be revealed tonight than ever the House of Utrecht and the history of power has been ready to admit, choosing to lie about offering civilisation, morality and order to the world while poisoning, stealing and enslaving even its very own peoples for its private gratification. We take back our hearts, our minds, our spirits which you have stolen through force and deception, we take back our tales, our myths, our heroes, our histories, which you have appropriated for your own glory. We take back all powers which we have ceded to you. And here tonight we take this house!"

As I spoke, small children, mostly black, but some from other ethnic groups, Arab, North African, Middle Eastern, Jewish, Indian, South East Asian, Chinese, children of the world who for whatever reason had been uprooted from their homes and countries, silently slipped into a semicircle behind my Dionysus, becoming the chorus of classical drama, quietly singing in improvised harmony, humming, chanting, as if relating, echoing, repeating words and phrases of the monologue, such that I, Chár Dionysus, seemed to have imbued them all with my spirit.

Nyaba Buli stepped forward and led the leopards away behind the children, while other Maenads and Satyrs restrained Mercantor in the shadows of a dark corner, pulling on his long topcoat, stroking his chest,

---

96   Assisted by the opening speech of Dionysus in The Bacchae by Euripides.

his face, his hair and pouring him strange cocktails to silence his anxieties and fears. Had he heard the name of his nemesis, or was his paranoia producing hallucinations again?

The congregated throng was gradually sliding towards becoming a gin-soaked Hogarthian mob, mostly propping themselves against or tottering drunkenly from table to table, avoiding puddles of liquor. The wild actions of the satyrs had started to blur distinctions between what was being performed and the audience. Who belonged to the troupe of performers and who did not? Noisily standing at the back of the hall, several unkempt, grubby and dubious personages in ragged cotton trousers, old and worn sailors' jackets, tattered military topcoats, and tricorn hats, pushed their way forward.

Watching them approach, the auctioneer picked up his clubbed walking stick and raised it above his head. These violent opportunists, ready to murder, torture, and beat into submission anybody who came between them and their greedy need were undaunted by the defence offered by the auctioneer who suddenly spun around and to the astonishment of the guests, cracked the club end of his walking stick across the head of the Greek God, a crack so loud, some in the audience felt nauseous. Dionysus's knees gave way and the harbour thugs grabbed him under his armpits to stop him collapsing to the floor. The auctioneer and traders laughed dirtily together, ripping off the golden skirt, and casting the ivy crown towards the crowd. Blood trickled down from the back of Dionysus' head onto his shoulder and down his chest. One of the pirates produced some sacking from a shoulder bag, which between them they pulled over his head, pushing his arms through holes cut in the corners of the sack. He was now dressed in crude sackcloth. While the slave traders still held him upright, the auctioneer stepped forward, laughing to himself, and occasionally looking up and grinning, then laughing aggressively, violently at the crowd as he paced around his victim, occasionally kicking him.

Again, laughing:-

"Dionysus Shitonicus!" he shouted, laughing all the more, "Ladies and gentlemen, who would like to buy this fine example of African manhood. Straight out of the jungles, out of the trees where brutish instinct flourishes and civilisation and culture have never entered. It is my Christian conviction, with proper training, all is possible! Even this lost and miserable soul bereft of intelligence and education can become, however meagre, part of our blessed world! You want to know if he is fit, coming from that filthy disease-ridden part of darkest Africa? (The auctioneer forced open his mouth to look inside). Perfectly healthy teeth. As for hitting him over the head with my cane, no, don't worry, they have very thick skulls." He grinned. "They're not far from being apes, you know, let's face it! (He lifted the front of the sack to pull back his foreskin and check his genitals). Look! No venereal disease, no infection. (Turned him around and forced him to bend over). No worms, no infestation. See?" (The harbour criminals grabbed his ears, back of the neck and hair and pushed me/Chár/Dionysus/him to my/his knees.) So, who will start the bidding?"

(Now that we are into the drama, identities start to slip and slide, just as they were doing for the audienced guests.)

Three people from the crowd came forward to examine the slave's body, his muscles, more closely, just as a photographer might do the body of a young woman for a fashion shoot. Some got up so sickened, they couldn't watch any longer, equally they couldn't quit Utrecht House, so simply left the Great Hall for the Parlour. Such upset now existed amongst the guests that they had even started shouting at and abusing each other. Some thought it was oh so funny to enter into this Georgian excess, others not. It was as if they were trapped in some nightmarish circus of horrors. They had all stepped back three hundred years.

Mercantor was led to the centre of the hall, hardly able to stand thanks to the massive self-inflicted intoxications, to sit next to the Deputy Commissioner on one side and Robert on his other. It is indeed astonishing how the superficiality of polite good manners is deployed to polish the surface of an unspoken contempt, or outright fear, but acknowledged by an equality of power and wealth. So, here, Mercantor, whilst uncertain of Robert's political power, was aware of his considerable wealth and personal confidence - to throw away so much money on a painting of doubtful provenance and value and to destroy it, you had to have a certain amount of nerve and self-belief. Hence it was possible on the part of Mercantor to greet Robert politely even though Robert had just destroyed what had been a family heirloom of historical significance. And on his other side was the second highest ranking officer of the Metropolitan police. It was like the rasping of sandpaper on a glass windowpane, something was wrong and discomfortable, discomforting, discordant; he was held in a silent double bind, frozen into a bleak and despairing silence.

"Let the drama unfold," said the Deputy Commissioner, smiling.

It came in waves, that feeling of doubting his own understanding or interpretation of events. The rasping, grating relations with Robert, the disturbing conduct of the auctioneer, whom he wondered if he recognised. Was he the creepy little arsehole on the train drinking blood, or was he the intern he had beaten up in a drunken frenzy for failing to find his nemesis? And was it the black, black, black tribal who had escaped the wipe out of his silly little tribe for the greater good of global gross domestic product, was it him being sold in this garish auction? Was he here, the nemesis? Was he the astonishing Pan? Was he one of the satyrs? He had threatened to find him, so what better way to remain invisible and stalk the enemy than in a crowd of lookalikes? As he looked around, blocks of colour tended in brief instants to separate and stand out in oblongs, or multi-sided shapes, separating themselves from a coherent set of circumstance into a disturbing cubist vision. Would his reality eventually deteriorate into the nightmare of abstract expressionist scribble?

Before the bidding could begin one of the houseboys, standing with a large silver tray of cigars, cigarettes and snuff near the scene of the auction, took a couple of steps backwards as the auctioneer, loud gestures, wide paces and high-pitched bellowing of exclamatory monetary evaluations of the beaten and bruised slave, backed into him. The boy tripped and fell, dropping everything clattering to the floor. The noise hit the marble walls, splintering and glancing through the yellow air, cutting, slicing, and freezing every movement, gesture, and speech of all assembled. All eyes turned towards the boy and the auctioneer who had started pacing, prowling around the prostrate child, like a wild animal around its cornered prey.

"Why, I know you!" shouted the auctioneer. "It's William! Little WILL - I - AM! Freed at last from the bondage of that painting of privilege, you are here to haunt us with your tales of misery!"

"What the fuck?" exclaimed Mercantor to Jolanta, the other side of her Commissioner. "What are you doing? This is supposed to be celebratory, your series of tableaux, not digging up the dirt on family history!"

"It's a satire, don't worry! The auctioneer is so funny, don't you think, his exaggerated gestures, the flapping wig, the Punch and Judy manner of dealing with the violence?" Jolanta looked at him quizzically, "Are you feeling okay? The blacks of your eyes are really dilated. You look pale. Too much cocaine, eh?"

" . . . . feel pain, you know, these picaninnies!" the auctioneer was addressing the crowd. "We Europeans can do whatever we deem fit with these subhumans, cursed as they are by their skin, by the blood-sodden land they come from, by their primitive lives, lacking in any refinement, education, sensibility, barely above the instinct of animals. They have to be whipped into some sort of civility, which this dumb creature clearly lacks." He was practically spitting and screaming.

The auctioneer started prodding then beating the child as he lay prostrate and brutally silent.

"Well, ladies and gentlemen, boys and girls, what should we do with him? I've been told his mother caught a fever on the transporter. The boy watched as she was thrown overboard and ripped apart by sharks. They say he hasn't uttered a sound since then. But that is no excuse!"

He looked around,

"Oh, yes, Madame, sharks would always follow the slave transporters. Sometimes several a day of the freshly dead or dying were thrown overboard.

"Ah, poor William! At least before now, you had a headstone, but now nothing! Wiped from haunted memory and the vicious reality you knew."

The auctioneer took out a huge silk handkerchief and pretended to cry, wailing loudly, and bending back and forth with each ululation. Slowly a few guests started to laugh at the mockery of weeping pity, until finally everyone was laughing and the auctioneer, turning towards the crowd with a cruel grimace, guffawed loudly too.

Suddenly, satyrs appeared, running amongst the tables and raucously filling glasses with an opaque and fizzing pale green cocktail.

"And now, Lords, Ladies and Gentlemen, before we dine on the blood and brains of children, the chef-d'oeuvre of the Mercantor dynasty. . . . " he raised his arm to indicate where attention should follow.

Suddenly the current scene gave way and projected onto the white wall of the Great Hall were scenes from the Kibish Valley.

"What the fuck!" shouted Mercantor, glaring at Jolanta. "What are you doing?"

Jolanta looked puzzled. "It's . . . your . . . . land. You and your investors . . . .and the Chinese. It's . . . . international development. You were Secretary of State . . . . remember?"

"Fucking stop this now!" he was panicking.

"What's wrong? You were helping to improve the Ethiopian economy, bring it into the modern world."

"He's here isn't he?!"

He jumped to his feet looking around the room at the reactions of the guests. They were sitting relaxed after the comic brutality of the auctioneer, now there were images of happy bare-breasted women with lip-plates, beads, patterned scarification and stylised hair, little smiling naked children, primitive round huts with conical thatched roofs. A few of the guests glanced at Mercantor wondering why he seemed distressed.

"These people, dear friends, we have been helping, by introducing education and medical services, access to markets and employment." Mercantor seemed almost hysterical, tearful, pleading. "Some of them are even working in our coffee plantations."

There was a murmuring amongst the guests who seemed to have settled disputes between each other. Many but not all were known to Mercantor. He had presented the event organisers, the three sisters, Red Windmill Events, with a list and they had also suggested others, art collectors, critics, and gallery owners. On his list were mostly influential party members, the Prime Minister and members of the Cabinet, plus various wealthy nobility, basically the people running the country and managing its wealth, most of which they had spirited away into anonymous offshore accounts in the Cayman's, Detroit, the Virgin Islands, and Panama and were of course still doing so. By now, they were all so well-oiled that apart from harrumphing into their Martini glasses neither knew whether they should be expressing any adverse opinions about the event or not. The wonderful bull dancing had set the tone of edgy excitement and the darkly comic slavery stuff had added a nervous uncertainty. No one was leaving out of indignation. Besides, there was no transport nor communication with the outside world. What harm could come to any of them? But what was this strange display of madness coming from their host, most of whom expected and wanted him as the next Prime Minister? They all knew they were having their arses kissed with this riotous party.

"Come along, Jimmy, my boy. Don't be a cunt!" shouted one of them, "We're having an absolute riot here, this evening. Well done! Someone help him powder his nose, for fuck's sake!"

Everyone laughed.

Suddenly the black slave, the beaten and wounded, sick Dionysus, kneeling in cudgelled submission, shouted out:

"He is lying! They are dead!" I shouted from behind the heavy curtains of blood dripping down my/his face and into his eyes. "All these people are dead! Murdered! Massacred! I covered their bodies myself with giant banana leaves, palm, whatever were around. He, Mercantor, wanted our land. The Ethiopian government wanted the promised millions from the International Development fund. Between them they colluded to destroy Beyahola village."

One of the merchant slavers smacked me/him across the back of my/his head and I fell to the floor.

"This is nonsense!" shouted Mercantor, "I never once demanded any massacre of anyone, village or people! This is typical of black sub-Saharan African mentality! You try to invest in their country, bring them into the modern world and once it is set up and profitable, they want to rob you of any benefit through lies, insults and criminal accusations."

"But these are not lies!" Amanishakhete stood to her feet, unable to contain herself. "A civil servant who has fled Ethiopia was with you and the Ethiopian Minister of Interior and has reported exactly your conversation with him.

"You bullied them, saying: "You are the government, aren't you? Sometimes when all else fails you have to simply requisition the land by force. They have no deeds, no legal documents to say the land is theirs, do they? Really, they are nothing more than just squatters."

"We've tried persuading them," came the response, "offering new land, more cattle, money. They're not even interested in money! We've even threatened.'"

"Well perhaps you should do more than just threaten. Empty threats are meaningless." You, James Mercantor, had insisted.

"Shortly afterwards, the same civil servant to the Ethiopian Minister of Interior saw emails agreeing to fund uniforms and AK 47s. And your assistant who quit working for you, John Chivers, remember him? He remembers sending those emails." She looked around the room, "John! Where are you?"

Someone stood up and stepped forward, removing his Georgian wig to become Chivers.

"And so what?" Mercantor was on his feet and striding around the room. "There is no direct link of provision for improving local police and a supposed massacre, for which you have no proof!"

"Look! Look at the images! Here are the bodies! Here is your proof! And plenty more from elsewhere!" retorted Amanishakhete.

"And what do we care?!" shout the Foreign Secretary, jumping to his feet. "I've known Jimmy since we were at college together. Most of us know him and have worked with him. He's a jolly good chap. And we've always looked out for each other. Don't imagine you bunch of dirty foreigners are going to change that. We all have money in Utrecht Capital Investments. You and your little black worms are not worthy even to gather up the crumbs under his table, whose sole aim is to lift you out of your primitive misery and persuade you into under-paid slavish employment and the illusion of achieving greatness, which your very nature denies you!"

The Secretary stood up threateningly, laughing cynically. He looked around the room for support. Three others immediately stood up with him.

Black young men in coarse and unkempt khaki uniforms, entered the hall from all directions, shouting crude commands at everyone. Armed with what appeared to be machine guns, they started firing randomly in the air. A couple of supposed bullets hit the central chandelier, shattering most of it into tiny shards, leaving only a wounded skeleton hanging in the centre of the ceiling. They grabbed the Secretary, brutally ripping off his topcoat and with rope around his neck dragged him to one side. His supporters who had stood up with him fled the room. Tables had been arranged around the sides of the Great Hall and the shards of crystal fell onto the tapestry on the empty floor. A few screams went up from the crowd, but most held their breath persuading themselves this was still only theatre. Quickly satyrs arrived with brooms and pans to clear the damage, pulling the corners of the tapestry together and dragging it backstage, behind the arras. The arced group of small children behind the auctioneer, the slave and slave traders, started crying, howling as the soldiers herded them together, tying ropes around their necks and marching them in a circle around the hall with the Secretary forced to follow them on his knees. Dionysus, dragged to his feet, picked up the body of little William and was led away also. The inebriated and somewhat dishevelled Georgian audience were wide eyed in horror, some started weeping.

There were moans of discontent and finally two Georgian men stood up and complained that things had gone too far, it was time to put a stop to this ugly horror. They were immediately grabbed by some of the soldiers, bound and forced to follow the crying children in this parade of terror.

As they completed the circle of the hall, the podium for the auctioneer and what remained of the Zoffany painting had been removed and replaced by a stage set of a bridge and trees.

Cries and screams of panic could be heard as the children were led up onto the bridge. The auctioneer provided the context for the drama, mentioning the Dizi people, employed as police/soldiers, Dibdib forest, Beyahola village, the Akobo river where the bodies of the children were thrown. Loud blows could be heard as their skulls were cracked open by the butts of rifles or rocks, and the little bodies thrown over the side of the bridge. Blood started to splash the khaki uniforms of the police/soldiers. Finally, they took their rifles and started shooting the older children and adults. Slowly the stage-end of the hall was filled with smoke and the smell of gunpowder.

Silence. And from this grey-yellow cloud slowly emerged the houseboys, footmen, satyrs, maenads and bull-dancers, immaculate in their livery or magnificent in their satyrs' and bull-dancers' semi-naked dress and demeanour, carrying lit candelabra to pose on and around the tables, all speaking quietly in hushed whispers when needed, returning the light of sanity to the room and guests who were finally able to examine each other and themselves through their glazed, intoxicated eyesight, now so desensitised that much had to be left to dimmed imagination to see unkempt and displaced, exaggerated curls and waves of gaudy wigs, their eyes hidden by smears of grotesque makeup and the vulgar display of unmerited privilege in their torn and dishevelled costumes.

Stunned silence and the vapours of drunken shame and guilt fell throughout the hall.

From between the dissipating clouds of smoke, as if at a great distance and eternal in their approach, appeared the figures of Chár-Dionysus and Little William, carried on my, Chár's shoulders,[97] and accompanying us, the two young leopards. I had now shed the sackcloth and was wearing a red silk wrap around my waist. Likewise, William had shed his livery and was wearing the same. Both of us were wearing crowns of vine and flowers.

"My name is Chár. Chár, from Beyahola. One of seven who escaped death and are forever burdened with that charge of being alive. Soon my peoples' retribution will be fulfilled, but my dying mother's wish will always be with me and my brothers and sisters: I carry all their names with me, in my heart, their wishes, their dreams and all that they want from me, the living and the dead of my people.

"This little one," I lifted little William down, speaking quietly and smiling into his trusting eyes, "he is my baby now, my baby brother and like me, has lost his home. He was found in Calais and brought here by friends. Little William, Mercantor's William, was mute; forced to watch his mother swallowed by monstrous greed and vicious cruelty. This little one suffered similarly and cannot remember his name. It was also the fate of my father to lose his mother at that age. But, unlike the English, who fear they will lose their homes, their jobs, their country even, by being kind to

---

[97] I must make it clear that when I write here about Chár Dionysus, in the 3rd person, it is because I have become the Dionysus of the drama and as such am no longer, in this theatre of madness the Chár of Beyahola. I have become many, perhaps even all the names in this history of terror.

poor and destitute, parentless children, my people, the people of Beyahola, cared for him with love. He became the son of all families, the brother to all the children. This little one," he indicated the mute 'William', "will have that same love and care. When my mother was dying, she instructed me to make a new tribe, a new collective, a new community. Already we are many! It is right, therefore, that as histories, stories, tales, and mythologies go full circle, that he takes the name of my father, Menenge Kórrò. Thus, I name him. And since he is now the son and brother of us all, the spirit that binds, that his name should mean Dark Spirit, is right in this moment. My Juliette, Wóhólò Tagí, Nyàbà Bulí, Jolanta, Amanishakhete, Lihua and many more all agree this should be his name."

The little one looked up at me and smiled, wrapping his arm around my legs and leaning his head against my thigh.

"Is that okay, little Menenge, little Menenge Kórrò?"

Menenge Kórrò nodded his head.

Then, Dionysus addressed the crowd once again:-

"My satyrs are coming around the hall with leaflets detailing web sites you can visit to verify the genocide of the Suri people that took place just a few years ago.[98] The British government continues to provide funds through the Department for International Development to the Ethiopian government for the continued seizure and exploitation of tribal lands, land of my people and my neighbours. James Mercantor has considerable investments in that exploitation as does Utrecht House Capital Management. Should any of you, our guests, have investments

---

[98] The web addresses on the leaflets were:-

https://www.oaklandinstitute.org/land-wars-ethiopia-accused-massacring-civilians-clear-way-foreign-farms

https://strugglinginjustice.wordpress.com/2013/01/09/the-suri-massacre-genocide-commited-by-the-ethiopian-government-and-army-in-southern-ethiopia/

https://selamlehulum.blogspot.com/2014/11/

https://www.vice.com/en_us/article/mbwnb8/land-wars-ethiopia-accused-of-massacring-civilians-to-clear-way-for-foreign-farms

Please note, everyone, on the vice.com page there are photos of dead bodies after the massacre, which some might find upsetting.

through Utrecht House, we suggest you withdraw them. Very shortly, the operations of Utrecht House as an investment company will be wound up."

Satyrs and Maenads started distributing the leaflets to every table. Menenge Kórrò and I, we also joined in going from table to table. And, out of curiosity, and because they, my leopards, had decided to make us their . . . and now we reach a problem: talking about whatever sentiment, or feeling leopards might have in human terms such as friendship, being brothers, family, etc. is absurd, but they were certainly devoted. The two leopards followed.

"Do not touch my leopards," I suggested. "They like Nyàbà Bulí but maybe they will not like you. And of course, they love Menenge Kórrò, he is their baby brother. Where is Juliette?"

*   *   *

"You have destroyed me!" said Mercantor to the three sisters. He was white with grief, anger and humiliation.

At which point, the train journey flashed before Mercantor's eyes, and the blood.

"The train journey to Bristol, I remember now!" said Mercantor.

Chivers and Nyàbà Bulí, still in his Nijinski costume, the remains of the yellow-ochre paste, dried, flaking, contrasting with his black skin, the transformation of white devil to black angel, arrived to join the group.

"My wife, Juliette," explained Chár, responding with contempt to Mercantor, "wanted to meet you. and so did I, face to face with the monstrously puerile. Of course, I could have killed you, but what unimaginative revenge that would have been, Jimmy. Juliette prefers the father of her first born should not be a murderer. The revenge you suffer is far greater than childish murder. Now, you have become nothing."

"Like the empty hole at the centre of that Zoffany family portrait, sucking away anything of value." said Rémi, laughing. "We were all there, Chár, Nyàbà Bulí, Juliette and I, and that's where we met the nice Mr. Chivers."

Mercantor glanced at Chivers with the same look of distain he used for all his immediate servants, civil or otherwise.

"Mr Chivers has told us all about your relations with Mr. Ferrier, all about having his nurses followed, all about the burning of Place Pigalle," said Amanishakhete. "It is a good thing we rescued Mr. Ferrier otherwise who knows what mishap might have arrived to him."

"It was largely his statement to the police that got the prosecution and pursuit of Chár dropped," said Jolanta. "In fact, according to my partner, John . . . . you know John, don't you? The deputy commissioner for the Met. He's here somewhere, in Georgian dress like the rest of us, checking whose been snorting all the coke and where it comes from."

"You accuse me of burning down that shit-hole of a brothel!"

Amanishakhete turned back to Mercantor: "What do you know about Place Pigalle, then, James? A brothel, you say? You actually know Place Pigalle?"

"Nothing!" came a confused reply, Mercantor realised this magnificent Sudanese woman had understood his self-betrayal.

"I don't remember you ever visiting our Place Pigalle." said Lihua.

It suddenly occurred to James that there had been more than this black insurgent pursuing him.

"We have been waiting a very long time for this," declared Amanishakhete, staring into his eyes with burning grotesque hatred. "You and your like, your alliances, your exclusive clubs, your turning of everything into objects of exploitation, not just the Earth, the land, animals, vegetation and the seas, but humans also. You deliberately separate yourselves, you and your . . . Bullingdon boy mates, in order to exploit and abuse.

"We look at you! Jolanta, Lihua and I, we recognise you. But you have never recognised us, which is why we can get so close. Reducing everything and everyone to objects results in your going blind. For you, all black people look the same, for you, women all become the same sex object, subject to your abuse. You, when you were a student, you and your Bullingdon club president were the big beasts, up for anything, treating people with absolute disdain, referring to them as 'plebs' or 'grockles', and the police were always called 'plod'. Women existed for your violent abusive entertainment."[99]

"And still you don't remember!" rejoined Jolanta. "Nineteen eighty-seven? We were still only teenagers, freshly smuggled into the country and yours was the first party our pimp, our owner, sent us to."

Mercantor suddenly had a distant memory of fucking a young Chinese girl on the dining table of this event, amongst bottles, dirty plates and delicately prepared food smeared over the walnut table and his ugly, pudgy white flesh, while others bayed, and howled like dogs, several screaming and laughing as they burned her naked body with cigars, and as Mercantor fell off her and the table to vomit on the floor, another dropped his trousers to mount her and still others watched on, masturbating.

"Afterwards, all of us, Lihua, Jolanta and I had to be cared for in hospital, of course a private hospital owned, practically, fortunately, by your father. Ever since, Lihua can no longer have children, for which she continues to wait in painful longing."

She spat at him. The very least he deserved.

Accusations were piling up. Even if it was not possible to prove his links to all these crimes, dealing coke and arranging drugs parties at his house were enough to put him away for a good few years, but proof of violent abuse, so many years ago . . . his links to genocide? The Furies[100] were flying in flames around his head. "The Erinyes, that, under earth, take vengeance on men," they are "the act of self-cursing made spirit", no longer the invocation of the curse but the curse detached, wreaking its own bitter revenge.

"And our home, Place Pigalle, which you had burned down, this was where your friend, our pimp, had kept us, bought in large part in payments for your evening of so-called entertainment. Our owner, the pimp, what did we do with him? Before his . . . demise, we managed for

---

99   https://www.theguardian.com/politics/2019/jul/07/oxford-bullingdon-club-boris-johnson-sexism-violence-bullying-culture.

100 The **Erinyes** (/ɪˈrɪni.iːz/ *ih-RI-nee-eez*; Ancient Greek: Ἐρινύες, sg. Ἐρινύς *Erinys*), also known as the **Eumenides** (Εὐμενίδες, the "Gracious ones"), are chthonic goddesses of vengeance in ancient Greek religion and mythology. (from Wikipedia)

Place Pigalle to become ours. Your cocaine dealer, whose body was found on your estate, eaten by wild boar, after Chár had crucified to the floorboards his mate, that thug, Brankovitch, we moved into the house they had practically destroyed with their violence, the house of Ms Evelyn Tutt, who is here also. When Zelusz, drug dealer and pimp, turned up to collect the young Kenyan girl, Lankenua, he had left with Brankovitch, and we all knew his intentions for her, I guess he reminded us too much of our pimp from all those years ago. You and he are alike, although he has already been eaten by equal greed to yours, like you, governed by avarice, self-entitlement and malevolence, with no humanity. A sterile world you live in where the complex beauty, transformations of the Earth, its nature, wealth and life are reduced to two values, commodities and capital."

"Fucking Marxists! Never worked, did it." Mercantor, laughing raucously, stood up to back away and parade his arrogance for the drunken herd. "So what are you going to do? Kill me also?"

Rémi Wóhólò Tagí and Nyàbà Bulí followed Mercantor, like two psychiatric nurses to restrain any psychotic violence.

Lihua jumped up angrily: " Yes! Yes!" she screamed. All three women were seething with repressed anger, and which for Lihua had suddenly burst the dam of suppression. "I hate him! I hate him! I see that torture every night! I want him to suffer as I did, his genitals ripped apart so that he is never able to have children, and that the rest of his life is pain and mental suffering!"

She ran at him howling and clawed at his face. He had fallen backwards, the claw-marks from her attack already bleeding. Rémi Wóhólò Tagí took her in his arms to restrain her. She immediately burst into hot tears of anger.

As Mercantor overcame this moment of panic, a sneer of contempt appeared on his face.

"James," Jolanta wanted to explain, as if to a small child, "After this evening, you will already have become nothing! All those titles, status, wealth and even your sanity will have disappeared. You can no longer be that great, powerful, deluded monster. But we intend to help you. You are establishing a charity; it was announced this evening. Leave it to us. We will arrange everything. That charity for refugee children will be based here. It will save your name! You are going to give Utrecht House to us - to the charity that is. Everything is arranged. All these children here now, they've moved in. They have no intention of leaving! Before you have even noticed, this place, the world, even you will already have changed." Jolanta smiled, laughed. "And you thought you were going to be Prime Minister!" she declared.

"And Chár," Amanishakhete wondered, "our perfect prince, our Dionysus, what does he want? Here in your silly civilisation, you ignorant people can think I am crazy, but I have been waiting for him for two thousand years! Yes! Many lifetimes! Waiting for him to come and paint the world differently. What will he decide?"

"Who paid for the destruction of my village?" I demanded. "The Ethiopian government? The British Government through International Development, you as director of the fund? Your willing, your demanding the end of a problem and that end being murder, genocide even, how different are you to the Dizi people's captain, Mihret? In my country, I would certainly kill you. It would be an eternal shame if I did not do this."

"Just prove it! Prove I called for murder! I haven't even heard of this person Mihret, nor the so-called Dizi people!" Mercantor howled. "You see? You can't, can you?"

"Sure, you did not kill," said Rémi, "but you have blood on your hands. All that spilling of blood by your ancestors and by you as government minister has produced great wealth, exclusively yours."[101]

---

[101] The problem of acting at a distance, is that it absolves both those doing the actual killing by removing responsibility and those coming to collective agreement over action, the Department for International Development, the Ethiopian government, and other powers willing this change and the confiscation of Suri land. Where in all that does final responsibility lie? It becomes so dispersed that we can only say it is an inevitable consequence of the nature of hierarchically structured civilisation. We offer up our will to this machine of highly unequal distributions of power. Our will becomes its will, until a reversal takes place and its will becomes ours. How to measure guilt? We are back in the world of measuring, counting the cost, debt and resentment. The cost, all those lives, had produced a great profit, for Mercantor and others. But was there a debt? An unpaid debt to the Suri people? How did notions of money, debt, paying for one's sins creep into thinking about justice? Is justice just another way of distributing resentment? This issue concerned Rémi and me over many nights of discussion. Rémi being a philosophy student, introduced me to these problems: Is civilisation always and necessarily hierarchical? Is justice the civilised way of dealing with resentment? The position was ideal for thinking about these problems since I did not come from a civilisation; my life had not been blighted (Rémi's description) by being 'civilised'.

A crowd had assembled around this impromptu trial. All the guests, except those so inebriated, their faces remained in puddles of alcohol on their tables, watched and listened. James knew he was condemned.

"Goodnight, James, we're leaving, before the place is raided!" said the party chairman. "The PM wants a resignation immediately after the weekend and I guess you'll be resigning from the party and as constituency MP. Any excuse will do, preferably health. Interesting evening. We cannot have the government, nor the party brought into disrepute, associated with all of this, now can we?"

Lihua and Claudine led some of the guests out onto the balcony where lamb was being barbecued for whoever remained. Others gathered closer around the group surrounding Mercantor, as if jury to his tribulations and demise. All the participants in the drama sat around Chár's feet and smaller ones on his knees.

"Where are my leopards?"

"They've been taking care of the barbecue with Juliette," Nyaba Buli joked, with a smile. "They are well fed."

Jackson Pan Nyaba Buli left the group and returned very soon with the two young leopards held on leashes. They made their way through the small children, who were undisturbed, and threw themselves on the floor amongst them, occasionally licking the faces of those little ones nearest.

Certainly, revenge is repressed anger. At the same time as the younger children gathered around my feet, I could feel the faces from my village crowd around behind me, some damaged and bruised, some quietly weeping and crying, some too bloody, but all were turned towards Mercantor, who attempted to stand up, feeling a weakness in the others, a moment of reprieve in his inquisition.

"So, what are you going to do? Why hesitate? Kill me in your country, fine, but here in England? You can't, can you?" he sneered. "Someone such as I, is far too much in the public eye to just disappear, rotting under banana leaves in an obscure jungle."

The insult was too great. I jumped across the low walnut table and punched him in the face, tears jumped from Mercantor's eyes and blood spurted from his nose.

.

"And you, do you still want to kill me?" I shouted.

Mercantor, his body contorted into knots of conflicting greed, public standing, egotistical self-image, contempt, and humiliation laughed briefly with hysterical despair.

"Want you dead? Yeh! But kill you with my bare hands?" He swayed in indecision. "What do I know any more?" he started screaming, nonplussed, bound in the twisted torturous flames of his Furies.

Some could see them, the Arinyes, the Furies, they told me, just as I had seen the flames around the Bodhisattva. Others also saw them, at least indirectly through the winces of pain and cries as they bit into Mercantor's face, and there were even brief seconds when their presence flashed into an unusual visual periphery.

Mercantor was now completely lost. He jumped up and ran towards a wall where crossed swords, military sabres, were hanging high above easy reach, swords he had known since his childhood when his aunt had explained the glories of the family history. He seemed to crawl vampire-like up the wall until grasping one by the hilt while the other clattered loudly on the white marble floor, he staggered, screaming with anger, at Chár. The cats were already on their feet hissing and baring their teeth. Their backs arched and fur along their spines standing on end, they moved towards him sidewards, crab-like, with their paws crossing each other as they stepped slowly towards Mercantor with the utmost menace. Both Nyaba Buli and Wóhólò Tagí took hold of them around their necks to restrain and best protect them. The group scattered, the Sisters pulling small children out of Mercantor's path until finally he tripped. The blade spun above his head, still in Mercantor's grip, and, as little Menenge Kórrò, who had jumped up in front of Chár shouted: "Don't! Stop!", the blade sliced through the air and finally into Menenge's ribs.

The cats were furious seeing their baby brother attacked and were struggling and hissing angrily to evade the grasp. The female, with yellow fur and black markings soon shook herself free of Jackson's arms, jumped at Mercantor, knocking him to the ground and was ready to rip out his throat when Jackson jumped to grab her and pull her away. I shouted to Rémi and Nyaba to take the leopards outside, while I leaned forward to lift Menenge Kórrò into my arms. It was as if the entire hall shook like the interior of a bass drum, struck by the clap of a mallet. Even the walls were stunned as every candle flame flickered in horror and all, Gods and humans, of every race and creed, were wide-eyed and immobile at the abject stupidity of arrogance.

Reaching to and exposing the white bone of a couple of ribs, penetrating no further, the four inch long cut hesitated in the silence before a thin stream of blood ran out of one corner of the cut and down little Menenge's belly, the Furies dived into Mercantor's chest releasing a thin high-pitched whine of intense agony as James realised the monster he had become. Howling and screaming, he turned and fled out of the terrace doors, over the balcony balustrade, into the near gardens until he disappeared into the black of night.

*   *   *

"We can't! We can't take him to a hospital!" declared Jolanta. "He would immediately be taken away from us by Social Services, Immigration, the Police, the nasty government and disappeared into a prison camp for illegals. Once we have proper charitable status, we'll be able to deal with all that bureaucratic government run racism. But just now . . "

Amanishakhete had spent enough time around doctors and nurses when tending Ray Ferrier to know how to deal with a superficial skin wound. There were no marks on the rib bones. Lihua found a First Aid box in the kitchens. Once cleaned with alcohol, the wound needed half a dozen stitches to hold the two sides together. Little Menenge was very brave while this happened. Juliette was at his side, holding his hand while Amani sowed the skin, closing the wound. Asked if he wanted anything while this was happening. Mute, silent, without even a sigh of discomfort, he indicated he needed his leopards. Nyàbà Bulí and Wóhólò Tagí quickly found them. They quietly came and sat next to him, watching. Who was he surrounded by while this took place? First of all, he was on Chár's lap with Amanishakhete on her knees opposite, intense attention written across her noble face, either side of her were Lihua and Jolanta, Juliette was next to Chár, holding Menenge Kórrò's hand, the two leopards were next to his head with Nyàbà Bulí and Wóhólò Tagí, Claudine, Robert and Charles were standing behind Chár and Juliette, with Chivers, Herbert Brunt, and Jolanta's partner, the Deputy Commissioner. Never had so many people cared for little Menenge Kórrò, in fact no one, when he had been in the camps around Calais, there was only a turning away. All were still in their party costumes such that the whole scene could easily have been a painted tableau from the eighteenth century, perhaps even an alternative Historia Sacre of Caravaggio.

* * *

A peace descended on the hall. To the conclusion this event, which like the stitches of Menenge's wound, tied together to heal a thousand-year history of many terrible events, all participants and guests resorted to simple gossip and occasional remembrances. All were punishèd! All were punishèd! And by association, bound by guilt, absolution, forgiveness, and gentle smiles of a mutual understanding. Wives turned to husbands, "get rid of those shares. . . . Give them away . . . . to a charity! . . . . I don't know . . . . the Church. And hopefully some good will come out of this!" Everyone felt the need to embrace each other.

Satyrs arrived with red wine for the tables, as footmen and houseboys served the entrée, which consisted of a bouillon prepared from a stock using lambs bones with conventional herbs, introducing the bone marrow and red Burgundy and finally when the bouillon had cooled, a measure of lamb's blood. Sitting in the centre of the bowl of bouillon was a small poached lamb's brain, served with crusty bread.

At the same time as the service, the little children from the chorus and the older ones who had been dancing with bulls, arrived and joined the various tables of guests with smiles. The guests were astonished, dumbfounded firstly by the drama they had seen, and then taken aback at being joined by these young ones, who happily tucked into their bowls of soup, dipping the bread and spooning down portions of the soft blancmange-like brains, or spreading it on their bread. At the same time, the guests felt reassured, comforted by the children's open, trusting, friendly manner. Fear of all things foreign, particularly the dish presented to them at this moment, had suddenly left them.

"What is your name?" said one little boy to his Georgian neighbour at table.

"I'm the Prime Minister."

"Aren't you hungry? Don't you want to eat?"

"Of course! I am happy to share food, drink soup and break bread with you!"

"Did you like our play?"

"I thought it was brilliant! All of you were so good!"

Jolanta arrived.

"Prime Minister, is everything okay? Are you comfortable? I see you have a little friend here." she said with a smile.

"That's right! And what a lovely little person he is, asking if I was hungry and whether I had enjoyed the children's drama."

"I hope everything has been to your satisfaction."

"Revelatory, I think is the word, revelatory. I will personally take action over what we have learned tonight, but you do realise the CPS[102] are unlikely to act, since the crime took place in another country, Ethiopia, which denies that this massacre ever happened. I had been made aware of it at the time of the Amnesty International incident. The investigation into that is ongoing but the young Ethiopian refugee attending who was initially portrayed as a terrorist himself by the press is no longer under investigation. I guess he is here, is he? The star of the show? Your Dionysus has told us he comes from the same village that the Amnesty-Survival meeting was about. . . Is it him?"

"I couldn't possibly comment, Prime Minister. Our Dionysus, as you call him, is a respectable naturalised French citizen. But let us turn our attention now to the future; embarrassment for your government was wrought foolishly by the ex-minister. There will be discreet ways of resolving these difficulties, believe me."

The Prime Minister looked at Jolanta in awe of her astounding confidence at assuming management of these stunningly anarchic events and wondered whether he should appoint her as his special adviser. After all, what does a good prime minister do but manage the anarchy of arriving history for, hopefully, the beneficial outcome that all deserve. A stone had been fired from a sling to burst through his forehead and open a truth that had always been before him, but unseen. Mercantor, failing to understand this about history and the unfolding of the future, had

---

102 Criminal Prosecution Service

attempted to control events for a selfish few, primarily himself, and had crashed into the brick wall that is humanity.

"Prime Minister, I need your support for our current project, the children's charity. Discussions are ongoing with Viscount Bone, but we are expecting to use Utrecht House as a home for refugee children, a form of resolution, absolution even, for this series of terrible events. It is our intention to empty the refugee camps around Calais of all their children and bring them here. Viscount Bone will be retiring from public life shortly and devoting himself to the charity. We hope you will give your support to this project and ensure its smooth conclusion. "

"Of course!" he feared refusing. "A noble and just penance! His actions were foolish, as you say, and this project will absolve us all from the shame of his actions." The Prime Minister didn't need long to reflect on the evening's events and his own associations with Mercantor to make his decision. "Could you arrange for my car to be at the entrance. I'll spend a little while longer chatting to my new friend and finishing the soup before I leave."

« Tout est pour le mieux dans le meilleur des mondes possible, comme disait Leibnitz, »[103] commented Jolanta.

The Prime Minister hesitated as he amassed his French to understand: "Yes, indeed!".

*   *   *

"Je suis épuisé! I am exhausted!" I declared, throwing myself onto a chair and smiling.

"What of Mercantor?" asked Juliette, with that look of dependent confidence that only honest love can express.

"Don't worry, Juliette. I'll find him later when the rain has cooled his madness. Nature can judge him, take care of him and direct him."

"You two were magnificent!" said Claudine, addressing Rémi and myself. "What you presented with all the children, was terrifying but

---

[103] "All is for the better in the best of all possible worlds."

beautiful. I didn't know you had become an actor, Rémi. And Chár, my darling Chár, Nathalie would be so proud and, please, accept my apologies for ever doubting you and for all of my silly prejudices."

Rémi had sat himself next to me and put an arm around my shoulders. I leaned towards him and kissed his cheek.

"I am surrounded by art," declared Claudine, laughing happily, "surrounded by living, mythic history!"

"Oui, ma Cherie, " responded Robert. "Finally, you appreciate what these young people are capable of."

"He is your partner, the Deputy Commissioner?" asked Claudine. "How lovely! Such a gentleman!"

"He proposed to me the other day."

"What?" shouted Lihua. "And you didn't tell us! How exciting! What did you say?"

Everyone turned to Jolanta in anticipation.

*   *   *

Fleeing the house having cut a wound into the side of innocent Menenge, Mercantor fell over the balustrade of the terrace twisting an ankle as he attempted to control his fall. He didn't know why he was running and was certainly directionless. He could hear himself whining, with occasional terrified stifled moans. He had been destroyed, not in a physical sense, he was still his body, but in the social world of determinations and definitions. Every vainglorious aspiration about governing the country, being at the forefront of commercial exploitation of east Africa, leading the country into new and powerful economic relations with China, rightly being feted wherever he went, all of that had turned to the ashes of delusion. He became aware of his arms flailing in the black and humid air. It was the Furies, those yellow balls of flames which twisted and spun like angry hornets around his head. For over a week now he had been bingeing on every alcohol and his personal brick of cocaine. Every nightmare, ugliness, and terror was bursting through his skin.

Suddenly, blindly, and hurriedly taking the next chaotic step his foot only found empty space. He fell forward into the stench of carrion and faeces. He screamed into the moonless, starless black night, which only seemed to feed off his madness as he heard the scurrying of animals around him. Remembering angrily, and then hysterically, that he had asked his manager to poison them, he guessed emptiness beneath his foot was an entrance to a badger's sett. Destroying Beyahola village, murdering the Suri people, exterminating badgers anything which got in the way of his cherished, sanitised world of commodified free-for-all global markets, had caused him to trip and fall.

"Fucking bulldoze it!" he thought, laughing madly at the ugliness of all that was left of the nasty spirit that had infected his being since his first faltering steps into the world.

"World leader!"

In contempt and self-loathing, he rolled around amongst scraps of rotting bones and remains of dead meat and shit. He had now become nothing more than that himself, so he felt. A large drop of water hit his forehead. And another. There were heavy beasts moving around not far from him. Cattle looking for shelter under trees? Was he near where Zelusz had been eaten by wild boar? He tried to liberate his foot from the badger sett, but the pain was so great it immobilised the entire leg. He felt the earth squirming beneath him and slowly climbing over him. He heard screams, shouts of death and horror. Rain started falling more heavily now. Terror rushed through his veins, such that his heart was pumping so violently, he could no longer breathe, only rapid short breaths of desperation. There was a moment of blissful reprieve when suddenly all fear and suffering was taken away; it was as if the hand of God had touched his head. Unaware of this terrible fate, his brain choked with warmth as his skull filled with hot blood.

James was unconscious for a while, at least he thought he was. The last thing he remembered of that night of the purging of history was the cold heavy rain and being woken by distant thunder. He opened his eyes to a flash of lightning and saw the faces of two leopards looking down at him and behind them the naked torso covered with sparkling raindrops and the head of Dionysus, bedecked once more with ivy and flowers.

I reached down between the leopards and lifted him in my arms.

A Bentley drew up outside Bristol infirmary and a trolley carried him into Accident and Emergency.

Later that night, Menenge Kórrò slept between Juliette and me, with the leopards at the foot of the bed. And in the morning, little Menenge laughed as the young leopards jumped onto the bed to lick our faces to wake us. Slipping into consciousness, the trees, and jungles of Dibdib came to me once again, and all the ghosts, the spirits of all the people of Beyahola followed me into the real as tears of the past ran down my face.

"C'est fini!"[104] declared Menenge Kórrò, climbing onto my belly and shaking me.

"He has spoken! Menenge has spoken, Chár darling!" said Juliette. "C'est fini!"

*   *   *

"Allô, Maman?"

"Allô?" repeated Nathalie. "Chár? Is that you, mon chou?"

"Oui, c'est moi. Nathalie, I have news! You and Charles, you're grandparents now."

"Oh là là! How wonderful! Does he have a name yet?"

"His name is Chobbosa (meaning 'kiss')."

"And your affairs in England are finished now, are they?"

"For now." I was certain. "Nathalie, I can't wait to eat your chips once more. The best chips in the world!"

"Well, you have to come back, mon cher![105]"

"We arrive at yours, our home, with Charles, Rémi, Robert and Claudine."

---

[104] It's over!
[105] my dear

"Ah, bon? When is that?"

I turned towards Robert: "How long will it take, Robert, to get to Charles and Nathalie's?"

"Robert says it'll take about three hours."

"Really? So fast?"

"We're coming in his plane. He knows a field near yours where he can land, it's a field of Monsieur Morel, Juliette's father, that's what he says. So, Grandma Nathalie, are you happy?"

"Very happy, of course! Now, listen, mon chou, my darling, you bring me very good news, but, unfortunately, I have to bring you bad news." There was a long pause. "Dieter has died." Nathalie waited for the horror to sink in. "His brother phoned me. He knew we had been close friends of his and he wanted our help. He wanted to understand what Dieter had said, the last words he had spoken before he died, and what did he mean, if anything. He had said:

" I hope I pronounce it well enough, Chár. Some of the words I remember hearing you and Rémi speaking between you. He had said: « Añi kidi-kari chár menenge. Añi kóbá kórrò. »"[106]

« Parfaitement, Maman. »[107]

"We knew he was very ill and one day the cancer would take him . . ." Nathalie continued talking, explaining, as her voice slowly faded from his attention and a great cry of pain shook the walls of Utrecht House and reached out as far as the Dibdib forest where two leopards, one black and one yellow with her leopard spots heard the cry and howled also until every nomad leopard in the world repeated the terrible pain in their hearts.

*   *   *

"Three months after the party, now in Chár's Sologne, Jackson Nyaba Buli completed the outcomes of our Bacchanalia for Nathalie:

---

[106] I am together with the leopard spirit. I follow the dark.
[107] Perfectly, Mum.

"James Mercantor had been living at home now for a while. As soon as his condition stabilised and only physiotherapy remained, following his catastrophic stroke, the hospital moved him back to Utrecht House, which was now known as Beyahola White Rock, home for child refugees.

"Much noise had been made in the media about his sudden life-threatening brain haemorrhage and immediate quitting of the government and all political life. Considerable praise was heaped upon him for setting up the charity. Herbert Brunt, acting as his spokesman had explained how Lord Mercantor deeply regretted the massacre of the Suri people under his watch as Secretary of State for International Development, being unaware of the murderous actions of one tribe against another in Southern Ethiopia. Had he been aware he would certainly have intervened. This was why he was now quitting political life and devoting his time and estate to his charity for child refugees. The charity was currently in discussions with the Home Office to bring the remainder of child refugees in the camps around Calais to their new home. His decisions and wishes had the full backing of the Prime Minister, a long-time friend and colleague of Lord Mercantor, a man renowned for his devotion to his country and the welfare of all.

"During his stay in hospital, he had been regularly visited by Lihua, Amanishakhete, Jolanta and her husband-to-be Deputy Commissioner Jack Henshaw and little Menenge Kórrò. Although he could not speak and was wheelchair-bound, James always seemed happy to see the little boy. It was as if the ghost of William in the now non-existent Zoffany painting had been freed and likewise James himself.

""Why does Uncle Jimmy's face look funny?" asked Menenge Kórrò.

"Lihua had found an old wicker three-wheeled bath chair, which I had cleaned and repaired and which James preferred to the conventional modern wheelchair. Menenge Kórrò was sitting on his knee and had been reading, or rather telling him the story, with the help of pictures, about how the leopard got his spots[108]. Many of the children would give James their attention, wheeling him around the house or out onto the terrace, showing him their toys and telling him whatever story came into their minds.

---

[108] Simplified version of the Rudyard Kipling original, with plenty of pictures for the very young.

""He is happy. He is trying to smile. I've told you before about his accident." replied Mama Lihua, now mother to all the children, just as Amanishakhete and Jolanta were also.

""When are Chár, Juliette and Chobbosa coming back?" wondered Menenge Korro.

""Very soon," I replied. "They'll be here for the wedding, in any case."

"I had now become the father or big brother of all the children at Beyahola White Rock House and always had a few following me around, including Marlon and Lankenua. I had been persuaded against using cow's urine on my hair by Lihua who took it upon herself to maintain my mass of uncontrolled orange dreads.

""But that's a long time!" complained Menenge Kórrò.

""You want to come and find them with me, in France? See where they are living? Speak French with Grandma Nathalie?" I offered.

"Yey! Let's go!"."

Some Suri vocabulary

The Suri people have no written language. Hence, what is written and recorded about their language has been by anthropologists and linguists. The phonetic alphabet used in such records can vary. I have discovered two such records of Suri vocabulary. As far as Suri grammar is concerned, I was able to discover one such work on the internet which has since disappeared. The vocabulary is listed in more or less the order in which it appears in the text, rather than alphabetically. It includes all words used in the text plus a few that I expected I might use at some point of writing but which finally may not have been.

Inye	You
aňi	I
ganyu	my (pl)
nanu	my (s)
aranjinya	foreigners, white people
Shodigái	full moon
Tagí	moon
wóhólò	naked
chàlli	good, right, clear, beautiful
Gerthi	bad, ugly, wrong
Wongái	come!
Duríyaye	dance
Baragadúy.	owl

Ɓúrrà ganyu	my testicles
bùrrà	egg
dormì	penis
ɗolé	anus
sugum	buttocks
way-tugó	nipple, waya-tuga nipples
wáy s., wáya pl.	female breast(s)
nyangí	vulva
nyábí	ear
nyábí-l:tenì	ear-lobe
búttɔ	to lick
gíróng	nose
guidú	navel
lésshuí	clitoris
kwengɔ	belly, stomach
Bulí	warrior
challá, challanya	bead, beads
chíktɔ	happy
choga	to have sex, to fuck
chó:ré	hair

derre	bead belt
erí**ʔ**	human skin
hídɔ	to want, to desire
híní	heart
kálugey	armpit
nyangí	vulva
huya, chobbosa	to kiss
tugo	language, mouth, lips
nyàbà	blood
ré:	body
wongái	come!
bo:ni-kabaré:	fig
anyane	to fear
baragaráy	enemy
barári	hot, forceful dangerous (said of certain people, plants and sacred objects)
ber	spear
bi:ka	to break
búgáʔ	hyena
wolé	bull
cháchá**ʔ**	to give back, to return; to revenge

dákká'	to hit
déllé	stupid, dumb
ɗolmɛ́	frog
ééééi	yes!
erra	to die
e:sɛta	to think
hiri	man, husband
huya, or chobbosa	to kiss
ingàrɛn	I'm not sure, I don't know
kágadau	to remember
kálugey	armpit
kwáɔ'ɔda	to kill, murder
kidi-kari	together
kinineggiɔ	perhaps
kóbá	to follow
kórrò	black, darkness
korrong	throat
lameyɔ	1/ to want 2/ to look for
lé:thu	to dislike, to hate

múmɔ	face, forehead
niyá / lokóyindo	to be angry
ressɔ	corpse
sábba⁷	head
tággá	to know
wolokoyndɔ	to be angry
woylenyɔ	to be able
tényéydá	to create, to make
tiráyna	to play
árrà	to see
mé:yá	now
menenge	spirit
buhógi	witch
hídɔ	to want, to desire
í:she:	all right
ngandono⁷ / no⁷	he/she/it
kegeyndɔ	ugly, bad, repulsive
gorí	very, truly, completely
hìnì, hóhŭ	heart

bù   great, big

Web sites noting the massacre of the Suri people of Beyahola

https://www.oaklandinstitute.org/land-wars-ethiopia-accused-massacring-civilians-clear-way-foreign-farms

https://strugglinginjustice.wordpress.com/2013/01/09/the-suri-massacre-genocide-commited-by-the-ethiopian-government-and-army-in-southern-ethiopia/

https://selamlehulum.blogspot.com/2014/11/

https://www.vice.com/en_us/article/mbwnb8/land-wars-ethiopia-accused-of-massacring-civilians-to-clear-way-for-foreign-farms

https://freedom4ethiopian.wordpress.com/2013/01/10/654e3/

Printed in Dunstable, United Kingdom

76663317R00157